Praise for
The Black Knave

"*The Scarlet Pi...* ...ake an old story new an... ...master storyteller and a... ...er has taken a classic pl... ...tion, making her story ring wit... ...ticity, color, exciting action, her special humor and deep emotions."

—*Romantic Times* (Top Pick)

"An enjoyable read that easily kept me turning the pages. Nicely drawn secondary characters, and the budding romance between Rory and Bethia make Potter's latest a sure bet for historical readers." —*The Romance Reader*

"Ms. Potter has penned a fabulous romantic tale of intrigue and daring. This tale will keep the reader spellbound through each twist and turn." —*Rendezvous*

"Well-drawn, memorable characters, compelling action, and Machiavellian political intrigue add to a story that Potter's many fans will be waiting for." —*Library Journal*

"Patricia Potter takes Baroness Orczy's tale, puts a Highland spin on it, and delivers a rousing tale of intrigue, danger, and forbidden romance that engaged my interest from first to last page . . . *The Black Knave* was a most satisfying read, featuring a truly heroic hero and a heroine with real courage." —*All About Romance*

continued . . .

Praise for Patricia Potter

"When a historical romance [gets] the Potter treatment, the story line is pure action and excitement, and the characters are wonderful."
—Harriet Klausner

"One of the romance genre's finest talents."
—*Romantic Times*

"Pat Potter proves herself a gifted writer as artisan, creating a rich fabric of strong characters whose wit and intellect will enthrall even as their adventures entertain."
—*BookPage*

"A master storyteller, a powerful weaver of romantic tales."
—Mary Jo Putney

"[Potter] has a special gift for giving an audience a first-class romantic story line."
—*Affaire de Coeur*

"Patricia Potter looks deeply into the human soul and finds the best and brightest in each character to help them face the challenges put before them with courage and love. This is what romance is all about."
—Kathe Robin, *Romantic Times*

THE HEART QUEEN

PATRICIA POTTER

JOVE BOOKS, NEW YORK

THE HEART QUEEN

A Jove Book / published by arrangement with
the author

PRINTING HISTORY
Jove edition / July 2001

The Penguin Putnam Inc. World Wide Web site address is
http://www.penguinputnam.com

ISBN: 0-515-13098-2

A JOVE BOOK®
Jove Books are published by The Berkley Publishing Group,
a division of Penguin Putnam Inc.,
375 Hudson Street, New York, New York 10014.
JOVE and the "J" design
are trademarks belonging to Penguin Putnam Inc.

PRINTED IN THE UNITED STATES OF AMERICA

10 9 8 7 6 5 4 3 2 1

Dedicated to the memory of Ralph Cramer,
a true hero both on and off the battlefield

Prologue

Scotland, 1738

Neil Forbes had never believed in broken hearts. He'd never believed in love, either.

Unfortunately, he'd been wrong on both counts.

He realized his error as he stood before the Marquis of Braemoor and knew he had the first, and could never have the second. He wasn't good enough for Janet Leslie. He never would be.

He'd come into this room prepared to fight the marquis, to fight Janet's father and even to fight dragons for her. But he couldn't fight what he was or what he wasn't. He focused on the man facing him . . .

"Your mother was mad," the marquis said. "The taint runs in your family. Do you want to pass it on? That you even thought you could make such a marriage proves you are already afflicted."

Each word was like pounding nails into flesh. At twenty-four, Neil had never before considered the consequences of his mother's illness. He'd been a child when his mother, Cierra, had died. He'd known he was a bastard, conceived with a married lord not her husband, a lord who was brother to the current Marquis of Braemoor and who was long dead without any other blood heirs. Other than his cousin Donald and Donald's youngest brother, Rory, Neil was the only direct blood descendent in this branch of the Forbes family. That was the reason why he had been brought here, he knew, even though his bastardy made him an outsider. It was rumored that Rory was fathered by another man, that the marquis had been cuckolded by the wife he hated. Neil knew his role at the keep was to diminish Rory, a hammer over Rory's head.

"The madness was not confined to your mother," the marquis said. "Her mother also committed suicide, as did a brother. You say you love the gel. If you love her, you will give up this idea. You can never marry, Neil," he continued, then added solemnly, "I promised your grandfather I would make you understand that."

Neil felt cold. Very cold, despite the warmth in the hall. "You never—"

"I dinna tell you because I dinna think it necessary. You showed little interest in wedding."

"I donna believe you," he said. "I . . ."

"Your mother and her mother's blood was cursed. 'Twas the reason my brother would no take responsibility for you. You should be grateful that I did when your mother became so . . . ill." the marquis said. "That I gave you the Forbes name."

The words tattooed themselves on his soul. He remembered his mother sitting in a tower room, singing to herself, ignoring the child at her feet who was desperate for a response. But there had been no one inside that shell.

He realized now he couldn't risk the same thing happening to those who might love him. What if he became that shell? And what of the children that might be born of a union with him?

Why hadn't he considered it? Because he'd never been in love before. Because he had never questioned his young years when he had been shut away in a falling-down castle, hidden from other eyes. Because when he had joined the Braemoor household as a companion to the heir, he had known he had noble blood even if it was tainted by bastardy.

He had not expected to fall in love. He'd never wanted anything so desperately before. He'd never thought his soul would cease to exist without one particular woman.

And by some miracle, she'd felt the same. Janet Leslie last night had pledged him her heart.

Janet, who was like a summer sunset. Glowing with beauty, peace, tranquility. Donald had called her a mousy bluestocking. But that was because Donald liked full-buxomed lasses who didn't have enough wit to argue with him.

Janet . . . well, Janet was slender with light brown hair that gleamed when the sun hit it just right. Her eyes were a dark blue that seemed depthless to him, and she had freckles on her nose that he always wanted to touch . . . to kiss.

It had happened so fast. He'd been transfixed when she first entered the hall with her father. Even wearied from the journey, she had a grace and dignity that had held his gaze. She'd been there, he knew, to meet Donald, as a potential bride for the Braemoor heir. But Donald, though tall and handsome, had been drunk. Her eyes had been dismissive, and had turned to him . . . and something had happened. Bells had started ringing, nerves tingled, senses jangled. He'd known it was happening to her, too. Her eyes had widened and her lips parted in a half smile.

He'd known she was meant for Donald. Both the fathers wanted it. But that didn't matter. He was drawn to her as though she were a lodestone.

They'd managed to meet alone one peaceful afternoon. She'd slipped away from a hunting party, and he'd followed. They found themselves next to a bubbling stream, the water lit like diamonds by the rays of an afternoon sun. . . .

She was still mounted. He'd eased down from his horse and went to her, holding out his hands. She slipped into his arms and made no effort to move away. His arms tightened around her. Magic. Enchantment. Sorcery. Neil didn't know which applied, or mayhap they all did. He only knew he never wanted to let her go.

They met again. And again. They slipped up to the para-

pet at night, or met at a nearby loch, or explored caves that
dotted the moss green hills that surrounded Braemoor. They
talked. They kissed. They couldn't stop touching each other.
They wanted to do so much more.

But Neil remembered his mother who'd been ruined by
having a bairn out of wedlock.

"We will wed," he said. "My uncle wants an alliance with
the Leslies. He will agree if you do not accept Donald." He
tried to convince himself of that. He was, after all, a Forbes
in blood and carried the name.

She made a face. "My father has always said I would not
ha' to marry against my will. He wants me to be happy, and
Donald . . . frightens me." She paused, then, and her gaze
met his. "Even if the families do not agree, I will go with
you. Wherever we can. But," she added, "Father will agree.
I know he will."

He'd kissed her then. The skies shook. Or was it the thunder roaring across the heavens?

They'd both been wrong.

Neil hadn't known how wrong until a few moments ago.
Bastard. Madness. Taint. He could overcome the first. He
couldn't overcome the latter two.

He should have known, should have never allowed his
hopes—so powerful and unexpected—to defy reality. How
many times had his uncle told him he was lucky to have
been taken in, that he, Neil, owed a great debt to him? He'd
trained in arms with a Forbes clansman, then was brought to
Braemoor where he'd continued his training and had been
tutored with his cousin, Donald. In turn, he'd been expected
always to look after him.

And Neil had done as he was told. He'd tried to temper
Donald's cruelties, especially those toward Donald's brother
Rory. But any championing Neil did brought even more
grief upon the younger Forbes. So he had stood aside, refusing to participate in the bullying but doing nothing to
stop it.

He'd finally learned to keep his opinions to himself. He

took lessons with Donald and was grateful for that. He taught himself about the estate because no one else seemed to care. He'd found that he loved the land, and he read about ways of improving the yield. The old marquis laughed at his efforts, calling them pretensions, but still he used Neil to keep the books. Donald had never been good at sums and Neil's work saved him the cost of a servant.

Neil had, in fact, made himself so useful that he'd believed the marquis would not begrudge him this chance.

The marquis broke the silence. "And, of course, you know you will not inherit one farthing from me if you marry, if you risk continuing the madness. How would you support a wife? Particularly one with such a background."

And now his hopes lay shattered around him like so much glass. He realized he would never be more than a servant here. Even worse, he knew he could never marry.

He'd known he'd been born a bastard. God knew Donald had called him that enough times. Just as Donald had called young Rory the same. Except Rory had a legal father, if not a blood one. The fact that Rory's mother might have cozened her husband, the marquis, did not have the legal consequences of a child conceived out of wedlock.

But Neil had loyalty to the marquis who had taken him in. Blind loyalty, he knew now.

He'd learned in the past few moments that he was no more to the marquis than the least of the stable boys. His uncle had taken pleasure in the interview. Neil had sensed that. And he believed he knew why. In his foolishness, he had thought his uncle would welcome the marriage because the dowry would still come to Braemoor.

In his foolishness, he'd not considered the blow to his cousin's pride. Nor to the marquis's.

A penniless bastard with madness in his family had succeeded where the young lord had not.

After facing the sneer on the marquis's face, he considered leaving Braemoor. Yet he realized he was all that stood between a brutal marquis and his tenants, between Donald and his younger brother.

"Don't see the gel again," his uncle warned. "Now get out of here."

Neil left the room. How could he have been such a fool? He'd entered with such high hopes and expectations. And if it had not been for his mother, he would have asked Janet Leslie to be his wife regardless. He was good with the land, with animals. They could go somewhere else.

But could he really have asked her to give up everything and live in poverty?

More importantly, could he ask her to share the risk of madness?

He was supposed to meet her that very afternoon at the same place they'd met days earlier.

He couldn't do it. He couldn't tell her the reasons why he could not marry her. Even an indulgent father would not approve of madness. He didn't want—couldn't—ask her to defy her father. He remembered how she had touched his face, how she'd sworn to run away with him if her father, and his uncle—or either of them—forbade the marriage.

He simply could not do that to her. He could not ask her to make a decision like that. He had to tell her that he knew she would not receive the dowry, that his uncle would disinherit him. He would have to lie and tell her it mattered.

Otherwise, he feared, she would hope and wait and try to convince her father. Even if he told her about the madness, he wondered whether she would accept it.

No. He had to make it possible that she would find a love match with someone else. It would break his heart but might save hers. . . .

He'd never had a noble thought. He'd survived by doing the will of others. He'd not been heroic. But for the first time he was doing something selfless.

Even if she hated him for it.

Chapter One

Scotland, 1747

No one should pray for another's death.

Janet knew she would go to hell for doing it. She'd couldn't even confess her sins since Catholicism had been banished. It wouldn't have mattered, in any event. She couldn't repent them in her heart.

How could she have ever deluded herself about Alasdair Campbell? How could she ever have wed him?

But as she sat in the nursery, her body still hurting from the beating he'd just inflicted and rocking the cradle that held her young son, she knew exactly why.

In the next room slept three little girls. She'd fallen in love with them, not their father.

Oh, Alasdair had played the charming and loving father who'd needed a mother for his children. It was the one argument that had won her consent. She'd hungered for children.

After Neil's betrayal, she thought she would never again succumb to love's seduction. And she hadn't. She'd even thought her heart incapable of loving again.

She'd turned down every suitor paraded by her father. Two years passed, then four and finally six since she'd received the note from Neil, saying that he'd decided against marrying her, that her dowry would not bring what he had expected. He'd not even had the courtesy to tell her in person. Instead, he'd fled Braemoor, leaving only the cruel note behind.

She'd been shattered. Not only shattered, but she had lost her faith in her own judgment. She'd never regained what she had lost that day.

She'd known she would not—could not—love a man again. It was far too painful. But she loved children. Her heart no longer yearned for a husband because she no longer believed that men could love as she wanted to love, and be loved. But she'd also wanted children. She'd longed to hold a bairn in her arms, to watch a lass take her first steps and a lad mount his first pony.

And when Alasdair Campbell courted her, bringing his three young motherless daughters with him, she'd promptly fallen in love with them, not him.

And so she had agreed to marry him.

He was handsome and outwardly charming. His daughters had been too well mannered, too quiet for children, but she hadn't put the two together until it was too late. Even then, though, she may have taken the chance.

She had been completely beguiled by the wee lassies. They'd been silent and shy. But then, they'd lost a mother. She wanted them to smile, laugh, play. And so she'd given her consent despite her father's concern that the Campbells were Protestant and, in fact, loyal allies of King George, whereas the Leslies had favored the Jacobites.

Janet had become the new Countess of Lochaene, wife to the Earl of Lochaene. She'd soon found a household ripped by hatred, envy and greed. Her predecessor, Isabella, had died in childbirth when she bore Annabella. Or was it, Janet often wondered, simply an escape?

If so, it had been a disastrous one for her children. They lived in constant fear of their father; his mother, the dowager countess; and her husband's younger brother. The latter had been particularly displeased at the birth of her own son, Colin, ten months earlier.

Colin and the wee lassies were the only good things to come from her marriage. She loved the earl's daughters as if they were her own. She nurtured them, taught them, protected them—which accounted for her recent bruises.

Annabella, all of five years old, had failed to move fast enough when Alasdair had strode past her. In fact, she had been rooted to the floor in fear. Her older sister had stepped in and tried to push her out of the way, only to be struck by a crop.

She'd screamed and Janet had interfered, placing herself between Alasdair and the children. He'd gone red with rage.

"I'll do as I wish with my children."

"No," she said. She'd held her tongue so many other times. She'd realized defiance only spurred his bouts of rage. But she would rather be the focus of his rage than a child who didn't even know what she'd done wrong.

"No?" he'd replied, his voice friendly. But she knew what lay beneath it.

His hand clenched her arm painfully and he dragged her into his room. They didn't share the same room, for which she thanked God. She had an adjoining room, and she was more than aware of the women he took to his chamber. She was grateful each time because that meant he wouldn't enter hers.

She'd made an art of keeping out of his way, and more importantly keeping the children out of his sight. But this time they'd darted out the door, eager for a promised picnic. Janet had not realized Alasdair had returned from a hunting party.

He threw her on the bed. "You will never say no to me again," he said, as he flicked the crop still in his hand. "You have never learned your place, Jacobite bitch."

Her blood froze at the words. The last year had been a horror in the highlands. After the Battle of Culloden, every Jacobite family had been hunted and persecuted. Her brother had died fighting for Prince Charlie and her father's lands

and properties had been taken, but not before he'd died trying to protect them.

She'd had no one to protect her then, no one who really
loved her. No one but three little girls, ages five, six, and
seven.

And a memory. A memory of a lovely sun-kissed day.

She'd hung onto that as he'd torn clothes from her, as the
crop fell over her shoulders, then across her breasts, and finally her back. Then he'd taken off his own clothes and
dropped down on her, oblivious to the pain of her body.
Oblivious and uncaring.

She tried to think of something else as he used her. She
thought about leaving him, but where could she go with four
children under the age of eight? How could she care for
them? Feed them? Clothe them? She could leave on her
own, but then what of the children? Alasdair would never let
his son go. He'd comb the entire country before relinquish-
ing his heir. The lasses meant nothing to him. They were
lasses, worthless. But her son . . . he was something to mold
into his image.

Over her dead body.

Or his.

And he'd known it. His eyes had narrowed after he'd left
the bed.

"You haven't learned obedience to your lord yet, my dear.
How many lessons do you require, stupid wench?"

She'd glared helplessly at him just as a knock came at the
door.

Alasdair opened it to MacKnight, his valet. He had a bottle of brandy on a tray. His eyes widened as she frantically
tried to cover up her body with torn clothes.

"A little lesson, MacKnight. One you need to remember if
you are so foolish as to marry."

Janet had learned two years earlier not to give Alasdair
the satisfaction of tears. But as the door closed, she said,
"Someone is going to kill you someday."

"A threat, my dear?"

"Nay, a promise, if you hurt the children again."

"I will do as I wish with my children. You will not interfere again. I will expect you at supper this evening. I have some guests."

He left then, the door closing behind him with deceptive softness.

Janet lay still for a moment, her body aching from his abuse. She refused to cry. That would give him power. Even if he was not there to see it. After several moments, she rose, dressed painfully, then went to see the children.

The lasses were huddled in the corner, and her son was screaming. Fixing a smile on her face, she'd told them they would have a picnic the next day. She soothed her son, feathering his face with kisses. When he'd finally calmed, she put him down in his bed and helped the lasses into their nightclothes. She stayed to tell them a story and sing a lullaby. Finally, their eyes closed.

She sat next to her son, watching him sleep. Less than a year old and he already flinched at the sight of his father. She feared that one day Alasdair would lose his temper and seriously hurt one of the children. She'd seen him do that to a puppy that wandered in his way. She'd nursed it, found it a good home. She'd never allowed the children another pet.

She swallowed hard . . . and thought of Neil Forbes, of how different she'd once believed her life would be. But then she'd been nineteen, and believed love really existed. She'd believed in his gentleness, in his kisses, in his awkward but seemingly honest words, the sweet explosiveness between them. She'd been ready to give up everything for him. The disillusionment had been bitter and long lasting.

He'd had little then. And he had not been willing to settle for what little dowry she would bring. Now he was one of the wealthiest men in Scotland. He'd inherited the title of Marquis of Braemoor after the death of his cousin at the hands of the notorious Black Knave. His lands had expanded through his cousin's marriage. He was said to have the ear of Butcher Cumberland.

He hadn't needed her at all.

But he hadn't married. She knew that. There had been talk of trying to interest him in her husband's younger sister. Braemoor had rebuffed all overtures. He obviously was hoping for an even more advantageous marriage.

He could have anyone in Scotland now. Not only was he wealthy, but he also cut a fine figure. She remembered his height, his raven hair that had curled around her fingers, the dark eyes that were always cautious until they looked into hers.

She shook her head of the memories. He had not been what she had thought. He was probably no better than her husband.

Then why did he haunt her dreams so?

Loneliness sliced through Neil as sharply as the blade tore through the meat on the table at the wedding party.

He stood in a corner and watched the merriment as one of his tenants danced with his new bride. A fiddler played a lively tune and ale flowed like a river.

He would leave soon. He knew he was not an enlivening influence on the celebration. He knew he was respected though not particularly liked. He'd been alone too long, wary too many years to relax and enjoy the company of others.

It was one of his greatest regrets. Only recently had Neil discovered how deep his cousin's friendships had run, what great loyalty he'd inspired. Neil had learned that all too late. He wished now he'd looked behind his cousin's outer facade to the man beneath.

Rory, Neil knew, would have felt right at home here where he—well—felt like an intruder.

He'd felt an intruder all his life, even now that he was Marquis of Braemoor. It was a position that he'd always wanted and even thought should be his. He'd thought he cared more for the land and people than Rory had. In truth, Neil now knew it was he, Neil, who hadn't had the slightest idea of honor or courage or commitment.

In the months since Rory's supposed death, Neil had tried to rectify his own life, to make it mean something, but he didn't know how to make a friend, or keep one. He didn't know how to relax over a tankard of ale. When he tried, he'd been discomfitted and knew everyone with him was, too.

And so he maintained his distance. He tried to do the right thing by his tenants, keeping them on the land rather than evicting them as so many other landlords were doing. The last vestiges of the clan system had been broken at Culloden Moor. Clearances were common. He had to pay heavy taxes to the crown to keep the land, which meant he had to produce revenue. Like others, he'd turned some land over to grazing, but he'd tried not to turn anyone out.

The tenants knew that. Still, he realized he was never going to be their friend.

He gazed around at the whirling figures. No bagpipes. They'd been outlawed by Cumberland, as had been plaids. Instead, the men wore rawhide brogans and cheap breeches.

The music stopped and the dancers huddled in small groups, none of them near him. He sighed, then forcing his lips into a smile went up to young Hiram Forbes and handed him a small purse. "For you and your bride," he said.

The girl curtsied and Hiram looked surprised, then pleased. "Thank ye, my lord."

"I wish you many bairns," Neil said, even as he felt the emptiness in his soul, in his life. He would never have bairns, nor a wife looking at him as the young lass looked at her new husband. 'Twas obviously a love match, and he ached inside that he could never see that look again.

Once. He'd seen it once. He'd seen himself in eyes shining with love, and he'd felt ten feet tall. He'd never felt that way since.

He turned and walked away, well aware that no one asked

him to linger. He mounted his waiting horse, Jack. Back to the tower house?

That was a lonely thought. Since Rory and his wife, Bethia, left, the life seemed drained from the stone structure. On a rare impulse, he headed Jack toward the loch up beyond the hill, the one where he'd met Janet years earlier. Nine years and three months earlier, to be exact. She was married now, to a Campbell. She had a son.

The thought brought a familiar ache to his heart. He'd kept up with the gossip about her. He'd heard that her brother had fallen at Culloden where he'd fought for Prince Charlie. He knew that her father had died shortly afterward and that all his estates had been forfeit. He also knew that Janet's husband had not received the Leslie estates, probably because he had not joined Cumberland at Culloden. Instead, they'd reverted to the king who had awarded them to an Englishman who *had* fought with him.

He'd remember how much she'd loved her father. Unfamiliar with prayer, he nonetheless had stopped in the small chapel next to the tower house and prayed for her and the man he'd once hoped would be his father-in-law. He doubted whether God had heeded his prayer; he'd not been practiced at such an undertaking. And he had his own doubts about the value of prayer and even the very existence of God. He'd seen too much cruelty, too much inequality, too much killing. If God permitted such injustices, then what use was He?

Still, for Janet's sake, he'd tried. *Little enough.*

It was very late afternoon when he reached the loch. The sun was setting, spreading streaks of color across a cinnamon sky. The last rays colored the loch with a sprinkling of gold and the surrounding hills were dark with heather.

The quiet serenity of the Highlands usually quenched the ache inside him. Tonight, it sharpened the pain, deepened it until it overtook everything he was. It smothered him. He saw Janet Leslie, her brown hair framing a serious yet delicate face, her eyes banked with quiet fires of passion. He saw the shy smile, thought of the sweetness of her touch, remembered how it had turned sensuous, yet never lost its gentleness.

God, how he longed for her, for someone to touch, to talk to, to share the simple pleasure of a sunset.

"You and me, Jack," he said to the horse. He'd named the beast as a reminder of Rory. The stallion was as duplicitous as his cousin—calm one moment, all rebellion the next. Wild and longing to be free.

Everything Neil wanted to be but couldn't. He was grounded in responsibility, in practicality.

Rory's disguises from his days as the Black Knave were still hidden in a cottage now abandoned. Neil knew he should destroy them, but he'd never quite been able to do so. They represented something to him, a reminder that never again should he judge another human being so heedlessly.

He watched the sunset fade into dusk. A mist rose over the lake, softly eclipsing it.

He turned Jack toward Braemoor and thought again of Rory. Would he ever be as courageous as his cousin? As bold? Even as honorable? Or was he just fated to plod along, waiting for the madness that had overtaken his mother?

He walked Jack down the treacherous path back to rolling land, then mounted. He urged the animal into a trot, then a canter and finally a gallop. He wanted to leave the ghosts behind.

But he knew they would always lurk deep inside.

Alasdair Campbell, the Earl of Lochaene, died in the wee hours of a Friday. He died in agonizing pain.

Janet had been summoned by a servant and hurried to his bedside. His mother and one of his brothers were at his side.

"The physician has been summoned," Alasdair's mother, the dowager countess, said.

The earl was no longer handsome. His face was pale and

distorted, his hair lank, his body twisted with agony. He screamed with pain.

"Dear God," Janet whispered. "What happened?"

The dowager countess, Marjorie, looked at her with suspicion in her eyes. "He was well earlier."

As mistress of Lochaene, Janet had often attended sick and wounded members of the household. She'd done the same back at her own home.

She was alarmed at the white in her husband's eyes, the obvious pain he felt. For all his faults, Alasdair was not one to moan. If he said he was sick, he was really sick. She recalled her thoughts three days earlier. She'd wanted him dead.

But now faced with just that, she knew she didn't want it at all. She did not want to be responsible for another's death, even that of one she despised.

She had no idea, though, what was wrong with him. His servant said he'd been sick since last evening with pain in his stomach, that he'd been vomiting.

Marjorie glared at her. "What did you do to him?"

A chill ran down Janet's back. "Nothing. I have not seen him today, and he was fine yesterday."

"Exactly," the dowager countess said. "Nigel said you were in his room yesterday when he took up a tray."

Janet nodded. Her husband had been drinking. He'd commanded her presence along with another bottle of brandy after a day of hunting with his brother, Reginald. She'd been forced to stand as he had steadily drunk its contents, as he'd recounted all her failures as mistress, wife and mother. He'd then ordered her to his bed, but thank God he'd passed out before he could do anything. She'd left, retreating to the safety of her own chamber after checking the children. Colin had been awake, staring solemnly up at her from the cradle she'd insisted on keeping in her room. She distrusted Molly, the woman her husband had employed to care for the children. The woman, Janet thought, had been employed more to keep her husband's bed warm rather than to take care of the children.

She'd been grateful for that in the beginning. It meant fewer visits to her bed. But then she'd seen the woman strike Annabella. She'd tried to discharge her but Alasdair would not hear of it.

"I will get some herbs," Janet said.

"No," her husband said. He groaned, then looked up at her with wide pain-filled eyes. "What did you do?" he asked. "What did you put in the brandy?"

All the eyes in the room went to her. She felt the blood drain from her.

She started to shake her head in denial.

"Get her out of here," her husband said.

Reginald glared at her, then took the several steps to her side. "Ye'd best leave," he said.

Janet realized instantly that she had no choice. "The physician?" she said, knowing that the only one was in Inverness, hours away.

"He has been sent for," the dowager said, her brown eyes glittering with malice. She'd never liked Janet, had shown only disdain for her Jacobite family. Janet knew her husband would never have married her without the dowry her father had provided, along with hopes that he would some day inherit her family's property. The fact that it had been taken by the English king had been a bitter disappointment.

Only the birth of her son had kept him from divorcing her. He'd wanted a son more than he wanted to be rid of her.

What a bitter bargain she'd made.

She didn't know what time it was, only that it was predawn. Colin was asleep in the nursery, the lasses in the room next to his, and she did not want to wake them. Nor did she wish to return to her chamber. She lit a candle from one in the hallway and carried it up the steps to the parapet of the sprawling ancestral home of the Campbells of Lochaene. 'Twas a smaller dwelling then her childhood home, smaller even than Braemoor. The rock edifice was built for defense, not for comfort, and its rooms were small and bare, the circular stairs steep and uneven. No tapestries warmed the rooms, nor carpets the floors.

When she'd come to Lochaene as a bride, she'd tried to convince her husband to purchase a carpet for the nursery. The floors were so cold and the wind often cut through the windows. She'd discovered then that he cared far less for the comfort of his children than he did for his frequent trips into Edinburgh and the horses he'd buy, then often ruin.

But now she wanted, needed, the cold jolt of night air. She left the candle inside the door so it would not flare out, then went out onto the parapet. The sky was threatening. Large bulbous clouds rushed across the sky and masked the stars, though torches lit the courtyard this night. She couldn't see beyond them, but she knew the land well. Mostly bare moors and low lying hills, the land had been cleared of its farms and the crofts and turned to shaggy cattle and sheep. It was a lonely place, dark and gloomy with none of the wild scenic beauty of her home.

Forced by the cold to return to the questionable warmth of the interior, she went to the nursery. Colin was still asleep. She next checked on the lasses.

"Mama," Grace said from her bed, wriggling to a sitting position. Grace, at seven, was the oldest of the sisters, a grave, slender waif of a child who, though timid on her own behalf, could be fierce in defense of her sisters and baby brother.

She loved the lasses as much as if they had come from her own body. Grace with her quiet dignity, Rachel who wanted nothing as much as to love and be loved, and little Annabella who was all mischief.

Janet went over to Grace and placed the candle on the table. She sat carefully as not to wake the other two girls, then gathered Grace in her arms, holding her tight. She felt the lass relax and snuggle deep against her. In minutes, the lass was asleep, but Janet couldn't relax. She wanted to be downstairs in Alasdair's room. She knew what he had implied, but she couldn't believe he really meant it.

It was still dark when she heard a knock on her door. She gently replaced Grace into the bed and padded over to the door, opening it.

Molly stood there, her face drawn and pale. "I was sent to tell ye. The earl is dead."

Chapter Two

The day of the funeral was as dark and dismal as the event.

Alasdair had been dead for four days. Janet had forced herself to perform the necessary tasks expected of a wife. She'd closed his eyes and placed coins on the eyelids to keep them closed. She washed and anointed the body and clad it in the *deid-claes*.

A joiner had straightened out the body and measured it for a coffin. It had arrived earlier today.

Janet attended to it all in a state of numbness. She kept remembering the wish she'd made days earlier. Guilt warred with relief that he was gone, that the children would be safe.

He looked different. Even peaceful. He'd been a handsome man when she'd wed him. In four years, he'd grown large and his face red and puffy with drink. Now he looked as she had first seen him. It made her wonder whether she'd had anything to do with his descent into drink and cruelty or if he had always had it in him. Certainly, his family was short on love and compassion.

Word had gone out about the funeral. She realized that there would be numerous people attending, if not out of love for or respect for the Earl of Lochaene, then out of curiosity about his widow.

She knew about the rumors. She knew they were being

spread by her sister-in-law and the dowager countess. Murder was whispered. Gossiped. Passed on from family to family in the Highlands.

Poison was mentioned. Arsenic. Caffeine. Belladonna. Opium. But the physician who arrived after the death could not swear to its cause.

When the local sheriff arrived, murder was mentioned but nothing could be proven. A servant had overheard her threatening the earl; the earl was a healthy man who suddenly succumbed to an unknown ailment. Both facts cast suspicion, but nothing was conclusive.

It was suggested that Janet's room be searched, and the sheriff had done so. They found nothing in her room but did find arsenic in her sister-in-law's room since she used it for her complexion. It was a substance Janet had disdained and now was relieved she had.

Still, the rumors persisted. Janet knew that many believed her guilty because she would have the most to gain from the earl's death. She wondered whether it was only a matter of time before her husband's family convinced the authorities to do more than question.

Because of the inheritance laws, her son inherited. Alasdair had made no provisions for a guardian and thus she gained control of Lochaene. It was a control she hadn't sought.

Yet on the day Alasdair was buried, she'd never felt such a sense of freedom. Guilt warred with relief. She was free. The lasses were safe. Her son would grow up with love.

Neighboring lords—either out of curiosity or loyalty— had been arriving for the past two days. She had ordered food and drink prepared after a battle with Marjorie.

"You should be hiding in your room in shame," Marjorie had said.

"I have nothing to be ashamed of," Janet retorted.

"My son was in good health."

"Your son ate and drank too much."

"You were a poor wife."

"I gave him an heir."

"Then poisoned him?"

Janet forced herself to stare into Marjorie's glittering eyes. "*I* am Countess of Lochaene now. I will not tolerate those kinds of accusations."

"I am not finished with you," Marjorie said. "I told my son not to marry a Jacobite."

"But he did, did he not? That there was no inheritance is no' my fault. Complain to his grace, the Duke of Cumberland."

"Whore."

"Say that once more and I will force you to leave Lochaene. And now I go to see about the arrangements."

Keeping her head high, she marched to the kitchen. Once out of Marjorie's sight, she slumped against the wall. She did not like confrontations. But she'd known in that moment that Marjorie was her enemy and would do everything she could to destroy her. She would not let it happen. She had four bairns to protect. That would make her strong.

She'd been weak for so long.

No more.

Neil called himself every kind of a fool. He probably wouldn't even reach Lochaene before the rites. But he had heard the rumors and he hadn't been able to help himself.

If there was one thing he knew, the girl who had touched him so tenderly years ago wouldn't, couldn't, be capable of murder.

He also knew that, coming from a Jacobite family, she would have precious few friends these days. If he couldn't do more, at least he could offer friendship. He didn't let himself believe he meant anything else, considered anything else. Nothing had changed. He could never marry. The taint was still in his blood. But he knew what it was like to be alone in a hostile household.

And Rory had taught him something about honor. So he had ridden over to his tacksman, Jock, and asked him to assume authority at Braemoor while he was gone. Jock had looked at him with amazement but had agreed.

Then Neil had saddled Jack.

He knew Janet would not welcome him. But the rumors worried him and instinct told him Janet may need help. She may well refuse his, but he had to extend an offer. He wondered whether Cumberland would be there. Neil detested the man, but he had been the recipient of his goodwill, mainly because of Rory. That small advantage might also help Janet.

It brought a rare smile to Neil's lips every time he thought of the irony of it. Rory had flummoxed Cumberland so well and thoroughly that the king's brother never realized how he had been taken, that the man he'd rewarded was the man who'd been a thorn in his side for more than a year.

And now Rory was probably somewhere in the colonies, flummoxing someone else. His cousin had done something fine. Neil, on the other hand, had become a mole on his own property.

It was time to emerge.

The great hall filled on the day of the funeral. Janet bore the ceremony and *draidgie* with the stoicism she'd learned in the past few years. As was the custom, she did not attend the burial. Wives did not. Instead, they stayed at the manor house and prepared the food and drink for the *draidgie* that followed burial.

But she grieved. She grieved for what could have been and was not. She grieved for her hopes and dreams.

She even grieved that Alasdair's life had been so wasted.

And she grieved for the lasses, for the expected mourning that would eclipse their lives even further. She had a black mourning dress she'd made when her father died, and plain black dresses had been hurriedly stitched together for the three little girls. She hated to see them in the dark clothes, for they looked sad and lost and uncertain.

Thank God all the visitors would be gone soon.

She went out to get some fresh air. The great hall smelled of stale ale and sweat and unwashed bodies. The lasses were back in their nurseries. One of her first acts would be to replace Molly.

Mourners—or curiosity seekers—were still approaching. She watched one small group come in, and she bade them welcome then invited them in for food and drink. A lone rider followed them.

She smiled automatically, then started. Memory prodded her. Her heart started to pound.

It could not be.

He was bareheaded, his hair dark as a raven's wing even in the late afternoon sun. His seat was easy, his posture comfortable, his large but hard body familiar. It had been in her dreams often enough.

She wanted to run inside. She didn't want him to hear the rumors. She didn't want him to see the paleness of her face, nor her too-thin body.

He rode straight up to her and dismounted. A boy who had just taken the other horses into the stable for food and water appeared to take the reins.

"I'll do it," he said in the deep rich voice Janet remembered so well.

She curtsied. "Welcome to Lochaene, my lord."

"Countess," he acknowledged, then softer, "Janet. Are you all right?"

He was so big, so tall. Overwhelming. But it was the softness in his voice that disarmed her. For the first time in days, she felt tears gather behind her eyes.

His hands remained at his side, and yet she felt a warmth she'd not felt since she left her father's house.

She looked up at him. "We did not expect you," she said with what she hoped was a cold, detached voice.

He hesitated, then said awkwardly, "I thought to pay my respects."

She wanted to turn away but she felt transfixed, as if rooted to the ground. She remembered the last time she'd seen him. He'd leaned over to kiss her, then promised to meet with her the next afternoon. He hadn't.

He looked travel-worn now. His hair fell over his forehead and his face had turned dark with bristles. His dark eyes were tired and his mouth looked as solemn as it ever did. It was difficult to think of him as cruel, but the end result of their meeting had been cruel. Cruel beyond bearing.

She looked beyond him. To the left. To the right. Anywhere but into his eyes.

"You are welcome," she said. "Some guests are staying in the great hall. There is food and drink." Hospitality demanded the words, but her heartbeat became irregular.

"My thanks," he said softly.

Her fingers bunched into fists. She couldn't find words, nor could she move. Why did he affect her this way after so many years?

"I am sorry about your husband," he said.

Her gaze was drawn back up to his face. It was granite. But then it had always been hard to read. It had relaxed only when her fingers had touched it. Her body quaked at the memory. She'd been so bold then. So reckless. She didn't think she would ever be reckless again.

"I am a mother now," she said. She had to say something to interrupt the intensity of his gaze.

"I ha' heard."

"Then you must also have heard the rumors."

"Aye, I've heard some. But I do not put credence in them."

"Then you are among the few."

"Mayhap there are more than you believe."

She hesitated, finding words difficult. The chill had left her. She felt only heat. Heat from regret. Heat from embarrassment. Heat, God help her, from a desire that apparently had not dimmed over the years.

And on the day of her husband's funeral. She was damned for sure.

Suddenly blinded by the first tears she'd shed since her father died, she whirled around. She did not care if he noticed, nor if he thought her rude. She just had to get away.

She went inside, past the hall where she could hear the ongoing revelry, up the stone staircase to the first floor where her chamber was, then up to the second where the nursery was located.

Alasdair's brother Reginald and his wife also had rooms on the first floor, as did Archibald, the third brother. Marjorie had a small cottage house away from the tower.

She went up to see the bairns. The nursery consisted of a small room where her son stayed except when she took him down to her own room, a sitting room that doubled as a play room, a bedchamber the lasses shared, and a tiny anteroom where Molly stayed.

Grace, the quiet one, was reading a book Janet had borrowed from the vicar. Her husband had not approved of lasses receiving an education. In truth, he had little himself, and there were no books at Lochaene. Janet was teaching her daughters to read with what books she could borrow.

Rachel was gazing out the window at the rare activity in the courtyard and Annabella was playing with a doll. They all looked up as she entered the room, Annabella getting up from a chair and scampering over to her.

"Where is Molly?" Janet asked. She'd told the girl to stay with the children. She should have known better. One more reason to discharge her.

"She leave us," Annabella said forlornly. "I doan think she likes us."

"Did you get something to eat?"

Annabella shook her head.

"Would you like some meat pies?"

"Aye," Rachel said.

"And some pastries?" Annabella said hopefully. Then her face fell. "Father would no' like it."

"Your father has gone to heaven," Janet explained for the sixth or seventh time in the past four days. She sincerely doubted it, but she hadn't wanted to scare the children with visions of another place. A small lie. A kind lie.

After her much greater sin of wishing her husband dead, she dinna think God would be too outraged at this small one.

"Will we go there, too?" Rachel, the curious one, asked.

"Not for a very long time, love."

Janet looked toward Grace. "Will you look after your little brother?"

A smile lit Grace's face. She loved nothing better than to be asked to do something. "I will," she said.

Janet knelt and held out her arms. The three girls crowded inside them, the small bodies warm, their arms clinging. They'd all been starved for love when she came to Lochaene. She hadn't been able to spoil them while their father lived. He'd seemed to object to every small gift or gesture. She would make up for it.

But now hugs were important to them. And to her.

Neil's appearance had opened a wound that ran deep and wide.

It was all she could do to keep the tears banked behind her eyes, to hold in the hurt she thought she had conquered.

A few kind words had torn down all the barriers she'd so carefully constructed. She didn't know why he had come, but she knew she had to be careful.

She also realized Neil Forbes was now a marquis, a higher rank than that of her husband, but he didn't look like a marquis. But then he never had, and she recalled that his indifference to clothes was one of the things that attracted her. He'd worn saffron shirts open at the neck and a great tartan plaid that was now outlawed. He'd looked rugged and handsome.

And now? Though his clothes were stained with travel, she'd noted they were of good quality. He wore a dark blue waistcoat over a linen shirt with blue trousers tucked into dusty boots. Unlike most of the other lords, he did not wear a wig. Instead, his own hair was a little shaggy, as if he couldn't be bothered with it.

Neither had there been any softening in his face despite his kind words.

She steeled herself against seeing him again. She would endeavor to stay away from him. Surely he would not stay long, especially since it seemed he'd brought little with him.

Janet slowly untangled herself from the children. "I will be right back," she promised.

She made her way down the stairs. All the servants had been recruited to help with the food and drink for the many guests. Molly, she thought, was probably servicing one of them, or one of their servants, in the barn. Another problem to be solved.

The great hall was more boisterous than ever. She hesitated. She did not have to pass it to go into the kitchen but her eyes were drawn to it. Not it it, she knew, but to one of the newly arrived guests.

The Marquis of Braemoor was talking to Marjorie. He happened to look up then, as if he expected her. His gaze met hers, and for a moment she thought her legs would give way. The intensity in his eyes reached across the room. Voices in the room seemed to slow, and she wondered whether it were just the effect he had on her or whether her presence had actually lowered the amount of conversation.

She turned and left, wondering what Marjorie was telling him, what others were saying. A poor wife. A bad marriage. Poison. She could almost hear Marjorie's sharp words.

Why did she care what he thought? He hadn't wanted her years ago and it had broken her heart. He was a very wealthy man, according to rumor, a favorite of Cumberland who had little use for most Scots. That reminder should dampen any warm memories. She despised Cumberland. So why was she reacting like this?

The unexpected kindness? God knew it had been a long time since she'd known any.

The kitchens were full of workers, most of them hired only for this day. The food costs alone would mean she would have to be careful the rest of the year. She hadn't seen the books yet, but she suspected that her husband had spent more than the revenues.

Pies were coming out of the ovens. She took one along with three meat pastries and a crock of milk. She hadn't eaten this day, and she did not think she could. Surprisingly, the Marquis of Braemoor was at the stone steps, looking as if he'd been waiting for her.

"Can I be helping you with the tray?" he asked.

Nay. "Aye," she said, leaving pride behind for a moment. She hadn't realized how much she needed a kind word, nor someone who had known her father. "If you can take the crock of milk."

She led the way. The wall sconces had been lit and they spread shadows on the stone. She stumbled once, her foot catching on an uneven piece of stone, and she felt the strength of his arm steadying her.

It's the day of your husband's funeral. She kept reminding herself of that.

They reached the top of the second set of steps and she led the way to the nursery. He had one hand free and he opened it. . . .

"Ma . . ."

The exclamation stopped suddenly as three pairs of light blue eyes looked at the Marquis of Braemoor. He was taller than Janet's husband and solidly built. Annabella dove behind a chest, Rachel ducked into the room next door. Grace paled. Only Colin was undisturbed, and that was because he was sleeping.

Janet looked up at Neil. He had a panicked look on his face as well.

Janet put the tray loaded with pies on a table, then held out her hand to Grace.

"Grace, this is the Marquis of Braemoor."

Grace took a few faltering steps, hanging back as much as she could.

"He won't hurt you, love."

Grace did not look convinced.

Then he knelt and held out his hand. "I am Neil."

Grace curtsied but remained at a distance. Neil rose, looking as uncomfortable as a man could. "I had best leave."

"Thank you for helping me," Janet said.

He nodded and disappeared out the door.

"He's verra' big," Grace said.

"I know, love," Janet replied, "but . . ." She had started to say "he's not like your father."

But she did not know that. He had betrayed her once before. And certainly her husband had not been what she'd thought. How could she be so foolish again. It had just been his sudden appearance . . .

And the only kindness she'd known in far too long. But he'd been kind before. It meant nothing.

Nothing.

Neil felt like a monster. He'd not been around children since he was a child himself, if indeed he had ever been a child. But he'd never considered himself a frightening figure, or that children would hide from him.

Feeling their fear, he'd tried to extricate himself from the room as quickly as possible. But not before he saw a glimpse of sympathy cross Janet's face.

By the devil, he never should have come here. He'd known it all the way here, and yet something had pulled him like a puppet master pulled strings. He'd especially known it when he'd seen her lean against the gray stone of Lochaene.

She'd looked drawn and tired. Her eyes were circled with dark rings. And yet she'd drawn herself up with that same grace and dignity he'd remembered. A spark flashed in her dark blue eyes, but then it had fled, leaving dark, unfathomable pools. There was no hint of the laughter he remembered, the tenderness. Her face was handsome, though. The high cheekbones and fine delicate lines made it one of those faces that improved, rather than deteriorated, with years.

Anger had flickered in her eyes when she'd recognized him. He was sure that were it not for the rules of hospitality she would ask him to leave. Instead, she'd straightened her back, and defiance and pride shielded her face. The hint of tears, though, almost undid him.

He'd hoped she would be happy, that she would make a good marriage. The night he'd heard of her marriage, he drunk himself into a stupor but he'd wished her well. He'd heard stories of her husband, and they had not been pleasant ones.

Still, he'd hoped, and yet the moment he'd seen her face, the spirit drained from it, he'd known it had been false hope. His . . . sacrifice had been in vain.

It had been all he could do to keep from taking her into his arms. But nothing had really changed. Oh, he was a wealthy man now, and he bore a title, but the madness still haunted his past, would always do so.

And so he had kept his voice measured, his arms to himself. In the great hall, he'd listened to the rumors, the charges. Marjorie Campbell, the late earl's mother, had seized upon him the moment she learned his identity.

"We are honored by your presence."

"My condolences on the loss of your son," Neil said. He also considered telling her he was a friend of the countess, but then he probably would not learn anything. And, in truth, he was considered no friend by Janet Campbell, not if her measured greeting had been any sign.

He'd allowed the dowager countess to believe that her family was important enough to draw a marquis to her son's funeral and listened as she regaled him with all her daughter-in-law's faults.

"She could even kill the children," the woman had muttered, not caring whether anyone had heard. He'd been appalled by the depth of the animosity in the hall, by the way the dowager countess had moved from visitor to visitor, spreading the poison as she went.

Then she'd moved closer to him. "I hear you have the ear of His Grace, Lord Cumberland. You should ask him to look into the matter."

"What about the authorities here?"

She waved her hand in disdain. "They fear to do anything, but His Grace could rule that Lochaene should go to Reginald, my oldest son. 'Tis only right."

He'd had to swallow the bile in his throat at her plotting on the day of her son's burial.

"I will tell him all that has happened," he promised and tried to sidle away.

She followed. "She is a Jacobite, you know. You tell His Grace that. I am sure he would prefer this land in the hands of a family who has been loyal to him and his brother, King George."

"I am sure he values loyalty," Neil agreed, knowing full well that Cumberland valued nothing but his own power. He would toss these people off their land in a second if he thought he would gain from it.

He drank one glass of not very good ale, then had a need for fresh air. It was then he noticed Janet trying to balance a heavily laden tray.

Without thinking, he rushed to her aid, and was surprised when she accepted his offer.

But up the stairs and into the nursery, he was all arms and legs and awkwardness. He knew his size terrorized the children, or was it all men? He knew that look in their eyes, the fear of being hit. Bloody hell, he knew it too well.

He'd wanted to leave but he could not. He saw her face as she tried to reassure the children. Her too-pale, too-thin face relaxed, and those dark blue eyes filled with love. And tenderness. The kind he remembered from those brief days together. The years between those days and this one disappeared, and he was seized with a need and longing so great his legs almost buckled under his weight.

He stepped outside. He had to, before he made a great fool of himself. He knew he had to leave. This night. Or he would break the vow he'd made. But first he had to let her know she had a friend.

It was the least he could do.

He thought of Rory, who had repeatedly risked his life to save others, people he didn't know, people he'd once fought. He wished he had only a measure of Rory's character. And yet how many years had he decried his cousin as a wastrel and fool? Even a coward. He should have seen under the facade, should have taken the time to find the true worth.

He tried to help others now in his own stumbling way. He'd tried to better the lives of his tenants, tried to influence neighboring landlords from clearing their lands. But it was so little compared to his cousin.

What would he do if someone came to him for help? Would he risk the people at Braemoor for strangers? It was a question without an answer.

Several moments later, he heard the door open.

An exclamation escaped Janet when she realized he was still there, standing in wait for her.

She quickly moved away. Little this day had hurt as much.

"I will not be touching you, lass," he said. "I just wanted you to know I'll be leaving Lochaene this night."

Her mouth formed an O in surprise, but she did not reply.

"I did not mean to frighten the wee ones," he said. "I did not think I was that fierce."

Her face did not soften. "They have no reason to trust men," she said. "And neither do I."

Another blow. He knew he had wronged her, and now he knew that he probably should have told her the real reason he had done what he had years earlier. He'd truly believed then that it had been the kindest thing to do. And now . . . there was no reason to explain. Nothing had changed. And it would accomplish little. He would not hurt her again, and he needed the distance her anger insured.

Still, he had to let her know that he could help. "Janet, if you need anything, if you need . . . a friend, or if you ever need help, come to me." It sounded stiff, even to him.

"I do not need help. Not from you. Not from anyone." Pride radiated from her body while a sheen fogged her eyes.

"I . . . just want you to know that I will be at your call. I *can* help."

"Aye. I understand you are a friend of the butcher."

He put a finger to her lips. "Do not let anyone else hear that."

"I would expect that from one of his lackeys," she said. "Now if you will excuse me."

"Janet," he started.

"Lady Lochaene," she corrected.

"Lady Lochaene," he said obediently. He was doing this all wrong. It had been a mistake coming here. But he'd never been good with social niceties.

She lifted her chin. "If you do not mind, I wish to spend time with my son."

"No' until you hear me out," he said.

"I have heard you. I do not need your help. My son is the new earl."

He hesitated, then said, "I have been asked to intercede with Cumberland to have the lands stripped from him."

She stilled. "He canna do that."

"Not if I have anything to say about it. But you must know that your husband's family is plotting against you. I meant it when I said you have a friend."

Her gaze bore into him. "One I can depend on? I think not, my lord."

He deserved every word, and more. No matter how noble his intent years ago, he'd obviously hurt her far beyond what he'd believed. Bitterness had edged her words when she'd said neither she nor her children had any reason to trust men. She made it clear that he had done nothing to make her feel differently.

What in God's name had Campbell done to her? Worse than what he'd done?

He couldn't help himself. He lifted his hand and ran a finger down her cheek, feeling its softness.

She flinched.

Pain twisted inside him. He stepped back, nodded, then went down the stairs, straight out to the stable.

He'd delivered his message.

It was time to go home.

Chapter Three

Janet remembered Braemoor's words. She remembered the intense look on his face, as if he were willing her to believe him.

But she knew she couldn't. She did not think she could ever believe a man again. She certainly never intended to depend on one again.

Her first thoughts were for the children. She dismissed Molly and promoted a lass who'd worked in the kitchen. She'd always been kind, and kindness was the quality that Janet wanted most.

She also had a battle with Reginald, who'd wanted to move down into her husband's room. She'd said no, that the children would move there. She wanted them close, and she installed young Colin's bed in her own chamber. She found the lasses a puppy—a herding dog—from one of the drovers, and a kitten from the barn cat.

Grace's face lit like a thousand candles in the night.

She immediate snuggled the puppy in her arms as Annabella took the kitten.

With shining eyes, Grace looked up at her. "What should we name him?"

"That is up to you. The three of you have to agree on both names."

"I want one, too," Rachel said, looking uncharacteristically disgruntled.

Janet hadn't thought about three animals. Now she knew she should have.

"They belong to all of you," she said. "You can take turns playing with them. Then we will see."

Rachel looked only a trifle mollified. She went over to Grace and started to pet the puppy. "He is a wee thing."

"He will soon be large enough to be trouble," Janet said wryly.

"Oh, he will never be trouble," Grace said. "He will be very, very good."

"We can call the kitten Princess," Rachel offered.

Annabella objected. "That's ord'nary. She is not ord'-nary."

"Why don't you wait a few days," Janet interjected. "Then you can come up with two very fine names. You can make up lists."

The lasses looked at each other. Grace, then Rachel, nodded. Annabella stuck her chin out pugnaciously. "*I* want to name the kitty."

Janet looked at the two older lasses. They nodded.

"All right, then," Janet said with mock seriousness. "You can tell me your decisions next week."

When she left the room, the three were crooning over their new charges, giggling as she had never heard them giggle before. She leaned against the door outside for a moment, just listening, particularly to Grace. Of the three, she had always seemed unable to be a child and regarded every person with a wariness that disturbed Janet.

When she went downstairs to fetch some milk and bread for the animals, she overheard the cook arguing with a tradesman about the bill and she stepped in.

He glared at her. "I willna be sendin' more goods here."

After he left, Janet questioned the cook.

"Ain't no one been paid for months," she said. "I would

leave except for my husband herds sheep and we have a croft here. If I left, we'd both be driven from the land."

Janet went from there to Reginald's room. He had taken over the management and the books without asking her. She had allowed it because she wanted the time to spend with the children. Now she felt ready, and well enough, for war.

He wasn't there. He was off on a hunt, said his wife Louisa as she nursed her baby who would soon be six months old.

Janet grinned down at the child. Children delighted her. Their innocence gave her joy. She would like several more children, in fact, despite the pain of delivery. Louisa had said she never wanted another. But that feeling usually wore off.

"He looks well," she said.

"Aye," Louisa said shortly.

"You will ask Reginald to find me when he returns?"

"Why?"

"I want to go over the books with him."

Her eyes narrowed. "Why would you do that? It's a mon's business."

"It's my son's business, his inheritance."

Louisa glared at her and Janet left. She should have checked on things before now. She went down to the stables. One lad was feeding the horses. The barn itself was in need of cleaning; the stalls were filthy.

She went down the aisle. The horses looked thin.

"Have you been feeding them their oats?"

"We donna have any," the boy said.

She remembered his name. Kevin. Kevin McDougal.

She went over to one of the stalls. The animal stuck his head out and she ran a hand down his neck as he nickered softly. She used to ride frequently but Alasdair had disapproved, as he disapproved of so many things she enjoyed. She might as well have been locked in her room. Why hadn't she rebelled?

Because she feared Alasdair would take it out on the children. They had always been the weapon he'd used to control her.

"Why have the stalls not been cleaned?" she asked.

Kevin looked rebellious. "There is only me. I canna do everything."

"I will help you, then."

"You, my lady?"

"Aye, I'll not have them stand in this filth. And I will see if I can get you some help."

Kevin did not look optimistic at the prospect. "Lord Reginald said no one was needed."

Reginald was not a lord. He was the honorable Reginald Campbell. Janet wondered who had instructed the lad to call him lord. Was it pretension? Hope?

She was beginning to see the depth of the problems facing her. She'd been lost in a mixture of conflicting emotions during the past few days. She'd been intent on quieting the fears of Alasdair's daughters, of relishing the time she had with Colin. Her sense of freedom had warred with guilt that she'd not done better with her marriage.

But she had no intention of handing over her son's estates to the care of the Campbells. Reginald was an ambitious, mean-spirited man and his wife, Louisa, was his match. Their only redemption was their infant, David.

She sighed, wishing for an ally. Any ally.

If you need a friend . . .

She needed so much, most of all a friend. A *trusted* friend.

Neil Forbes was not that. He could never be that. The devil take him for appearing out of nowhere. She'd tried to banish him from her thoughts over the years, but it was for naught. She kept remembering standing next to him in the stables at Braemoor. He'd known each of the horses. He'd never let them be neglected.

Janet wished she'd known more about what was going on. But her husband had all but kept her a prisoner. The cook had disregarded her orders in favor of those of the dowager countess. She'd been able to teach the bairns, to play with

them, to care for them. And only that because her husband
had so little concern for them. As long as she kept them
away from him, he rarely interfered, except for commanding
that they sleep apart from her. He did not want clinging children, he'd said often enough.

In the beginning, she'd protested. Then she discovered
that the more she protested, the more he took it out on the
bairns. But, she wondered, mayhap she should have tried
harder.

But her heart had been wounded, first by Neil, then by her
father's and brother's deaths, and finally by her husband.
How many times had he told her how inadequate she was?
She had made the children her world.

She couldn't do that any longer. To make their world safe,
she had to make her own safe.

Until now, she hadn't realized how immense that task
would be.

She knew nothing about managing an estate, and she did
not trust anyone in the family to do it for her.

And now she'd just offered to muck out stalls. As if that
would help in any measurable way. But mayhap in a small
way. A beginning. A small stab at control, at independence.

A pitiable one.

Still, she felt excitement well inside her for the first time
in years.

Mayhap mucking out the stalls would help muck out her
mind.

Upon his return to Braemoor, Neil spent several hours with
Jock, who was one of four tacksmen at Braemoor. They
leased property from the marquis, then in turn rented it to
the crofters. Three of them, Neil suspected, cheated their
tenants. Jock was the one honest one who cared about the
people who rented from him.

As the new marquis, Neil had the right to cancel the
leases held by the tacksmen. Contracts varied throughout the
Highlands; this one continued only through the lifetime of

the marquis. Once a marquis died, the contracts were no longer valid.

Jock could lose his livelihood and he knew it. He fidgeted until Neil said, "Sit down, Jock."

Jock sat down, looking as if he were facing the hangman. "Did I do something wrong, my lord?"

Neil studied him for a moment. He was a fine-looking man, tall and strongly built with a shock of red hair and honest blue eyes. Neil knew he was in his mid-thirties and was a distant kinsman; he'd inherited the position of tacksman from his father, who'd died five years earlier. Like Neil, he had no wife; unlike Neil, there was no reason for that to be true. At least as far as Neil knew.

"No," he finally said. "I wanted to thank you for looking after Braemoor while I was gone." He hesitated, then offered, "Would you have a glass of brandy?"

Jock looked as if Neil were about to poison him. Afraid to take it. Afraid not to take it.

Neil sighed. Rory had had such an easy relationship with people around the estate. It must be a talent, having friends. A talent he'd never cultivated. He'd been too busy walking the sharp edge of a knife. He poured a dollop of brandy into a cup and handed it to Jock.

"I wanted your opinion," he said.

"My opinion?" Jock replied dumbly.

Neil realized then he'd never once asked for the man's opinion since he assumed management of Braemoor. Before Rory had left, Neil had never been quite sure of how much control or responsibility he actually had, and he'd been bitter that Rory, not he, had inherited.

He'd always believed he had a love for the land and husbandry that his predecessors had not. They'd cared only for the money the estates had brought. Rory had cared, but Neil had not known that until it was too late. Neil had done what he thought was expected: extract what he could from the earth and try to do little harm in the process.

Then Rory's body—or what was thought to be Rory's

body—was found on the coast, assumed to be the latest victim of the Black Knave, and suddenly Braemoor became
Neil's. The poor relation, the orphaned bastard, was suddenly lord. He'd visited all the crofts, but he hadn't known
how to put the tenants at ease. He hadn't been able to express his concern for them. He hadn't been able to translate
his hopes to them.

He felt like a fraud, and knew they must feel the same.

But now over the months he'd developed a plan, one he
hoped would help every soul who lived on Braemoor.

Poor Jock looked like he was about to be consumed by a
dragon. He clutched the cup with hands so clenched they
were white.

"Ye are no' goin' to be clearin' the land, are ye?" Jock finally ventured, obviously convinced that was the reason for
this interview.

"Nay," Neil said. "No one will be evicted."

Jock's frown cleared but his brows remained furrowed.
Neil couldn't blame him. His uncle, the old marquis, had
paid precious little attention to either the lands or the tenants. During Rory's brief tenure, he acted the fool and indicated no interest at all in Braemoor. In truth, Rory had no
reason to care about it. Neil had been given full responsibility, and he'd thought then that it was merely because Rory
hadn't wanted to be bothered. It wasn't until later he'd discovered that Rory had thought he would be a good steward
of the land.

During those months, though, he'd tried to do what he
could for the tenants but had felt unable to make any real
changes that would improve their lives. Now, for the past six
months, he'd been developing a plan. He finally had all the
parts ready. Six months of work, of planning.

Rory's marriage had brought additional land to Braemoor,
land already cleared of tenants, mostly through the carnage
committed by Cumberland.

Neil planned to entice some of his current tenants to move
to those lands and tend cattle and sheep. Braemoor's lands

would continue to be farmed. He knew there were too many families on Braemoor to survive only through farming, but if some would voluntarily move, then Neil could make the best use of all the lands now under Forbes control.

He just had to make the offer attractive enough to entice some of the young men to move miles away. He'd already decided to provide cottages, a cow and other livestock to anyone willing to move. He would give them a percentage of the profits of the sale of stock they tended.

It would mean that those who stayed could keep more of their yield.

Ultimately, he planned to offer to sell plots of land to the crofters tending it. He'd already checked with a solicitor. 'Twas legal, if unprecedented. He knew it would not be popular among the land owners—nor with Cumberland—which is why he hoped to keep his plans quiet for the moment.

His proposal, he knew, was revolutionary. The land would not produce as much revenue as it would if he cleared it all off. But he should have enough to pay the taxes, and that was all that mattered to him. He had no need for money, clothes, jewels, or riches. Though his title and lands drew people to Braemoor, and no end of offers of marriage, he knew they did not seek *him* out. He had not wit nor charm, nor social graces, but that bothered him not a whit. He did have a passion for making changes.

He outlined his scheme for Jock, whose eyebrows furrowed closer and closer together.

"A share of the profits, my lord?"

"Aye," he said simply.

"A cottage? Livestock?"

"Aye."

"Why would ye do tha'?"

"Because the prospect of having a share of one's own labor should make our people more productive."

"The prospect of losing wha' they have would be havin' the same effect."

"Fear instead of reward?" Neil asked. "I donna believe so."

"I ha' never heard of the like," Jock said suspiciously.

"Nor have I," Neil admitted, permitting himself a small smile. He hoped it came out that way. God knew, he seemed to scare everyone to death, even wee lassies. That experience still stung.

Suspicion oozed from the man sitting across from him. The tenants had received little from the Forbeses over the years except demands for more and more rents. "Wha' about the other tacksmen?"

Neil had been watching them carefully for the past year. He did not want them at Braemoor. "I will not renew their leases," he said. "I will pay off the remaining terms."

"They will no' be happy."

"They've been cheating the crofters."

Jock looked surprised, and Neil realized the man had not thought he knew what was going on at Braemoor. In truth, he knew everything that was going on.

"I want you to take over their leases," Neil said. "You are a fair man. I can trust you, and more importantly, the crofters trust you."

"But ye be wantin' some to leave."

"The land is too crowded. There is not sufficient land on Braemoor for all the sons being born here. I am offering a new opportunity for them to start households of their own on vacant land. I hope you can persuade some of them."

"For a cottage, and a cow and space to garden, I am thinking ye will have some volunteers."

"We will run cattle and sheep on the new lands and put most of Braemoor into grain, build our own mill. The crofters can have gardens of their own and keep all but ten percent, which will come to me." He hesitated, then added, "Eventually, I want to enable them to purchase their land for a fair price."

Jock's eyes widened. He dropped his caution. "Are ye flummoxing me?"

"Nay, Jock. I have too much land for any one man. I ha' no children to leave it to. I want it in the hands of those who've worked it all these years."

Jock stared at him in shock.

"This last is between you and me for the time," Neil said. "My hold on Braemoor may be tenuous. I do not want word reaching Cumberland and give him reason to suspect my loyalty to his wishes."

Jock nodded, still obviously dazed. Still not altogether comprehending.

"Will you talk to the other tenants—except about the sale of land?"

"How do I know ye will keep your word?" Jock said.

It was an unusually brave thing for a tacksman to say, and Neil respected him for it. "I shall put it in writing if you wish," he said. "It will be a contract."

"I donna put much stock in that," Jock replied. "The nobs always find a way around it."

Neil had to smile. That had been his experience, too. "What would you like?"

"I will have to think on it."

"Then you do that, Jock. And talk to the others. Will you do that?"

Jock hesitated, then said grudgingly, "No harm in tha'."

"Now will you drink with me?" Neil asked.

Neil found himself going to the cottage once inhabited by Mary Forbes, who had grown herbs for the tower and for the nearby village. It had a deserted, forlorn look. He knew he should give it to someone; it was a waste such as it was. But it held secrets that he'd been loathe to give up.

The furniture was still in place, even plates and cups. It had been rumored that Mary was a witch, and no one had wished to test the theory. The devil looked after his own.

The fact that she'd completely disappeared, along with the village blacksmith and Neil's own cousin had created no end of speculation. Had the blacksmith and herb grower been involved with the Black Knave? Had they been partly responsible for the death of Rory, the Marquis of Braemoor? No one but Neil knew that Rory and the Black Knave were one and the same. It was a secret he would take to the grave.

The key to the secret was the clothes hidden beneath the dirt floor of the cottage in a secret compartment. Neil had thought many times about destroying it. If Cumberland ever discovered that he'd been outfoxed by the Forbeses, both Neil's own neck and the estates would be forfeit. And yet . . . yet . . .

He brushed aside the dirt, finding the boards that covered the cache. He pulled them up and looked inside. A black cloak, black trousers and shirt were there, along with a British uniform. And a deck of cards.

Neil had found several other decks in Rory's chamber. He'd destroyed those. Now he picked up this deck. *New.* His fingers went through them, pausing at the queen of hearts. He closed his eyes.

How he envied Rory who had *his* heart queen, the lovely Bethia.

Neil very carefully replaced all but the deck of cards. He tucked the deck into his belt.

Then he covered the cache and went to the door, pausing only a moment before closing the door on his regrets.

Every muscle in Janet's body ached.

True to her word, she'd put on her oldest dress and had helped the boy muck out stalls all day. For a while, at least, the animals would have some comfort. She'd also found a chest of coins, and she'd ordered oats.

Then she went back into the house. She said a quiet thanks that she'd encountered neither Marjorie nor Reginald's wife, Louisa. They no doubt would regard her with horror. They would, in any event, when they heard that she had worked in the stables. But she felt a surge of satisfaction. She had awakened something inside herself.

For a moment, she remembered earlier days, days when

she'd been a young girl out riding with her father or brother, and later, when—with the help of a stable hand—she'd slipped off alone to ride the moors and hills. She'd had dogs, a mare of her own, a family who loved her.

Then it was all gone. And she had lost part of herself with it, and even more after years of being Alasdair's wife. Only the wee bairns had kept her going, but they had not kept alive the independent, adventurous, curious girl she'd been. Because of the girls, then her son, she'd survived, was even able to love. But she'd walled off a sizeable part of herself.

But now she felt a stirring, and she wasn't going to let anyone spoil it. Tomorrow she'd demand to see the books. She'd already taken other steps. She'd taken one of the housemaids, Lucy, as her own personal maid. Clara, who had been promoted to nursemaid, was doing very well. The children liked her and that was Janet's main criteria.

Now though, she longed for nothing more than a bath, then to tell the lasses a story. She determined to buy some books for them. Her father had made sure she had an education, and she would continue to see that her lasses did. Weight seemed to lift from her as Lucy brought up buckets of water and after a few *tch, tch, tchs* at the sight of her mistress poured them into the hip bath.

"Thank you," Janet said, surprised that the girl still blushed with pleasure when she did so. "Will you ask Clara to bring Colin to me?"

"Aye, my lady," Lucy said. "I can bring him, myself," she said shyly.

"I would like that," Janet said. Because she'd been so dirty she'd not stopped in the nursery where Colin had stayed while she worked in the stables. Now she missed him. She missed, in fact, every minute she did not spend with him. He was getting to the curious stage now, crawling and putting everything in his mouth. She loved the trusting way he looked up at her when she picked him up. He'd never had that look for his father, and she regretted that.

She quickly washed the dirt and muck away, pleased that

she had tucked her hair under a cap while working. The hot water soothed the aching muscles.

Then the door opened and Lucy set a sleeping Colin in the cradle Janet had moved next to her own bed. She got up, dried herself off and stood for a moment in front of the flames in the fireplace.

She put on a nightshift, padded over to Colin and looked down at him as Lucy left the room. She reached down and picked him up, noticing how much heavier he was getting day by day. Before long he would be toddling all over Lochaene. One day, he would be its lord. And she vowed he would be a good one.

His eyes opened sleepily and he smiled a slow, lazy smile. Maternal instinct surged in her.

Nothing would ever hurt him. Not while she had a breath in her body. No matter what she had to do.

She sang a low lullaby until his eyes closed again and she gently placed him back in the cradle. Soon he would be too big for it.

Despite her weariness, she felt restless. She checked Colin once again, then headed out the door, up to the battlement. It was a clear night. The stars would be out, as would the full moon.

She quickly mounted the stone stairs. One hundred and twenty of them. She'd counted them many times. She reached the top of the tower.

The sky was a carpet of dark blue sprinkled liberally with stars. A few lacy clouds darted in and out like children playing hide-and-seek. The wind was sharp, bracing. She heard a stone clatter somewhere. She swung around. Shadows bobbed and weaved but she saw nothing. She heard the wind. Only the wind.

Yet she found herself shivering, and not from the cool, night air.

She took a last look at the full moon riding high in the sky. It was at its best, a huge bold ball decorating the heavens. The cold air stung her but it also made her feel alive. She started to move away from the edge when she saw a shadowy figure, saw it start toward her.

The lack of words, of greeting or apology, alerted her. She darted toward the stairs, making it just seconds before the shadow, and she flew down the steps. After reaching the third landing, she slowed and listened. Nothing. No sound behind her.

Her breath was coming in fast, hard gusts. Her heart pounded. Her legs felt weak. She would have sworn the figure had meant her harm, had meant to sweep her off the parapet. Her legs felt weak. She stood. Still listening.

Then she went down the stairs. She would find a servant downstairs and ask him to go up with her.

There was no one on the second floor where her rooms and Reginald's were. She decided to try his door.

She knocked. Louisa opened it.

"Reginald," Janet said. "Is he here?"

"No," Louisa said. Her eyes narrowed. "Is something wrong? You look pale."

Janet had no wish to explain herself to Louisa. She just shook her head and closed the door and continued down to the main hall. There she found MacKnight, who'd been her husband's man. She didn't know his first name, had never heard it.

"Will you look up on the battlement?" she asked.

He looked at her curiously, but bobbed his head, "Aye, my lady." He took a torch from one of the wall sconces and led the way up. She followed him up the steep, stone steps.

She wasn't surprised to find it empty. She took MacKnight's torch and looked around the battlement. There was no sign anyone had been there.

Her foot hit a pebble and it went skidding across the stone.

"My lady?"

She felt cold. And alone.

"Thank you," she said.

She led the way back to her chamber, then gave him the torch. An oil lamp lit her own chamber.

"Would ye be wantin' more wood?" MacKnight asked.

She realized then she was shivering. She looked inside her room. Colin was still asleep, a thumb in his mouth. The logs in the fireplace were blazing. Several more logs lay alongside.

"No," she said, "I am fine."

"If ye be needing anything . . ."

"I'll call you," she said with a small smile.

Uncertain, he stood there for a moment, then bobbed his head and backed out of the door.

Janet went to her son. He had kicked off the bedclothes. She covered him, leaned down and kissed him. It would be hard not to hover over him forever.

She looked down at her hands. They felt ice-cold.

Then she went to the window and looked out. *Quiet.* Everything was quiet. The few servants were abed. No strangers were outside lurking.

Had she been mistaken upstairs? And if not, who had been up there?

Chapter Four

Janet confronted Reginald. He'd arrived home sometime in the morning and was coming out of his room.

"I want to see the household books," she said.

He gave her what she was sure was meant as a reassuring smile. "Now Janet, you do not want to bother yourself with that. I will take care of everything."

"That is very kind of you," she said, holding her temper. "But Lochaene belongs to my son, and I feel responsible. I believe I should know what is happening."

"'Tis a mon's business," Reginald said. "The servants and tenants would no' pay mind to a lass."

"Mayhap," she said, "but that is not your concern. Our debts are not being paid, the horses are not being fed. I want to know what rents are being paid and what are owed."

Reginald's face turned the shade of a ripe apple. "You are a woman," he said.

"I have not been under the illusion of being anything else over the past twenty-seven years," she retorted. "But my son is an earl, and I am Countess Lochaene."

"My brother died before his time, before"—he added with emphasis—"he made a will."

"The estate is entailed," she said calmly, though her stomach was roiling.

"But a guardian could be appointed," he said. "A *competent* guardian."

She felt as if he had hit her in the stomach. She wondered whether that was where he'd been the past several days. Trying to have himself appointed her son's guardian?

Then, she knew, she could lose Colin. She would never, ever let Reginald and her mother-in-law control her son.

She saw the expression in his eyes. He hadn't meant to tell her that. So he hadn't been successful yet. But that was the plan. It was written all over his florid face. Or was it just one of the plans? Could last night have been another?

A chill crept up her back. If Marjorie and Reginald had control of her son, they would control Lochaene and its rents. And they could bring up her son as an angry, greedy selfish man, after their own image. She would die before she would let that happen.

But one thing was true. Reginald, as a man and as a member of a family loyal to King George, would have far more influence with Cumberland and the English king than a Jacobite widow. Law meant nothing in the Highlands today.

Reginald turned away. She had no doubt that he and Marjorie had been plotting together and had meant to tell her nothing until they won.

"The books," she insisted. She was not going to let him get away with his arrogance, not however long she had as countess.

"No," he said flatly.

"It is my right."

"Not for long." He turned around rudely, as if to go back in his room.

"I will go to the solicitor."

"He was Alasdair's solicitor and he agrees with me that a woman is incompetent to run an estate." He went into his room and closed the door behind him.

Janet was so angry she could not move. She stood there for a moment, wondering whether she should pound on the door, demand to see the books.

And if he continued to refuse?

What could she do except look like a fool? She was not large enough or strong enough to take them from him. Nor could she ask any of the servants to risk their positions, or worse, to do it for *her*.

Was he lying about the solicitor?

Fear played havoc with fury. Lochaene was not personally important to her. It was important only because of Colin and her three stepdaughters. And they were everything. If Reginald was appointed their guardian, he could send her away. He could limit her contact with her son. Dear God. She'd believed that once the authorities had not brought charges against her that she was free.

Alone. She was so alone. And she could lose the children.

If you need a friend . . .

How could she go to Neil? He had made promises before, then had abandoned her. How could she trust anyone who would do that?

Or could he be a part of some devious plan? He had shown up so unexpectedly.

But as she explored her alternatives, she kept coming back to his offer. She detested the idea. She could barely stomach it. How could she ask him for help? The very idea ripped through her pride.

Think of Colin, Grace, Rachel, Annabella. Think what would happen to them if their uncle gained control over them. In just the past few days, their smiles came faster. The wariness was fading from their eyes.

Pride should be nothing compared to their welfare. At least, it was a chance.

Or should she call on the solicitor first? Mayhap Reginald was bluffing.

Yet every time she reviewed the situation she saw little hope. Could she afford the time?

She went up to the room occupied by the lasses. She had offered to replace her husband's great bed with smaller ones, but her daughters had clamored to sleep together. They felt safer that way. They were up, eating their morning meal. Colin gurgled happily at seeing her, and she lifted him up in her arms.

The lasses looked up at her with hopeful eyes. "Can we go to the fair?" Rachel asked.

Janet looked toward Clara, whose face flushed.

"There is a fair in the next village. Kevin said he would take us if your ladyship approves."

Janet raised an eyebrow. "Kevin?"

"Aye, my lady," Clara said, her blush deepening.

Janet smiled. She remembered how she had felt with Neil, how her heart had pounded and her soul soared. He had been so unlike any other suitor. Quiet yet full of depth. Or so she had thought. She jerked the thought from her mind.

"When?"

"Tomorrow after he finishes his chores." Clara stared at her hopefully.

"Can we go?" Annabella asked again. Her arms were full of kitten. "Pleathe."

"Yes, Mama, please," chimed in prim Rachel.

Janet hesitated.

Clara's face fell, and Janet understood she wanted to be with Kevin. Janet tried to decide whether that was good or not. How much protection should she give Clara? How wise was she in the ways of young men? How wise was any woman?

Janet looked at the girls. "I will think about it. In the meantime, would you like to go to the vicar's and borrow a book?"

"Oh aye," said Rachel blissfully. She was the little scholar among them.

"We will take the pony cart," Janet said.

"Can I drive?" Grace asked.

"I was hoping you could care for Colin," Janet said, knowing how much Grace liked playing mother.

"Can we take the puppy, too?" Rachel said.

"I think both of them need some rest," Janet replied gently.

"But the vicar will like them."

"Some other time," Janet said, thinking of the horror of the pony cart with a baby, kitten and puppy.

The prospect of an outing made the bairns' eyes sparkle. They all liked the vicar, Timothy McQueen, who somehow managed to annoy no one, partially because he lived in his books and demanded little of his parishioners. He had helped her in little ways, secretly loaning her books she hid from her husband.

That was as brave as he got. He was in midlife with a mother to support and was totally dependent on Lochaene for his living. He had survived by asking nothing of her late husband. The only time he had ever gone against Alasdair, she thought, had been regarding the books and even then with a promise from Janet never to let her husband know.

Despite his timidity, he was a good man, and Janet liked him. She knew he wanted to be braver, to fight for his congregation, but somewhere in time he had lost his will to fight. Just as she had.

He was in his garden when they drove up. His face broke into a smile when he saw them and he went over to the pony cart, taking Annabella and swinging her to the ground, the the same for Rachel. Grace handed Colin to him, then clamored down on her own.

"And to what do I owe the pleasure of this visit?" he said, beaming at Janet.

"I hoped to borrow some more schoolbooks," she said, knowing that he taught the village children in addition to presiding over the church. "Rachel races through them."

His slightly moist gray eyes regarded her somberly. "Trouble?"

"Aye, I think so."

"My mither has some pastries inside," he told the lasses. "She will be verra happy to have someone to eat them."

The three hesitated. "Go on," she urged them, and took Colin in her arms. They did not need more prompting.

Once they had disappeared inside the small house, Timothy led her into the church and they sat on a bench. "What is it, my lady?"

"I think Reginald is going to try to have himself declared guardian of the children," she said.

He looked distressed. His loyalties were going to be tested again. She felt guilty at asking him, but she had to know. "I have heard rumors," he admitted.

She swallowed hard. She had hoped he would say something else. Hoped against hope. "Could the court do that?"

"They will do what the Duke of Cumberland wants them to do," Timothy said sadly.

"I cannot let Reginald and his mother control my son."

He shrugged helplessly. "The good Lord will protect you."

"The Lord left Scotland years ago," Janet said bitterly.

"You must have faith, my lady."

"I will take my son away first."

"And the lassies? They need you."

"If I'm dead?"

His eyes widened. "What do you mean?"

"I think someone tried to kill me last night." She quickly told him about the figure on the parapet.

"Could ye have seen a shadow?"

"Nay."

Distress crossed his face. "I do not know how to advise you, my lady. Do ye not have someone to turn to?"

She wanted to say nay. She had thought about this moment since her encounter with Reginald. "There may be someone," she said cautiously. "I do not know how to get word to him."

His face cleared. "I can see to that," he said.

"I do not want to get you in trouble," she said. "But I do not know who to trust at Lochaene."

"I do have a few people I trust," Timothy said, "and 'tis little enough to do. I regret . . ."

"Please do not," she said. "I know my husband threatened

to discharge you and that you care for your mother. I know how . . . persuasive he could be."

He put a hand on her shoulder. "The lasses have fared well with ye," he said. "I would not like to see that light in their eyes quenched."

Janet bit her lip. "If I can write a note . . ."

"Aye. And ye must have a sweet, too."

She swallowed hard. "Thank you."

"Can ye rely on this person?"

"I do not know," she said. "But I know no other way."

"Who is it?"

She hesitated, but he would know when he had the message. "The Marquis of Braemoor."

His eyes widened. "A powerful friend."

"In truth, I do not know if he is friend or no', but I have nowhere else to go. All my father's friends died at Culloden."

He nodded. "He will get your letter within three days."

Neil rode over to the new properties. They had been seized from a Jacobite after the Battle at Culloden and came to Braemoor as the dowry of Rory's wife. Neil had half expected Cumberland to take it back after Rory's death and his wife's flight, but the Black Knave had not been seen since Rory's disappearance and the duke had somehow attributed that fact to Rory. It had been tragic that the marquis had died in the crown's cause, but Neil had been permitted to keep the properties.

There had been no one left to farm the newly acquired properties. All had been killed or driven from the land. Neil had been too occupied with events at Braemoor to do anything about it, but now that Jock was beginning to share his enthusiasm he felt he could start buying sheep and cattle. First he had to comb every part of the land, decide where cottages should be built and what land should be planted.

The manor house had been burned. There was nothing but a pile of stones. Much of the land was rock and unfit for farming. He saw several crofts, but they were little more than hovels. He wanted something better for his tenants.

Satisfaction surged inside him. He'd felt Jock's excitement when he'd come back after talking to the tenants. Ten young men, all of them bachelors, had agreed to move. Two of them wanted to marry but hadn't had the means until now. They'd lived in already overcrowded crofts.

After talking with each one, he'd caught their own anticipation of having chances they never thought to have. Most had believed they would be cleared from the land. And, if not, the younger sons had little hope to make a living from the land. They had thought to leave Scotland as so many others had.

The land was mountainous and good for little except grazing. But it was very good for that. Streams meandered the land and rock fences were already in place. Craggy mountains framed the horizon, and the hills were purple with heather. He spent one night on the ground. He woke at dawn and watched the sun rise over the mountains. He wished Janet was there beside him, watching the pink rim turn into gold. Saddling his horse, he wondered whether she would always accompany him in his thoughts.

He wondered how she was faring. As a young widow, she should have a choice of suitors.

He forced her out of his thoughts, knowing that she would not stay banished, then saddled his horse. Another day and he would be back at Braemoor. It was not home, though. He did not think it would ever be home. There were too many bad memories there.

As he rode his horse into Braemoor's stables, he noticed an unfamiliar horse there. He unsaddled his own mount before Jamie, one of the stablelads, came to rub him down. He paused a moment to watch the boy, thinking how much he had grown in the past year. Rory had asked him to look out for the boy, who had been abused by his father. One of Neil's first acts as marquis had been to buy an indenture from the father, then banish the man from Braemoor.

"There's an unfamiliar horse here."

"Aye, my lord," Jamie said. "A messenger came for you two days ago. "He has been staying in the great hall."

"He did not leave the message?"

"Nay. He said he was told to wait for an answer. He has been working here with me. He comes from Concarnie."

Concarnie was near Lochaene.

Without more conversation, he strode quickly to the tower house. He was met there by Torquil, his butler and valet, though Neil seldom had need for the latter. He preferred taking care of his own person, including shaving. But Torquil had needed a position and had been unwilling to take charity.

He was a thin man who looked gloomily over the world. He rarely smiled. And he always muttered as he went about his duties. Now he met Neil at the door, his nose wriggling with indignation. "There be a lad to see ye. He says he has a letter for ye, but he willna leave it with me."

He nodded. "Jamie told me."

Torquil snorted and any other time, Neil would have smiled. He knew how protective Torquil was of his position in the household. And of Neil himself. In truth, Torquil had a kind heart and siphoned off food to give to those who needed it. Then he roared about missing food. Everyone pretended they did not know of Torquil's small kindnesses. It was a gentle game to let Torquil believe he was truly feared and regarded as a crotchety guardian of his master's interests.

"It is all right," Neil said. "Where is he?"

Torquil glowered. "He's been sleeping in the great hall. He came not long after ye left. I dinna know what to do with the ruffian," Torquil said.

"You did right," Neil said. "Is he there now?"

"Aye. He did work some in the stable this morning," Torquil said grudgingly. "Said he wanted to earn his keep."

Neil kept a smile to himself. A gleam of approval glinted in Torquil's eyes despite his disparaging "ruffian."

Neil merely nodded and went into the great hall. A lad was at the great table, eating a plate full of stew. At the sound of boots, he raised his head, then scurried to his feet. "Ye are the Marquis of Braemoor?"

"Aye. You have a message for me?"

The lad, no more than sixteen, reached inside a torn, worn wool shirt and took out a sealed letter. "From the vicar in Concarnie," he said.

He'd expressed the thought earlier that Concarnie was near Janet. Neil took the envelope, tore the seal opened and glanced to the bottom of the letter. *Janet Campbell.* Not "Countess of Lochaene."

"Go back to your meal," he told the lad.

He went out the door, past Torquil's inquisitive face and up the stairs to his own chamber. He wanted to read the letter in private, even as he wondered why Janet had chosen this means to send it. Why not a messenger direct from Lochaene?

He remembered her face, pale and thin. Her eyes, which he'd remembered as soft and full of wonder, had been cautious, wary. The softness was there only when she spoke of the children.

He reached his room, poured himself a drink of brandy from the bottle he always kept there, then sat down at the table. He fingered the parchment for a moment before starting to read. He could almost feel her reluctance in the first sentence, and it sent streaks of pain through his heart.

> *You said if I ever needed a friend . . .*
> *I do fear that I need help. I am asking for it not for myself but for four innocent children. I will understand if you consider it not your business. But mayhap a simple word from you to Lord Cumberland may help safeguard the future of my son and his sisters.*

His stomach tightened as he read on. He sensed how desperate she must have been to send the letter. Damn the Campbells of Lochaene. Damn their souls to hell.

"Torquil," he roared.

Torquil, who'd obviously been hovering nearby, appeared at the door.

"I am leaving again. I will stop by Jock's cottage, then be gone at least four days, mayhap more."

"Ye will eat first," Torquil said. "I have already set a place for ye."

In the dining room, no doubt. Neil had never felt comfortable supping there. In fact, he had never been included at the table when the old marquis had ruled. He always took his meals with the clansmen in the great hall. It had suited him well enough.

But now—mostly to pacify Torquil—he took his meals in lonely splendor in the family dining room. A misnomer if there ever was one, he thought. The old marquis, now dead nearly two years, had hated his second wife—Rory's mother—nearly as much as she had hated him. She had, in truth, hated her husband enough to tell him that Rory was not his son.

Even now, Neil recalled the shouts and screams, the brutality. God, he had hated it. Sometimes he felt the room still echoed with those bitter voices, the raw accusations.

"My lord?" Torquil asked again. "Your supper?"

"Aye," Neil said, knowing the man would nag him until he did. He went into the dining room where a place was set at the end of a very long table.

Torquil gave what was for him a smile and hurried from the room. Neil sighed and poured himself a glass of wine. He did not like the delay, but Torquil was right that he needed to eat. Torquil was, in truth, usually right.

He had found Torquil months ago when, on an odd whim, he went back to his mother's family home some seventy miles away. Even as a lad, he had remembered the desolate falling down wreck of a home on the edge of the sea. His

mother was an only child, and she had died in madness.
When her father died, there was not enough left of the estate
to save. The land reverted to the crown for taxes. But no one
had wanted the damnable thing. The castle had been a
drafty, mean place and the land too poor to grow or graze
anything. Locals said it was even haunted and they kept
away from it.

It was probably the castle that had driven his mother mad,
he'd thought when he'd visited there. He had wandered up
steps to the tower where she had lived until one day she
threw herself out a window, or so they said. That had been
more than twenty years ago. Her father died six months later
with no more issue, and word passed that the castle was
haunted. No one had lived there since.

He had wandered through the wreckage, trying to remember. But all he could recall was his silent mother sitting
in a chair, rocking. He remembered being told he was fortunate that a kinsman would take him in as a companion for
his own son.

He recalled riding away. He had turned back and seen his
mother's face in the window. That was the sum total of his
memories of this place.

As he was about to leave this second time, Torquil had
appeared seemingly out of nowhere. He had once served
the family as a groom, he said. He was nearly sixty, thin to
the point of emaciation and dressed in little more than rags.
The clothing was clean, though, and his lined face clean
shaven. He said he was the caretaker, and he was allowed
to live in the stables in exchange for looking after the property. He had been doing just that for the past two decades.
Probably, he added honestly, everyone had forgotten about
the estate. And him.

Neil had taken an instant liking to the man who looked as
if he had not had a decent meal in as long as he'd cared for
the property. It was unusual for Neil to accept someone so
readily, yet he had found himself asking if Torquil would
like to come to Braemoor.

And so Torquil had gone with him to Braemoor. He kept entirely to himself, but was as reliable as the sun appearing in the sky each day. He had started as a coachman but soon moved into the house when the former butler had become ill. He soon became indispensable, but never said anything of his past life or even memories of the last family he served. When Neil asked about the past, he mumbled that it was too many years ago, that time had jumbled his mind. . . .

Torquil appeared with his meal. "I will prepare some clothes for ye," Torquil said. "What will ye need?"

Neil paused. He would go to Edinburgh first. His Grace, the Duke of Cumberland, was there, currently in residence at Holyroodhouse. He would make it clear that the countess was under his protection, then he would pay a visit to Lochaene.

"I am going to try to see Cumberland," he said.

"Your best clothes, then?"

Neil nodded. He had purchased some clothing after inheriting Braemoor, knowing that on occasion he would need it. But he still didn't feel comfortable in the silks and satin. He far preferred the outlawed kilt. Still, he had a pair of dark blue satin breeches and a light blue doublet, and dark waistcoat. It was fine enough material for Cumberland's presence.

As soon as he finished eating quickly, he shaved as Torquil prepared his better clothes for travel, then pulled on his riding clothes: plain buckskin breeches, plain woolen shirt and jacket. 'Twas somber wear, especially with the boots he preferred, but it suited his taste.

Within the hour, he went to the stable where Jamie had already saddled two horses, one for the young lad and the other for himself. They mounted and trotted out of the courtyard.

He hated taking time to stop at Jock's but the man knew he had gone to inspect the new lands. Trust was still a fragile thing for both of them, and he could not disappear for days, perhaps a week, without an explanation.

Jock was not at his cottage, and Neil took another two hours to find him. When he did, Neil tossed Jock a leather purse full of coins and told him to get what was needed to build the cottages on the new property. He drew a map, indicating where he believed the best locations were.

"Should I no' wait for yer return?"

"Nay, I donna know how long I will be gone, and we made promises."

Jock just looked puzzled.

"Someone I . . . know might be in trouble."

A small smile tugged at Jock's mouth. "You be taking care of 'em, then. I will see to things here."

"I know you will," Neil said. And he meant it.

Cumberland eyed Neil with haughty amusement. "I see you have none of your cousin's taste in clothing."

Neil had stopped at an inn to change clothes before requesting an audience with Cumberland. Internally, though, he squirmed with discomfort. His personal contacts with Cumberland had been minimal. Rory had manipulated him, but Neil had none of Rory's talents for subterfuge. He only knew how to state his case bluntly and he felt much like a ruffian in the princely surroundings that was Holyroodhouse. The thought was too close to reality for comfort.

"Nay, my lord," he said simply.

"You asked to see me?" Cumberland said impatiently.

"Aye, Your Grace. I am here on behalf of the Countess of Lochaene."

"Ah, the newly bereaved widow," Cumberland said. "And what is your connection with her?"

"My uncle and her father were friends."

"Her father was a Jacobite," Cumberland said coldly.

"And my uncle and I fought beside you," Neil reminded him. He knew he was stepping on shaky ground but he steeled himself for whatever was coming.

"You have never married," Cumberland said thoughtfully.

Neil went still. He had not known what Cumberland was

going to say, or do, when he'd approached his adjutant for an audience. Now he wondered what to say. If Cumberland knew about the madness in his family, would he continue to support Neil's claim of Braemoor?

"I've been in no position to marry," Neil said. "I had nothing to offer until my cousin died." He hesitated, then added, "In your service."

"There are whispers that she might have murdered her husband."

"There are often whispers, but I know the countess. 'Tis a ridiculous accusation."

"A woman cannot run an estate."

"Then appoint me her guardian."

"You are busy at Braemoor," Cumberland said. "Reginald Campbell is willing to take responsibility."

"Forgive me, Your Grace, but I think his ability . . . and reliability . . . is in some question."

From his facial expression, Cumberland had caught his meaning. Reginald Campbell had avoided the king's service. "His family has always been loyal to the crown."

Neil wished again he had Rory's ability with words. He tried to use the one argument he thought would appeal to Cumberland. "I believe, Your Grace, I could produce more taxes for you than the Honorable Reginald Campbell."

Cumberland's eyes were like ice. "If you are so interested in her welfare," Cumberland said, "you could think about marrying her."

"Her husband has been dead only these past weeks. She is still in mourning."

Cumberland's eyes narrowed. "I told Campbell I would consider his request."

Neil had made it his business to know about the Alasdair Campbell's family. Janet's husband had declared for King George but Neil did not remember seeing him at Culloden. His brother, Reginald, had been in England.

His stomach tied into a knot. His heart beat faster. He knew that Janet would be furious about what he was about to do, but he needed to buy her time. "I do have an interest in the widow," he said. "I was planning to wait a proper amount of time."

Cumberland regarded him with steely eyes. "How is Braemoor faring these days?"

"Very well, Your Grace."

"No problem with the tenants?"

"Nay."

"I must say I miss your cousin, even if he was a popinjay. He always brought me fine brandy."

"I will endeavor to do the same."

Cumberland allowed a small smile, then returned to the subject at hand. "I will appoint you temporary guardian for the young earl and will allow you a short time to court the new widow, Braemoor. But you will be responsible for seeing that Lochaene pays its share of taxes. The army needs money."

"Aye, my lord."

Neil bowed his way out of Cumberland's chamber.

Once outside, he tried to relax. He was not sure what he had done. He had provided Janet with some time, but he knew she would not be pleased with the conditions attached. She most certainly would not happily view him as a prospective husband.

Nor could he even consider marrying her. He would not be able to keep away from her. He knew that. And nothing had changed since that day he'd learned about his past, about his family.

But he'd bought her time, time to find another champion.

In the meantime, she would have to accept his protection. He did not think that would be easy for her to swallow.

He heard a snort of laughter and was surprised to realize it was his own. It had no humor in it, though. He'd just spun a web that might well trap them both.

Chapter Five

Janet gazed out of her chamber window. She'd had no more success in prying the books away from Reginald than on her last attempt.

She had ridden to see the solicitor but he had given her no help. He, too, had insisted that a woman had no head for business or management. It was "unfortunate" that after her son's birth her husband had not made provisions for a guardianship. Her brother-in-law was assuming that role, and she should be grateful.

She fumed with helpless indignation.

It had been more than a week since she'd sent her letter to the Marquis of Braemoor, and she had heard nothing. She didn't know whether she felt disappointment or relief. Certainly, she had been right in her assessment of his concern.

But she had not found a way to get around Reginald's refusal to acknowledge her rights to Lochaene. He had even gone so far as to tell the grooms that they were not to accept orders from her. If she did not acquiesce, he implied he would press murder charges against her.

The bairns—except for Grace, who was in the kitchen—were down for the afternoon. Janet knew she had to get away from the tower, from its cold, gray stone walls and the bleakness of the rooms.

She went to the stable and chose a mare. Kevin was not there, but a rough-looking man came up to her. "The master said ye were not to ride alone."

"I will do as I wish."

"Nay, mi'lady. I 'ave my orders."

She could only surmise that the solicitor had reported her visit and Reginald wanted no more interference. "Then you may ride with me," she said.

"I got work 'ere," he said rudely.

"Where is Kevin?"

"I donna know who ye mean."

"He worked here yesterday."

The man shrugged.

"Your name?"

"Bain."

"Have you tended horses before?"

"Aye."

"Then let me see you saddle this horse," she said.

He started to walk off.

"You take one more step, and you will leave Lochaene."

"Ye 'ave no authority."

"I do not know what the *Honorable* Reginald Campbell told you, but I am the Countess of Lochaene. My brother-in-law has no authority to forbid anything. My son is earl."

She did not know whether or not it was the anger in her voice, but he hesitated. She saw sudden indecision in his eyes. "You do not have to saddle the horse," she said, "but I would advise you to consult with my brother-in-law again before denying me my own property."

That did it. He obviously thought her incapable of saddling her own horse. He shot her an angry look, then lumbered toward the tower. As soon as he was out of sight, she found the lightest gear and quickly saddled one of the two mares. She'd done it often as a young girl; her father had thought she should learn everything in handling a mount.

With the help of a mounting stone, she settled into saddle, hooking her knee around the saddlebow. She walked the mare through the stable doors only to see Bain coming toward her. He started to run toward her. A shout spooked the mare who broke into a trot, then a wild gallop.

Janet allowed her rein. It suited her purposes that Bain believed the horse was spooked. She would blame everything on him.

She allowed the mare to run until they were out of sight, then she slowly but firmly reined her in and slowed her to a walk. Then she headed toward the mountains. One afternoon. Just one afternoon. She felt the tears welling behind her eyes. She told herself it was frustration. She'd never believed in self-pity.

Janet rode into the mountains, toward a waterfall that fell into a pool below. A mist fell over the gray-green mountains, and it washed out some of the anger. Her hair fell from its knot and lay damp across her face. It had been so long since she had felt this kind of freedom.

She rode for another hour, until she was drenched through and through. The air had turned cold and slashed through her wet clothes. Janet shivered and turned back. It was time, more than time to return.

Halfway back, she saw smoke curling from the chimney of a croft. Neatly plowed rows in front looked empty, unplanted.

She rode the mare up to the croft, slipped from the mount and knocked on the door.

It opened, and a man who looked to be in his late middle years stared at her blankly.

"I . . . am Janet Campbell," she said, uncertain about either her welcome or even her own intent.

"The countess," the man sneered. "I know rightly who ye are," he said coldly.

A woman pushed beside him. "And she be soaked an' shiverin', Angus." She pushed him aside. "Come in and warm yerself."

The inside of the croft was dark, the sides blackened by peat fires. The smell of peat permeated the interior. She looked at the table. It was full of bowls. Her gaze went around to four small, thin children.

"Will ye 'ave some hot soup?" the woman said.

Janet heard a grunt of protest from a corner. An older boy leaned against a wall. "Ain't enough fer us now," he said.

"Hush," said the woman.

"Nay," Janet said. "I just saw your fire, and the fields outside. They are not planted."

"There is no seed," the boy said. The older man, apparently the father, said nothing.

Janet swallowed a bitter breath. It was the lord's responsibility to provide the seed. She wondered how many other crofters had not received their allotment. Without seed, they could not pay rent. Without rent, they would be evicted.

She had heard of the clearances, knew that many landlords were clearing their land to raise cattle and sheep. She'd even heard her husband speak of plans to purchase more livestock. She had not realized, though, that he was starving out the tenants.

And yet the woman had offered her what had to be sorely inadequate for her family. They all looked starved.

"I thank you," she said, "but I am not hungry."

"No' for our poor offerings," the boy muttered.

She wanted to reassure them that she would take care of their needs, that she *would* provide seed, but how could she promise anything? How could she give them help when she could not help herself, when she had to steal a horse to take even a ride? Anger fermented inside her. No wonder Reginald hadn't wanted her to explore the holdings.

"Are the other crofters . . . not getting seed?" she asked.

"Do ye not even know?" the boy said contemptuously.

"John!" The woman said in rebuke.

"Why? Wha' are they goin' tae do tae us tha' they ha' no' already done?" He moved closer to her. He was a tall lad of eighteen or nineteen years with a hank of black hair falling over his forehead. "As fer yer question, many have already left. The ones tha' ain't are starvin'. My mither and her mither willna leave. So we stay and starve until the sheriff comes."

She felt his hatred radiate through her.

Janet wanted to back up, straight out the door. But she had been cowardly enough these past few years. She did not know if she could have done something, but she could have tried. *It would only have made him angrier, more determined to do what he planned to do.* But mayhap she may have been able to slip some food to the tenants.

I will do something. I have to do something. For Colin's heritage, his inheritance.

She straightened her back. "Thank you for your hospitality," she said.

"But ye are still wet," the woman protested.

Janet heard a snort from the boy. "She will soon be warm an' well fed."

She turned to face him. "You are right," she said softly. "I wish . . . I could do the same . . ." She felt the too-familiar tears coming to her eyes, and she backed away, going out the door and nearly running to her horse. With the help of a stump, she managed to mount, then looked back. Six thin faces stared at her from the doorway. Thin and resentful. All but the woman, who merely looked weary beyond her years.

She turned the mare away. In some way, she would regain control of Lochaene. And then no man would ever control her, or her actions, again.

She swore it.

Neil rode hard. The lad, Tim, was riding one of Braemoor's horses; the lad's own decrepit beast was stabled at Braemoor until it had been well fed and rested.

The vicar apparently had given Tim a sovereign to deliver the letter. Neil intended to add several more, and mayhap give him employment. The lad had told him his father could not find work, and there were three small brothers to feed.

Neil could not help but realize the changes that had overtaken Scotland since Culloden. He was fully aware, of course, of Cumberland's rampage across the land, killing every Jacobite he could find and burning both crofts and manors. He remembered the ceilidhs that he had attended as Donald's aide and bodyguard. He could almost hear the plaintive sounds of the pipes and spirited fiddles, see the Highlanders in their plaids and women in their clan tartans. They were all banned now.

The hills and mountains seemed ghostly reminders as the mist closed around them. Many of the Highland clans—all of those which were Jacobites—had been decimated. He closed his eyes, seeing them as they were earlier at Culloden. Proud and brave and stubborn. They had been the best of Scotland. To the day he died, he would regret his part in it. *He would try to make his own kind of atonement, just as Rory had.*

He reached Lochaene in late afternoon, finding it an uproar.

An angry Reginald Campbell was berating someone outside the doors. He looked up as a dusty, damp Neil rode up.

Neil had left the lad with his family in the small village a few miles distant. He did not want anyone to know that Janet had written him. He came, though, with an order from Cumberland.

Campbell regarded him balefully, obviously not remembering him from his brother's funeral. But Campbell had been drunk then, Neil remembered. Neil's travel-stained clothes obviously did nothing to assist the man's assessment of his visitor.

Neil dismounted. "Campbell," he said, not even granting him the "honorable" title.

The man bristled, his gaze flickering contemptuously over Neil. "It's 'my lord'."

"I think not," Neil said. "I understand the new earl is but a bairn."

" 'Tis none of your concern," Campbell said as he turned away.

"Aye, but it is," Neil said with equanimity. "I have been

appointed guardian of the young earl. I believe it was at your urging that the Duke of Cumberland decided a woman could not competently manage such an estate. I owe you a debt of thanks."

Color drained from Campbell's face. Then, just as rapidly, color flushed back into it. "You lie."

"You will take back that word, Campbell. No one calls me a liar without consequences."

Campbell's face turned even paler. "*Who* are you?"

"Oh, did I forget to introduce myself? So sorry. I am the Marquis of Braemoor. You can call *me* 'my lord.' And I have not heard your apology."

Neil knew he should not take such pleasure in tormenting the man, but it seemed little enough for the misery he'd obviously caused Janet. A taste of his own medicine should be instructional.

"*His Grace* would . . . would not . . . it cannot be . . ." Campbell blustered.

"It is," Neil said with no little sense of satisfaction. He did not think it would last and so he enjoyed this moment. He suspected that despite his good intent, Janet was not going to be delighted with what had just happened. She had asked for assistance, but he was sure she had not intended to trade Reginald for him as her child's guardian.

His stomach knotted as he even thought about it. "Where is the countess?"

"We are looking for her. She went riding hours ago."

"That is unusual?"

Reginald muttered something to himself.

"I did not hear you," Neil said sharply, sensing something he did not like at all. Janet had merely said Reginald had been trying to gain guardianship, nothing more. Had he also made her a prisoner in her own home?

"Some of the tenants could be . . . dangerous," Reginald said. "They are lazy, resentful. My brother had evicted some of them."

Anger coursed through Neil. He could barely contain it.

Yet he suspected he needed to be careful. Reginald Campbell came from a clan held in high esteem by the duke. If this particular branch did not share in that regard, 'twas not to say they could not gain support if he overplayed his hand. He was walking a very thin rope.

"I'll go with you to look for her," he offered.

Reginald frowned as recognition finally dawned in his eyes. "You were here for my brother's burial."

"You are a little late in remembering, but aye, I was here."

"You know the countess?"

"Aye, our fathers were friends."

"And now you believe you deserve these lands. *My* lands." Indignation shaded the charge.

"I believe the rightful earl deserves these lands. I am merely here to assure he will get them. Now I believe I need a fresh horse to look for the countess."

Neil noticed Reginald's fingers were bunched in fists.

A shout distracted him. He turned and watched a figure on a horse trot toward him. A groom ran toward her. She leaned down and said something, and the servant moved aside. Then she saw him.

Her eyes widened. Her cloak was sodden, her hair clinging loose to her cheek. He went over to her side, and held out his hand to her.

She hesitated for a moment, then took it. She was cold, shivering. Her blue eyes were uncertain. He quickly released her. "You are cold, my lady."

She ignored his observation as she pushed hair away from her face. "My lord. I did not expect you."

"Did you not, my lady?" he said in a voice too low for Campbell to hear.

"Nay."

That comment pierced, too. Despite her request, she obviously had expected him to refuse. But then why should she not? Hadn't he abandoned her before?

Shivers ran through her body again. "You should warm yourself," he said. "We can talk later."

"You are staying?"

"Aye, my lady."

"Reginald?"

"Reginald has no say in the matter."

Her eyes widened at his tone. He saw her glance over toward Reginald, who was glowering.

Then she turned toward the manor house.

He watched her go, the sodden clothes wrapped around her like a castle wall, her back stiff with pride, her hair wet and tangled under a drooping bonnet. Even so, there was a graceful dignity about her even now.

Neil watched her go through the door and knew that he'd not tamed the wild, burning yearning inside him.

Janet was shaking. Shivering, really. And not from the cold.

Her letter to him had been born in desperation. She'd been truthful when she'd told him she had not expected much. At most, she'd hoped that he would speak to the Duke of Cumberland on her behalf. She certainly had not expected him to suddenly appear at Lochaene.

What did he want?

And what did he mean when he said Reginald had no say in the matter?

She heard a light knock on the door and opened it. Lucy stood there, looking most anxious. "Everyone has been looking fer you, my lady."

"So I understand," she replied wryly. "Has no mistress ever gone for a ride before?"

"That new groom . . . he said you stole a horse."

"How can I steal my own horse?" she said. She looked at Lucy. Servants always knew more than anyone realized. "And what happened to Kevin?"

Lucy's gaze looked away. "He was dismissed, my lady." She hesitated, then said hurriedly, "Can you do something, my lady? His family depends on those few coins."

When Lucy looked at her again, Janet saw a sheen of tears in her eyes.

"Well then we will try to do something about it. But first help me change these clothes."

Lucy ducked her head. "Aye, my lady." She helped Janet untie the ribbons to her dress, then handed her a dressing robe. Then she went to the hearth and placed more logs in the fire.

"How long has the marquis been here?" Janet asked.

"The marquis?"

"The Marquis of Braemoor."

"I think he must have just arrived."

Janet clenched her fist. She could not even imagine how she'd looked as she had ridden in. A nearly drowned rat was a good description. Her hair was wet and matted and steaming down her face, her costume soaked. She told herself that her appearance really did not matter. What *did* matter was his reception. She wished she had been cool and well dressed and well coifed and had swept down to meet him.

He was probably thanking God in heaven that he had not married her.

"My hair," she said, summoning all her courage. She had to know why he had come, why he had said what he had about Reginald. "Can you do something with my hair? I must go back down."

"But ye are still shivering."

"It doesna matter," she said.

"I will do my best, my lady."

An hour later, Lucy handed Janet a mirror. Her hair had been tamed into a braid that Lucy then twisted in a circle at the back of her head. A few damp tendrils framed her face, but Janet knew her face looked thin and pale, her dark blue eyes too large and shadowed. She pinched her cheeks, trying to bring some color into them.

Not for him, she told herself. For her son. For the lasses.

Then she put on a plain dark dress devoid of trim which, she knew, made her look even more colorless. But she was still in mourning.

"Thank you," she told Lucy, then headed up to the nursery. Three blond heads looked toward the door as she walked in. Grace was holding Colin, who gave her a happy baby grin and held out his arms toward her. She went over and picked him up, hugging him close to her.

Annabella came running over to her, her lower lip stuck out. "I worried," she said.

"Well you donna have to worry any more, sugarplum. I just went for a ride."

"Uncle Reggie was angry," Grace said in her own careful way. "He thought we might know where you went."

Janet hugged Colin closer to her. "He dinna hurt you?"

Grace shook her head but Janet saw the fear in her eyes. She should not have gone. It had been selfish of her, but she had so needed to escape the prison the manor had become. It was probably that, and more, for the children. A place of fear.

She closed her eyes. *Let Braemoor be here to help.*

But at what price? She knew now that everyone wanted something. He would want something, too.

She only hoped it would not be too high a price.

She gave Colin a last hug, then put him back down on the floor with Grace. Then she hugged each of her stepdaughters, one at a time. Annabella came last and planted a wet moist kiss on her cheek.

With that touch of sweetness, she could, she would, do anything that would protect them.

"Stay here," she said. "Lucy will bring up your supper."

Grace nodded and Janet's heart lurched. They had all learned to be little shadows, darting away from any quick movement. Their world as so small, so gray, so full of fear. She had done what she could to protect them, but she had not been able to erase the anxiety that never quite left their eyes.

The Marquis of Braemoor was waiting for her in the withdrawing room, MacKnight told her after she descended the steps. The withdrawal room was off the great room and seldom used by a family that had not liked being together.

She bit her lip, then opened the door.

Neil Forbes was sitting in a chair before a fire, his long legs stretched out in front of him. His dark hair looked as if he'd combed it with his fingers, and though he had changed clothes they looked more as if they should be worn by a merchant than a lord. His shirt was linen but devoid of lace or trim, and he wore simple trousers that were molded against powerful legs. Black boots encased his feet and lower legs.

She stood at the door, aware that he had not yet noticed her presence, which gave her a moment to study him. He should have looked relaxed as he sprawled out in the chair, but he did not. She sensed a coiled restlessness in him, that he was no more comfortable in these surroundings than he had been at Braemoor years ago.

Then, though, she had thought him reserved and quiet, even shy. It had been those qualities that had appealed to her, that and an unexpected gentleness she'd never known in a man before. After Donald's leering drunkenness at Braemoor, it had been appealing.

And a lie.

He turned, as if sensing her presence, and unwound his tall body and stood. He bowed slightly. "My lady. I did not hear you."

"Have you come from Braemoor?" she asked.

"Nay, from Edinburgh," he said.

Her stomach clenched. The last time she had seen him she'd rudely rejected his help, and she'd had to pocket her pride when she'd written the letter. She'd never thought he would reply, particularly in person, and now she had to eat even more pride. She did not know what to say. Finally, she gathered her wits. "You received my letter."

"Aye," he said. "I was away from home when the lad arrived. Or I would have been here sooner."

He was apologizing.

"I dinna know who . . . to turn to," she stammered. "Everyone—"

"You need no' explain. I know about your father and brother. I was sorry to hear about them."

"Why? They were Jacobites." The bitterness rushed out unheeded. She knew the Braemoor Forbes had fought alongside Cumberland at Culloden.

"They were good men," he said quietly.

She wanted to believe him, to believe the sincerity she thought she heard beneath the words, but she had believed them once before, and he had wanted only her dowry. How could she believe him now?

Yet he was here, and her body reacted to his presence as it had years earlier. The air was suddenly thick with strong emotion. She felt regret and loss and anger and resentment.

He took a step toward her and raised a hand, caressing her cheek with the back of his fist.

"I had hoped you were still no' so bonny."

"And you, my lord, are still a liar." 'Twas a cruel, unwise thrust. But her body was betraying her. So was her heart. She had to do something to force him to step away, or she would throw herself in his arms. And she would never, ever do that again.

He stepped back as a muscle leaped along his tightened jaw. She wondered whether she had just made the biggest mistake of her life in insulting someone she needed so badly. Desperation warred with need, defensiveness with want.

He must have seen the sudden caution in her eyes, because he took a second step back. "I have news," he said. "I am not sure you will be pleased about it."

Her heart seemed to stop, then beat harder. "Reginald won his request," she said flatly, hoping against hope it was not true.

"Nay, but His Grace *has* appointed a guardian."

Her heart stopped. She did not like the way he said it, as if something worse was coming. She could not imagine anything worse than Reginald gaining legal control, but obviously . . . "Who?" she whispered.

He turned away and stared at the fire. His stance was coiled, controlled. She had never known anyone so in control of his emotions, of his every thought. Even . . .

"*I* was named guardian of your son," he said softly.

Janet felt numb for a moment. Stunned. Her stomach roiled. What had she done? She'd exchanged one keeper for another, one thief for another. He had betrayed her once again. How could she have been such a fool? "How could you?" she whispered.

He turned back and his dark eyes met hers. "It was the only way, my lady. I also said I had . . . an interest in you. Cumberland is not going to let so much land remain under the control of a Jacobite."

"And I gave you a gift with my letter," she said bitterly.

"I have no interest in Lochaene," he said. "None other than to see that it is kept for the rightful heir. I did not mention the letter to His Grace. I merely said my uncle was your father's friend and would wish me to help."

"And did he believe that?"

"I doubt it," he said. "But he wants to insure that the land stays in loyalist hands."

"*Your* hands."

"Aye," he said.

His calm demeanor infuriated her. She wondered why she had ever thought he might help her, why she could trust him. *Desperation.* It had been desperation, plain and simple, and she had delivered herself into his hands. "Your family seems to be uncommonly fortunate in receiving stolen lands," she said bitterly.

"I have no intention of stealing your lands, or your son's heritage," he said. "You trusted me enough to ask for my help. Trust me now."

"I dinna trust you," she said bitterly. "I had nowhere else to turn. I had hoped only that you would ask Cumberland to name me legal guardian. No more. Certainly not . . ." Her voice broke off. She needed to trust someone. But she had trusted him with her heart and he had shattered it. If she could not trust him with the most precious thing she had, how could she trust him with what belonged to her son?

"Janet?"

She winced at the sound of her name on his lips. Too many memories. "I will never trust you again," she said. "I made that mistake once. I canna do it again."

His lips tightened, but he did not defend himself. "I will look for someone to help you manage the estate," he said after a moment's silence, "but I will make it clear that you make the decisions. By necessity, I will be required to stay here occasionally. Cumberland wants accountings from me, and I donna want any problems with your brother-in-law. I will try no' to be in your way."

"And what do you expect in return?"

He took a step backward as if she'd hit him. Then he smiled, but only one side of his lips turned up in an expression both wry and vulnerable.

Vulnerable as a snake. She had to remember that.

"Have you told Reginald?"

"Aye, he was not happy."

"He has threatened to press . . . charges against me."

"Not unless he wishes to be cut off altogether," Neil said, "and he and his family told to leave. I will make that clear."

She leaned against a wall. He could be ruthless. And she still did not know what he wanted, what he expected. She recalled Neil's words, that Cumberland thought he had an interest in her. The implication was, of course, marriage.

Not again. She would never marry again. She would never put herself at the mercy of a man. And he had made it clear years ago he had no interest in her.

Except now she may have something he wanted. More land? A wife that met Cumberland's approval? A mistress?

"I have no choice?"

"Nay," he said.

She closed her eyes. She had leaped from the pot into the

fireplace. How could she have been so foolish? Somehow she should have found a way to outwit Reginald. She did not think she could outwit this man with the cool, cautious eyes, the man she no longer recognized.

"How long do you plan to stay?"

"Until Reginald understands his position and you have the help you will be needing."

She raised an eyebrow. "You mean someone who will report to you."

He shrugged. "As I rode here, I could see the land has been neglected."

"Do you propose to help the people who live here or clear the land?" she asked.

"As I said, the decision will be yours."

"And if I wish to try to run Lochaene myself?"

His eyes appraised her. "Do you think you could?"

"Aye," she said. "Better than my husband."

"From what I've seen, that would not require much skill," he said dryly.

She bristled. "I do not remember Braemoor as being much better."

He regarded her steadily. "I did not realize you noticed."

"Because my attention was elsewhere?" she said. "You flatter yourself, my lord."

He leaned against a wall, his legs crossing. "In any event," he said, "you are right. Braemoor was in need of improvement. I am making changes."

"Evicting your tenants?"

"Culloden ended the old system," he said. "Too many lands have been forfeited and changed hands. The old traditional obligations of clanship no longer exist. Not at Braemoor. Not here. Not anywhere in Scotland. 'Tis better for many to go to the new lands in America."

"So sayeth a man who owns a good part of Scotland," she said. "You do not care if they starve in the process."

"My lands are none of your concern," he said, his eyes darkening. "You should be worrying about your own."

"They are not mine. They are my son's, and I want him to care about the people whose families have lived here for centuries."

"A noble goal," he said, "though probably impractical."

She wanted to hit him. He sounded superior and supercilious. Everything she attributed to his cousin years ago. Had he changed so much? Or did wealth truly corrupt?"

"I do not think so," she said.

"And the first thing you would do?"

"Get some seed to the tenants. And some food."

"Where are the estate books?"

"Reginald has them. He has refused to hand them over to me. He expected to be appointed guardian."

His face hardened. "After I see him, we will go over them together."

"You dinna answer my question."

"About running Lochaene? It would not be easy, my lady. Men are no' so ready to take orders from a lass."

She glared at him. "My husband has nearly destroyed Lochaene. I could not do worse."

"The point isn't not doing worse. It is doing far better."

She bit her lower lip. He sounded so sure of himself. Confident. Ruthless. She still did not know what he wanted. There had to be something, a missing piece of a puzzle.

His gaze bored into her. And found her wanting? Did it even matter?

"You have never married, my lord?"

His lips firmed into a tight line and he was silent for a moment. "Nay. I had naught to offer until my cousin . . . died last year." A mask smoothed over his face, and he turned back to the fire. "I will require a room, madam. And food. It has been a long journey. We can talk again after I see the books."

Janet lifted her chin. She had just been dismissed in her own home. She had her answer about assuming control.

"The children have my late husband's room. I wanted

them close to me," she said. "I would not like to see them moved."

"And I would not wish to see them move. I am used to plain surroundings, my lady. I do not require much. Any room will be sufficient. A bed and a table. And some food. We can discuss the estate on the morrow."

"I will have a room prepared," she said cooly, but she did not feel cool. He had turned away from the fireplace and approached her, and she saw the shadows in his eyes. As he came closer, heat rose in her. An almost palpable tension stretched between them and she wanted to reach out, to smooth the lines around his eyes. She did not think they came from laughter.

Remember what happened before. You thought he wanted you then.

Her stomach quivered. She stiffened her back and took a step backward, her hand reaching behind her for the door.

Then, to her shame, she turned and ran. Escaped from him. From her own thunderous feelings.

Chapter Six

Neil spent a most unpleasant hour with Reginald, who still protested the guardianship and presenting the books to Neil. The man had been drinking and was belligerent. It was not until Neil threatened to ask Cumberland for some soldiers that Reginald grudgingly handed over the books.

When Neil emerged from the study, a servant—a young woman—showed him to a room.

The mistress, she said, was with the children.

While not luxurious, the room was clean and, as he requested, had a table and chair as well as a large bed and a wardrobe. A decanter and glasses were on the table, and he poured himself a glass. Port. Not particularly good port, but he welcomed its warmth as he sprawled in the chair and opened the large ledger book.

Neil had kept the books for Braemoor even before assuming the title. He was scrupulous about them. He looked at Lochaene's books and even his first cursory glance found trouble. There had been no entries for several months. What rents were mentioned were obviously overly high for this unfertile ground.

Long overdue bills were stuffed between the pages of the book.

He would have to do an inventory, determine what could

be sold to raise enough coin to buy seed. Either seed or sheep. He had no idea from the state of the books how many sheep or cattle Lochaene claimed.

It was perfectly evident that he would have to loan funds to the estate to give it any chance of succeeding. He wondered how he could do that without Janet's knowledge. She would want to refuse. She'd made it clear she'd wanted nothing from him except to convince Cumberland to give her guardianship. That he had emerged with it had made her more than a little suspicious.

He knew it had galled her to ask him for help; it must be magnified three times that by now. To hand her money would only further destroy her pride. Yet he knew from the books and the state of the property that it could not survive without a large influx of money—and soon.

He'd been a fool years ago, thinking that she would readily forget what had happened and marry well. Part of that belief had been his own lack of faith in himself. What woman would really want to risk the madness that tainted his blood or share the poverty of his position then. He had sought to protect her, and now he realized he had struck a mean blow that had never healed, perhaps had even led her into a loveless marriage.

In the end, he hadn't protected her. He'd had damned little experience at being noble, and so he'd been completely inept at that, too.

Bloody hell, but he had made a mess of everything.

Eventually, she would have to accept his financial help if she wanted any inheritance for her son, but it would cost her dearly. And he had already cost her enough.

A knock came on the door, and he felt a momentary anticipation. Janet?

He rose and went to the door. The same servant who had shown him the room had a tray loaded with food.

"Your mistress? Is she dining tonight?"

"She is eating with the lassies," the girl said.

"And you are . . . ?"

She curtsied neatly. "Lucy, my lord."

"Then my thanks, Lucy."

She bobbed and blushed. "Ye are welcome, my lord."

"Will you ask your mistress if she can go riding over the property with me in the morning?"

"Aye, my lord."

He nodded and shut the door, placing the tray down on the table. There was a roasted chicken, sweet potatoes, boiled buttered carrots, and a fruit pastry. He was surprised at how good it was. But the food left a bitter taste in his mouth. He was damnably tired of eating alone, of being alone. Perhaps he had even hoped . . .

But that had been an unwise hope. He needed to stay away from the countess. He'd come close today to making a fool of himself. But the fire in those dark blue eyes was like a flame to his moth. So was her fine soft skin and the lips that trembled ever so slightly. He remembered the feel of them in vivid detail. The years had peeled back as if they had never existed.

He tried to dismiss the image and concentrate on the changes. But they, too, were dangerous. He was as attracted to the woman she was today as he had been to the lass she had been. He had hoped that would not be true, but he'd known it was the moment he'd seen her again. His heart still spun out of control. Reason fled. He'd realized how much he wanted her beside him.

He'd hoped that he could come for a day or so, settle the fact that he, not Reginald, was the young earl's guardian. He would find someone to help her, but then he could be gone. But now he knew he could not do that. Reginald's enmity ran too deep. The finances of the estate were too tangled. No matter how intelligent Janet was, she would not be able to unravel them without help. He would not stay, but he would have to make frequent trips back.

And each would be a visit to hell. He remembered an old Greek tale. Tantalus, that was it. He had offended the gods, and he was condemned to stand up to the chin in a pool of water in Hades and beneath fruit-laden boughs only to have the water or fruit recede at each attempt to drink or eat.

Mayhap that was his punishment for Culloden, for protecting a bully, for closing his eyes to misery.

He finished his meal, took another sip of port. Then he paced. When he had ridden onto Lochaene, he'd seen unplowed fields, empty pastures, abandoned crofts. How bad was it? The groom had been a hulking, inept man. Neil had tended his own horse, knowing that he wanted the man nowhere near his horse.

He took the oil lamp from his room, went down the stairs and out to the stable. No one was there. He set down the lamp and went through the stables. The stalls needed cleaning, and the horses moved restlessly, which meant they'd probably not had enough to eat. He checked around for oats and found only hay.

He swore to himself. Matters would change on the morrow. He would bring the young lad who had fetched him to Lochaene. He'd had a fine eye and a way with horses.

Neil had reached the back of the stable when he heard a noise. Someone else had entered. The groom? A stableboy? If it was one or the other, Neil meant to upbraid him. He lowered the flame in the lamp and moved into the shadows without really knowing why. Instinct? Curiosity? Caution born of an uncertain childhood? He could not remember when he had not listened. There had been too many blows. Too many insults.

But then he heard *her* voice, low and melodic.

Janet was talking softly, obviously to one of the horses. "I will get you some good oats," she promised. He heard a noise of a stall opening, then the sound of rustling straw. He stepped out of the shadows.

The Countess of Lochaene was mucking out a stall!

She obviously did not see him as he leaned against a wall for a moment. He wondered how often she had done this, and how critical he had been of the stables. That she had done it before was obvious. She was as competent as his own stablelads.

Bloody hell. He'd wondered what her life had been like these past few years. He'd wondered whether she had loved her husband. Certainly she had been pale the day of the burial. But now he wondered whether her life had been plain hell.

His chest ached. He stepped out of the shadows and moved carefully to the stall. He did not want to startle her. Then he waited until she looked up.

When she did, a startled cry came from her mouth. Her eyes narrowed in the thin light from a lantern. She wore a plain, nearly threadbare dark dress that did nothing for her. Yet it could not hide the slender curves of her body, nor the graceful way she moved, even holding a heavy pitchfork.

"Is it your custom to sneak about at night, my lord?"

"Is it your custom to muck out stalls at midnight?"

"Aye, when there is no one else to do it."

"What happened to the grooms and stablelads?"

"They were not paid and one after another left. One, Kevin, was fired because he allowed me to take a horse, but he had no' been paid for months, either. The last one"—she shrugged—"he probably lost his position for the same reason, but he was no loss."

"Here," he said, holding out his hand for the pitchfork she was using.

"You, my lord?"

"Better than *you*, my lady," he replied. "And I've probably had a lot more practice. Did you intend to do them all tonight?"

"Just the mare. I rode her hard today. She deserves a comfortable stall, and I wanted to see that she had feed. I canna find any," she added despairingly. "I ordered some."

"Hay will do for tonight. I will send someone for feed in the morning, and then we shall keep it locked," he said. "I know of a young lad who would make a good groom."

"So would Kevin," she said. "He needs the money for his family."

"Then we will have both," he said. "What in the hell kind of landlord was your husband?" he said.

Her chin set stubbornly and she did not answer as he quickly cleaned out the old straw and easily lifted a bale and scattered it around. "Done," he said as he left the stall.

"There are twelve others," she said.

"I've done my share of cleaning stalls, my lady. I will leave the rest to other hands. It will be done tomorrow. I will bring Tim here and see whether we can find your Kevin. Now I think it is time for us to be abed."

Her eyes met his. He wanted her to say she was pleased he had come. He should not want that. But he did. He wanted to feel needed. Wanted. The desire was raw. Intense.

But she looked away, her dark blue eyes as deep as the midnight sky. And as revealing.

"Did Lucy tell you I wished you to go riding with me this morning?"

"Aye," she replied cautiously.

"And your answer?"

"Do I have a choice?"

"Are you not accustomed to having one?"

"Nay," she said.

He watched her swallow hard, and he suddenly knew why it was so important to her that she had some control. She obviously had had none. God himself only knew what she'd been through these past few years. Obviously her husband had cared little for his properties and even less for his tenants. And his wife . . . ?

Her eyes held scars. Everything about her, even the stiff pride, was like a suit of protective armor.

He thought how free she had been years ago, how she had delighted in a sunset, or the trail of rays across a loch. She'd had a glow when she looked at him that made him feel like a giant of a man when he'd been little better than his cousin's servant. How he wanted to see it there again.

He did not think it would ever be there for him again. And it could not be. But he wanted that glow back for something. For anything.

"After the morning meal, then," he said, disregarding the fact that she had not agreed at all.

"Aye," she said without enthusiasm.

"I bid you good night," he said, taking her lantern.

She walked alongside him to the manor house, but he sensed her reluctance every step of the way.

He stopped at the door. He wanted to tell her about the books, but she had to be tired. He would leave that distasteful chore until tomorrow.

But she looked up at him. "You talked to Reginald."

He nodded.

"You have the books, then?"

She waited for him to answer.

"Aye," he finally said. "I just glanced through them."

Her eyes suddenly looked hopeful. "I . . . can get seed? It will soon be too late for the tenants."

"It is late for planting," he said dubiously.

"But without it they have no chance at all," she said.

"We will talk about it in the morning."

Her eyes pleaded with him, and he hated that, because he knew how much she loathed him. Finally, she nodded. "Is your bedchamber adequate?"

"'Tis fine, and so was the meal."

She tried a small smile that went straight to his heart. Then she seemed to gather her dignity around her, and he felt she had moved a thousand miles away from him.

She made her way up to her room. Colin was sleeping there, his breathing easy; his breath, when she leaned over to brush his cheeks with her lips, was sweet. There was something about bairns, an innocence so pure that it made her heart ache.

She had almost believed Braemoor. She tried to think of him that way. Braemoor. The Marquis of Braemoor. Not Neil. Not the young man she'd so desperately loved. She still could not quite believe that he had appeared out of nowhere, not only out of nowhere but suddenly to take such an enormous place in her life. She only wished she knew what he wanted. Or was he in league with Reginald in some way?

She had not told him about the incident on the battlement. He would think her hysterical, for one thing. For another, she still did not know where his loyalties really lay. Was he totally Cumberland's man? Reginald's accomplice? Or most unlikely of all, her friend? And if it were the latter, did she really want to rely on him again? He was a man without honor. She had to remember that.

Colin opened his eyes. They were dark blue like hers. Not his father's light blue ones. She prayed he wouldn't inherit any other of his father's traits, either. Or had it been Alasdair's heritage that had made him what he was? Love, she thought, begets love. Hatred begets hatred. Alasdair grew up in a household full of greed and jealousy. So had Reginald. Neither had known anything else.

But Colin would. And so would the lasses. She undressed down to her chemise. She had eaten earlier with the lasses, and had promised them an outing on the morrow. That was before she'd received the summons to ride from her son's new guardian. She had no choice but to do as he requested, particularly if she wanted to help the tenants.

How long did he plan to stay? How much would he control? How much would he take from what belonged to her son and her stepdaughters?

And why, considering all these questions, did something inside her respond to him?

When she was with him, her heart pounded harder. Her senses came alive. Her breath came in ragged bursts. And she felt a warmth in places that had been ever so cold before.

A ride tomorrow. He had given her little choice. Janet went to the window and looked out. It was silent below, quiet. Lochaene had never been home to her. Within several months of coming here, she'd realized she had made a mistake. And yet . . . mayhap not a mistake at all. Grace, Rachel and Annabella had enriched her life. They had needed her as much as she needed to be needed. And Colin. She knew she would not exchange him—nor the lasses— for anything in the world.

She also knew she did not want to be alone with the Marquis of Braemoor in the morning.

Mayhap, the presence of three lasses might assuage the unexpected yearning within her.

And even make him rethink the length of his stay at Lochaene.

Grace's steady stare, Rachel's many questions and Annabella's barely contained exuberance might disconcert him. And she *wanted* to disconcert him. She wanted to tear away that steady gaze and controlled face. She wanted to know if there were really any emotions in him.

Or whether he was just as empty as she'd thought these past eight years.

Neil knew she hadn't wanted to come with him this morn. He tried to tell himself it was a necessary part of his new duties, but lately he'd been cursed with an honesty that didn't permit such self-deception. He wanted to be with her, whether she wanted to be with him or not.

It was a hellish admission.

And it kept him awake the rest of the night. He had to curb his need for her. She was so newly widowed. Even if she were not, he had no right. Ever since that disastrous interview with his uncle years ago, he'd not been with a woman. God knew he had not wanted to present a child of his with his own dilemma, with the possibility of madness. 'Twas best to end the line with him.

Abstinence had not been a burden. Until he'd met Janet,

he'd been like any young man, wenching and bedding any
willing woman, but he'd always come away with a disqui-
eting sense of emptiness. And after meeting Janet, every
woman since paled in comparison. He'd known that cou-
pling would only lead to self-incrimination and an even
deeper sense of aloneness.

He'd thrown himself, instead, into managing the land,
first for the old marquis, then Rory and finally himself.
He'd found a sense of worth in it. He'd also found a kind of
release. He hadn't had to be anyone but himself. He did regret the fact that he'd not learned, if indeed it could be
something that was learned, to be at ease with others.

Only Janet had drawn him out. Only Janet had found in
him qualities he'd never known existed. Only Janet had accepted, and loved him, for what he was inside.

But that was eight years ago.

The window was open, and he took a deep breath of fresh
air. He knew he was playing with fire. He knew that nothing had changed—for him—in those years. It was as if he
had just stepped backward in time.

He was rushing toward disaster, but he was unable to
save himself. He knew that he was telling himself he was
trying to help her, that he was trying in some way to redeem
himself. But it wasn't true. He was doing it for himself.

He finally lay down, but he knew he would not sleep. He
could only think of seeing Janet in a few hours. Of spending several hours with her. It might be all he ever had.

Grace was reluctant when Janet asked if they would like to
go on an outing with the marquis. She had an abiding distrust of men. "I want to stay here," she said reluctantly.

Hiding behind children. She should be ashamed of herself.

"Can we take Di'lah and Samson?" Annabella countered.

They had finally decided on names for their new pets.
Rachel, the small scholar, had indignantly declined the
names of Princess, Baron and Ginger. Like Annabella, she

believed the new additions for the family were extraordinary and as such should have special names.

Since the children had just heard the tale of Samson and Delilah, Rachel decided the new pup had to be named Samson despite the fact he was all awkward legs. So then Grace decided on Delilah for the kitten, which was probably among the homeliest orange kittens ever created.

Pleased that they had finally agreed on something, Janet had tried to keep the twitch of her lips barely visible. But whenever she heard Di'lah called, she smiled inside. The lasses loved them so, and even Colin, who was crawling everywhere, kept going in their direction, oblivious to a smooth wet tongue and a scratchy one.

But she might well be pushing her luck if she added the two to today's mix. The marquis might well refuse to take any of them, but she had not wanted to present them at his door if they did not want to go.

Rachel's gaze went from Grace to Annabella, then to Janet. Janet could almost feel the want in her warring with fear. They had been little more than prisoners themselves these last months. "He's very big," Rachel said. That apparently had been her one impression of the marquis.

"Aye," she agreed, "but he willna harm you."

"Does he want us to go?" Grace asked, putting her finger on the crux of the matter.

"I have not asked him. I wanted to know if you would *like* to go first."

"How?" Grace asked again.

"We would have to take the pony cart," she said, planning for the marquis to ride his horse beside them. That way she would not have him by her side, not be tempted by wayward feelings.

"Do you want us to go?" Grace asked.

Leave it to Grace to ferret out her intentions. And she would not lie to them. She'd had too many lies in her own life. "Only if you want to go."

Rachel stood. "I will go."

"Di'lah?" Annabella insisted.

"We will see," she said, wondering how much tolerance the marquis had.

Annabella pouted for a moment, then gave Janet one of her angelic smiles that would melt the heart of anyone except her own father. "Awright."

Grace nodded solemnly.

Janet left them to their morning meal. Now to convince the marquis.

She wondered whether he was up yet. It was an hour past dawn, but her husband, and even Reginald, rarely were up this early. But when she went into the kitchen she found him, and a lad she did not know, eating at the servants' table, much to the obvious chagrin of the cook and her helper.

The marquis stood and the lad scrambled to his feet. "This is Tim," he said. "He and I shared a ride from Braemoor. I have employed him as a groom and dismissed the former groom. And a man named MacKnight."

"When . . ."

"This morning. I rode to Tim's village. We brought back some oats for the horses."

He must have left in the wee hours of the morning. "You woke the merchant?"

"*We* woke the merchant," Braemoor said, a small smile tugging at one side of his mouth. "He did not protest overmuch when we paid the bill."

She could not help staring at him. His hair was tousled, his clothes still damp from an early morning mist. He had not shaved yet, and dark bristle shadowed his face. He looked like anything but a marquis this morning, except, perhaps, for the gleam in his eyes.

Janet suspected he was waiting for her to protest his high-handedness in employing someone without her consent, but at the moment she was simply pleased that at least the horses would be well fed today and the stalls would be cleaned. This was not a battle she wished to fight. She suspected there would be other, more important ones to come. Choose your battles, she warned herself. *Do not let your attraction to him make you choose unwisely.*

So she merely nodded and took perverse satisfaction in the sudden puzzlement in his eyes. "About this morning, my lord . . ."

"Aye?" he asked cautiously.

"I was hoping we could take my daughters with us. They have been out so little, and this would be a grand adventure for them."

She watched as the gleam sharpened in his eyes. They glowed like a polished onyx.

"And how, madam, do you propose that we ride the estate with young lasses?"

"We could take the pony cart. You can ride alongside."

He raised a dark eyebrow. " 'Tis not exactly what I had in mind, my lady. There is much to see, and a cart will slow us considerably."

"There is a family . . . not too distant that can probably tell you more than you could see riding the entire estate."

He studied her for a moment but if he was disappointed, she did not see it in his eyes.

"Very well," he said. "If I am not satisfied, I can always delay my return and we can ride out tomorrow or the next day."

Mate and checkmate.

He sat back down. "Will you join us for the meal?" he said, challenging her.

She looked around the kitchen. The cook looked stunned; families did not eat with their servants. But Janet had always liked the warmth of the kitchen compared to the cold formality and long table in the small dining hall.

Reginald and Louisa would have apoplexy.

She sat down, avoiding his eyes, knowing she would see triumph there.

She comforted herself by acknowledging she had won at

least one of her battles. She would not be alone with him. Today, at least.

And for some reason she wanted to coax a smile from him.

But to smile, you had to have a heart.

And she'd discovered years ago that he had none.

Chapter Seven

Neil realized what she was doing, that she had no interest in being alone with him, that in truth, she would go to great lengths to avoid it.

He shouldn't have expected anything else. She thought he had betrayed her years ago, and now again. He only wished it did not leave such a persistent ache inside him.

He tried to ignore it as he and Tim had found the governess cart and backed a mare into the traces. He ran his hand along its long, rough neck. "Tim will groom you when we return," he promised, "and you will have some fine oats for supper." The mare nickered as if understanding. Animals often did understand, he thought, and far better than humans.

He'd always been comfortable with animals but he'd never let himself love one. 'Twas only lately that he allowed himself the luxury of caring. But even then he had something inside that held him back.

If you care about something, it will be taken away.

Like his mother. Like his dog when he'd been whisked away from his mother's home when he was a small lad. Like a horse that had been his but which Donald had admired and taken. And then when he'd thought he might have a chance to marry someone he loved, that, too, was taken from him.

Even now he resisted selecting a favorite horse or owning a dog for that reason. How many times had he told himself he did not need anyone or anything.

It was enough that he had come to believe it, even though it left an aching hollow place inside.

He'd also steeled himself against his own acts, those he'd once thought he'd committed in the noble purpose of loyalty. There had been nothing noble about those few hours at Culloden. Nothing honorable about obeying orders to kill every Jacobite, wounded or not. He kept remembering his contempt toward Rory when his cousin had thrown his sword down and walked away. He, too, had believed his cousin a coward when indeed it was himself who was the coward.

It had taken him far too long to discover that courage was not might, that it was going against might.

He'd basked in self-hatred for a long time after Culloden, after the slaughter there. After Rory left, he'd found his own path to redemption. But redemption, like real courage, was a quiet, unheralded thing. It had also taken him a long time to understand that, too.

When the cart was ready, he stabled the horse he'd ridden earlier, then turned to Tim. "Take care of the horses, then see if you can find a lad named Kevin and bring him back to help you. This stable requires more than one groom."

"Aye, my lord," Tim said.

"And see what you can learn about this family," he said.

"Ye wish me to spy?"

"Not if you are not comfortable with the role," Neil said. "But if you discover anything I should know to help rebuild Lochaene, I would be appreciative."

The lad's face smoothed out. "Aye, I can do that."

Neil studied him for a moment. "Keep those principles, lad. They will serve you well."

The boy turned several shades of red, then shuffled off back to the stables where there was far too much work to do.

Neil waited patiently, wondering if all the children would be coming with them. He had hoped to see most of the estate. That would be impossible with the governess cart, which could only travel established roads. Using the cart meant he would have to stay at least another day. He had no intention of leaving until he felt Janet had the people she needed to run the estate.

What he really wanted to do was whisk her away to Braemoor where she would be safe and well cared for. But that would be unfair to her and to her son. He intended never to wound her again.

He heard a shrill puppy bark and looked toward the door. He winced as he saw the parade. Janet was still dressed in a dark dress with a high neck and long sleeves. A gray shawl finished the somber costume. She held Colin in her arms and three little stepping-stone girls followed them. A gangly black-and-white puppy rushed toward the cart and barked at the pony, which stamped his left hoof as if to bolt. An orange kitten was clutched tightly in the arms of the youngest lass. Trailing behind them all was a young woman, obviously a maid, clutching a big basket.

He sighed. He had no idea how to talk to bairns, and the dog was yapping at the pony. The kitten wriggled her way out of the lass's arms and dropped to the ground to chase the dog.

"Samson," Janet said, stamping a black booted foot on the ground, raising dust to float in tiny particles around them all.

Neil leaned down and caught the kitten. "Samson," he said dubiously.

The smallest lass shook her head in disgust. "No . . . Di'lah."

Neil turned his gaze to Janet who was regarding him solemnly, waiting, apparently, to see if he was going to kick the puppy or drown the kitten.

"I should have known," he said wryly and placed the kitten back in the grasping arms of the littlest lass. "Miss Annabella, I assume?"

She gazed at him uncertainly for a moment, then grinned with a mouth devoid of two front teeth.

He could not help but smile back. He reached out and picked her up, kitten and all, and set her in the cart. He went back to help the others, but the oldest lass had already scrambled up and the middle one shrank back against Janet. Instead he picked up the puppy, which reached up with his tongue and tried to lick his face.

Neil held him away. "Is he to go, too?" he inquired.

"Aye," she said. "The children would not leave them. And this is Clara," she said. "She is nurse to the children."

His eyes went to the basket. "'Tis not for us," Janet said. "'Tis for the family I mentioned. They are in need of food."

It was a challenge again, as if she dared him to refuse to take food to a hungry family. Bloody hell, but her opinion of him was obviously as low as that of a snake's belly.

He took the basket from Clara and placed it in the front of the cart, then reached for Colin. For a moment, she clutched the bundle closer to her.

"I do not harm children," he said softly enough that the others could not hear.

Her eyes searched his, then she nodded. She handed Colin to him, then stepped into the cart. She reached down to get her son, her fingers touching his briefly as she took the lad, then she jerked away as if his hands burned her.

Neil dropped his hands, then helped Clara up. She looked surprised as he offered his hand. Flushing all shades of red, she took it as she stepped up into the seat.

Neil looked at the full governess cart. Janet had the reins while Clara held the bairn. One of the lasses had put the kitten in a basket. Another—the middle one who had shied away from him—clutched the puppy as if her life depended on it. None of them looked at him with friendly eyes.

He sighed. It was going to be a long day.

If Braemoor had been displeased at Janet's tactics, he did not display it. She recalled how angry her husband used to get when she did anything to interfere with his plans, whether she knew she was doing so or not. He'd been particularly angered when she'd placed herself between him and the children by sending them on a false errand or some other such distraction.

Now she was placing the children between herself and Braemoor. And except for some obvious awkwardness on his part toward the lasses, he seemed perfectly amiable toward the situation.

Braemoor mounted a large gray gelding. For the barest of instants, she recalled the ride they had taken together so many years ago. Neil Forbes had been an easy rider, comfortable in the saddle and thoughtful of the animal. They had raced across the low hills before stopping at a loch where he'd kissed her. She'd never felt so free, so joyous, so natural.

And then she discovered it was all a lie.

A lie. Remember, you cannot trust him, no matter how pliable or amiable or accommodating he appears to be. Remember how gentle he had been. And it had been a lie.

No, she did not want to remember that at all.

She forced her gaze away from Neil as Annabella squirmed into the seat between Clara and her.

"I like him," Annabella said.

Annabella rarely expressed a good opinion about anyone, mayhap because she'd not been around that many people she could like. She *did* like the vicar.

The vicar and Braemoor. More like an angel and the devil.

Why was he being so accommodating?

"Do you?" Annabella tugged on her arm as she posed the question.

Janet looked down at her. The small pixie face gazed up at her with such complete guilelessness and trust that she wanted to say, "Aye." But the word simply would not come. "We do not know him that well," she said cautiously.

"He's big," Rachel said as if that said it all. Big, to her, was frightening. Her father was big. Her uncle was big. And Braemoor was larger than both.

"That doesna mean anything," Grace said with big sister knowledge.

Janet was always amazed at Grace. She was a quiet, slender lass who said little but when she did, it was always unexpected. And, usually, some little piece of wisdom popped out.

"You are right," Janet said. "It doesna mean anything. Deeds are always more important than appearance." She instinctively flinched at the primness of the statement.

"He does have nice eyes," Grace ventured.

Janet had thought so once, too. But she was startled that Grace, who had shied away from Braemoor, had noticed.

She had not been looking at his eyes. In truth, she had been trying to avoid them.

She fervently hoped that Braemoor, who was riding ahead of them, had heard none of the conversation, but then he was too far away. All the saints above, she wished her heart would not continue to beat erratically when she looked at him. How could she still feel this way when she knew what he was? When she knew how faithless he was? And how do you warn children to protect their hearts? She did not want them to doubt everyone they met. Nor did she want them to accept everything.

There was such a fine line between hope and heartbreak.

She had given him directions toward the croft she'd visited just a few days earlier. But with the large cart, it was far past noon before they reached the croft. No chickens scratched in the dirt. No pig wallowed in a pen. The croft appeared deserted until they stopped just feet from the door.

The door half opened and a small face peered outside.

Janet watched as the Marquis of Braemoor dismounted. So easily. So fluidly. She closed her eyes. She did not want to admire anything about him. But then he was next to the cart, lifting Samson down, then Annabella who held out her arms to him.

The croft door widened further, and the older man she'd met earlier came out and stood belligerently, hands at his hips. "What do ye want this time? To take more of our food?"

Janet felt the man's hostility. She understood it. She'd understood it before.

This time Janet took Braemoor's proffered hand as she climbed down from the cart. He'd taken the riding gloves from his hands, and the heat of his skin seared through her own thin gloves. For a fraction of a second, she felt his protection, even his warmth, and she wanted it. Dear God, how much she wanted it.

But she could not take it. Or believe in it. Or rely on it. She would never rely on anyone but herself. She gathered up her courage and moved away toward the tenant. "We brought you some food."

"We donna want charity from the mon who is destroyin' us."

"The former earl is dead," she said. "We will have seed for you this week if you wish to go ahead and start planting. In the meantime, there will be no rents for a year."

She had not talked to Braemoor about her decision. She had not wanted to give him a chance to gainsay her.

"Angus?" she said. "It is Angus, is it not?"

"Aye," he said reluctantly, obviously a little mollified that she had remembered his name. His eyes narrowed as his gaze moved to Braemoor beside her. "Who is 'e?"

"An acquaintance," Braemoor said stiffly. "I am only providing escort."

A sudden surge of gratitude flowed through her. He could have said he was now in charge of the entire estate. But she knew the tenants would soon hear the truth of it. "He is the Marquis of Braemoor, my son's new guardian."

"Ye are in charge?" Angus asked.

"No," Braemoor said softly. "This was my lady's plan, and she will be in charge of Lochaene."

"A lady? I heard tha' the earl's uncle—"

"You heard wrong," Braemoor said. "He will have nothing to do with the affairs here. If you need anything, you come to the countess."

Angus frowned. "A woman no' has the . . ." He trailed off.

"Yes?" Braemoor raised an eyebrow as the man paused, obviously wondering whether he was saying too much. "You were about to say?"

Janet watched as Angus dropped his gaze. The door behind him opened and Angus's wife sidled out and stood shyly, and apprehensively, beside her husband. "Are ye here to tell us to leave?"

"Nay," Janet said after glancing at Braemoor. "We are here to bring you some food and tell you seed will be here later this week so you can start your planting. 'Tis not too late, is it?"

Angus regarded her steadily. "Nay. The land is already furrowed. We need only seed for sowing. And the other tenants? Them who is left?"

"The same. We should have enough seed for them all. If not, we will get more. Can you take it to them?"

"Ye would trust me tae do that?"

"Aye," she said. "And you can tell them they can hunt and fish the property."

Suspicion crept into his eyes again as they searched for an ulterior motive. The deceased earl had forbade all the tenants from doing either. Poaching was a hanging offense. "For truth?"

"For truth," she said.

For the first time, a hint of a smile played around his lips.

He looked toward Braemoor for confirmation, and Janet realized that trying to run Lochaene on her own would be more difficult than she thought. Braemoor, though, made no sign whatever. No nod. No denying shake of his head. No smile. No frown. He was allowing her to handle it, to succeed. Or fail.

Which did he want?

She wished she knew. She wished she knew why he had

convinced Cumberland to give him guardianship. She wished she knew why he had ridden out last night and bought feed with his own funds. She wished she knew why she felt a . . . kinship with him when she should be suspecting his every mood.

Regret? Apology? Men like him did not have regrets or make apologies. She knew that much from living with the Campbells. Even her father, who'd loved her, had never apologized for anything in his life.

He had to have some reason. Some purpose. She was not going to succumb to the attraction that had once enraptured her, which still, for some reason, hovered between them. He cared only for land, for money, for title. He'd said as much years ago.

So she fought the appreciation she felt now, the authority he was so obviously conveying to her.

Angus was shifting on his feet, obviously awkward, uncertain. He'd been discourteous, then incredulous. It was obvious he did not know how to act.

But his wife did. She curtsied. "Thank ye, my lady."

"You are welcome," Janet said. "Thank you for sharing what little you had." She returned to the cart and took the basket of food and returned. "There is flour, bacon, potatoes, several fowl. If you need more flour, just send one of your lads to the manor."

The woman's face twitched as if she were trying to hold back tears. She just nodded.

Janet returned to the cart, and climbed back on the seat with the children and snapped the reins. Her presence, she knew, was an embarrassment. In seconds, Braemoor was riding beside her.

"Where now, my lady?"

Just then Colin started to fidget. "There's a waterfall not far from here," she said. "We can stop there and rest." And she could feed Colin. There were some rocks up there where she could have some privacy. She wished now that she had brought an extra basket of food. Braemoor had made it clear he would not leave until he saw everything he wanted to see, and she had only delayed him today.

She wanted him gone as soon as possible.

He still stirred feelings in her, and in those few moments talking to Angus she'd felt a companionship, a bond. They had been attuned to each other in a way she'd not known since those halcyon days she'd tried to wipe from her memory.

He rode next to her, a silent sentinel. She stole a glance at him, but he was looking straight ahead. That moment, or moments, obviously had meant no more to him than those days a lifetime ago.

Pride for her swelled inside him.

She had handled everything very well. All her instincts were good. It had taken him far longer to find that tiny connection between landlord and tenant. Mayhap because for so many years he wasn't the landlord but merely representing him. He had never been able to promise anything, particularly in the later years when the old marquis was determined to clear the land.

He'd watched Janet, her face so earnest, and his heart had thumped so loudly he was afraid she would hear it. That would have been disastrous. The fact that she cared so much for the tenants warmed him. He had wanted to step in when the crofter had been rude and even a bit threatening. It had taken all his control to remain silent.

But he wanted to give her Lochaene. He wanted to give it to her with all she needed to make it work. That meant loyal people around her. And she had to build that loyalty herself. He couldn't do it for her. He'd learned that if nothing else in the past year. Once done, he could return to Braemoor and complete what he had started there. And then what?

God's blood, but the prospect was numbing. Years stretched out in lonely succession. He looked at the cart full of children clutching pets, and he ached. He yearned to hold young Annabella and feel the sweetness of a hug. He wanted

Grace to look at him with trust in her eyes, and Rachel, well, he wanted to tell her the stories no one had told him. He'd known that in a startlingly short time. He detested the way they looked at him with fear, and he'd wondered what their life had been like. And Janet's.

Bloody hell, he knew. And he was determined to do something about it without hurting them even further. And that meant he could not get too close to them. He could not expose them to potential madness.

He kept just behind the front of the cart, ready to give protection if protection was needed. Hungry, angry tenants could be dangerous. So could Cumberland's soldiers who still roamed the Highlands.

He tried not to look in her direction, but to study the barren ground. What land was not furrowed was stark, rising up into heather- and gorse-covered hills. Good grazing land. Probably far better than farmland. But grazing land did not support people.

They went by a second croft, but it was deserted. They stopped and he went inside, but it was obvious from the scurrying of small animals that it had not had human habitation for the past several years. He came out. "They are gone." He shook his head. "The estate books are so poor I could not even tell how many crofters you have. There is no record of tacksmen."

"There are none," she said. "Alasdair did not think it was necessary. He had discharged the ones who had been there for years. I think he wanted to force everyone to leave."

"Those lands that have been abandoned can be used for sheep," he said.

She looked up from her seat on the cart, her eyes narrowing.

"They are gone, lass. You canna bring them back."

Her bleak gaze met his. "I donna even know what happened to those on my father's properties. The property was confiscated. Alasdair had thought it would come to him, but it was given to some Englishman."

He said nothing as she clicked the reins of the cart and they started again. But he decided then to make a trip to her father's old lands and see what he could find out. Perhaps bring some crofters, if anyone had survived Cumberland's purges, back here.

In the meantime, they would stop to eat. Unknowing to her, he'd already packed some food in a corner of the cart. He hadn't known how long they would be out.

He looked toward the sun. It was at least an hour since noon. They could eat when they rested the animals, then turn back toward the manor. He would spend tomorrow going with Tim to distribute seed and take a look for himself at the condition of the fields. He would also make it quite clear that if Janet chose to come, they would use horses, not a governess cart.

The sun was bright, the blue sky washed clean by a morning mist. It was a rare lovely day in the Highlands, and Janet felt herself relaxing as they neared the waterfall she'd seen yesterday. She had already surrendered the reins to Clara and now crooned a lullaby to a hungry Colin.

But as they neared the waterfall, she sat up in her seat and looked at it with fresh appreciation. The fall ran down a heather-covered hill, tumbling along over water-polished rocks. The sun's rays caught the mist from water, forming an ethereal rainbow, and the pool looked as if diamonds had been spread over its surface.

She had not been struck by the rugged beauty of the hills yesterday, but perhaps because they had been partially veiled by the heavy mist—and her tears. But now the sight of the fall surrounded by purple heather and golden gorse lifted her spirits. She had lived here now for four years and she had seen very little of the property. She had never gone for a ride with her husband, and he had forbade her going by herself. Her few outings had included one trip to Edinburgh to see Cumberland, then a hunting party at the home of one of Alasdair's friends. She'd hated every moment of it, and

he'd told her how embarrassed he'd been at her lack of cordiality when she tried to shake off the advances of his
friends.

But now she looked at Lochaene with different eyes.
From the manor battlements, she'd felt Lochaene was her
prison. Now it could be her freedom.

If she could rid herself of Reginald's jealousy and now
Braemoor's interference.

Even though, she had to admit, it was helpful interference.

He had dismounted and moved over to the cart. "If you
will give the lad to Clara," he said, "I'll help you down."

"You take Colin," she said. She held her son out to him.
He stood there for a moment, looking uncertain; looking, in
truth, as if she were trying to hand him hot coals. A look of
panic darted over his face. Then he reached out and took
Colin, holding him as if he was a piece of glass. Awkwardly.
Clumsily, but with—she would swear it—tenderness.

Colin wailed, reaching back up for her. But she turned
away, climbing down herself, then helping Annabella and
Rachel as Clara stepped down on her own, clutching the
basket holding the kitten.

Janet turned to take her son.

In those few moments, her son and Braemoor had apparently come to an understanding. Colin was gurgling, and
Braemoor was looking at him with unabashed yearning.

But the instant he looked up to see her standing there, a
curtain fell over his eyes and without a word he started to
hand Colin back to her. Colin wailed again and held his
hands back toward Braemoor.

"Traitor," she whispered in Colin's ear, hopefully in a
tone too low for Braemoor to hear, but she left her son in
Braemoor's arms.

But Braemoor was distracted by Samson who promptly
lifted his leg on Braemoor's boot.

"Bloody hell," Braemoor said. It was mildly said, but the
effect was immediate. Rachel snatched the dog up and

clutched him in her arms. "Please do . . . do not hurt him," she said, backing up, terror written all over her face.

Her timid Rachel was ready to do battle for the pup. Annabella was trembling. Grace placed her thin little body between Braemoor and Rachel.

Janet looked at Braemoor. Her husband would have killed the dog, and the girls knew it.

She took the few steps to stand next to Grace and looked at Braemoor. "He is just a puppy," she said.

"I know," he said in a voice so low that she barely heard it. His eyes had darkened to that particular color of onyx.

Grace didn't move. She was used to her father who often preceded a blow with a calm, almost loving demeanor.

They were so brave. All of them. Not for themselves, but for a poor nondescript puppy.

Janet swallowed, the air passing with difficulty through a rather large lump in her throat. "I . . . I'm sorry," she said.

"Why should you be sorry?" he asked. "*You* didn't relieve yourself on my leg."

His answer did not remove the combined anxiety for the puppy. "I sorry, too," Annabella said.

"You can beat *me*," Rachel offered in a small trembling but determined voice.

They were all looking at him. A muscle throbbed along his tightened jaw. He *did* look large and angry. For a moment, she wondered whether she'd been so wrong about him years ago. She had been wrong about so much. She did know she was not going to let him hurt either the dog or the children.

"I donna think I want to beat anyone," he said. "Nor a pup."

"Truly?" Grace asked in a strained voice.

"Truly," he said. But he did not smile. In fact, she saw building anger in those eyes.

The lasses had not been convinced. She did not know whether or not she was. She had once believed Alasdair incapable of hitting a child. She'd been quickly disabused of that notion.

The fear of the children was palpable despite the softness of his voice and his words. Clara, several feet away, also appeared rooted to the ground, her arms clutching the kitten's basket to her bosom.

The ghost of her husband was all too real.

Even Colin had started wailing.

She looked at Braemoor's face, at the eyes that had darkened with anger. *And she knew.* Clouding out that anger in his eyes was vulnerability, helplessness. She realized then the anger had not been directed toward her or the children, but at whatever had turned them so fearful. And the vulnerability came because he had no idea how to cope with the immediate disaster.

In the past day, she'd learned that the young man whose uncertain sincerity had so appealed to her had turned into a competent, forceful lord, one becoming accustomed to getting his own way and not above using raw power to accomplish his aims.

But now he was faced with a situation he had no idea how to handle, and his gaze held an appeal, and a muscle ripped along his tightened jaw. Her heart shifted, opened just a crack. She would never trust him with her heart again, but she knew she could trust his words here and now. She leaned down, picked up Samson and stroked him. The small animal had caught Rachel's fear and was trembling.

"It is all right," she said soothingly.

Rachel's stiff back, obviously ready to accept a blow, slowly started to relax. Grace reached down and took Annabella's hand. Clara shifted and loosened her grip on the basket.

It was as if a tableau had been unfrozen.

She saw Braemoor swallow, then made a small bow. "I must ask pardon. A gentleman should never swear in front of ladies. I hope you will all accept my apologies."

"But . . . your boot?" Grace managed.

"My boot has seen far worse, I assure you, lass," he said. "I was just startled, 'tis all. I am not accustomed to being around so many fair young lasses."

Colin had stopped wailing and was now looking at the marquis with interest, his hunger evidently temporarily forgotten.

"I think you can put Samson down," Braemoor said. "I have no intention to do harm to him."

Her gaze met his. The appeal was still in them and she saw something else as well. *Pain? Even bafflement that she and four children would believe him capable of hurting them or a puppy.*

How deeply ingrained was the fear Alasdair had built in them all. She wondered whether the girls would always flinch when a man came close, or exhibited even the slightest expression of anger.

Even she, who had known him, had experienced a moment of fear. Not for herself but for the others.

And he had seen it.

Chapter Eight

Neil struggled to control the fury roiling around inside him.

He'd seldom seen such stark fear in faces so young. Seeing it in Janet's eyes had been like a fist in the gut. But in the faces of the children, it was almost too much to bear.

He wished the Earl of Lochaene still lived. He would have pulverized the man.

The wee lad squirmed in his arms. He was small, and Neil feared he might unintentionally hurt the bairn. And yet the boy felt good in his arms. Especially when he smiled.

Some of his anger faded at that grin. He sighed. It was foolish to waste his energy on a dead man. Campbell had gone to his own judgment. But he did wish the man a particularly agonizing afterlife.

It was painful to realize that he'd caused fear in bairns, and in Janet as well. She'd been uncertain whether he might hurt either the lasses or the pup. What in the hell had Lochaene done to her? To his own children?

He felt an unexpected moisture on his arm and looked down. He'd just been watered again! This time by the bairn.

Janet apparently saw it, too, and regarded Neil's shirt with dismay.

"Do not look that way, lass. Even I know that bairns do not know whom they are wetting any more than that misbegotten animal." In fact, rather than anger, he felt an odd tenderness at the thought of such complete innocence. He'd never held a bairn before, had never been the recipient of such a guileless contentment. He tried a smile to put her, and the children, at ease but he knew it was a poor excuse of one. He had damned little practice at it, and he knew immediately he was not succeeding. Hell, the children still looked frightened half to death.

Janet lowered the puppy to the ground, and Samson went running back to Rachel. As she straightened, their gazes locked for a moment. Janet gave him a long, level look, then something lit in her eyes, the eyes he remembered so well. The ground seemed to tremble under them for a moment, or mayhap his legs were none too steady. Eight years had passed and yet his tongue was as tied as the day he had met her. He felt the same leap of his heart, the same sudden recognition.

Then she reached out and took the lad, and he immediately missed the feel of him.

"I have to feed him," she said. "Clara will look after the children."

He raised an eyebrow. "You do not trust them with me?"

"I can tell you are not used to children."

"Nay, you are right there," he replied wryly.

"I thought not," she said. "What have you been doing these past years?"

"Serving my cousin," he said. Feeling the necessity of destroying that intimacy they'd just shared, an intimacy neither of them could afford, he added, "and fighting Jacobites."

"For the English king." It was not a question.

"Aye."

"My brother died at Culloden. Could it have been by your sword?"

Pain twisted inside him. He had not met her brother, only her father whom he had admired and liked. "I canna say, my lady. 'Tis possible."

"And now you are wealthy and can ask favors of Cumberland and take what you wish. How did that happen?" She'd heard rumors about the poor cousin who had become the Marquis of Braemoor, but there had been few details.

"Donald died of wounds at Culloden. My cousin inherited, and he too died in the service of the king. Cumberland appreciates that kind of loyalty." The latter wasn't true. Cumberland appreciated nothing from Scots. But the lie served him at the moment.

"How?" she said.

"The Black Knave is said to have killed him."

She wondered how she had not heard that particular piece of information. It must have happened at the time that Colin was born, when her son was the center of her world. She'd heard of the Black Knave—everyone had—but in this household he'd been considered the worst type of villain. A murderer. A thief. A traitor.

Then she caught his wording. "Is said?"

He shrugged. "It could not be proven. But my cousin had gone after the Knave, and his body was found on a beach. Cumberland believes that he might have destroyed the Knave since no one has heard from him since the night my cousin's body was found."

"And murder is a reason for gratitude?"

"If it is a traitor to the crown, aye."

He flinched at the look in her eyes. And yet he knew he could never reveal the entire truth about the Black Knave.

The lad in her arms fidgeted, and she shifted the weight. "I have to feed him," she repeated in a cool voice and turned away.

Colin squirmed in her arms. He was ready, she knew, for a fit of temper. She turned around and headed away, toward privacy beyond the hill. She felt Neil's gaze going straight through her.

She also felt her breasts throbbing with milk. Most women in her position hired wet nurses. But she'd wanted to nurse her own child and Alasdair had not objected. He had, in fact, been pleased. Where he was often vicious toward his daughters, he'd doted on his only son. And it had given him a new threat against her. Taking away her son.

She had only recently started to wean Colin with gruel mixed with honey. Another few weeks and he would not need her in this way. And, despite the discomfort, she would miss it. There could be no other feeling like this.

Reaching a spot out of sight, Janet found a stone to sit upon. She shifted Colin on her shoulder, holding him close to her for a moment. She was trembling. How *could* she feel anything for Braemoor when he'd just told her that he had killed Scotsmen at Culloden? Possibly even her brother.

She remembered the day a messenger had arrived at Lochaene, telling her of his death. Alasdair had not gone to Culloden despite Cumberland's orders. He'd claimed that duty demanded that he stay and guard this land that lay to the west of Cumberland. It was nothing but cowardice. She also remembered his words when she was told her brother was dead: "One less Jacobite."

Janet tried to shake the memory from her heart. She undid the ties of her dress, and in seconds, Colin was sucking with a lustiness that made her ache. There was always pain, but there was also intense pleasure. And satisfaction. She held him close, wanting desperately for him to feel safe.

She wished she understood Braemoor, and what he wanted. He had shown no particular desire for her, although there could have been a hungry look in his eyes earlier. But he was stingy with his emotions, and she couldn't tell what he thought.

Nor what he wanted from her. He'd indicated no interest in her as a woman. He certainly did not need her properties; he was probably among the wealthiest Scots in the Highlands. Lochaene was small compared to his holdings. And poor.

And she no longer believed in fairies. Or angels.

Colin finished and gave her one of his sweet smiles. He

was, she thought, the most handsome bairn in Scotland. "No one will ever hurt you. Not if I can help it," she promised him as she tied the front of her dress and settled her shawl around her shoulders.

She heard the waterfall from here. The sun was still warm and Colin was drowsy. She heard laughter, childish laughter from around the hill, and she started. It had been a long time since she had heard her daughters laugh that freely.

She stood and carried Colin back to the others. Annabella was giggling, Grace had a smile on her face, and Rachel was grinning.

Delilah had somehow escaped from her basket and was chasing Samson in circles. Chasing the little orange kitten was the large, awkward figure of the Marquis of Braemoor. He dived for the kitten, only to find himself holding empty air.

Grace, Annabella and Rachel were rooted to the ground, not helping at all. Clara, too, was staring, a dumbfounded look on her face.

The marquis rose from his undignified position on the ground, and brushed off the dirt and gorse, then looked toward the kitten again, which was altogether too close to the pool. Then Samson saw her with Colin and came running toward her. The kitten followed, and she swooped down with one hand and retrieved her while holding Colin in the other.

"Did you lose something?" she said.

His face colored. "I thought I could . . ."

She tried to choke back the laughter that welled up in her throat. He looked crestfallen. He obviously felt outwitted by a kitten.

"He told us not to move," Grace explained.

"I thought they might fall into the pool," Braemoor explained.

"I see," she said as she handed over the kitten to Grace. "Keep her in the basket," she admonished her oldest daughter.

Grace's face creased into a smile. "Aye," she said, then curtsied to Braemoor. "Thank you, sir."

For the slightest moment, his face creased into an answering smile. It disappeared all too quickly, almost as if he was embarrassed by it.

"I think it is time to eat," he said.

She shook her head. "There is nothing."

"Aye, but there is, my lady. I thought we might be out longer than you expected. There is a basket in the back of the cart in the box."

She gave Colin to Clara and looked in the back of the seat. A basket, topped by a blanket, had been pushed under the front seat, out of sight. She started to pull it out, but Braemoor took it from her. Grace and Rachel spread the blanket out on the ground as Annabella clutched the kitten.

Janet checked the basket. There were several roasted chickens, cheese, bread and some pastries. There were also some cups that she used to scoop up fresh water from the fall.

She would have expected the bounty from the young Neil Forbes, but not from the older, dignified and unapproachable Marquis of Braemoor.

But once the food was laid out, he did not partake of it. Instead, he walked away, disappearing among the hills.

The lasses were giggling in a way Janet had never seen them do before. She didn't know what Braemoor had done, but something had made them relax. Whatever it was, their fear was gone. That much was obvious. Rachel cuddled Samson, feeding him pieces of bread while she ate chicken. Annabella put Delilah in her basket and grabbed a pastry. Grace was very gracefully taking small bits of chicken. Clara balanced Colin in one arm and took a chicken wing for herself.

Janet discovered that she *was* indeed hungry. But she wanted Braemoor to join them. It was his feast, after all. And he must be hungry. And tired, if he had taken that early morning ride into the village. He showed no sign of it, though. He showed little sign of any emotion or condition.

She ate a piece of chicken, then left the others and walked

in the direction he had gone. She was as drawn toward him as a bee was to honey, even though she knew better. He was not honey. He was someone who discarded her years ago because he could not get what he expected.

Had he changed in those eight years? Or was he still playing games she did not understand?

She went around the hill, not far from where she had nursed Colin moments earlier. She saw him quickly moving away, his stride easy and effortless. He was facing away from her, could not see her, could not know she was there, and yet she felt as if there was some invisible rope reaching between them. He looked alone, as alone as she had felt so many times, as she still felt. She had Colin, and Grace and Rachel and Annabella, and yet she had never been whole since the day she had been abandoned by Neil Forbes. And now she was worse than Samson, running after him like a demented puppy.

She stopped and watched him meld into the heather and disappear.

Reginald met Neil as he entered the manor. Janet, Clara and the children had gone ahead while he helped Tim unhitch the cart, then gave him instructions about delivering seed.

In truth, Neil wanted to avoid Janet. He'd run away this afternoon, or nearly so. Just her presence did something to his heart, to his plans. So did the bairns. Their laughter filled some of the emptiness. He wanted more. He wanted to see amusement in their faces when he knew they had known too little of it. He wanted to see Janet's eyes crinkled with joy, as it had been years ago.

In self-defense, he had left them. He brooded alone among the rugged rocks and bracken and wild heather. And when he returned, it was time to return to Lochaene. They had not seen all he wanted to see and he would have to stay another day. Mayhap a second or even a third. He could not leave her yet, not until he felt there were enough people to protect her.

On their return to Lochaene, he assisted Janet and the small lasses down, then helped Tim care for the horses. When they'd completed rubbing down his mount and the horse that had pulled the governess cart, Neil reluctantly returned to the manor house. He was met by Reginald, who apparently had been waiting for him.

To his astonishment, the man had a smile on his face. His manner was more than cordial. "I asked the cook to prepare a fine meal tonight," he said. "We wanted to officially welcome you. I realize that . . . I was not . . . gracious earlier. 'Twas the shock, you understand."

Neil did. More than Reginald Campbell would ever know. With some painful familiarity, he recognized much of himself in Reginald. The sense of entitlement, the absolute conviction that he could succeed where his cousin could not. A year's difference in birth meant the difference between power and dependency. It was a world where fate was more important than competence or character. He knew the resentment, the jealousy, the hopelessness of being a poor relative.

He nodded. "I understand. Cumberland's decision had to come as a surprise."

"We are pleased that my nephew has such a distinguished guardian."

Now that, Neil thought, was a trifle much. He could not even imagine the effort it took Reginald to utter such words. He himself would not have been capable of such a statement. He wished he knew whether the man had actually adjusted to what had happened or was simply biding his time.

"I will try to see that the entire family prospers," he replied.

Reginald's face relaxed a trifle, and Neil realized Reginald was concerned about his initial reaction and whether or not he had offended Neil and, consequently, Cumberland.

"I will have to dress," he said.

"You knew the countess before?"

"Aye, but only briefly. She and her father stayed awhile at Braemoor when she was but a young lass."

Reginald Campbell nodded. "We are honored to have you here, and if there is anything my wife or I can do for you, please just let us know. I would be most pleased to work with you. We both have the best interests of my nephew at heart."

"That is most kind of you," Neil said wryly.

The smile on his face broke and for a moment he looked bewildered. "I would have made a good guardian."

"I am sure you would have," Neil said, and he thought that Reginald meant it. Campbell had lost much: prestige, control of lands. Perhaps worse was loss of face by having an outsider appointed guardian. "I do not think Cumberland doubted your ability. He knows me. He did not know you."

Reginald simply nodded, a smile still fixed on his face.

Neil again felt sympathy. But after looking at the books, he knew the man was incompetent if not venal. Still, he had no wish to humiliate him. "I must change clothes," he said again.

"We will dine in an hour," Reginald said. "My wife planned the meal herself. And I do not believe you have seen our son. He is only a few months of age."

Another potential heir.

For a moment, Neil felt trapped in the past. He shook it off, then nodded and headed up the stone steps to his own room.

A hip bath was filled with hot water. Janet's orders, no doubt. He wondered whether she was enjoying the luxury of a bath herself. The thought stirred a tormenting desire.

The meal tonight would be agony, just as the day had been, just as every moment at Lochaene had been and would continue to be.

He discarded his clothes and slipped into the hip bath, hoping the still-warm water would quiet the demons inside him, even as he knew nothing would.

•   •   •

Janet stayed with the lasses as they ate, then put Colin to bed. But then she indulged herself with a bath and afterward Lucy pulled her hair back and tied it with a dark ribbon and topped it with a small lace-edged cap.

Janet looked at herself in the mirror. She wore a plain dark dress since she was still in mourning. Her face was thin, as was her body, except for her breasts which swelled with milk. She thought herself rather plain, and her husband had constantly told her as much.

She sighed. She did not know how she would get through the coming meal, how she could sit opposite Braemoor and eat. Flashes of the past kept darting into her mind. Good ones, terrible ones. She wanted to remember the note she'd read, not the neat bow he had made to her daughters today. She wanted to remember his hurtful words, not the vulnerability she saw today.

She had not told him about the cloaked figure on the battlements she'd encountered before his arrival. For one reason, she had no proof that he meant harm. And she did not want Neil to remain. It was too . . . unsettling, too . . . unpredictable, too . . . too painful to see him.

Still, she pinched her cheek to put some color in them and she smoothed back her hair. She did not use powder as her sister-in-law did.

Then she stiffened her back and went down to what she suspected might be the most difficult meal of her life.

Reginald had to swallow his pride. Nothing had hit him quite as hard as Braemoor's sudden and unexpected appearance nor the news that he, rather than Reginald, had been appointed guardian.

He knew of the man, but only slightly. Braemoor apparently did not venture far from his estates. No one knew much about him, and he had tried desperately in the past day to find out more. He had, in fact, ridden ten miles to try to gather some information from Strathmore, an Englishman who had recently been given Jacobite estates. He needed to find a weakness and exploit it.

But Strathmore knew no more than he, and his dismissive attitude was galling. At the end, however, he had agreed to find out what he could about the Marquis of Braemoor.

Braemoor certainly did not look like a lord. He did not have the social graces, nor did he dress like one. He looked like some loutish blacksmith. He was, Reginald had been told, a bastard who for some unknown reason had been named heir by the recently deceased marquis who, himself, was an upstart.

This Braemoor had Cumberland's ear, and Reginald intended to find out how and why, and to get some of that ear himself.

Reginald had hoped to inherit the title himself. His brother had produced only daughters before marrying the Leslie girl for her dowry. In addition to the sizeable dowry, there had been a future promise of additional lands. That came to naught after the uprising.

Damn the woman for bearing a son and taking what should be his. He had thought he could have everything anyway, at least until the lad reached his majority, but Braemoor's interference had ended that.

Louisa had been even angrier than he. She had never liked Janet, had felt her sister-in-law thought herself better than she, since she was the daughter of a merchant. As a second son with no title and no wealth of his own, he'd had few choices. And Louisa had brought a large dowry herself. She had a tart tongue, though, and bad temper, and she often took it out on him by refusing him her bed.

Being named guardian would have solved so much.

But now Louisa had convinced him that their best course was to mollify Braemoor. Once the man returned to his own estates, Reginald could siphon off funds and still control the estate. He had to convince Braemoor that he would be a fine manager in the man's absence.

The first meeting had not gone well. He had not been very

good with books, and neither had Alasdair. He, like Alasdair, had intended to empty the estate of the remaining tenants and turn the land to grazing.

And he would be, for all purposes, the laird of Lochaene. Louisa had said it was only right. Why should a Jacobite Leslie control Campbell land? God's truth, she was right. He would bide his time until Braemoor left, then offer his help.

Louisa had spent much of her day in the kitchen, a rarity, although one of her finer points was a knowledge of food. They had prepared a feast for Braemoor, including the last of his brother's finest wine. Enough food and wine, and perhaps the oaf would go home and take care of his own business.

His motives were still unknown. Did he want Lochaene, or did he have an interest in the widow? He'd certainly shown no sign of the latter, and Janet was not very appealing. She was far too thin, her face too austere. So it came back to the land.

Mayhap, Louisa prodded, he could discover more if Braemoor were to partake liberally of the wine.

It was the only hope he had, unless he wished to live the rest of his life as a supplicant and poor relative with no funds of his own. His wife had hoped to be countess one day. He doubted if that would happen now, but at least he might loosen some funds. Some new dresses, a carriage, a trip to Edinburgh might make her loss less severe.

He went to oversee the preparations.

Even Braemoor's best clothes were severe, Janet noticed. He wore dark blue except for a linen shirt and plain neck-cloth. They were like crows next to parrots. Both Louisa and Reginald were dressed in the finest clothes, which meant a red gown for her sister-in-law and a bright green waistcoat for Reginald. The dowager countess, Marjorie, was still in black mourning, but she wore family jewels that were dazzling. They were all obviously trying to impress their visitor.

The smile inside her, however, quickly dissipated. She'd been surprised at learning of the banquet tonight, since she had not ordered it. She'd also heard from Clara about the fit Louisa had had when Braemoor had announced he'd been named guardian.

But then, Louisa had always been a bit on the sly side. It was obvious they had harnessed their resentment long enough to try to impress Braemoor. For a moment, she had worried about that, but then she knew in some corner of her heart that Braemoor would not fall for such a ploy. If he had demonstrated anything in the past few days, it had been a confidence he'd not had years ago, and determination to follow through on his word. He'd shown that last night when he'd traveled into a village to get oats for the horses.

He would see through them. She kept telling herself that. Nonetheless, she was surprised at his cordiality toward her brother-in-law, and obvious deference to Louisa. Mayhap he did not see the edge of contempt in their eyes.

Louisa had been very careful with the seating. She had taken away the chair at the head of the table so they sat two on one side, three on the other. She placed herself next to Braemoor. Wine was poured immediately.

"I hope you enjoy the wine, my lord," Louisa said. "It was Alasdair's best."

"I'm sure it will be satisfactory," he said, taking a sip, then returning the glass to the table.

Janet badly needed a sip. She needed a gulp, and yet she knew she could not afford that. It was quite obvious that Louisa and Reginald had a plan tonight. She hoped it was as obvious to Braemoor as it was to her. But he did not know them as she did. And neither, she reminded herself, did she know him now.

Everything he had done puzzled her. She had expected nothing but greed when he had shown up at her door. Why else would he take on such a position? She had asked for his help because she'd had nowhere else to turn. She had meant for him to talk to Cumberland. She had meant a tiny boon.

She had not meant for him to take over her life, or that of all of Lochaene.

Had she created a monster that would devour her and hers?

He was quiet and watchful, which he always seemed to be. He was as polite to them, as he had been to her. He kept every feeling, every emotion, to himself.

A pox on him.

She only knew she had to keep her own feelings every bit as private. She'd learned to do that as wife to Alasdair Campbell. He had quashed what joy of spirit she had. She had learned to measure every word, every action, and still she had incurred his wrath. She swallowed now, wishing she was not so timid, that she had not learned so many lessons so well.

But she had. So she sat and observed, uncertain as to whether those scenes today with the children reflected Braemoor's true character. Or had his character been in that note he'd written her years ago? It had been curt, unkind. She remembered every word. It was ingrained in her mind.

I withdraw my suit. Your father as well as my uncle are opposed to the match. There would be no dowry or inheritance. I am sure you understand.

When she had asked to see him, she'd discovered he had left for London on some errand for his uncle.

She had *not* understood. She had not understood anything at all. He had declared his devotion, had said he did not care about a dowry. Lies. All lies. He *had* cared about the dowry. Janet had lost her faith that day. She had lost it in love, in hope, in her own judgment. Her marriage to Alasdair had been yet another mistake, another blind step.

"And you, my lady—what do you think?"

Janet jerked upright in her chair at Braemoor's question. She had missed the previous conversation, lost as she was in her brief unhappy visit to the past. "Of what?"

"That sheep would be more to our advantage," Reginald

said with an exaggerated patience as if repeating the conversation showed her inadequacy.

"More to whose advantage?" she said, wondering whether he was aware of Braemoor's promise of seed.

"To Lochaene, of course," Reginald said. "All our neighbors are turning over the land to sheep and cattle. 'Tis the wise and frugal thing to do," he added, casting a quick look toward Braemoor.

"And our tenants?"

"They can find work in the cities," he said, obviously confident that he was gaining Braemoor's ear.

"I do not think it is that easy," she said. "And they have children."

Reginald stiffened. "So do we, my lady, and we must ensure that they, too, have a future."

"Not at the expense of others," she snapped back.

"Those are words of . . . a sentimental woman," Reginald said, his face reddening. It was obvious that he wanted to say something more.

Braemoor, as usual, was silent. His face did not, by so much of a twitch, betray the slightest indication of approval or disapproval. She wanted to hit him.

"They are the words," she said, "of the Countess of Lochaene. I have talked to some of the tenants. They are receiving seed for their planting."

Reginald's face turned white. "You did not consult me."

" 'Tis no need," she said.

Reginald turned to Braemoor. "Surely, you do not approve?"

"Aye, but I do," he said calmly. "I advanced the necessary money. It appears that Lochaene has been neglected . . . or mismanaged these last few years. The books are dismal. I hardly think the countess can do any worse."

"You malign my son," Marjorie said, rising from the chair. "And he recently dead. Perhaps by foul means." Her gaze rested on Janet. "Surely, you cannot . . ."

Braemoor looked at her with a steady gaze and said nothing for a moment. Janet tensed. She did not know what he had heard, what he suspected. Her husband's family had been spreading suspicions. She shouldn't care what he thought . . . she shouldn't. But she did. She looked down at her hands. They were like marble, stiffened and unmoving.

"By foul means?" Braemoor said.

"Aye," Louisa said eagerly. " 'Twas unexpected and without warning. A stomach ailment. The physician said . . ." She hesitated, leaving the words lingering with all their implications.

"Said what?" Braemoor asked.

Had he really not heard? Was he deliberately tormenting her?

"It could be . . . poison," Marjorie said with some satisfaction.

Braemoor's eyebrows furrowed. "Did the authorities investigate?"

Janet's heart pounded faster. Could he actually believe . . . ?

"Ah . . . there was no . . . proof . . ."

"Surely Reginald would not . . . do such a thing," Braemoor said calmly.

The room stilled. Janet's heartbeat slowed, almost stilled. Bewilderment, then anger, flitted over the faces of others in the room.

Reginald pulled away from the table and half-rose in indignation. "Surely, sir, you are not accusing me."

"Of course not," he said blandly. "I just said so, did I not? But he would be the only one to benefit."

"How so?" Louisa said. "His wife threatened—"

"She did? And why was that? Surely he did not mistreat her? And Reginald, I suppose, expected to be named guardian. 'Tis simple deduction."

Three outraged faces stared at him. He sat back, a guileless smile on his face, his gaze going from one to the other, studying each one. He had quite neatly outfoxed them. Unless they said Alasdair had mistreated her, they indeed became the prime suspects. And yet nothing he'd said was defensive of her.

Braemoor had changed in the years since she had met him. One of the qualities that had attracted her as a girl was what she believed was his blunt honesty. Had she been that big a fool? She was finding him far more complex than she had ever thought possible. It was not a thought that comforted her. The thought continued to nag her: what did he want from her?

"Let us speak no more of poison," he said. "The wine is too fine to ruin it with such unpleasantness." He lowered his gaze to his food and started to eat again, completely oblivious to all the stunned reactions around him.

And hers, Janet knew, was no less troubled than those of the others.

The Marquis of Braemoor was playing all four of them against each other.

The question was why.

Chapter Nine

Neil looked over at Lochaene's manor house from astride his horse. A full moon rode the sky behind the bleak stone edifice, and he could see the flickering of lamps inside several windows. He saw one flicker in what must be the nursery and he knew in his heart that Janet was there.

In his mind's eye, he saw her bending over each girl, pulling a cover over her, giving a light kiss.

He closed his eyes against the scene, against the bitter longing inside him, the ache that deepened every moment he stayed at Lochaene. He wanted so much and could have so little.

After the dreadful supper had ended, Janet had quickly left. He had changed clothes, then gone out to the stables and saddled a horse. He needed to get away from the prying and greedy overtures of the Campbells. He needed the fresh, stinging air, the uncluttered skies, the purity of the Highlands. He needed it to clear his mind and cleanse his soul.

He had done what he could for Janet this evening. He had purposely been silent this day, wanting to determine how much she could handle by herself, whether she could indeed manage Lochaene on her own. How much did she actually need him—or, more accurately, his skills? She had made it quite clear she did not want any more from him, that, in fact, she wanted him gone as quickly as possible.

And now he would be. He'd put the Campbells on notice tonight. He would establish credit with the local merchants, but only if items were ordered by Countess Lochaene. He would also send several reliable people from Braemoor. It was all she needed. She had the strength to do what needed to be done, and the ability, he thought, to work with the tenants. The best thing he could do now was leave her and return to Braemoor, follow through with his own plans and his own life.

He would remember every moment here—with the possible exception of supper tonight. He'd even savored being wet upon by puppies and bairns. There was something truly pitiable about that, that he needed personal contact so badly that he would enjoy such indignities. The simple fact was that he was nothing—not even an uncle or godfather—to anyone, and for a few moments he'd been included in a family outing, even if the family had been somewhat reluctant.

There had been few family intimacies at Braemoor. His uncle had been a rough, intolerant man who had virtually imprisoned his wife and doted on only one thing: his son who was little more than a bully. Neither had known how to love. They only knew how to conspire against others.

Just as the Campbells conspired.

All except Janet and the children. The girls were not hers by blood, but he'd noticed the gentle affection—love—between them.

He was a lord. He'd once thought that would be enough. That security and riches would be enough. It was ironic that none of those things was more than a willow branch in the wind. No substance. No meaning.

Neil reached in his pocket where he kept the deck of cards he'd taken from the cottage at Braemoor. For the life of him, he didn't know why he kept them, nor why he kept the heart queen at the front of the deck and the spade jack—the black knave—at the bottom. He did not gamble. He'd never had enough funds as a lad, or even a young man, and he'd thought other pursuits more important. For instance, being the best at arms. It had been his only worth to Braemoor.

Mayhap he kept that deck to remind him of his past, of Rory's redemption, and of those few glorious days with Janet when he'd thought all things possible. But he was not Rory. He had not his cousin's verve or skill or recklessness. He wondered how many people Rory had actually saved from the gallows or imprisonment. The legend he had become placed the number in the hundreds. But then the myth, as myths do, had grown and facts were exaggerated. Although the Black Knave had not been seen in months, he was still rumored to be secreting Jacobites from the country.

Rory had masterminded his own death by the Black Knave; no one realized they were one and the same. A body thought to be Rory's had washed ashore, and many whispered that the Knave must have died also. But rumors of the Black Knave persisted, and Cumberland continued to keep a price on his head.

His cousin must laugh every time he thought of outwitting Cumberland and keeping the Knave alive as a symbol of hope. Neil had only come to know of his cousin's dual identity in the last days of the deception, and he'd been both stunned and awed at the audacity of a man he'd despised as a fool and rogue.

"Ah Rory," he said to the harsh wind blowing down from the mountains, "I hope you and your bonny Bethia are well in the new world."

In a rare moment of whimsy, he dismounted and took the knave and the heart queen from the deck and put the two cards back in his pocket. He held out the rest of the desk, allowing the wind to pick them up and carry them off into the hills.

Then he mounted again. He would ride until he, or the horse, was exhausted. Mayhap then he could sleep.

• • •

Reginald drank. He tried not to listen to his wife. Or to his mother.

"You should have gone directly to Cumberland," his mother said.

"How would I know that His Grace would appoint someone outside the family," he said defensively.

"There is something between those two," Marjorie said. She had retired with Reginald and Louisa to their rooms to discuss the conversation. "I can see it in their eyes. And why else would someone of the Marquis of Braemoor's wealth bother with Lochaene?"

"She never left here," Reginald reminded her. "Alasdair saw to that."

"Still, there is something very odd about this," Marjorie persisted.

"He came for Alasdair's funeral," Louisa said. "I talked to him then. He just said he came to pay respects."

Marjorie pondered that for a moment. "I did not know Alasdair knew the man."

"He just recently inherited," Reginald said.

His mother raised an eyebrow. "Do you think they were lovers?"

"I donna know, but I will find out." A sudden thought occurred to him "Mayhap Colin is his."

"It would not matter," his mother said. "My son claimed him."

"Demmed mon," Reginald said. "What in the bloody hell does he want? He is not the most conversational of men. And his clothes. They are more suited to a merchant than a lord."

"He is said to be a bastard," Marjorie said contemptuously. "You can see the lack of breeding. And we have to cater to him. If only Alasdair—"

"Blast Alasdair," Reginald said. "He's all you ever cared about. He is the reason all this is happening. He and his lavish spending."

"How can you say such things?" Marjorie retorted. "And he just in his grave."

"It does not change the facts," Reginald said bitterly. "He left us nothing."

"How long will he be here?" Louisa asked, obviously seeking to cut through the tension radiating at the table.

Reginald shrugged. "He has not said. He seems to be taking over the property. Apparently he employed a new groom all on his own. As if he were master here." He heard the resentment in his voice. "He did not even consult with me. He's even buying seed without giving weight to my opinion of emptying the land. I did not know until supper tonight. The upstart."

"His cousin—the mon he succeeded—was said to be a gambler and rogue, but he is thought to have killed the Black Knave," Marjorie said.

"This Braemoor does not look . . . formidable," Marjorie said meanly. "He has no . . . presence. He is a bore."

"Our Janet does not think so," Louisa said with a snide smile. "She kept looking at him."

"Mayhap his reward has already been given," Louisa said slyly.

"My son has been dead less than a month," Marjorie said in a low pained voice.

"They were alone all day today," Louisa reminded him.

Reginald's lips quivered with indignation. "All alone?"

Louisa shrugged. "The children were with them. And that Clara."

"Hmmm," Reginald said. "I wonder if His Grace would be interested. 'Tis disgraceful. Poor Alasdair must be turning over in his grave. I always said he shouldna have married a Jacobite."

"He did not know her family was Jacobite," Marjorie defended her late son.

"I will try to find out how long he plans to stay," Reginald said. "If it is to be a long time, we will plan a ball to introduce him. Then we can find out more about him. He does not provide much information."

The other two nodded.

"If only it were not for the lad," Louisa said in a low voice. "Then you would be in line for the succession."

"Aye, but he is healthy," Reginald said. "I do not think we can expect anything there."

"There would be nothing left, either," Louisa said caustically. "Janet apparently has his ear, and she appears to want to give everything away."

"Everything that should have been ours," Reginald added. "And she nothing better than a murderess."

A silence settled around the table. They had tried to have Alasdair's death declared a murder but the physician had said he could not be sure. It was not arsenic, he said, because he would recognize the symptoms. But as to any other poisons, there was no way to be sure.

"If only she had been barren," Louisa said.

"Colin is *my* grandson," Marjorie said, straightening. "Alasdair's son."

Reginald threw a warning glance toward Louisa. "We are only saying that by rights the guardianship should be in *our* family, not be given to a slip of a girl nor some bastard outsider."

"I canna disagree with that," Marjorie said. "I do have friends. I will write them and see whether they will intercede with His Grace."

"We will pray it is not too late," Louisa said piously. "This . . . Braemoor could loan money, then call in the debts. We may have nothing left. That, indeed, could be his plan."

Marjorie nodded. "I will journey to Edinburgh and talk to His Grace myself. He may not even realize that Reginald could manage things here well, and that it is both his duty and right."

Reginald felt some of the tension fade away. His mother could be quite formidable and persuasive and she was a member of the powerful Campbell family. While they were but distant to the powerful Campbells, the name should mean something. "Perhaps you should also visit our Campbell cousins," he suggested.

Marjorie nodded. "I will leave tomorrow."

Reginald nodded his head. Mayhap there was a way out of this catastrophe. Perhaps there was more than one. He had to have money of his own, not just what Janet felt like dispensing. If he could sell some of the land, then mayhap he could invest in some venture that would make him independent. It was the devil's own punishment to be a second son, a poor relative living on largess. He just did not know what he had done to deserve such.

All had been said. Marjorie would have the new stablelad prepare the phaeton to take her to the dowager's house on the edge of the property.

After a servant had been sent to the stable to have the phaeton readied, Reginald poured himself a brandy and his wife and Marjorie a glass of sherry. Reginald lifted his glass. "To freedom," he said.

"To success," his mother added.

Janet told her daughters a story, then sang a lullaby to Colin and held him close after nursing him.

She should be content. She had the children. She had her own son in her arms. She now had the independence she'd so longed for.

It should be enough.

She couldn't remove from her mind, though, the image of Braemoor holding her son, the look of tenderness and vulnerability on his face, the stark longing in his eyes. An image she wanted to see?

Why did her skin burn and her insides quiver when he touched her, her heart remember the kiss they had exchanged years ago and long for another? Nothing about him had indicated he returned the interest at all.

What if he were roaming again tonight? What *if* he did not seem to sleep any more than she had since his arrival?

Colin fell asleep and she placed him in the cradle next to her bed. She liked to reach out at night and just touch him, reassure herself he was here and well. Then she went to the window and looked out. A flicker of light shown from the barn. Someone was there.

How late was it?

Past midnight, she thought.

Perhaps she should see what was happening down at the stables. But that, she knew, was only an excuse. She would not go. She had made fool enough of herself these last few days.

Go down.

No.

But she found herself putting on her shawl. She checked Colin. He had already kicked off his covering and she replaced it and leaned down, touching the soft skin of his face with her own. Dear God, how she loved him. And she loved her daughters, each one with all their own lovely qualities. If nothing else, she would make sure they married men they loved.

Janet felt something wet on her cheeks. Her eyes stung. Was there really such a thing as love?

She used the shawl to wipe away the unwanted moisture, then left the room, taking the stairs slowly. She hesitated once more at the door. It was probably the new lad. Tim.

In any event, she needed fresh air. She took the several steps outside. The air was bracing, cold. Then she saw the light go out. A second later, Braemoor emerged from the stable. He stopped when he saw her.

Janet felt as if the world had stopped. She backed up against the door, ready to escape inside, but her legs did not move as he approached her. Why had she come out here?

He wore no jacket against the cold, and his hair was tousled, several wayward strands falling over his forehead. In the moonlight, his face looked shadowed, darkened by afternoon stubble. He looked reckless and even dangerous. He'd never looked that way to her before. As a young man, he had been vulnerable and steady and gentle. In the past week, he'd appeared in many guises. She'd even believed that some of them were treacherous.

But *dangerous*?

For the past several days, he'd merely watched and studied and held his own counsel in a particularly maddening way. He'd given away nothing at all at supper tonight. He had not championed her, nor had he championed the others. He'd just watched.

"My lady?" he said. "It is late."

"I might say the same to you," she said. "I saw a light in the stables and thought I should see if all was well."

"It seems to be," he said. "I talked to Tim earlier. He found your Kevin, and he is coming back. I'll be sending several men, too."

"To spy?"

"Nay, my lady. To help. You may dismiss them anytime you wish. I thought I had made it clear. You may do whatever you like. I only ask that if you have any difficulties that you send me a message."

"And you will come as you did this time?"

"Aye," he said simply.

"Why?"

"Call it a whim, my lady. I do not care for your relatives."

"They are loyal to your Cumberland."

"A good reason to suspect them."

She took a step back but was stopped by the wall. "I thought you were close to Cumberland."

"He had an admiration for my cousin, not particularly for me. I never did understand it. My cousin was, as he liked to say, interested only in his own welfare. He was, as you probably heard, a profligate and womanizer."

"And you did not approve?"

"No, madam, I did not. I thought Braemoor deserved more."

An odd statement, and a telling one. Janet took a moment to absorb it. Braemoor deserved it. Not he. Not Neil Forbes, the Marquis of Braemoor. She looked again at him, at the plain clothes, the lack of pretense.

Nothing made sense. If he had been so concerned with her dowry, with inheritances and titles, why did he not wrap himself in their trappings now that he had them?

Silence stretched between them. So did the awareness that she'd sensed earlier today. He was not indifferent to her. So why did he act as if he were? Because she was so recently a widow?

"You have been riding," she finally said. She had to shatter the intimacy building between them.

"Aye. I needed fresh air after that meal."

She had to smile. She, too, had needed air. But she'd had three little girls and a wee bairn to look after.

"You cannot be referring to my husband's family."

"Of course not. The room was just a bit . . . stuffy."

"And the fresh air helped?"

"Aye," he said simply.

"I would like to ride at night. I have not done it since . . ." Her voice faded. She had not done it since that one night at Braemoor she'd met him.

"I hurt you years ago, madam," he said unexpectedly. "That was not my intention."

"Is that why you are here now?"

"Guilt? I hardly think so, my lady."

"You used to call me Janet," she said.

"That was a long time ago."

"Centuries," she agreed. "I learned much during that time. But you still have not told me why you are going to so much trouble."

"So much trouble?"

"Aye," she mocked him by using his own simple answer.

"It is no trouble at all. I do not like the Campbells."

"All Campbells or just this branch?"

"I think all of them would be accurate," he said judiciously.

"So this is just a game?"

She saw a shadow cross his eyes but then his mouth moved into a wry, cynical smile. "Aye. I have been taught by the best to play."

Disappointment flooded her. For a second, she'd thought . . .

"You have a fine son," he said. "And bonny lasses."

"They like you."

He looked surprised at that statement.

"Samson wetting on you helped," she offered.

He raised an eyebrow and she thought again how . . . handsome he looked when he did that. "Definitely not my charms," he said.

She raised an eyebrow this time. "Charms?"

His lips did crack slightly then, even turned up around the edges. Something shifted inside her. How could she care so much after what had happened, what she knew about him? How could she really trust him again?

She tried to move. "I should go inside."

He was blocking her. Even if she could move. He was close, too close. A distinctly musky smell enveloped her. The air grew dense. Despite the chill in the night, she felt warm. She wanted to touch him.

Her gaze met his. His eyes were fathomless, still inscrutable. His face was like a statue. Nothing moved now. But then his hand moved and the back of it brushed her cheek.

"My lord?" Her voice was a whisper.

He reacted as if it were a slap in the face.

He stepped back. "I will be leaving after having one last discussion with your brother-in-law," he said in that cool voice she hated.

"I thought you wanted to see more of Lochaene." What was she doing? Practically inviting him to linger. Incomprehensively, she felt a far greater loss than when her husband died. She had grieved for Alasdair as she would for any man, but not for him as a husband. She'd felt no little guilt about that fact, but she could not deny it.

"I have seen enough, and you do not need me, lass," he said.

She did need him. She needed parts that he probably did not even realize existed inside him.

She would not beg, so she merely nodded.

"I have business at Braemoor," he added. "As I said, I will send someone here to help you."

"I would rather try Angus," she said. "'Twould be better if I had someone from the property."

He looked dubious.

"You said I could make my own decisions. Was that the truth, or another lie?"

She was beginning to know that muscle in his jaw. It was the only telltale sign that anything bothered him. He did not have to ask her what lie she meant. He nodded, then said, "I will return in a fortnight."

"I would not be wishing to keep you from your own affairs."

"Lochaene is now my affair," he said. It was an unkind reminder. "If you have but need of me—"

"I will not."

She was grateful that he was silent at that latest boast. She'd obviously had need of him. He had repaid what he obviously considered a debt. Either that, or he had some nefarious plan in mind. She was not quite sure which she preferred at the moment. She wanted to dislike him, to despise him. It was easier to live with the memory that way.

Still, he did not turn away. She felt the impact of his presence throughout her entire body. How could she still be attracted to him?

But the unfortunate fact was she was, and far greater than even eight years ago. Age, perhaps battle, had written lines in his face. Small wrinkles jutted out from around his eyes, and his jaw was leaner. He had a confidence now when once he had youthful bravado. His eyes were the same dark, deep mystery, and they more than anything had not changed, except they were far more wary. He reminded her a little of a hawk, and the danger that image conveyed stroked treacherous places inside her.

The truth was she did not want him to leave, and that was the worst thought of all.

"Thank you for being kind to the children today," she said, putting off the leaving just one more moment.

"It was not that difficult, Countess."

"They have not had much kindness from men."

Neither have you. She saw the realization in his eyes. It hurt. She did not want his pity.

His fingers touched her cheek again, brushing away a curl that had fallen from her braid. They hovered there for a moment, then he leaned down and touched her lips with his. Electricity ran through her like lightning through an oak. Heat puddled inside as she instinctively responded to his caress. Gentle yet so maddeningly persuasive, seductive, searching. She tried not to respond, but her body betrayed her. Her arms reached around him.

Her entire body was alive with need. She told herself it was for the tenderness that her husband had never shown. That it was loneliness. Mayhap it was all of them, but she had never been quite so alive. Her lips responded to his, and her mouth opened as his kiss became hungry, demanding. But it still had a tenderness that had never colored Alasdair's advances. Her husband had just taken. He'd never explored, invited, seduced.

She turned her eyes upward to Braemoor's. In the moonlight, she saw a pain so strong it ripped her apart. Her fingers tightened against the back of his head.

His kiss deepened, and the tenderness erupted into an explosiveness that echoed in every part of her body. Lips became almost frantic with the need to touch and feel and taste. The need burned straight through her, and nothing else mattered. Not betrayal, or resentment, or fear. Her body melded to his, and her lips opened, allowing his tongue entrance as her hands went up around his neck, tracing her fingers along his back. It was as if she'd been seized by a storm of feeling and tossed around with no will of her own.

She felt his hands moving around her body, and she felt it tense with expectation, with an eagerness new and unexpected. She tried to take a deep breath, to return to sense, but his tongue was devouring her mouth, his hands burning paths everywhere they touched. Her own body had become a natural adjunct to his, bending and yielding, her own hands and mouth as greedy as his.

Magic wrapped itself around them, a magic she'd experienced with him years ago, but this sorcery was even stronger, more demanding, more painful. A sob built deep inside her. How could she need him so?

A month after her husband's death. A month after the relief she'd felt that no man would again invade her body with no care for her. She felt herself shuddering. How could her body and heart and mind be at such odds.

She wanted to clutch him with all her might, to keep him with her. But he was as much a phantom as the man the Highlands had called the Black Knave. A myth.

With a cry, she pulled away from him. She stood, her body trembling, aching, wanting. She fought back the tears that had been far too close to the surface since he'd arrived. She'd thought she could never be affected by a man again. And now she felt like a mindless puppet.

He stepped back, looking at her with those dark unfathomable eyes. "I apologize, Madam. I did not mean for that to happen."

Then why had it? If neither of them had wanted it . . . why?

Sweet Mother in heaven, but those tears were threatening again.

Braemoor stood there silently for a moment. He looked down at her, and she almost thought she could hear his heartbeat. She wished she could read his eyes, but she could not. They were as barred to her as his heart. She'd been a moment's fancy. An easy kiss stolen from a love-starved widow. Once he'd proven his prowess, he had little interest. Pain ripped through her. She straightened, lifted her chin. He would never know how much that moment hurt her.

But it was Braemoor who finally turned away. "I am going to walk awhile," he said.

She was clearly not invited. Nor did she want to be, she told herself. It was better that he left before she did anything foolish. She turned toward the door.

He nodded, "Do not forget. If you have need of me . . ."

It would be a good day in hell before she approached him again.

She did not answer him but slid inside the door. She closed it, then leaned against it as if her body could keep him out. Why did she always lose all her senses around him? And why did the good memories push away the bad? Especially when he had just made it obvious that he was only paying back a debt. He evidently had no interest in her as a widow, either. Her estates were not so large. In truth, she had to admit, they were very small indeed compared to his own.

Had he expected more? The Campbells had properties throughout Scotland, most of them stolen, she knew. Had he come here thinking that Lochaene might be a treasure to drain?

That must be it. And now that he had discovered differently, he was leaving as fast as his horse would carry him. She would, most likely, not hear from him again.

Good riddance, she told herself as she finally moved away from the door and started toward the steps. She repeated the words, even as the tears finally fell.

Chapter Ten

The gunshot came out of nowhere. Then another.

The blows knocked Neil off his horse. He tumbled for several feet, his head hitting a rock. He saw blood coloring his breeches and felt it running down his cheek. He realized it was only a matter of seconds before the pain hit him. He knew, from battle, that there was usually a moment's numbness.

It came quicker than he thought.

He forced himself to slump and lie absolutely still. Would the assailant venture down to see whether he had succeeded? Or figure that this path was so isolated that no one would find him in time to save him? He prayed for the latter even as his mind worked feverishly. He had taken this path through the Highlands because the route was faster, even though often dangerous.

Bandits roamed these Highlands, as did bands of fugitive Jacobites who hadn't been able to escape the country even eighteen months after Culloden. They needed money for their escape to France.

He had been a daydreaming fool. The morning mist had cleared and the mountains had been deceptively peaceful with their fields of heather and gorse and tumbling waterfalls. He'd been thinking of Janet and last night's unwise kiss. How could he ever have permitted himself to commit such a selfish act? But she had been so appealing in the moonlight, her face turned up to his. . . .

He'd regretted it instantly and yet he had not been able to stop himself. He had touched her face, and then. . . .

And then . . . he should have walked away. But he had not, and now he would remember forever the way she had invaded the deep private part of him he'd tried to keep locked tight. He would always remember the way her lips felt, the way her body had melded to his. She had not wanted to kiss him, but there had been something so instinctive, so irresistible. He had even let himself think for a second that . . .

But what was a marriage without intimacy, without physical love?

He was visiting that particular hell when the sound of a musket ripped through the air and a ball into him.

Lost in his thoughts, he had forgotten these Highlands could be as hostile and lawless as any place on earth.

The pain struck him now with a fury. He heard voices and he struggled to hold his breath. A kick landed in his ribs and he forced himself not to react.

"E's not quite dead," he heard a voice say. "Should I finish 'im?"

"Search him first. The woman said he would have money. If he does not, we might hold him for ransom."

Neil forced his body to go limp and his eyes to remain closed as fingers probed his clothing. They found his much-depleted purse of coins, and he heard the disappointment in their voices. Then a grunt. "Tae bloody cards. We was promised more tha' this."

Neil heard the sound of boots approach. Not a steady gait. Damn, but he wished he could open his eyes. There was a moment's silence. "The queen and knave?" The voice was puzzled. And, to his surprise, obviously educated.

The pain was boiling inside him now, and he felt the loss of blood. He tried to will his assailants to leave.

A foot prodded him again, this time more gently. "If you still live, it will pay you to open your eyes." The educated voice again. "Otherwise, I will plunge this sword through you."

Neil believed him. He opened his eyes.

"Dem me, but he was playin' dead," said the other man.

"Who are you?" The man who had prodded him asked. Neil tried to raise up to see his interrogator. The man was dressed in peasant's clothes, a poor wool of nondescript color. His face, though, was striking. A scar ran down one side, giving it a perpetual smile. His hair was a dark russet color, tied in a queue at his neck. He was probably in his late thirties or so, but it was difficult to determine with the scar. His eyes were a dark blue.

Neil tried to move, but the pain was agonizing. The musket ball, he thought, must still be inside him.

The man over him seemed not to care. "Who are you?" he asked again. "And I might warn you that your life weighs on the answer."

"Neil Forbes," he said, afraid it sounded more like a groan than actual words.

"Are you Braemoor?"

"Aye," Neil said, seeing no advantage in denying it. Those cards, for some reason, had stayed this man's hand.

"Damn, if this isn't the devil's own work," the man said. He stooped and turned Neil, loosened his cloak, then jacket with far more care than the other man had shown. *Why?*

He took a knife from his belt and quickly cut open Neil's trouser leg. He muttered something to himself, then looked back at him. "One ball's still inside the leg."

"So what?" the second man said. "Why not finish him?"

"I have my reasons, Burke," the man with the scar said. "Come and help me get him off the path. I doubt whether there will be any more fools coming this way, but you never know."

If Neil hadn't felt so damn bad, he might have resented the description of him. He had no idea why his title had apparently changed this man's murderous impulses, but he was not going to quarrel with it now. He had too many things he wanted to do, and far too many debts to pay before he met his maker.

"Can you stand?" the stranger asked.

Neil tried, but he felt a rush of blood pour from his wound and pain turned into burning agony. He pushed up, though, and the russet-haired man put an arm under his and hoisted him to his feet. "God, but you are a heavy one," he said. "Burke, help me."

The other man took the other side and they half carried, half dragged him down out of sight of the road. The fire in his leg spread throughout his body. His head felt as if someone was hammering it. The pain almost blocked out the questions in his mind. Almost, but not quite. One of the men said a woman had set these two on him. And why now was the bandit trying to save the man he'd just tried to kill?

"Get my flagon," the stranger told the man called Burke, then turned to Neil. "I have to take that bullet out," he said.

Despite his best efforts to stay upright, Neil dropped to the ground. "Why? You just tried to kill me."

"I did not know you were Braemoor," he said. "We were told an English toff with plenty of Scottish gold in his pockets would be riding this way."

"You shoot without making sure?"

"Better than being shot. Or hung," the bandit replied with a shrug. "And I find myself in need of scratch."

"My horse?"

"Unhurt. The blood on him is yours. At least I might salvage a horse in this bloody mess."

Burke returned with a flagon and musket in his hand.

"Get him something to bite on. I donna want to bring the entire English army down upon us."

"Who are you?" Neil asked.

"A man trying to survive," the well-spoken bandit said. "You had the queen and knave. You can think of me as the king."

"King of bandits?"

The man just shrugged and offered the flagon. "Drink well, Braemoor. This is going to hurt like the furies."

Neil did so. He knew what was coming. He'd taken a sword thrust once, and some nasty slices while in training. Between waves of stabbing pain, he knew he was losing consciousness. He'd lost a lot of blood. Mayhap too much. The voice of his assailant-turned-benefactor was fading.

But then the flask was taken away, replaced by a piece of wood. Obediently, he bit down on it when told. His world exploded with agony and a mist of red blinded him. Then he sank into darkness.

Braemoor was gone. Janet wondered whether he would ever return. He had not even said so much as a good-bye. Or mayhap he had said it early this morning outside the manor. He'd said too much with his actions. And yet not nearly enough.

A conundrum.

How could she distrust someone, and yet want him so much?

Lucy had reported that he had met with Reginald early in the morning. Her maid had heard Reggie's loud voice but had not understood the words. She had not heard Braemoor's voice which meant *he* had not shouted. But then he never did. Was it simply because he did not care enough?

He certainly had not cared enough to linger this morning.

She knew she should take what he had offered and make the most of it while she could. He had given her freedom, credit to make some changes at Lochaene. He had given her everything she had asked for. Just not everything she had longed for.

Janet scolded herself for being so greedy. She had so much more than she'd had a month ago. Most of all, she had her children.

But now the losses seemed added one upon the other. Her father. Her brother Alexander. Friends. So many of them gone. Some dead at Culloden. Others put to the horn. Hunted by the English and their own countrymen.

The absence of one traitorous Scotsman should mean nothing to her.

She had risen later than she'd thought. After she had left Braemoor late last eve, she'd nursed her son and thus Colin had not woken at daybreak, as was his custom. When he did wake her with hungry demands, she went to the window and looked out. It was long past daybreak.

Janet ate breakfast with the lasses, answering their questions as well she could. Where had the gentleman gone? When would he be back? Oddly enough, they seemed disappointed that he had left without telling them good-bye.

Then she went out to see Tim, and was pleased when she saw Kevin there also. He acknowledged her by doffing his hat. "Tim here said ye asked fer me," he said.

"Indeed I did," she replied. "And I am happy to see you back. No one can discharge you now except me. Remember that."

"I saw MacKnight yesterday in the village," Kevin said. "He was in his cups. Said he would get even. Blamed yer ladyship fer being discharged."

"It doesna matter. Can you and Tim handle the stables?"

"Aye, my lady. Now tha' they 'ave their oats, the beasts are happy. Tim is deliverin' the seed. 'Tis a foine thing ye are doing."

"It is no more than their due."

The boy looked startled at the comment but said nothing more.

"Does Lucy know you are back?"

Kevin blinked rapidly, then grinned. "Aye. I saw her this morn."

"I expect your intentions to be honorable," she said.

"Oh, aye, my lady. Now tha' I have a position again I intend to ask fer her hand."

"You will have my blessing," she said. "The marquis, when did he leave?"

"Early this morn. 'E left this fer ye." Kevin handed her a letter sealed by the Braemoor crest.

She nodded.

"Would ye want me to be saddling a horse for ye, my lady?" he asked. "Or the phaeton?"

"Nay," she said, clutching the letter in tense fingers. "Not now."

She took the letter and hurried back to her room. She wanted to read it in private. What if he was denying all that he had offered?

Lucy was rocking Colin.

"The lasses?"

"Clara is with them," Lucy said.

"They need a governess." 'Twas a thought—nay, a strong belief—she'd expressed to her husband. He had decried it. "Lasses need no education," he'd told her.

But now . . . now she had choices. She hoped. She opened the letter and read it slowly.

I will establish credit for you in the village. When the first crop comes in, you can repay the loan at no interest. I have made the situation plain to your brother-in-law. He understands that you have the final word at Lochaene. If you have need of me, you need only to send a messenger.

Braemoor

His title was scrawled at the bottom of the page. Not Neil. Nothing personal. Only a cool letter of agreement. She wanted to crush it in her fist, but instead she looked over the room to find a secure place for it. A loose stone on one side of the room would do. She worked it loose, then put the letter inside in case she needed it.

Lochaene was hers. She was free for the first time in her life.

Then why did she feel so empty?

• • •

Pain radiated through Neil. He wanted to retreat back into sleep but that too was haunted. He saw the Culloden battle-field, heard the cries of the stricken, the moans of the dying, the sound of sword against armor and the even worse sound of it piercing flesh.

His sword.

Then a voice. *A woman said he would have money.* How many people had known he would be leaving this morning in time to alert someone? There were three women at Lochaene, but none but Janet knew when he planned to leave.

The very thought caused more pain than his wound.

"Braemoor." He heard his name called. Again and again. He tried to ignore it, to slip into the oblivion that blotted out the wrong roads he had taken.

The voice continued to nag at him. Challenging him. Why? Why did a bandit care whether or not he lived or died?

For that matter, why did he care himself?

But then another internal voice goaded him. *You've made promises at Braemoor.*

His mouth was dry, so dry he could barely make a croaking sound. His eyelids were heavy, and it required an amazing effort to try to open them. His leg burned as if all the pitchforks in hell had been thrust inside him, and his head felt little better. He was hot all over despite the chill in the air.

A wet cloth bathed his face. It was a gentler hand than he'd felt before.

He tried to focus. On one side was a young lass of no more than thirteen years. On the other was the man who had cut the ball from his leg.

"Ah, you are finally awake, Braemoor?"

The eyes in the scarred face were cool, almost indifferent. Neil wondered why he was still among the living.

He moved, barely stifling a groan. He sensed he could not

show weakness to this man who had ambushed him and had obviously intended him to die. What had stopped him?

Neil tried to move. The pain intensified, stabbing at him. "Why?" he managed to ask.

"Why did you have those cards?"

The cards. For some reason, those cards had saved his life. Those cards and his name. He had thrown away the other cards in a moment of fancy. Fate?

"Someone must want you dead, my lord, since we were told a wealthy gentleman would be traveling through these parts," the man said in a mocking voice.

"And why . . . am I not?"

"You answer my questions first. Why did you have those cards?"

"I like them," Neil said.

"Not a good enough answer."

"Where am I?"

"A cave far away from any British soldiers. Or turncoat Scottish ones. Do not expect any help."

"I never . . . have," Neil said.

"You fought with Cumberland?"

"Aye," Neil said, knowing that one word might be his death sentence. This man was unquestionably a fugitive Jacobite. And a bandit.

"Wise answer, my lord. If you had said otherwise, you would be dead."

"I still do not understand why I am not."

"Do not hold too much hope, my lord. It is still likely to happen."

Neil could not think of anything to be said after that dire prediction.

"I have heard the name of Braemoor whispered," the bandit said. "And I know what the jack of spades means to some."

Neil tried to move again. God, but he was thirsty. "Water?"

The man nodded to the girl who quickly got to her feet

and disappeared from his view. Seconds later she appeared with a cup. The bandit took it from her, and put his arm under Neil's head, lifting it slightly. But the cup came no nearer Neil's lips.

"You have not answered my questions yet," his captor taunted him.

Neil closed his eyes. The man obviously thought he had some connection with the Black Knave. That much was obvious. He was not going to take credit for Rory's acts. He'd dishonored himself enough.

"Where were you coming from?" the bandit said.

Neil puzzled over the question. "Lochaene," he said. "Near Inverness. Did not your informant tell you that?" he said bitterly.

"What informant?"

"I heard you say . . . the woman had said I was carrying money."

The man swore under his breath. "I did not know the message came from Lochaene. One of my . . . compatriots told me he obtained information from a high-bred royalist."

"Compatriot? Or fellow thief?"

"Oh, he is a thief, all right. He just does not have the courage to do the work himself. He gets others to do it for him. I pay a small fee for information."

"So you can ambush and kill Scotsmen?"

"So I can ambush and kill traitors," the man corrected him.

"Murder is murder." Neil knew he was goading the man, but he could not help it. The reference to a woman still bothered him. So did the man's indifference to life.

But then he'd been rather indifferent to life himself for a number of years. All he had wanted was the marquis's approval. Now he felt he was looking himself in the face, and he did not like it. He just did not know why he was not dead.

But the man merely shrugged. "Were you at Culloden?"

"Aye."

"Then you, too, are a murderer."

"Then why did you dig a musket ball out of me?"

"You haven not yet answered my question. Why the cards?"

"Many people have cards."

"Not just the black jack . . . the knave. You could be arrested on that fact alone."

"I also had the queen," Neil said.

"Do you really wish to die?"

"Nay, but I am not the Black Knave. He is dead."

"And how do you know this?"

"He has not been seen in months."

"I have need of him," the bandit said unexpectedly.

"Sorry to disappoint you," Neil said. "I know nothing about him."

Surprisingly, the man gave him a sip of water, and another. Neil swallowed greedily. "My thanks."

The man merely nodded, stood and walked away with an unsteady gait.

The young girl moved back to his side and washed his face.

"What . . . is his name?" he asked.

She shrugged. "We call him Will, but no one knows his true name."

"We?"

"There are ten of us. Will takes care of us."

"More water." Dear God, but he was thirsty. And hot.

He closed his eyes. *Braemoor.* What if he never had the chance to do what he wanted with Braemoor? He had no heirs. If he were to die, the lands would fall to the crown, and probably be given or sold to an Englishman who would most certainly clear the land. Everything he had planned, had wanted to build, would fade away and it would be as if he never existed.

And Janet? What would happen to her?

The young lass returned with water. He sipped it, but he felt as if he were burning up inside. He could never have enough and too soon the cup was empty. He closed his eyes.

He would bargain with God. He needed a few more months. A year.

Or would he be making a bargain with devil?

Will did not know what had stayed his hand.

He had made killing his life's work. He had come as close to death as one could at Culloden, where he'd suffered such grievous wounds that he was passed by Cumberland's soldiers who were giving death blows to the Jacobite wounded. An old woman, looking for her son, had found a flutter of life in him, had enlisted some help and then hid him. He'd taken over a year to heal, and even now he bore a scar on his cheek and he would never be able to walk naturally again. His leg had never healed properly. Even worse were the memories of the battle, of a British lance going through his best friend, of the slaughter of others.

He hated the English with every drop of blood in his body. He hated their Scot allies even more.

The man Will once was, the lord he'd been, was believed dead. He knew that. His family was gone. His face was so scarred that he could never escape notice. His crippled leg was another constant reminder of months of pain and of the man he once had been. Bitterness and hatred had crowded out every other emotion.

So he had supported himself, and other refugees, by killing every traitorous Scot and bloody Englishman he could find and relieving them of whatever goods they carried to help the desperate young stragglers he'd found in the Highlands.

He'd hope to see them to safety, but he was too visible with his scars. But he, too, had heard of the Black Knave and had hoped to convince him, by force if necessary, to take his small and pitiable band to safety. He did not know who else to trust, and he did not have the financial resources to buy loyalty.

His prey was the lone wealthy traveler who disappeared into thin air. 'Twas a cowardly way to live, but he had so little regard for his victims he did not care. And, he told himself, he had no choice. He could not take prisoners, nor could he let his victims live and tell of his existence.

This man was the first he had spared. Only the card, the hope that this somberly dressed Scot might know something of the Black Knave, had saved him. Will prayed it was not a mistake.

He also wondered why the man had been at Lochaene. He knew the estate, knew about the Campbells who lived there. One of their people, in fact, had been among his informers who alerted him to possible victims. Rewards were small, but still coveted in a part of Scotland where people were dying of hunger. But he was cautious. One person told another who told another. In the latter case, Burke, who had been with him, had received the message from a man named Bain who in turn said he had been given information by a lady. The lady had understood the implications of the information, he'd said.

It must have come from Lochaene—but from which lady?

He knew about the families that ringed *his* forest. It was only wise to know that.

Braemoor. Why had that word stopped him? What in his mind had stayed his hand? *Another whisper.* A connection to the Black Knave.

The man himself was nothing extraordinary. He'd been careless like the others. His clothes were somber but of fine quality. The lack of bluster had been on his side. No begging or pleading or promises that were never meant to be kept. All of those would have invited a quick death.

The lack of them had puzzled Will. And then, of course, there were the cards, and the prickling in his mind at the name of Braemoor. All his concern might be for naught. The man was warm, and Will knew the wound was festering. Without help, he might well die.

No loss that. Another traitorous Scot.

Someone wanted him dead. A royalist household.

Why?

Will did not like puzzles. He did not like his hesitation. He did not want to worry about the life or death of an enemy. He'd killed his conscience long ago.

But questions nagged at him. Was it the countess at Lochaene who wanted him dead? Or the dowager countess? It made a difference to him.

But Braemoor had been as close-mouthed and cautious as Will had learned to be.

He will die without help.

The old woman who had nursed Will was dead, killed by some drunken English soldiers. He had been hidden up in the loft of a barn. He'd heard the whole thing, but had been unable to go to the woman's assistance. That weighed on him, too.

He made a decision. He would leave the matter of Braemoor's life or death up to the Countess of Lochaene. If she wanted him dead, so be it. If not, mayhap she could save him. And if Braemoor did live, he would owe Will a very large boon.

One Will intended to collect.

Chapter Eleven

Janet rode in from visiting the last two of her tenants. There were twenty families remaining where once there had been more than a hundred. She did not know them personally but she knew the kind of people they were. Proud. Hard-working. Devoted to family and land.

They were, she knew, much like those on her father's land, land now in the hands of some Englishman. Her father had known every tenant on their land. They all came to family celebrations: birthdays, weddings, births. They had mourned together as they had celebrated together. She knew how much they loved their hard but beautiful mountains. She knew how they treasured their plaid, and pipes and dance. They had been clansmen, and her father had been one of the few remaining chiefs who had felt an obligation to them. Even before Culloden, the traditions had been changing. The tragedy at Culloden—and its bloody aftermath—had only speeded the process.

But while she had known every family on her father's land, she knew few at Lochaene although she had lived there three years. Her husband did not have the same relationship with his tenants as her father had. Alasdair, in truth, cared nothing at all about any of them.

But now she had the power to change things. She had

been trying to visit each of Lochaene's tenant families, to convince them to stay, to tell them they could hunt and fish without fear. She had given sweets to children who'd had none for a very long time. She'd tried to inspire a trust long since gone.

She had even given an older tenant—McNann—the position of butler to replace MacKnight. Reginald and Louisa had both protested. He had no training and looked like a ruffian. But she overrode them. She wanted someone *she* selected, and he needed additional funds for his brother's family.

Except for the argument over McNann, there had been something like peace at Lochaene since Braemoor had left nearly a week earlier. Reginald and Louisa had been unusually pleasant, and she had tried to be the same. She only prayed it lasted—for the children's sake if not her own.

Anxious to get back to the children, Janet nudged the mare to a faster pace. Colin was drinking cow's milk now in addition to her own. He still clamored, though, at her breasts for milk, and they remained sore and swollen. She hated to give up that bond between mother and child, and yet she knew if she was going to be successful in managing Lochaene, she needed more freedom.

Janet decided to go across the field. She would have to jump a low rock fence, but that challenged her. It had been far too long since she'd ridden across the fields with her father and brother. She leaned forward on the horse, flicked her crop lightly, and the mare stretched out, racing toward the fence. Up and over. Flying.

Suddenly, the saddle started slipping. She kicked her feet clear of the stirrups, then tried to pull the reins, but the horse was spooked. The mare's gait faltered, then she started running as both the saddle and Janet began to fall. She twisted and threw out her arms to cushion her fall.

Stunned, she lay on the ground as the horse continued to run toward the stable. She tried moving. Though parts of her body ached, everything worked; she did not believe anything was broken. She stood and limped over to the saddle and looked at the girth strap. It was torn.

The tear was ragged. It could have been simply worn. Nothing at Lochaene had been well tended for years. Or, a cut could have started the tearing process. If it had separated during the jump rather than on the landing, she might well have been killed.

Donna think about it. But she had to. If anything happened to her, what would become of her son?

Janet thought about that night on the rampart, the shadowy figure. She had not mentioned it to Braemoor. Mayhap, she should have.

She shivered, fear sending cold waves through her.

It was an accident.

She stood unsteadily, tried a step, then another. She was about half a mile from the stables, but she suspected someone would come looking for her when the horse returned. Should she wait? Or walk? Suddenly, she thought of her son.

What if this was no accident? And if it were not, if she was in the way of someone, then so was her son.

She put the torn cinch over her arm. She would ask the smithy in the village to check it. Then she started walking painfully toward the manner. She wanted to hold Colin, to feel him safe in her arms.

Neil screamed Janet's name through the haze of heat and pain. Thirsty. He was always thirsty. Janet was lost in his dreams, in his nightmares. They were intertwined. He saw her on Culloden Moor, covered with blood. Someone was coming toward her with a sword and he tried to stand in front of her, but something blocked him. She was being surrounded. There was blood everywhere. His own. Hers.

"Braemoor!"

He tried to open his eyes but the lids were too heavy.

"I'm sending you with Burke," he heard a voice say. Will's voice. It seemed to be a long way off. "You need more help than I can give you. Braemoor—do you hear me?"

Neil tried to hear, to listen. The voice commanded it. "If you live, you owe me," the voice said. "I will claim the debt."

And then he was being moved, carried, lifted on a horse. Pain was a living, burning thing inside him. He wanted to protest but there was not enough left inside him, not enough sound or voice or will. Neil was vaguely aware of being tied to a saddle, but then everything—even the nightmares—faded into nothingness.

Janet clutched Colin to her tightly, so tightly he started to whimper in protest. Reluctantly she put him back into the cradle. She had not been able to tear herself away from him since her return to the manor house yesterday afternoon.

Tim had met Janet as she'd neared the manor. He was mounted on a horse, and when he'd neared, he slipped down and ran to her. "My lady, are you hurt?"

"Just some bruises," she said.

"The horse returned tae the stable withou' a saddle," he said.

"The saddle slipped off." She handed him the cinch. "I want you to take this to the smithy and have it repaired. Ask him to examine it first. I want to know how it came apart."

The lad's eyes grew large but he merely nodded. "Would ye like to ride back?"

Janet shook her head. She was almost back, and it would be as painful getting into the saddle as it would be to walk the remainder of the way.

Tim took the reins of the horse and they had returned together. Louisa was outside pacing anxiously, and she had quickly run over to Janet. "I was so worried when the horse came in."

"Reginald?"

"He left this morning on some business," Louisa said.

And Marjorie was away, visiting friends near Edinburgh. Had Reginald done something to the cinch before he had left? Louisa wouldn't have. She feared horses. She would never go near them, and Janet thought she would not know a cinch strap from a stirrup.

It was only an accident, she told herself again. Nonetheless, she ran up to the nursery. Grace and Rachael were reading, the kitten and puppy intertwined in an unlikely ball at their feet. They both looked up at her, horror on their faces as they saw her soiled dress and dried blood on her arms. Annabella was napping, as was Colin. She knelt next to Colin's cradle and listened to his soft breathing, then kissed him lightly so he would not wake.

Clara looked at her torn clothes and a small cry escaped her lips. "My lady? What happened?"

The question was echoed in the children's faces.

"Just a wee fall," Janet said. "I just wanted to see you all before . . . changing clothes."

Rachel ran over to her. "You are hurt."

"No more than a few scratches, love." She leaned down and hugged Rachel. "You have to expect that when you ride. And you know what? I am going to look for a pony for you two so you can learn."

She had not thought of that before, but she did not want them to be afraid because of her fall. She should have changed before coming up here, but she had not been able to wait to see whether they were all right. The last thing she wanted was for them to fear riding. It was one of the great joys of her life, and she had missed it sorely when Alasdair had limited her access to the horses.

Rachel's face lit. Grace looked apprehensive. It was not unusual. Grace was the worrier.

Janet leaned over and tipped up Grace's chin with her fingers, then soothed out the tiny little worry lines. Grace was so incredibly dear. "I truly am all right," she said. "It was an adventure."

Grace did not look convinced.

Janet sighed. "I am going to take a warm bath and then we will eat supper together up here. Would you like that?"

"Oh yes," Rachel said.

Grace nodded somberly.

Janet leaned down and scooped up Colin despite a small whimper of protest. She was not going to let him out of her sight tonight. "I will ask cook to prepare a meat pie," she said, knowing that that was a favorite of the lasses. "And a sweet."

She went down to her chamber. Lucy had met her just inside the manor house after she arrived and had already heated water for a bath. The hip bath was steaming.

Janet put Colin on a rug on the floor, knowing she had to keep an eye on him. He was crawling everywhere now. Then she gratefully accepted Lucy's help in undressing—removing the riding dress, stockings, chemise, then drawers. She stepped into the bath and sunk as far as she could, letting the hot water soothe the bruises. It stung the scratches, but she did not mind. She was alive. Her son and daughters were well. That was all that mattered at the moment.

Janet tossed and turned, often reaching out to touch her son. She did not know what hour it was when she finally rose and went to the window. Wispy clouds played among the stars and moon, casting shadows across the courtyard.

She sat on the window seat. Had today's mishap truly been an accident? Perhaps she might know more after the smithy saw the cinch. *Sleep*. Get some sleep.

But she continued to look out. She hated to admit that she missed Braemoor. Yet she did. Far more than she wanted to. She felt alone and isolated, and there was a strength about him she had not remembered or, mayhap, had tried to forget. In her mind's eye, she saw him striding across the courtyard, or riding from the stable with such complete assurance. And that kiss. That infernal kiss. Just recalling the feel of his lips against hers sent sparks through her body. He'd made her feel safe. But more than that, he had made her feel as if she could do anything.

Then she saw movement on the road into Lochaene. Two fast-moving horses. She watched as they stopped in front of the stables. The rider on the first horse leaned over the other, which was loaded with some kind of bundle. In a second, the bundle fell, and the rider raced away, the second horse behind him.

The bundle moved.

Apprehension prickled along her spine as Janet ran down the staircase and opened the heavy doors. She ran over to the bundle. A body.

She immediately recognized Braemoor's clothing, but the blue cloth was brown with dried blood. The face was dark with black bristles. He was mumbling but made no sense. She leaned down and touched his forehead. It was burning.

Janet ran to the stable where Tim and Kevin slept and woke them. Tim came with her while Kevin went to get their new butler.

She sat next to Braemoor along with Tim. She put her head down to his heart. His body was burning with fever. Blood crusted his face and hair, and the one leg of his breeches had been torn away. A bloodied bandage covered the upper half of his leg.

When McNann arrived, she got to her feet. "You and Tim take him up to the second floor. The blue room. Kevin, you ride for the physician. Tell him he must come as quickly as possible."

Kevin went to saddle a horse as Tim and McNann struggled to get Braemoor to his feet. She followed them as they half carried, half dragged him inside, up the stairs and into a bed. Then they stood aside, looking helplessly at the wounded man.

Like most Scottish women, Janet knew a little of healing and herbs. As mistress of a household, she was often called upon to see to illnesses and wounds. One look at Braemoor chilled her.

Who had brought him here? And why? And how did he come to be so badly wounded? He had left four days earlier. She had thought him back at Braemoor. Where had he been these past days?

She leaned over the bed. "My lord," she said. "My lord. Do you hear me?"

His eyes were closed. But he mumbled something.

She unwrapped the blood-soaked rags around his thigh and looked at the ugly wound. It had been clumsily sewn and was red and raw. There was also a flesh wound on his shoulder, but that was already healing.

"Please stay here with him," she said to McNann, then hurried to the room her husband had used. His clothes had not yet been taken to the attic. She took out a nightshirt and drawers and hurried back.

"Help me undress him," she told McNann, handing him the clothes. A look of surprise crossed his face, but he did as he was told. He held Braemoor up while she tugged his tattered shirt from his body and pulled the nightshirt over. Then she left McNann to take off what remained of Braemoor's trousers and pull on a pair of drawers.

When all was accomplished, she turned to him. "You may leave," she said.

He backed out. "Aye, my lady," he said.

Lucy appeared then with bowls of steaming water. Clara came behind her with bottles of herbs. They put both on a table, then hesitated.

Lucy hung back but Clara came over and together she and Janet bathed his face. He moaned and tried to fight them but he was obviously unaware of his surroundings. He mumbled something, just as he had before, and she leaned down to hear. "Neil," she said again, well aware it was the first time she had mentioned his given name in the past eight years. "What is it, Neil? What are you trying to say?"

"Jan . . . et." She could barely make out her name.

"Aye, it's Janet," she said soothingly. She went back to the table and dipped the cloth back in the water, then squeezed it tightly before taking it back over to him. She washed the area around the oozing foul-smelling wound, then rinsed the wound itself.

He groaned but did not fight her this time. She prayed she

could stop the spreading infection. Please God it did not turn to gangrene. When she was satisfied the wound was clean enough, she left his side and made a poultice of lint dripped in oil and placed it on the wound.

Clara returned with more water and Janet poured a little into a cup, lifted his head and tried to make him drink. He needed liquid. He swallowed, though his eyes remained closed. She got a little more into him, then stopped. "He will need rest and a dram of bark every three hours," she told Clara.

"I will stay with him," Clara volunteered.

"Nay," Janet replied. "You get some sleep. You have to watch the children tomorrow."

"Are ye sure, my lady?"

"Aye, he came here because of me. The least I can do is watch him. You and Lucy get some sleep. I hope the doctor will be here before daybreak." And in truth, she wanted them to leave. She wanted to be alone with him.

He was very ill. He would probably die. She did not know how to stop the fever. She could sew up a wound when necessary, dispense some herbs, but not much more. She could only stay with him, let him know he was not alone.

Clara seemed to sense that need. She left with Lucy, closing the door behind her.

She pulled out a chair and sat on it. She was still sore from her own mishap this day, but her minor pains mattered little. She reached out and touched his face. The bristles of new beard were rough against her hand, the skin hot to her touch.

He had been the sum of her hopes once. Then embodiment of her disillusionment. She had loved, then hated him. She had needed him, then resented him. She still did not know why he had come to Lochaene, or what he had really wanted.

The beard made him look both roguish and vulnerable. She had sensed that about him before and then wondered whether she was wrong. Had she just wanted to see something not quite so sure, so confident, so distant?

"Stay with me," she demanded of him. She wondered whether she should send anyone to Braemoor to inform them of his injuries. Was there anyone there who cared? She knew he had no family. But surely there was someone.

Everyone had someone. She had her children.

He coughed, then groaned. She offered him some more water and he drank it with more ease this time, but she knew it was instinct rather than consciousness. Did he even know where he was? Would he want to be here?

What had happened to him? Why did someone just dump him at her door?

And who?

But none of that really mattered. The only thing that mattered was making him well.

Through the rest of the night, she continually rinsed his face and his upper body with cool cloths. He mumbled, moved, fought the bed covering. But there was no lucidity.

She prayed. She had not done so in a long time. She thought God had deserted Scotland. But now she tried again, just as she had when her brother went to join the Jacobite cause.

"Janet." He had murmured her name several times. It seemed strange, since he had seemed to avoid it when he'd been here. Such a plain name. Yet it sounded like more in the raw agonized way it seemed jerked from his mouth.

She leaned down. She had called him "my lord" since his appearance. Mayhap something more personal might help. "Neil," she said softly, tasting the sound on her lips.

His lashes fluttered open. His eyes were swollen and red. They seemed to try to focus, then settled on her. Then his eyes narrowed. "Janet . . . ," he said again. This time it was as much a question as an acknowledgment of her presence. "Where . . . ?"

"You are back at Lochaene. Someone left you here last night. Can you tell me what happened?"

"Thirs . . . ty."

She went over to the table and poured more water into the cup she'd been using. She put her arm under his head, lifting it slightly, and put the cup to his lips. This time he drank greedily until it was all gone. Almost reluctantly, she removed her arm. "I will have to get you some more water down in the kitchen."

"Stay." It was more a plea than a command.

Then his eyes closed, as if the act of drinking and the few words had stolen what strength he had.

She sat back down next to him. "I have sent for a physician. I hope he will be here soon. Can you tell me what happened?"

"Shot . . . ambushed."

"Someone brought you here."

"The . . . outlaw . . ."

She tried to understand. "The man who shot you brought you here?"

"One . . . of his . . ." He stopped speaking for a moment, and a shudder ran through his body. She could see it move in his chest. An onslaught of pain? A memory?

Braemoor did seem to be a man who would shy away from a memory.

She leaned over. "Who was he . . . ?"

"Called himself Will," he said. "They . . . expected me."

"Why did he bring you here?"

But his eyes were closing again, his chest rising and falling. More easily? She did not know. She could only hope.

And wonder. He was ambushed. Then whoever ambushed him had brought him back. Had they thought him dead and were sending her a message of some kind? Or had it been some afterthought of compassion? Compassion was a rare commodity these days in Scotland.

But she would know no more until he woke again. He needed as much rest as he could get. She stood, then decided to go downstairs to fetch some more water. Some needed to be heated for a new poultice. She needed to drain as much of the poison as possible.

She hurried down the stairs with the pitcher, hesitating for a moment at the door. Then she opened it and looked outside. Dawn was breaking. Fog cloaked the nearby hills but the first light of morning had lightened the sky. It was cold, and she shivered in the hostile wind. But then Scotland was a hostile land, and now she felt it more than ever.

Janet closed the door and went back inside to the kitchen. The huge fireplace was always lit, and the cook and one helper were already busy preparing bread for the ovens built into the hearth. "I need some more water," she said.

Bridget, the cook, hurried to get it. "I heard someone brought the marquis back." The statement was full of questions.

But Janet had no answers. "Aye. He is ill. I was hoping the . . . physician . . ."

"He seems a good mon," Bridget said. "God will look after him."

Janet wished she felt her faith that clearly. Instead, she took the water, a more visible and viable sort of help. "Will you make some broth for him? Mayhap I can get him to eat."

"I will fix the best tha' can be made," the woman assured her. "If ye need anything else . . ."

The worry was evident in Bridget's voice. So someone else in the household cared about the marquis, too.

"Thank you," she said, feeling an odd pitch of her heart. The Marquis of Braemoor had seemed so alone to her, and never so much as when he was dumped like a sack of potatoes in the courtyard. She did not want him to be alone now.

She speeded her pace up the stairs. The door was closed. She was sure she had left it open. Mayhap a draft . . .

Janet pushed the door open and saw Louisa leaning over the sleeping marquis. "Louisa?"

The woman jumped as if Janet had been a ghost. Then she appeared to relax. "Oh, it is you, Janet. I rose early, and I heard about the marquis. I came to see whether he needed anything and found him quite alone. He appears to be very ill."

"He is," Janet said, "but the physician should be here soon. And the marquis is a strong man."

"So was your husband," Louisa said, shrugging one shoulder gracefully. "Men do not seem to fare well around you."

"I would suggest you go down and wait for the physician," Janet said coldly. But her heart was beating faster. Louisa was right. She did seem to be a Jonah. But she was not going to let Louisa know her words had affected her.

"Dreadful thing," Louisa said. "So much lawlessness today, and His Grace cannot seem to do anything about it." An almost satisfied look came into her eyes. "I really do not think you should ride alone any longer. Especially considering your fall yesterday."

"Your concern is touching," Janet said dryly. "I will be careful. I am sure the marquis would appreciate it also."

"Just remember what I said," Louisa said, sweeping out the door as if she were a queen. Which was, Janet knew, exactly what Louisa believed she should be.

She put down the pitcher, then closed the door and returned to look at Braemoor. He had thrown off his bed covering. She touched his face. Was it warmer than before?

Janet tugged at his nightshirt, urging it over his shoulders. No groan this time. Nothing. Fear ran through her, and her hands trembled as she touched him. His body seemed to be on fire.

What had Louisa been doing here? Louisa did not appear to have one compassionate bone in her entire body. Curiosity? And what was she doing up at daybreak? She seldom appeared from her room before noon.

"No!" Braemoor shouted. She leaned down and tried to keep him still so he would not disturb his wound. But his arm flailed out and caught her in the chest, and she went flying back, landing on the floor. All the parts that had been bruised earlier reacted poorly. Painfully, she managed to get to her feet and keep him from falling off the bed.

"Neil," she whispered, as she had earlier. It had quieted him then, but now it seemed only to excite him further. He shouted again, his words muffled, and he grabbed her wrist, squeezing it so tight she called out.

At the sound, he stilled. His grip on her relaxed. She leaned down with her body, her wrist still caught in his grasp. "Neil," she said again softly, "I am here. Is there anything you want? More water?" Her free hand touched his forehead, ran down the darkened cheeks.

His eyes opened again. They looked frantic until they focused back at her. "Janet. You . . . are . . . safe?"

"I am well," she said, "but I canna say the same for you."

His eyes went to the wrist he still held. He slowly let go and his gaze fastened on her wrists and the bruises there. "I hurt . . ."

"Nay," she said softly. " 'Tis nothing. You did not know what you were doing."

She stood and picked up the cup, returning to his side. "Can you drink something?"

"Aye. I think I could drink the ocean."

"You were having nightmares?"

His dark eyes were brilliant and glittering from fever. But he did not answer, only took some of the water, then fell back on the bed. She pulled back the cover she'd tried to replace and which lay halfway across him, and took the poultice from his wound. It was badly soiled. She quickly made another and carefully placed it on the wound. His body flinched at the new irritation, but no sound escaped his lips.

His body was still warm with the fever. She had made several drams of water mixed with bark and she took a potion to him. "it doesna taste as good as the water but it will help the fever."

He obediently drank it down, then lowered his head, but his eyes still watched her. "You . . . undressed me?"

"Nay, McNann did it."

"McNann?"

"Our new butler."

She watched him try to absorb that.

"Can you tell me how you got here?" she asked.

He shook his head.

"You said a bandit ambushed you."

"Aye."

"You said he knew you were coming."

His eyes closed again and for a moment she did not know whether he had lost consciousness again, or was just thinking, recalling, or even measuring what he wanted to say. Even now, he kept so much to himself.

"Neil?"

"Not 'my lord'?" he asked with a tiny hint of humor.

Poor as it was, it heartened her. But just then she heard noise from below.

She went to the window. The physician had arrived. He had been here when Alasdair had died, and she had sensed his suspicions. And now . . . he would probably think the worst of her for having nursed a wounded man who was not her husband.

"My . . . lady." She turned back toward the bed at his words. "Thank you. . . ."

They were back to her title. She had liked "Janet" far better. Nonetheless, she kept her voice cool as she replied. "I could hardly let you die."

His eyes lost some of their glitter. "In any event . . ."

"In any event, the only thanks I need is for you to get well," she said.

Their gazes met. His eyes were full of questions.

Why?

But she had no time to explore them, for Reginald and the physician stood at the door. She would have to wait to ask her own questions.

Chapter Twelve

The physician examined Braemoor, then drew her outside. "He is very ill," he said. "I will bleed him, extract the poison from him. But I can guarantee nothing."

"Nay," she said.

Startled, the man started to bluster.

"He has already lost a great deal of blood," she said. Losing more made little sense to Janet.

"I hardly believe you are qualified to make that decision," he said, squinting his eyes at her. "Your husband did not fare well under your attentions."

A chill ran down her back. Reginald and Louisa had done their work well. But she was not going to surrender.

He turned and went back into the room and stood at the side of the bed. Braemoor had submitted wordlessly to his examination, but now his eyes were angry. He obviously had heard the physician's words. He tried to sit up, but fell back down.

"You will do as the countess asks," Braemoor said.

"You should be bled. If not, I will take no . . . responsibility."

Braemoor squinted, as if having difficulty in focusing. "Then you have none," he said.

"I must protest, my lord."

"Then protest, but . . . do as she says."

"Her . . . husband . . ."

"Bloody hell, I . . . will not be bled," Braemoor said.

"Aye, my lord," the physician said, glaring at Janet. "Then I will leave some medicine to make you sleep . . ." He turned to Janet. "If he dies, I will report this to the authorities." He gave her a bottle. "Mix it with water and give some to him every two hours and keep changing the poultices. Keep him as cool as possible."

Then he left. Janet stood there, shaking. She wondered whether she had just condemned Neil to death.

His eyes were closed, as if the last few hours had completely exhausted him. For a moment, she panicked. What if she was wrong? Yet the physician had done nothing to help her husband, had not, in fact, even decided what had killed him. Still, she had hoped for some miracle.

She reached out and touched him. He was still so warm.

"Neil?" she said. But he had drifted away again. She sat next to him, worrying that she had made a terrible mistake. And yet . . .

Time passed. She did not know how much. She hesitated to change the poultice again for fear of waking him, and rest, she thought, would be the finest thing for him. What if she was wrong?

He started to move restlessly again. She sat next to him, sponging his body to keep it cool, changing the foul-smelling poultices, and talking to him even if she was not sure he could hear her.

Neil drifted in and out of darkness. When he woke, he had no idea how much time had passed. The world was a haze of pain and heat. But he still preferred it to the nightmares. To the faces he saw in his dreams.

He saw Will over and over again. Standing above him. Dirk raised. He remembered the pain when the man had probed for the musket ball. Most of all, he recalled bits and pieces of the man's words. He did not know how much had become jumbled in his mind, however. How much was true? How much were lies? And how much had been twisted by the confusion in his own fevered state.

A woman. He kept remembering that. The outlaw had said a woman had told him that he might be traveling that way.

And Janet's soft, soothing words became tangled in it. She kept drawing him back from the darkness. Her hands were so gentle. He even thought he had seen tears in her eyes. Why, of all places, would he have been brought here?

Janet's soft questioning had done nothing to sort out the confusion. He did know, however, that his first fleeting thought that she could have been responsible was wrong. She'd had more than a few chances to let him die. Instead, she seemed at his side every time he woke, her voice encouraging, urging, refusing to let him go.

Which meant someone else in this house must have informed the bandits. And if they rid themselves of him, what of Janet? Would she be next?

It was that thought that kept him alive, that made him fight against the darkness when all he wanted was to sink back into it.

He did not know how long he had been at Lochaene. The hours, mayhap the days, had faded one into the other. Janet, or one of the servants, had been with him each time he woke, offering water or the dreadful bark mixture. He remembered a physician, or at least he thought the man a physician. A dour soul.

He opened his eyes. The heat had subsided. He still felt warm, but his body was not on fire as it had been. His gaze searched the room. Then he saw Janet dozing in a nearby arm chair, her son propped in her lap, also asleep.

A cap covered much of her hair, and she looked wan, tired. The lad snuggled in the crook of her arm. He thought he had never seen anything so beautiful.

He tried not to make any sound. He was both thirsty and hungry, and he knew the latter to be a good sign. But he had no intention of waking her. He wondered how long she had been here, whether she had slept in her own bed. Sunlight was flooding the room, which was on the east. He thought it must be several hours past dawn.

Or what day?

He moved slightly, and he felt pain again, but it was duller now. His thigh was bandaged, and he was wearing a night-shirt again. Had it belonged to Reginald? Her husband? He tried to sit upright in the bed, and the room spun. He was so weak.

His hand went to his face. It was scratchy, rough. How many days' beard? How long had he been away from Brae-moor? Had anyone there been told of his delay? A hundred questions came to mind, and he did not like unanswered questions.

Neil moved again, and pain flooded his side, his head. But he stifled any sound. Instead, he silently tried to move each of his arms and legs. One arm was stiff, but the other seemed to work. He felt an embarrassing need.

He did not know how to behave in a sickbed. Nor had he ever had anyone care for him before. He had been wounded, but only hastily tended and stitched, and he'd needed no one to take care of intimate needs.

Someone had unclothed him, had washed him, helped him into a nightshirt. He knew she had changed foul-smelling bandages. He remembered her washing his face, her hand touching his skin. Or had that been the kiss nights earlier? Nights? A week? More?

He had to get back to Braemoor. So many things undone. So many promises to keep, particularly now that he was be-ginning to realize his own mortality. If he died, the proper-ties would revert to the crown, and he knew what that would mean to the tenants to whom he'd given hope.

And the men who had shot him. Neil had never believed in turning his cheek. His uncle had taught him it was noth-ing but a weakness. And yet, they had also . . .

Also what? And why? Again the questions descended on him.

He could not stay here. He put one leg on the floor, then the other. He tried to be silent and yet he saw Janet jerk awake, her eyes drowsy. Then they sharpened and focused on him. She rose quickly, keeping her arms around the still-sleeping boy. She very carefully laid him in the middle of the bed, then went over to Neil. Her hand touched his forehead, and she smiled shyly. Pure delight touched it, and warmth filled him. This warmth, though, was different from the bitter heat that had eaten at him.

"You are better," she said.

"Aye, thanks to you."

Her cheeks colored, as if she had never been thanked before.

"I was afraid . . ." Her voice faltered.

He was feeling dizzy again. It was all he could do to remain sitting upright, his feet on the floor. He did not dare stand. But he had to get word to Braemoor.

"How long?" he asked.

"Since you've been here? Three days."

"Since . . . I left . . . Lochaene?"

"You were gone four days."

So it had been near a fortnight since he had left Braemoor. "I must send word to . . ."

"I would have sent Tim," she said. "But I didn't know who he should speak to there. Can you tell me now what happened? You did not make a great deal of sense."

But it made no sense to him, either. "I was ambushed, shot," he said. "They came down, apparently to finish the task. There were two of them. For some reason, the leader decided not to kill me. At first, I thought he hesitated because I had so little money or jewelry with me, and they meant to ransom me. But then . . ." His voice trailed off.

"But then?" she prompted.

"I was feverish but I heard them argue . . ." For some reason, he felt restrained about saying anything about the other people in the cave. They were innocents. Or were they? But he knew he did not want the authorities to comb those hills for them.

"Argue about what?" She was insistent.

"I do . . . not remember. It is . . . mixed up." Why did he not tell her? Or send a message to Cumberland? Clear the brigands from the hills?

He had a chance but did not kill you. It was as simple and as complicated as that. He did not believe in turning his cheek but neither did he welsh on a debt.

"Has anyone informed the authorities?" he asked.

"Nay," she said. "Reginald said we should wait . . . until you felt better, that it might have been . . . an accident."

He tried to comprehend that. Mayhap the honorable Reginald had just hoped he would die first and no further questions would be asked. Nonetheless, he was pleased that Reginald had done nothing, regardless of his motives. He always fought his own battles and paid his own debts. And he intended to fight this one. And, if necessary, pay the debt.

How much do you owe an assassin who spares your life?

He tried to stand. He got to his feet, and the room started spinning again. He held out his hand. "Lass?"

Janet took it and he felt her warmth down to his toes. It crowded out the pain, the confusion, everything. He steadied himself.

"That is enough," she said.

But he did not let go. He took a small step, then another, taking strength from her, although she was a small lass. Still, she had an innate toughness. And he liked having her so close. He liked it too much.

He took another step, using her for balance. But then his legs seemed to fold, and he barely made it back to the bed. He did not want to crash down on her. Then he remembered a day ago. Or more. He had . . . hurt her. He swallowed hard as he sat heavily, still holding her hand. He turned it over, saw the black marks from where he had held her. Then he saw other marks. A faint bruise colored one side of her face, along with a scratch.

The sleeves of her gown came halfway down her arm and he could see more bruises and cuts.

"Did I do that?" he asked softly.

She looked down at them. "Nay. I fell from a horse the day you were brought here."

"The truth?"

"Aye," she said. "In your fever, you grabbed my wrist, but that is all."

He sighed, grateful, at least, for that. "You were riding alone?"

"Aye," she said.

He wanted to say something, but he had no right. She was not his wife, nor his charge. But nonetheless, he found himself saying very carefully, "Mayhap you should take Tim or Kevin . . . with you. Now that you are aware there are outlaws not far away . . ."

Her gaze met his. He had not known what weakness was until that moment. Her eyes were so bloody blue, her lips so seductive as her teeth worried them. Her hand was still in his, and the touch stirred every nerve inside him. But even worse was the way his heart reacted. With an aching awareness, he knew nothing had really changed. He still could not marry, with madness being a trait in his family.

And yet she colored his gray life like a master artist painted a sunrise. She lit every dark corner, even now with the doubt on her face. The thought that he might have physically hurt her would be far worse pain than that damned musket ball.

Despite her denials, he knew he was responsible for at least one of her bruises, and probably more than a few of much larger ones. And yet her hand rested trustingly in his.

"Tell me how I came to be here," he said, seeking to puncture the growing intimacy blossoming between them again.

"A rider came in and just dumped you. Like a sack of

potatoes," she added with a tiny gleam in her eyes. "Then he rode off. No one saw his face. He was riding your horse."

"How do you know?" he asked.

"I saw him. I was looking outside at the time."

Neil wished he had left the horse, too. It had been his favorite stallion. Another reason to find this Will.

Or would Will find him?

He suddenly felt very tired again. All his strength had been expended in those few steps.

She seemed to sense it and gently disengaged her hand. "Can you drink some broth?"

"Aye," he said. "And some water."

She handed him a cup full of water. She looked at the lad who was still sleeping on the bed. "Will you look after him while I get some broth from the cook? Just keep him between you and the wall."

"I think I can manage that," he said dryly.

She looked doubtful but then hurried out the door. He sat on the side of the bed, willing himself to stay upright. He leaned over and put a hand on the lad. Just then, Colin stirred, yawned, stretching out his small arms, then favored him with a sleepy grin.

Neil's heart melted. He held out a finger, and the lad clasped it tightly and pulled himself up with it, then crawled over to him.

The lad reached up and touched his face, then frowned. "Ah, you do not like my beard, either," Neil said.

The boy beamed at him and garbled something. All the loneliness Neil had known, all the emptiness inside seemed to fade, and his heart cracked open. A smile built inside Neil, and he found himself grinning back.

They were sitting there grinning at each other when he was suddenly aware that Janet stood at the doorway. She came over and picked up Colin, as if she feared he might hurt the bairn. He closed his eyes. *Fool.*

She did not say anything for a moment. Instead she played with her son, her hand meeting his in a mock contest of strength, then she set him down on the floor. He sat there looking first at his mother, then at Neil. After a moment, he seemed to make a decision and started crawling toward Neil.

Neil leaned over and offered a hand. Colin took it and struggled up on his wobbly legs, balancing on Neil's hand.

Janet did not move, but he looked up and saw her eyes. Moisture filled them and a haunting sadness marked her face.

Did she feel as if he had stolen something from her?

"He must trust you," she said stiffly.

She did not say anything else, but unsaid words shone in her eyes and he thought no silence could be as cruel. *He was not worthy of trust.*

He never would be in her eyes. It was a devastating blow, yet was that not what he wanted?

"You best take him," he said. "I should not like him to fall."

She approached her son just as he moved his hand. Colin let it go, and his mother took him, holding him tightly until the lad squealed in protest.

"'Tis the first time he has stood," she said, avoiding his glance and apparently trying to hide her own emotion, that moment of hurt that had radiated from her eyes.

That flash reminded him of how much he'd hurt her years ago. He had not thought then that his actions would be so damaging. Mayhap because he thought so little of himself, he had not thought her loss great. He had honestly believed that she would find a man far better than himself. The fact that she had not and that, instead, his actions had left her with such a deep wariness made him hurt beyond healing. He suspected it would be a festering wound for a very long time.

"Lucy will be bringing up some broth," she said.

"Thank you," he said and looked at Colin. "He is a fine lad."

"Aye," she said. "He does not usually take to . . . men like that."

That told him a great deal since the only men in the household had been her husband, her brother-in-law and MacKnight. And mayhap a few more retainers. He was really beginning to hate the dead man. And he did not know how to respond. There had been no children around Braemoor; he had always thought himself awkward when he came upon someone else's bairns. His size often terrorized children, and he had no easy manner. He remembered his clumsiness just days before with her lasses.

And yet, young Colin Campbell had favored him a smile. It seemed to him a great accomplishment.

Just then a young maid—Lucy, he remembered—entered the room. She dipped slightly in a curtsey and gave him a broad smile. "Ye look fine, my lord."

"Thank you, lass," he said.

"We all thought ye dead for sure, but my lady, she said ye would get well. And ye have." She set her burden down on the table.

"Clara said the lasses have been asking to see ye," she continued, sending a furtive glance at him.

A painful emotion crawled inside and wrapped around his heart, just as it had moments earlier when Colin had taken his hand so trustingly.

Janet hesitated. "He's still very ill," she said, looking at him. She was giving him an excuse. If he wanted it.

His decision. He knew he should say he was too tired. He should not insinuate himself into this family. Yet the temptation was too great. Three wee lasses had asked to see *him.* "If the countess agrees," he said cautiously. Then he rubbed his cheeks. "And if I would not scare them."

"I can shave you," Janet offered unexpectedly, then looked as surprised as he felt. "I sometimes shaved my husband," she added defensively as Clara looked astonished. "You are too ill to do it yourself. You need no more bloodletting."

He nodded, unsure what to say.

"But first drink the broth," she said. "You must regain your strength. Lucy will help you. I will take Colin to Clara and his sisters. They can come down later if you feel well enough."

Lucy brought over the bowl and sat next to him as Janet left the room. "Do ye need any help, my lord?"

"Thank you, Lucy, but no." He took the bowl with its spoon, and balanced it on his lap, then tried to lift a spoonful to his mouth. His hand shook and most of it spilled. Still, some made it to his mouth. The next effort was a little more successful. It was hot and flavorful and he took another sip, and another, until it was all gone.

Then he handed it to Lucy and, exhausted, he sank back onto the bed. Dammit, but he had to get well. Already, he knew he did not want to leave. He did not want to give up Janet's smile, fleeting as it was, or Colin's small hand reaching for him, nor those words, "The lasses have been asking to see ye." For a moment, he could close his eyes and imagine himself part of a family.

But reality had a way of quenching hope. He was an unwanted guest here; Colin was too young to know better; and the lasses—well, the lasses were seeing something in him that was not there. Janet knew that. Her wariness told him that.

Then he remembered something Janet had said earlier. "Lucy, the countess said she fell from a horse. Can you tell me anything about it?"

Her eyes clouded. "Only tha' she was not badly hurt." She hesitated, and Neil realized she was debating as to whether she should continue. After a moment, she did in a strained whisper. "My lady asked Kevin tae take the cinch into the blacksmith. He said the smithy thinks someone may ha' cut it."

"Cut it?"

"Aye," she said after a moment's pause. He knew then that she had not been sure whether she should have said anything. Fear shadowed her face. Only loyalty to her mistress, he thought, had prompted the warning.

Did Janet know yet? Had the boy told her? And if so, why had she not said anything to him?

It had happened around the same time he was attacked.

A coincidence?

He did not believe in coincidence. Someone had set the man who called himself Will on him. Someone apparently had wanted to injure Janet. The same someone? Seemed likely.

And there were the rumors that Janet's late husband had been murdered. Because the speculation had centered around Janet, he had dismissed it. Now he wondered if the speculation had a grain of truth. Just a different culprit.

He did know that he could not leave her here alone. He also knew he could not extend his stay away from Braemoor. Too many people depended on him. His goal was too important.

But Lochaene was equally as important to Janet and to her son.

How much was Lochaene worth? A life? two lives?

"My lord?" Lucy's voice broke his thoughts.

"Thank you for telling me," he said gently.

"Ye will not tell anyone I told ye?"

"Nay. You are a good friend to the countess."

Her cheeks reddened. "She is a good mistress."

She would be. He had seen her concern for the tenants as well as young Kevin. Concern was too rare a commodity these days.

Obviously afraid she had said more than she should, Lucy backed out of the room.

Once she was gone, he lay back in the bed, frustrated at his own weakness. His mind kept going over the conversation. He needed to see Will again, had to find out what the outlaw knew about the "woman" who had suggested he might be a good victim. It had to be the countess dowager or

Reginald's wife. But then Reginald could have passed the word through someone else.

He could not accuse a Campbell, a family favored by Cumberland, without proof. They would turn it back on Janet.

And Will? Neil would bet his last coin that Will was not the man's real name. Searching his hazy memory, he knew the man had been well educated, probably a lord, most certainly a Jacobite.

A light knock came on the door, and Janet entered with a fresh bowl of water and a razor. It was then he remembered that she had volunteered to shave him. Both pleasure and apprehension flitted through his mind.

She sat next to him and propped him up with several pillows. She regarded him somberly for a moment. "I think I like you as a brigand," she said with a slight smile.

"I do not think your lad does," he said.

"Well then, we have to do something about that. My daughters also want to see you, so we must make you appear civilized." She rinsed his face with warm water, then applied some soap. Her hands were gentle, but they ignited anything but gentle sensations. His gaze met hers and emotions shimmered between them. He felt his body stiffen, felt something glow inside him. Then her hands stopped, and he saw the same awareness in her face. Her tongue licked her lips in a gesture so innocent yet so sensuous that his breath seemed to stop.

She handled the razor with quiet competence, and in minutes she was through, moving away from him. He felt his cheeks, smooth now, and he felt far better. But that, he knew, was attributed far more to her touch than to cleanliness.

She tipped her head mischievously, regarding him. "You willna scare the lasses to death now," she said. "Are you well enough for them to see you?"

Pleased beyond reason that they, indeed, wanted to see him, he nodded. He would ask her about her fall later. But he *would* ask her. He wanted to know exactly what had happened.

She left the room and, in minutes, the three small lasses entered the room. Annabella carried wilted stalks of heather, Grace a bowl obviously filled with water, and the middle lass held the puppy and kitten, who were not happy to be at such close proximity to each other.

"We thought you would like some flowers," Grace said seriously as she carefully set down the bowl on the table.

"We want you to get well so you will take us on a picnic again," said Rachel, clutching the pets.

Annabella handed her squashed flowers to him. "I sorry you feel bad."

"I feel much better now," he said, regarding the flowers with a slight smile. Annabella climbed up. He flinched slightly as she jolted his leg. Yet her smile lit something inside that more than compensated for the discomfort.

"Thank you for the flowers," he said.

"We picked them just for you."

"They are beautiful," he said, deciding in this case that a lie was far better than the truth. But then they *were* beautiful, even in their squashed, wilted state. They were beautiful because they were so happily given.

"We are glad you came back," Grace said. "So is mama."

He doubted that, but said nothing. He really did not know what to say or how to answer. But then the puppy barked and tried to get up on the bed. "He likes you, too," Annabella said. "Do you have a puppy?"

He shook his head. "Nay."

"A kitten?" she said hopefully.

"I am afraid not," he replied.

"I think Samson has a brother," Grace said from her safe place at the end of the bed. "I think you could have him."

Three faces looked down at him with such eager hope that he could find no way to say no. He could only hope the brother had already found another home. He did not want a dog.

Or did he?

• • •

Janet kept telling herself nothing had changed as she took off her gown and put on a nightshift. She had looked in on Braemoor just before retiring. He was asleep, his breathing now easy. He was weak and exhausted, but he would live.

Janet had been mesmerized by the tender, yearning look on Braemoor's face when she had returned from ordering the broth and saw him with her son. She had stood in the doorway for a moment, watching the interplay between Braemoor and her son, and she thought her heart would break.

Colin's father had never looked at him like that. Oh, he had been pleased to have an heir, but Colin had been no more than a possession to him. He had never picked up his son, or expressed an interest once he'd ascertained that Colin was a perfectly formed bairn.

She never would have expected Neil to show an instant tenderness. But mayhap she should have. There had been something years ago that had beguiled her. She had thought she had imagined it, or that something had quenched those magic moments they had once shared. That young man would have laughed with her son, but Braemoor . . . ?

He had changed so much. But now she saw what she had seen then. She just did not know why he had left her with nothing but a cruel note eight years earlier. The fact that he had never married was strange. Most men in his position sought a wife if for no other reason than to produce an heir. So many things about him puzzled her.

And nothing so much as her reactions to him when she touched him or when his gaze rested upon her.

Could she still love him? Had she never really stopped?

It was obvious, though, that he did not return the feeling. He had kissed her, but it had been no more than a momentary lust. She had told herself that. And she never wanted to make herself vulnerable again. She had done it twice before, once with him, then with the hopes she'd had when she married Alasdair.

She'd continued to watch the man and bairn together, even as it hurt, even as she wondered what might have been had she married him.

Most likely, no difference. Her head told her that. She had learned that she needed only herself.

Reminding herself of that, she quenched the oil lamp and burrowed under her covers.

Chapter Thirteen

Neil walked around the room. The fever had faded. But he was still very weak.

Yet he could not indulge himself. He could not stay here.

Neither could Janet. But he had not told her that yet. He did not think she would take the suggestion well.

She had been here earlier. Her eyes had been bright when she saw him sitting up. "We are going to deeply disappoint the physician," she said. "I am sure he expects you to be dead by now."

"A good reason to live," he said dryly. Then he changed the subject. "I must get letters off to Braemoor. I will require a quill and ink and paper."

"Is that a request or an order?"

He realized then how curt he must have sounded. How long had he done that? Had he been that autocratic at Braemoor? Is that why he had never seemed to break the barrier between himself and the people at Braemoor? He had always seen the objective and been impatient with the steps it took to achieve it.

"A request," he said. "And I'll need Tim to take them."

"As long as it is a request," she said with a hint of a smile.

"I am not very good at being a guest," he admitted.

She regarded him solemnly. She still had said nothing

about her riding accident. He wondered whether she had any intention of doing so. "You are improving," she finally said.

"In which way?" he asked suspiciously.

"Your wound."

"And not as a guest?"

"You are not exactly a guest," she said.

"Nay, I forced myself upon you."

"Someone brought you here," she corrected.

"Aye. Because they knew I had been here."

"How?" she said. "How did they know to bring you here?"

Ah, that was the question. Should he tell her what he had heard, that a woman had told Will and his fellow knaves that a man was going through the mountains from Lochaene? How much had he said to her before? He did not remember.

And how much should he tell her now about his plans? He knew she was not going to agree easily. What had she said earlier: *a request or an order?*

She would most certainly see his plan as an order. She would most certainly object to being uprooted, along with four children. But he knew she was in danger here. Probably far more danger than she thought.

He wanted to confront her about her riding accident, but then he would betray Lucy's confidence. He would talk to Kevin and Tim first.

But before he could do anything, he had to have someone he trusted here at Lochaene. Unfortunately there were not many men who met that particular qualification. His tacksman, Jock, came closest to it, and now he would be asking the man to leave his own land and people. It would only be for a short time, until he could find an outside manager. But he knew Jock would not be pleased.

Nor would Janet.

Yet he felt the danger now. He sensed it. Janet would want to stay and confront it herself, but she would be alone. Enemies were in the household and few servants would have the courage to defy them. Jock, he knew, would. Jock had confronted him.

"My lord?"

He looked up, startled. He had been so lost in his own thoughts he had forgotten her question.

"Aye?"

"How did the outlaws know to bring you here?"

He hesitated, then shrugged. "The leader—his name was Will—said someone had told him that a wealthy 'nob' would be crossing the hills."

Janet frowned. "He did not say who?"

"Nay."

"What did he look like? This Will?"

He shrugged. "Tall, dark red hair. He had a scar across his cheek."

" 'Tis very strange he saved your life."

"I donna think he believed I would survive," he said.

"Still . . ."

"I think he had a twisted sense of humor," Neil said. "But he took my horse and what little coin I had, and I plan to reclaim both."

Her eyes widened. The thought that it might be concern for him both pleased and perplexed him. He did not want that. Or need it.

He *did* need to keep her safe. Her and the wee lad with the bright smile, and the three lasses who had brought him flowers.

"Will you fetch Tim?" he asked, trying to keep his concerns to himself. He wanted to know what Tim said about the riding mishap before he did, or said, any more. "I would like to send the message with him. He knows the way."

"By road, I hope," she said.

"Most certainly by road," he agreed. "No more treks across the hills."

Her eyes studied him for a moment.

"I would like him to go this afternoon," he added.

It was a dismissal, and he saw the old wariness return to

her face. "Aye, my lord," she said, turning on her heel and leaving.

Just as well, he thought, even as his insides twisted with an agony as hurtful as his wound had been. If she was dismayed at him now, God help him when she discovered what he was planning.

Tim twisted his cap in his fingers. "My lord? You sent for me?"

Neil had managed to sit down at the table. "I understand the countess had a riding accident."

"Aye," the lad said cautiously.

"And you saw the cinch?"

The lad nodded.

"Had it been tampered with?"

"Tampered with?"

"Had it been cut?"

The lad looked decidedly uncomfortable. Neil understood why only too well. Tim was a groom, and his words would mean little against that of gentry.

"Tim?"

"I like my position, my lord."

"And you will keep it, Tim. But I must know if the countess is in danger."

He nodded. "It could ha' been cut. The smith said he could no' say for sure."

"Have you told her?"

Tim shook his head. "She has not asked."

"I will tell her," Neil said.

"Wha' if she asks me?"

"Then tell her," Neil said. "I would not have you lie to her."

Relief flooded the boy's face.

"I want you to take a message to Braemoor," Neil added.

"My lord?"

"I want you to leave today. You can take any horse you

wish. I want you to find my tacksman, a man named Jock.
You are to bring him back here with you."

Tim's lips drew into a frown. Neil sensed what he was
thinking. Another employee. Mayhap to take his own position.

"I want you back. You are one of the few people I trust."

"In truth, my lord?"

"In truth, Tim." He took off his ring with the Braemoor
seal. "I donna have any coin to give you but this should give
you credit. I asked Jock to take care of you on the way
back."

Tim took the ring reverently. "Ye would trust *me* wi'
this?"

"None more," Neil said, wondering whether he was beginning to learn a little about trusting.

Tim gave him a crooked grin. "I willna disappoint ye."

"Come back in an hour and I will give you a message."

"Aye, I'll saddle a horse."

Neil slumped against the chair. Bloody hell, but even that
small conversation exhausted him. He sat there for several
moments. His fever was gone, but the pain remained. Every
time he moved, his leg felt as if a knife was twisting inside
it. He'd thought about taking Janet immediately to Braemoor. But he knew she would not go unless someone was
here to protect Angus and the other families. She might not
in any event.

Unless she came to realize that if she was in danger, so
might her children be, particularly her son. His death would
mean the title would go to Reginald. And someone here was
not above attempting murder.

If he had not been so weak, she might well have hit the marquis when he ordered her about. Ill as he was, he was already taking over Lochaene. Nonetheless, it probably was
quite reasonable that he wanted to send a message to Braemoor to tell . . . someone that he had been delayed.

It was the outlaw business she did not understand. Braemoor—she tried to think of him that way as protection against traitorous feelings—was not very forthcoming nor as angry as she thought he would be. Braemoor did not seem to be a man to take such things with equanimity. But it was none of her affair. Once more, he would leave, and she would move ahead with her own plans. She would, however, check her saddle cinch next time.

She could not believe anyone really meant her harm. A scare, perhaps. A fright to keep her from riding over the properties. She would just be very careful. She would also let the family know that Braemoor approved of her plans and would carry on if anything were to happen to her. She did not intend to be frightened away.

She sent Lucy to Braemoor with writing materials, then went to see Tim herself.

"We will miss you," she said. He and Kevin had made themselves invaluable in the past weeks. The stable was clean, the horses finally well fed. Both could ride and exercise the horses. And Kevin had been distributing food and seed to the tenants and reporting on their progress. Her granting permission to hunt, he said, had helped much. Janet realized they probably had been poaching previously, but now they could go after larger game and feed their families without worrying about hanging.

"I have a brother I can ask to help Kevin while I am gone," Tim offered shyly and, she noticed, hopefully.

"I expect we can put him to good use," Janet said. There was so much to do, and so few people to do it. But still, she looked forward to every moment. For the first time in her life she would be mistress of her own destiny. She could protect her children, her property, her tenants. If the price was loneliness, she was willing to pay it.

"Aye," Tim said.

"Did . . . did the blacksmith say anything about that cinch?"

Tim fidgeted. Then he nodded his head.

"And . . . ?"

" 'E said it could be a cut."

"Could or was?"

" 'E could no' say fer sure."

"Thank you, Tim," she said. "Be careful. Remember . . ."

"I know," he said. "The marquis warned me." Pride sparkled in his eyes, and she knew that Braemoor had placed it there.

"Go with God then," she said.

She watched as he mounted. He gave her a cocky grin, then trotted the horse out toward the door.

She went into the stable and to the tack room. She looked over all the saddles, the cinches, the buckles. Some were a bit frayed. She separated those from the others, putting them aside to be taken to the village and repaired.

When she left the stables, it was growing dark. She went inside and up to the nursery. Her daughters had been playing outside earlier, and now they were eating. With no little help from Clara, Colin was busy eating gruel mixed with honey. More of it was on his face, though, than in his stomach.

Four faces looked up at her.

"How is the marquis?" Grace asked.

"He says he is much better since you visited him," she said. " 'Twas a far better tonic than the doctor gave him."

Annabella giggled. It was a sound that went straight to Janet's heart. She giggled far too little.

Samson climbed over her feet, trying to claw up her leg, and she leaned down and picked him up. "Restless, are you?" she asked. He barked.

They were ready for another outing. Her preoccupation with Braemoor had meant neglecting them. Mayhap she could arrange another picnic tomorrow. But in the interim, a story might serve.

She still had to find them some new books, now that she had some credit. But she would be careful using it. Still, a book was worthy.

"What about a story?" she asked.

"Oh yes," Rachel said.

Janet took a sleepy Colin from Clara and sat down on the bed, the lasses surrounding her, puppy and kitten in hand. She looked at them, one at a time. Warmth filled her. For the first time, Lochaene felt like home. "Once upon a time," she started, "there was a princess . . ."

"Like me?" Annabella asked.

"Just like you, love," she said.

"And me?" Rachel asked shyly.

"Aye, and Grace, too. You are all princesses."

Colin squirmed, complained. Janet leaned down and kissed his forehead. "And you, my love, are an earl."

"A princess is better," Rachel said.

"I think so, too," Janet said confidentially.

"Are you a princess?"

"Nay. I am only a countess, and that means very little."

"But I love you," Rachel said with the earnestness that so set her apart.

"That is the nicest thing anyone has said to me," Janet said.

"I lob you, too," Annabella said, her lower lip sticking out, obviously annoyed at being upstaged.

Something hard stuck in Janet's throat.

Balancing Colin, she gave each of them a hug. More than anything, she wanted them to know love and safety.

"Once upon a time," she started again, "there was a princess who lived high in a tower . . ."

Marjorie arrived on the third day of Braemoor's recovery.

Her carriage—Lochaene's carriage—clattered into the courtyard and she regally stepped out, then waited as a number of boxes were handed from the driver to the new butler who had appeared at the door.

Janet watched from the garden at the side of the house where she had taken the lasses and Colin to play with Samson and Delilah. She continued to look as each box was taken inside. Most likely Lochaene would receive the bills, and Janet would have to find a way to pay them or risk further damage to their credit. She would, however, promptly inform each of the creditors and—if necessary—place a notice in the newspaper that no more debts from anyone but Janet would be honored. *Satan's pitchfork.* Marjorie had to be fully aware that tenants were going hungry. If it had not been for Braemoor . . .

But they couldna live off him forever.

Not that Marjorie would care. Not that any of the Campbells had ever cared. They'd picked the carcass until it was nearly clean.

Marjorie saw her, Janet knew, but turned her head away and went through the door. A chuckle started in her throat. She suspected that the dowager countess had depended on their "guest" being gone. She would not be pleased that Braemoor remained here.

But he *was* much improved, though his thigh wound made walking difficult. Still, she did not expect him to linger much longer.

She turned back to the children. The day was bright, the sun warm. Even Marjorie could not ruin this day.

But would she feel that way when Braemoor left?

She had not realized how much she cared until she nursed him. She had tried to tell herself it was naught but ordinary concern for a wounded man. But it ran deeper than that. Too deep. She *did* care. Passionately.

Be careful. Remember what happened last time.

The sun started to dip, and she gathered up Colin. He took her hand and tried to stand again, just as he had done for Braemoor. Still hanging on with one hand, he grabbed her other hand, then fell into her arms with a huge grin on his face.

Her heart thundered. She held him tight. Dear God, she loved him. After a moment, he wriggled. She released her grip on him and picked him up. He seemed to grow heavier each time she did.

Annabella leaned down and picked up Delilah, then fol-

lowed the two older lasses inside as Samson gamboled behind them. They all glowed from being outside, from playing with their wee pets. Balancing Colin with one arm, Janet
clasped Rachel's eager hand with the other and went inside.

Janet promised to tell them a story later, after she checked
on their wounded guest.

She went into the kitchen to get a plate of food and a
pitcher of fresh water. As she walked toward the steps,
raised voices drew her to the withdrawal room. The door
was only partially closed and she heard Braemoor's name
mentioned, then a muffled sound.

"Can you not do anything right?" she heard Marjorie say.

"There was nothing I could do," Reginald replied in a
voice that was part whine, part placating. "You were the one
who was going to change Cumberland's mind."

"His Grace is in London. But one of his aides said he
would do what he could to persuade His Grace to name
you—"

"Now there, you see," Reginald interrupted. "There was
no harm . . ."

Marjorie broke into his protest. "He also said, though, that
His Grace wants control of this land. Lochaene protects a
pass through the Highlands and there are still bandits and
Jacobites in hiding there. He believes Braemoor can clear
them and you cannot. Or will not." Reginald, like Alasdair,
had not heeded Cumberland's call to arms. There was a
long, accusing silence. Then Marjorie's voice again. "He is
said to favor a marriage between Braemoor and . . . Alasdair's widow. He wants Braemoor to have the property."

Another silence. Janet heard footsteps and she moved
away from the door and fled up the steps as questions darted
through her mind. Did Braemoor know of Cumberland's desire?

And why—if he did—had he not mentioned it to her?

*He wants Braemoor to have the land. Had Braemoor
thought of a way to get it without marrying her?*

She recalled the kiss the night before he left. He was the one who had broken it.

He did not want her.

Did he want her son's land?

She suddenly felt very alone again.

"No," Janet said sharply. "I will not leave."

"I'm afraid, my lady, you have no choice." Neil heard his own voice. Cool. Measured. Even indifferent. How could he sound so calm when his heart was being sliced apart by the look of betrayal in her eyes?

He had been sure of his position. There was no choice. He had known that when Tim and Jock arrived this afternoon, and Jock had reluctantly agreed to stay here until Neil found a permanent manager for Lochaene. He had continued to be sure until she looked at him with desperate, betrayed and unbelieving eyes.

"I talked to Tim," he said. "Your life could be in danger here."

"It could also have been an accident."

"Mayhap," he said calmly. "But I, too, was attacked. I do not like coincidences."

"That had nothing to do with me."

"It might have everything to do with control of Lochaene," he said. "I willna leave you here alone."

Something flickered in her eyes, and he wondered if she knew something she had not told him. But then her chin went up in defiance. "I can take care of myself. I have no intention of leaving my son's inheritance."

"It is for your safety. And his," Neil said, playing his trump card. "If you do not care for yourself, then think of the children."

"There is absolutely no proof anyone would hurt them. Or me, for that matter," she said, and he saw the shine of stubborn tears in her eyes.

"I must get back to Braemoor," he said. "And I canna leave you here alone."

"*Your* man will be here," she said angrily. She had not been happy when he told her that Jock would be manager.

"He canna protect you from the family," Neil said. "Neither can Kevin."

"So Lochaene becomes yours, under your stewardship. 'Tis what you wanted all along," she said. "To add land to your own holdings. But it belongs to Colin. And I will not be dependent on you or any other man again."

So there it was. He looked at the determined set of her jaw and realized he could not change her mind through cajolery. He had thought they had reached at least some semblance of friendship in the days during his recovery. But after his behavior years ago, he realized now she would never believe in his honor again. She would never believe in *him* again.

She glared at him with something akin to hatred.

But he could not stay here. Jock had told him there were doubts at home, and that the lease men and tenants were reluctant to leave what they had for something unknown, especially when the "lord" had disappeared. A trick, they said. Everything he had planned at Braemoor was in danger.

Jock had been none too pleased, either. He, too, wanted to be back at Braemoor, and he'd agreed to stay at Lochaene only on the condition that he be replaced as soon as possible. But Lochaene needed him more at the moment. The estate had been badly managed, its tenants ignored, while at Braemoor the tenants at least had land and food and fuel for the winter.

Neil had spent the last four days walking, trying to build his strength. He had even gone for a ride yesterday, despite the agony he felt when his leg had stretched while reaching into the saddle. It had not been ready. But he had to return to Braemoor. He could linger here no longer, allowing her to think that he might leave here alone. He would be forcing her, as her husband had done, to do things she did not want to do. And because of their past, she would never believe he was doing it for her.

"I will not go," Janet said again.

He sighed. He wished he had Rory's charm, his glibness. He did not know how to embroider the truth. "I am sorry, Janet. I am Colin's guardian. He is going with me to Braemoor. I cannot force you, but I *can* ensure his safety."

She looked at him with shocked eyes. She took a step backward. "You would not do that."

"I would and I will. We leave tomorrow. Jock will make sure all your orders are carried out here. He will work with the tenants so they can stay. No one will be forced out, and they will have everything they need."

"This is my home."

"Is it, Janet? Have you been happy here?" Another cruel blow.

"Happier than I was at Braemoor," she retorted.

A knife stroke to his gut. "I will try to make it better. I will get a governess for the children. There's the library . . ."

"And I will be a prisoner again," she said flatly.

"Nay," he said.

"Aye," she contradicted him. "And it is my own fault. I wrote you. I knew I could not trust you and still . . . I wrote you."

Janet took a step back as if she could not stand being in his presence, then turned and fled from the room.

Janet bit back her frustration. She hadn't wanted to run, hadn't wanted him to see her reaction.

She reminded herself of his ruthlessness. Reminded herself that this man had fought at Culloden, had killed men that might have been her friends, that he might have killed her brother. For a few days, she'd allowed herself to forget that, to shove it to the back of her mind. She'd thought she saw the old Neil Forbes in him, not the arrogant marquis who knew best for everyone, especially himself. She had been right when he'd first arrived. He wanted what was her son's.

And once more she was helpless. Just as she had been with her husband. He did have the legal right to take her son with him. He did have the physical power. And he knew that she would have to go with him. She would not leave her son in his hands.

For how long?

Or could he be right? Had someone tried to harm her? And if so, would they go after Colin? She had not told Neil about the figure on the battlements. It had frightened her but had not harmed her. Perhaps he'd had something to do with all of it. He could have cut the cinch on the sidesaddle before he left. He would know she was the only one who used it. Both Louisa and Marjorie always used carriages.

As Colin's guardian, he could easily fold Lochaene into his holdings.

Why had she not considered that? She wrapped her arms around each other as a chill seeped through her.

Had she invited the serpent into her garden?

Chapter Fourteen

Neil decided to join the family for supper. He had heard the carriage, watched the dowager countess make her grand entrance. It had been obvious that she thought he would be gone by now, and she could resume her role as grandame.

He was usually indifferent to people like the Campbells. He had been a servant to them. He had never cared enough to despise them. He had only tried to survive those early years.

Now he knew the harm they had inflicted on Janet and the children. How they had quenched the fire of their lives! And he, too, was guilty of it. Were good intentions a better excuse for betrayal than indifference or even evil? They all inflicted damage.

To his surprise, Janet joined them. Her eyes flickered slightly when she saw him. She apparently had expected him no more than he had expected her. He had heard from Lucy that she usually took her meals with the children.

She looked lovely. Although she was still in mourning, she wore a dark blue dress with just a small bit of lace. It was not fashionable. He'd learned something about that during these past years, too, but the color made her eyes bluer and the cloth moved gracefully with her body. He wondered why she had come to supper tonight. He had noticed she generally tried to avoid her relatives.

"Marjorie," she said smoothly. "How nice to have you back. Is there anything I can do to make the dower house more welcoming?"

Marjorie's face reddened and he smiled inwardly. Janet had, in effect, just informed her mother-in-law that she was not expected to stay in the manor, as the woman had obviously been planning.

Then Janet turned to Reginald. "I am putting a notice in the newspapers that Lochaene will no longer pay any debts that are not incurred directly by me."

Louisa half rose from the table. Reginald blustered. "You canna do that. It will shame us."

"You have done that yourself by making wagers and purchases you, and Lochaene, can ill afford," she said serenely.

Marjorie glared at her. "I am the dowager countess. I do have claims."

"Then your son should have settled them on you in his will."

"You know there was no will," Marjorie said. "He died too suddenly," she added, with the familiar accusation in her voice.

Fascinated, Neil watched. Janet was making it quite clear to everyone exactly who was in charge. He could almost sense what was coming.

"At my request," she continued. "My lord Braemoor has brought someone here to manage the estate. His name is Jock Forbes and he will have full control of our holdings until I return." Her voice was confident, easy. Her eyes betrayed nothing.

He couldn't have done better. She was a better actress than he'd thought. *He* almost believed her.

She knew she had no choice but to follow his will, but she was making it her own for when she returned. That she meant to return was obvious. That she meant to run her own affairs was equally obvious. She was quietly declaring war.

He had never admired her more.

Lochaene was hers, she'd just told everyone, including

him. And no one was going to take it away from her. She
might have to agree to his demands at the moment, but she
was also making it very plain that it was a temporary situation.

"And I want to thank the marquis," she added sweetly,
"for his protection." She allowed that to settle, then sprung
her next attack. "He must return to his estates, and he is still
very weak. I will be going with him in the morning to make
sure he does not exhaust himself and fall victim to a fever."

The three Campbells were looking at her as if she'd just
sprouted horns. Devil's horns.

"You are going away? With a gentleman? As your
brother-in-law, I must protest. It is not proper. What about
the children?"

"It is most kind of you to inquire," she said. "They will be
going with me. As well as Clara and Lucy," she said, looking at Braemoor.

"Aye," Neil said. "She will be well chaperoned." He did
not want to besmirch her name any more than Reginald had
already done. He also feared that Cumberland would take
the act as a possible first step toward marriage, which he'd
made clear he would approve. That, of course, was impossible. Even if he could marry, Janet most certainly would
never consent.

He felt trapped in a spider's web.

"I can manage things while you are gone," Reginald said,
obviously trying to extract something from the arrangement.
"It is my duty as your brother-in-law," he added piously.

"I do not wish to impose on you," she replied serenely.
"Especially since the marquis knew of someone superbly
qualified. We all owe him thanks, because when Lochaene
becomes prosperous again, we will all benefit and there will
be no need for such austere necessities as legal notices."

If apoplexy was fatal, all three Campbells in the room
would have expired. Marjorie took out her tiny salts box and
waved it under her nose. Reginald turned red, then purple.

Louisa sat stunned, hatred glaring from her eyes. "You cannot do that," she finally said.

Neil wanted to enter the conversation, but knew that would not be welcome. Janet wanted no assistance, particularly from him. She was, in fact, almost daring him.

He leaned back and poured himself a glass of wine.

She shot a glance at him, then her gaze returned to her inlaws. "I am not sure when we will return, but I feel certain that Mr. Forbes will do what is necessary for you to continue as you have."

"Which is poor indeed," Louisa said. "Your husband never meant us to be beggars in our own home."

"It would not have been necessary if you had used some judgment," Janet replied with steely determination. It was obvious she was throwing down the gauntlet.

Reginald had turned various shades of red. At the moment, he was ruby in color. "I am not going to be scolded or reprimanded by a gel, much less a Jacobite."

Marjorie gave Janet a withering glance, then turned to Neil. "Certainly you do not countenance this disrespect to her husband's family?"

He shrugged. "Disrespect? I consider it common sense."

Louisa coughed and wine came sprinkling out of her mouth.

Marjorie turned to Janet. "I have . . . friends. My husband was a Campbell."

"Then I suggest you visit them if you are so uncomfortable," Janet said.

Marjorie looked back at Neil for the smallest sign of support.

He yawned.

Marjorie bit her lip. "My lord . . ."

"Aye," he said.

"I plead with you to be fair. My son has just died and . . ."

"I realize that, madam. That is exactly why I have invited my lady to visit. This home contains too many sorrows. And Lochaene is far poorer than it should be. It has been poorly managed. If you and your family have any hope of improving your lot, you should be most pleased at the decisions she has made."

If he'd expected any approval from Janet, he was quickly disabused of the notion. She shot a look of distrust toward him that was no less fervent than the ones she'd just aimed at her relatives. It was fortunate, he thought, that they were too distraught to notice.

Marjorie obviously was weighing the advantages of stalking out or staying and trying to cajole Braemoor, whom she obviously considered an upstart and intruder.

Reginald had taken another glass of wine and sunk down in his chair, his gaze centering completely on the decanter of wine.

"Surely you would not take the advice of a woman above that of my son?" she tried again. "Janet has never conducted business."

"But she has the principal necessities: common sense and a care for the tenants who depend on Lochaene. Jock can do much of the rest. He knows farming and how to deal with tenants. That should please you."

"Please us?" Marjorie said. "You are beggaring us to add Lochaene to your own holdings. I heard that Cumberland . . ." She stopped suddenly.

"Cumberland . . . what?" he asked after a moment's silence. Janet looked at Marjorie, then at him. Her eyes showed no emotion. She was keeping that hidden deep inside.

Marjorie shrugged. "Just that he is in England."

"Then it is all settled," he said. "Let us all enjoy this fine supper."

When Janet explained to the children that they would be taking a trip, Annabella was beside herself with excitement. Rachel asked a million questions. Even Grace had a rare gleam in her eyes.

It distressed Janet to admit it, but mayhap a short trip

would be good for the lasses. It would, however, be a certain kind of hell for her.

She had desperately reached out for a shred of dignity. She could never allow her in-laws to realize she was being dragged off like a sack of potatoes. When she returned, she needed to have at least the image of authority. And she planned to return soon. Even if she had to sneak off in the middle of the night.

She just wished that she hadn't wanted to smile when he'd yawned at Reginald's plea. She'd even felt a little sorry for her brother-in-law. But maybe Reginald would come to realize that he had some responsibilities, too, and not only to himself.

But the thought of two days of close traveling with Braemoor was agonizing.

"How long will we say, Mama?" Grace asked.

Janet wished she knew. "Not long," she said, hoping she was right.

"We can take Samson and Delilah?" Annabella questioned, eyes wide.

"Aye," Janet said. They would be left at Braemoor's peril. All would go, or none would go. Mayhap when he saw the extent of the expedition, he would change his mind. And yet, he seemed to tolerate the children well enough. Even the animals.

They would leave in the morning, according to Braemoor. But she had said she would not go until she met with Jock Forbes first. She was not going to leave until she knew more about the man who was to administer her son's property.

She folded the last child's clothing into the valise. She regretted there were not more toys or books. She did remember Braemoor's library. She remembered being awed by it, but had there been children's books? She did not remember.

After finishing packing with Clara, Janet told a story she'd been told during her own childhood, then leaned over and kissed each of the sleepy faces. Then she picked up Colin and wished Clara a good evening.

Braemoor lounged outside, and his presence startled her. "Do you always lurk?" she asked.

"Only when stories are being told," he said.

Something about his expression told her that he had not heard many stories himself as a child. "It was not a very good one," she said.

"I liked it."

"Then you, my lord, are easily pleased."

He shifted his position, and a grimace crossed his face. It was obvious his leg was still painful.

"Are you sure we should leave tomorrow?" she asked. "Your leg . . ."

"'Tis not but a nuisance," he said. "We will leave in the morning, but Jock is in the withdrawing room. He will stay in the manor when we leave. Is there a room available?"

"Aye," she said. "I will have Lucy prepare one."

He hesitated.

"The children want to take Samson and Delilah."

"I had assumed as much," he said with the slow smile that was rare but devastating. At least when she did not consider the deviousness behind it. "We will take the post chaise."

"We cannot spare someone as coachman," she said.

"Oh, I think we can," he said. "Tim can drive. His brother seems to be doing well here, and he will return soon."

"What about Kevin?" she asked. Tim was his man. Kevin was hers.

He shrugged. "If you prefer Kevin, then you can have him."

"I do."

"No more protestations?"

"Would they do me any good?"

He looked at her with those dark, enigmatic eyes. "No." Then his lips turned up in a half smile. "I think your relatives will tread lightly now."

"Because of you or me?" she asked.

"You, my lady, were quite forceful."

"But you do not think me competent enough to manage Lochaene?"

"I think you are more than competent, particularly after supper tonight. It is not your mind or determination that worries me; it is your safety."

For a moment, his words ignited a small glow inside. No one had ever even acknowledged that she had a mind. But now she realized how manipulative he was, how little he told her, how much he had to gain.

Does he really? Lochaene is really of small value compared to his estates.

She was not going to give him the satisfaction of arguing with him. She'd realized earlier that she would not change his mind. She could only work around it. And she would do that. She had not surrendered, only retreated until she could find a better position. "I do want to meet this . . . Jock."

She followed him as he limped down the hall to the steps. She heard his heavy breathing and realized how much it must have cost him. She pushed back the billowing feelings of sympathy.

Jock was a large man with a kind, leathery face. He was sitting when she entered but he rose swiftly and nervously fingered the bonnet in his hands. "My lady," he acknowledged awkwardly. She knew he was no more comfortable than she. She wondered what Braemoor had told him. Did he realize how unwelcome he would be?

"Thank you for coming," she said softly and was rewarded with a smile.

"My lord told me ye wished tae keep the tenants," he said. "No' so many landlords feel tha' way."

"What do you think?" she asked.

"I rode the land today," he said. "It can be done, but there will be small profits to ye."

She nodded.

"I would like to purchase sheep for the abandoned areas," he said, looking at her, not Braemoor.

She knew they did not have the money to do so.

"Do it," Braemoor said at her side.

"We do not need charity," she retorted sharply.

" 'Tis no charity, my lady. It is a loan to be repaid with interest. I trust you to make it good."

"The land is none tae good for farming but fine for grazing," Jock said, as if the exchange had never occurred.

She hadn't wanted to like him. She did not want to like anything to do with the marquis, but instinctively she liked this big man whose oversized work-scarred hands fumbled with his cap. There was an innate honesty in his face, a directness in his eyes. He was not, she thought, at all like his lord.

"You have seen Angus?" she asked.

Jock nodded. "I can work wi' the mon. He knows his farming."

"We can produce enough to pay the taxes?"

"Aye, with enough sheep and cattle. There are few enough in this area. They will bring a foine price at Inverness and Glasgow. It will be taking four or five years to build herds but with good dogs, ye need but a few herders. And the tenants should produce enough to keep themselves, sell a bit, and provide a share for you."

"My family . . . might try to hinder you."

"My lord told me as much," Jock replied. "But 'e told me I make the decisions, and I will make the best I can for ye."

She was satisfied. As satisfied as she could be under the circumstances. Lochaene's people, she felt, would be safe with this man. He would not be easily intimidated.

But safe for whom? Jock Forbes's loyalty would be to his employer, not to her. If Braemoor wanted Lochaene to succeed, she had no doubts it would. But then would he leave it for her son, for Lochaene's true heir?

She could only try to return as soon as possible. Mayhap even convince Cumberland that her son needed no male guardian, that it was an imposition on Braemoor. Mayhap if she made so much trouble, Braemoor would want to get rid of her.

She said good night to Jock Forbes, who seemed uncomfortable in the manor. He would be even more so when he met the other members of the household, but she felt he could hold his own.

She still knew a deep resentment, though, that all control was being taken from her, that she was given no choices of her own. She also feared she did not know Braemoor's true motives and intent. It most certainly was, as Marjorie had conjectured, not marriage. He had demonstrated his lack of interest in her over and over again. The desolation that had swept over her eight years earlier at his rejection still lingered painfully.

She turned to him. "When do we leave?"

"First light," he said. "It will take us at least two days with the chaise."

She nodded and turned toward the steps.

"My lady?"

She stopped but did not turn back.

He hesitated long enough that she knew he had reconsidered whatever he meant to say. "Good evening," he said simply.

She wanted to retort that being forced to leave her home was not inducive to a good night, but thought better of it. Better to allow him to believe she had accepted his decision.

Janet, the Countess of Lochaene, mounted the stairs with as much dignity as she could manage.

Neil watched Janet ascend the stairs with no little dignity. Neil had been both amused and impressed by Janet's performance at supper, and then at the meeting with Jock. She was a strong-willed lass.

After she disappeared down the hall, he walked over to the stable. With Tim, he inspected every inch of the post chaise he planned to take the next day. The coach was faded, the interior scarred and the cushions slightly soiled, but it should get them to Braemoor. He then examined the harness and traces. He did not want any more accidents.

When he was ready to leave, he asked Tim to sleep near the coach rather than the back room the lad shared with Kevin and, since his return, Tim's brother, Dicken.

"I willna take my eyes from it," he said.

"Kevin will be driving the coach," Braemoor said. "I want you to stay here and help Jock. If there is any trouble, come for me."

Tim's face fell. It was obvious that he had wanted to accompany them. "I need you here more," Neil said softly. "And you will be here to teach Dicken what he needs to know."

Tim's eyes brightened. "Aye, my lord."

"I hope to leave at daybreak," Neil said.

Tim nodded, a red forelock falling onto his forehead. He was all freckles and bright blue eyes. At thirteen, Dicken was a younger version of him. Neither boy, Braemoor knew, had been to school; their labor had been needed too badly. But both were quick in mind, and Braemoor intended to provide a tutor who could teach them as well as the lasses.

When it was safe enough.

How long would he have the torture of seeing Janet every day, to watch her bend over her son with such tenderness and hear her stories when she put the bairns to bed? How long could he resist kissing her again, or holding out his hand to her? Knowing that she was taking it only under duress.

He returned to the manor house. Only a few lights flickered in the hallway. He wished there was a library here. He went into the withdrawing room. The fire was almost out. He placed a new log on it and watched a small flame begin to lick at it, then started to blaze. It had just been waiting for fuel.

He felt like that flame. The embers had been barely glowing inside, but a few days with Janet—with the children—that small flicker had grown into an inferno of need.

Neil poured himself a glass of brandy from the bottle always kept there, and watched the fire burn.

Chapter Fifteen

Janet had a lapful of children. She sat in the middle of one seat. Annabella was asleep, her head buried in Janet's skirts. Rachel had likewise stretched across the left side of the seat, her head resting next to her sister's.

Grace sat primly on the opposite bench, valiantly trying to read a book. Next to her was Clara, who held Colin. Looking wretched after the jolting, cold day-long ride, Lucy sat next to Clara, her hands clasping at the side of the carriage as it lurched along a muddy road. Samson sat curled up next to Rachel, and Delilah was safe in a basket on the floor.

Rain pounded on the carriage roof, and thunder roared. Each new volley changed the lurch of the carriage a little more as the horses strained against the harness, obviously ready to bolt.

Braemoor had stopped the chaise just as the thunder started and climbed aboard the driver's bench with Kevin. Janet knew both man and lad must be soaked, and it could not be good for Braemoor, who was still weak.

Blast the man for his stubbornness. They never should have left this morning with the heavy overhanging clouds, the thick smell of moisture, the electricity in the air. But a woman could never tell a man anything.

She wished she could keep from thinking of him being up on that platform just days after a near-fatal fever.

Yet she knew there was no place to stop along this toll road for another ten miles. They had seen only one soul and that was a frowning, crooked stick of a man who had hobbled out to collect the due. There had been no inn, no shelter.

She knew there was a far swifter way across the mountains, but the chaise could not navigate it even if bandits did not control the only pass.

Janet tried not to worry and concentrated on devising a plan of her own. She had to demonstrate to Cumberland that she was fully capable of taking care of her own affairs. But how? She did not know. Not yet. But she did know she would go to hell before she married again.

She could do little while the Duke of Cumberland was in London. But Braemoor's odd experience in the mountain had made her wonder. She kept puzzling over the fact that the bandit had released him without asking ransom. He must be a very odd bandit indeed.

Or a fugitive Jacobite who had somehow escaped detection for more than a year.

If so, he might be of assistance to her, and she to him.

It would be a fine line. She could be putting herself and the children in danger. And yet she was obviously already in danger. Her family? Or Braemoor? Both?

Of the two, Braemoor was the more likely suspect. Reginald was too bungling, his wife too concerned with clothes, and his mother . . .

Thunder roared again, and she felt the horses straining against the traces. The coach came to a lurching stop and Janet had to grab Annabella to keep her from falling. Samson barked. Janet opened the wood shutters, which covered the windows and had kept the rain out. The rain was so thick she barely saw the cloaked form approach.

"We canna go farther," Braemoor said. "The road is too slippery. I've pulled off and Kevin and I am going to tie the horses until the lighting stops." Through the pouring rain, she saw the strain in his face, the lines that had not been there this morning. He must have been braking with his wounded leg.

She gently rearranged the two girls on the coach seat and stepped out of the chaise, immediately stepping into mud and nearly falling as her feet slipped. She looked toward the front of the four-horse team. Kevin and Braemoor were both trying to sooth them as thunder boomed and lightning streaked across the dull gray hills cloaked by the falling rain.

A lantern hanging from a post shone eerily through the heavy rain.

One of the horses struck out, and she tried to soothe him.

"Go back inside, Janet," Braemoor said. "We are going to have to unhitch them. There's no place to tie them with the carriage attached, and we cannot risk them bolting."

Janet shivered. She knew how impossible was the task. But he was right. They would have to take the horses far off the road, and there was no way the carriage could make it over the soggy ground.

But instead of obeying him, she ran her hand along the neck of the lead horse which was quivering. "Quiet, my love," she crooned to him. "You have done so well and soon you will have a nice warm stall and lots of oats." The gelding shuddered but quieted at the sound of a familiar voice. She had visited them often at Lochaene and was familiar to them.

Once the lead horse calmed, the others followed suit. She continued to run her hands along his neck as Braemoor and Kevin freed them from the harness and led them into some shelter under the trees. He ran a line between them and hurried back to the chaise.

"Get inside," he said.

"Not unless you and Kevin do."

"There is no room. We can stay up in the seats with the oil cloth," he said.

"Aye, there *is* room. You or Kevin will have to hold one of the children but you will not stay out here."

He nodded, ruefully accepting her order. "Ah, you care, madam."

"Only in that I do not wish to stay here forever," she said, not wishing to show that she did, indeed, care.

He finally shrugged. He climbed back up onto the seat and took off the lantern, carrying it inside the carriage where he hung it on a hook and dimmed the light. He gave her what she thought might be intended as a smile but really was a grimace. He was shaking with cold. Still, he held the chaise door open for her, and held out his hand to help her in. She ignored it and climbed in again, picking up blankets from the floor as Braemoor and Kevin stepped in, water dripping from them in great puddles.

Braemoor had no business on the drivers' bench so soon after surviving such a grievous wound. Stubborn mule of a man! Why did men always believe they were invincible and leave it to the women to clean up after them?

Kevin was also concerned. His gaze met Janet's as they covered the marquis with the spare blankets as well as the one she'd used. The lad's concern was obvious.

Braemoor tried to protest but neither paid any attention to him.

Annabella stirred because of all the movement and she tried to crawl over to Braemoor's lap. Janet started to stop her but Braemoor shook his head and held out his arms. The little girl snuggled into his lap.

Human warmth was the best thing for him, Janet knew, and yet she was surprised at Annabella's boldness. Her youngest daughter had been warming up to Braemoor ever since her dog wet on him, but this was the first time she had made a physical overture. She was even more startled by the look in Braemoor's eyes. They were red-rimmed from exhaustion, but those dark, usually unfathomable eyes looked both grateful and inexpressively tender even as his body continued to shiver.

His shivering gradually eased. She wished she had something warm to give him to drink but their only food and drink was strapped atop the coach. Thank God it was protected by oilskin covers, but there was no possibility of heating anything.

She leaned over and pulled one of the blankets closer around him. Her fingers touched his arm, and they were ice cold.

Janet wanted to rail at him—far more out of concern for him than for themselves—but then, none of them would have been able to predict how heavy and steady this rain would be. Still, they could have waited.

He had wanted her away from Lochaene. That much was clear. She still was not sure of his reasoning. Had it been for her sake or his? But now it did not matter. For these minutes or these hours, he needed warmth. Would it ever be thus? Whenever she thought she could dismiss her feelings for him, something reached down and battered her heart.

Was that love? Did it truly never die? Even if it was not returned?

And how did one love a man she believed dishonorable? Who had proved himself dishonorable?

Looking at him now, her heart contracted. His hair was plastered to his head, his face was red, his mouth a grim slash of pain. She saw him wince as he shifted his legs, and she knew the price he must have paid in working the brake. Annabella's weight must be agonizing. And yet his hands were firmly around her, and when Janet reached to take her daughter, he shook his head.

She sat back. Apparently, Annabella gave him more pleasure than discomfort.

His eyes closed for several moments as Annabella snuggled closer to him. Kevin looked immensely uncomfortable, squeezed tightly between the marquis and Lucy who obviously adored him. Grace had moved to sit between Janet and Clara, who held Colin, while Janet held Rachel. Samson was trying to find a place between feet.

Rain pounded down at the chaise. It was late afternoon, and it was going to be a long afternoon and longer night. A chill had seeped into the carriage and small legs—and large ones—would soon become cramped.

Worse of all was the enforced intimacy. She had welcomed Braemoor's decision this morning to ride his horse rather than ride inside the chaise. But now their legs touched, their bodies were inches apart and when he had taken Annabella in his arms her heart had started to pound erratically.

She tried to turn her thoughts away from his dominating presence in the chaise. There were problems other than stiff legs and a lack of privacy . . . and the problem of Braemoor himself. He had been far too weak to make this journey at all, much less tolerate the rain and cold winds.

He opened his eyes just then and gazed at her. "This was no' the way I intended to travel," he said dryly.

Her heart lurched again at the admission. Though she had considered him arrogant to the extreme in demanding she accompany him to Braemoor, those odd little occasions of self-deprecation took her by surprise. They touched something deep inside her, made her wonder whether she had been wrong about him. He was far more complex, she had learned, than she had ever expected.

How complex? How clever?

She looked down at his leg. Blood was seeping through his trouser leg, and still he kept Annabella close against him. She eased Rachel from her lap and reached over for Annabella. "I'll take her for a while," she said.

Annabella protested slightly but was soon sound asleep in her arms.

Braemoor tried to stretch out his legs, bumping into Samson who protested with a bark. The marquis gave her a wry look and tried to fold them again. Janet noticed the bloodstain was spreading.

"You've opened the wound," she accused.

His gaze met hers, and he seemed to be asking a question.

But she had no idea what it was. The dim light from the lantern shadowed his eyes. "'Tis nothing," he said.

"It may be nothing, but it will ruin the coach seat," she scolded, using the cushion as a mask for her real concern. "Kevin, can you hold Annabella?"

"Aye," he said and took the lass, holding her much like a piece of glass.

Janet leaned over. The trouser leg was snug over his leg. She felt no bandage there. "I hope you have a knife with you, my lord," she said.

He raised one eyebrow in that inquisitive way he had. God's truth, she wished it was not as appealing as it was.

"I want to see how much has torn open," she said, "and unless you wish to discard your trousers . . ."

He grinned at her. It was a roguish smile, full of mischief, though the lines around it showed both weariness and pain. She had never seen that particular smile before, and it was as beguiling to her as a sunrise or sunset. A surge of emotion rushed through her as the air thickened between them and the interior of the carriage became as charged with expectancy as the storm outside.

No. She was not going to let it happen again.

She was not going to let him slide back into her thoughts, her heart.

"A knife," she said calmly.

"'Tis on my saddle, along with my pistol," he said, as if he had just remembered he had left all the means of defense out in the storm. That simple confession told her how weary he was. If nothing else, she knew Neil Forbes to be a soldier, one respected by Cumberland.

She started to leave the carriage.

Instead, his hand stopped her. His fingers wrapped around her wrist as strongly as if it were a bracelet of iron. "No," he said.

Kevin was shifting in his seat. "I will get it, my lord." Awkwardly, he set Annabella on the seat and inched his way out the door.

"Take this, lad," Braemoor said, and took the lantern from the hook and handed it to him. "Bring my saddlebags."

Kevin took the lantern and opened the door. Cold driving rain rushed in, and Janet shivered. The lasses had heavy cloaks and so did she, but still the interior of the carriage was very cold.

The thunder seemed to be receding, however. Mayhap if the lightning went with it, they could try to proceed. The horses would not be as skittish.

But Braemoor could no longer drive. That much was obvious. Neither should he be riding until the wound was restitched. And Kevin was still only eighteen.

Minutes passed. Janet glanced down at the trousers. The bloodstain was still spreading. If the wound had indeed opened, it might need cleansing. And she was restless. She worried about Kevin in this storm. She worried about the rest of them. After the storm had descended upon them, there had been no place to stop. They'd had some bread at noon and nothing since.

She thought about the food basket above. It was indicative of Braemoor's exhaustion and pain that he had not thought to get it before entering the carriage. She prayed the oilcloth had done its job and kept the food dry. Even if not, there would be spirits to warm Braemoor. He needed that, and so would Kevin when he returned.

Braemoor had released her hand. She gathered her cloak around her and put the hood over her head. With the lantern gone, he could not see what she was doing.

He was not quick enough this time when she opened her own door and stepped out. She remained on the step. She looked out but did not see any light from the lantern. The night was black, the rain still falling heavily. But the thunder seemed farther away.

With no lantern, or lightning, she could not even see the hills that rose on one side of the road, nor the edge that fell away on the other side. The interior of the carriage was totally dark.

Kevin, where are you?

At least there were candles in the basket along with food. If she could reach them. She stood on the step of the chaise and stretched upward to reach the top of the chaise and feel underneath the oilcloth.

Her hands touched cloth, but not the basket. She regarded the problem for a moment, then stepped down and, holding to the side of the carriage to keep her feet from slipping in the mud, reached the step leading up to the driver's seat. She climbed up, then peered under the oilcloth, finally finding the basket.

She worked it free and lifted it to the seat next to her, then tried to figure out next how to get it down with the contents intact.

She looked around again and finally saw a bobbing light distorted and fogged by the rain. It was obvious Kevin was having difficulty finding his way back. She stood and shouted as loud as she could, then saw the light approach.

Kevin climbed the step and peered at her. The lantern showed wide eyes in a white face.

"My lady," he said in a shaking voice. "I couldna find the way back till I heard your voice. I couldna see anything through the rain."

"Well now we are all safe," she said. "But I need help with the basket."

He nodded. "I will put the lantern and saddlebags inside," he said.

Kevin disappeared for a moment, then was back and reached up for the basket. "I will be back to help ye down," he said. She decided not to wait for him. She moved to the side and started to climb down. She had removed her gloves in order to find the basket, and now she could not find them. Her fingers were icy cold as they clasped the side of the coach. She felt the hood of her cloak fall away and her fingers slipping, then found herself wrapped in arms and clasped tight to a hard male body. *Braemoor.*

Despite the rain, they remained there for a moment, bod-

ies locked, his heat warming her. Her heart beat a tattoo and
her breath caught in her throat as rain splashed around them
and plastered her hair against her face. For a fleeting instant,
she felt alive, electrically alive. She looked up at him. Despite the darkness, she saw the angles of his face. She closed
her eyes as rain washed over them. It should have brought
sense to her, but it did not. Instead, it seemed to fold around
them, embracing them.

Then Braemoor let her go and, limping badly, hurried her
to the door of the carriage.

Everyone had shifted positions to make way for the basket and the newcomers. Grace was her usually cautious,
quiet self. Rachel was squirming, and Annabella was whim-
pering at having been moved so many times.

Colin was trying to squirm out of Clara's arms and
screaming to raise what dead might be out on such a hellish
night.

Janet was not quite sure which need required the first attention. One more look at Braemoor's leg decided her. She
saw him try to stretch it again, then draw it up quickly.
Blood had mixed with rain, and now pink water dripped
from his trouser.

"Grace, you take Annabella. Lucy, give Colin a cracker
from the basket and the lasses a fruit pie. Kevin, can you
find a knife in the saddlebags?"

The lantern was again inside and she saw Braemoor's be-
mused look as she issued orders. She glared back, challenging him to argue.

"I would no' dare disagree," he said.

Curses on the bloody man. He had an uncanny way of dis-
concerting her.

Colin was not appeased by the cracker. He continued to
scream. She still had milk in her breasts, and she knew that
since they had no cow's milk, her own would be the only
thing that would quiet him. Her eyes met Neil's, and he
seemed to understand.

"Kevin and I will wait outside," he said.

She looked at his soaking clothes, the exhaustion in his eyes. She shook her head. "Just . . . turn away," she said.

Both men did, and she untied her cloak, then the ties to her dress. Thank God she had worn this gown. In minutes, Colin was greedily sucking.

The closeness in the coach was daunting. She knew he could hear every sound, and she felt every part of her body grow red with embarrassment. At last, her son finished. In minutes, she and Clara had changed him and Clara took him in her arms.

The lasses were finishing their fruit pies and quenching their thirst with drinks of water which would, she knew, create still another unfortunate demand. Braemoor was eating a chunk of bread and drinking brandy.

She wondered whether the marquis had ever before traveled with four children, much less three women. But when she looked at him, the dim light of the lantern showed a wistful yearning that made her heart skip. Immediately he looked away. But she knew she would remember that expression.

Still, she tried to dismiss it as she tended to his own needs. She used the knife to cut his trousers, laying back the material to reveal the wound. The top end of it had opened, the stitching torn away. It looked raw and sore and was bleeding steadily.

She wished she had a needle and thread, but that would have to wait. Now it was important to stop the bleeding. She leaned down and pulled up her skirt and cut a strip of her petticoat, then tied it tightly around the wound. It was damp, and she was chilled, but that was not important at the moment. She carefully wrapped the cloth around the wound and tied it snugly. It was the best she could do at the time.

That and keep Annabella from crawling back up on him.

She prayed that the rain would subside.

But it seemed intent to continue.

Annabella wriggled some more. She did not have to say what she needed.

Janet glared at the marquis, pushing away that warm feeling she had moments earlier. She must look a fright. Her hair had fallen from the neat knot Lucy had so intricately entwined, and her cloak smelled of wet wool. The bottom of her dress was ringed with mud.

She could be warm in bed at Lochaene.

The tattoo of rain against the carriage seemed to slow imperceptibly. She had not heard thunder for the last few moments. Mayhap . . .

She tried to put the blankets back on Braemoor but he shrugged them off. "The lasses need them. And you."

"I haven't been foolishly riding on the seat of a carriage through a driving rain," she said.

He half closed his eyes and looked at her lazily. "Aye, no' one of my greatest accomplishments."

"And did you think about four wee children?"

"Aye," he said. "And their mother."

She looked at the children. Only Grace seemed to be listening.

Braemoor's eyes had a glittering intensity. "You were not safe at Lochaene."

"Neither am I safe on this road."

"Nay, but I couldna predict that."

"And you could the other?"

"Aye. I think so."

She sighed. "I have to take the lasses out."

He looked startled, as if he'd never considered such an obstacle. "I . . ."

"Nay. You will not. And neither can Kevin. She turned away from him and adjusted the hood. "Clara, will you go with me? I will take the lantern and you can hold on Rachel and Annabella. Grace can take my hand. We will have to stay together."

Braemoor squirmed. She had never seen him squirm before. Evidently, he had never been around small lasses before.

It was difficult to be angry at a squirming man.

She sighed, took the lantern down again, then stepped out. The rain was slackening but still steady. There was no more lightning, but the night was pitch black and the hills were shrouded in fog. Clara stepped out, then swung each of the children down.

Clara had not uttered a word of protest during the day and several other brief, wet trips. Janet thanked her angels every time she looked at Clara. Lucy was a fine maid, but she was as timid as a field mouse.

They stepped carefully no farther than behind the carriage. Shielded by both Clara and Janet, each of the lasses took care of their needs, and turned to go back. The door was open, and Braemoor held out his arms. He took each child and saw that they were covered with blankets.

Then he closed his eyes. Once back in her arms, Colin fell asleep almost instantly. All the lasses were soon asleep as well, and Lucy's head was nodding.

Janet would have liked to quench the lantern, but they might need it again tonight, and lighting it again with a tinderbox would not be easy. So instead she closed her eyes.

She was aware that her knees were nearly interlocked with Braemoor's long legs—far too aware, just as she was aware of the unexpectedly attractive scent of leather and horses and brandy.

But he was oblivious to her. Oh, how she wished she could shut him out of her mind as easily, apparently, as he did her.

It was going to be a very long night.

Buffeted by new emotions and reactions, Neil feigned sleep.

His leg ached from using it on the brake. He had hoped to get them to an inn this night, but he'd been too optimistic. He'd had no idea of the needs of such a family, of the number of times they would have to halt their journey, and then the storm that had threatened all day had been one of the worst he'd ever experienced.

He'd made a hell of a mess of the whole thing, but he'd

lived his entire life depending on his instincts. And his instincts had told him that she was in danger.

She had, in truth, turned all his instincts inside out. He no longer knew what was emotion, what was his overwhelming sense of protection toward her, and what was instinct. Had the former completely skewed the latter?

He'd never previously done anything in his life without thinking it through. He had obviously not thought this through.

All was still in the carriage. He half opened his eyes. Despite the cramped and cold interior of the coach, his companions were nodding off to sleep. Even Janet appeared to be sleeping, her son cradled by both her and young Grace.

He had tried to look away when she'd been nursing her son—and succeeded, but when he'd looked at her when she'd finished, he'd had a glimpse of her face and saw the tenderness on her face.

And he understood it as he had never understood anything before. Because tenderness had lodged in his chest when Annabella had crawled into his arms so trustingly and gone to sleep with her head against his heart. His leg had hurt like hell, but that was of little import compared to the other feelings. He felt as if a candle had been lit inside.

Nothing like that had ever happened to him before he came to Lochaene. He'd been totally unprepared for such feelings and how seductive they were. Not seductive in the sensuous way, but in so many other ways.

He had handled everything badly. He should have told her why he'd done what he had eight years earlier, that it had been for her sake, not his own.

But how do you tell someone that? And how do you tell her you come from a long line of madness?

And expect trust?

Chapter Sixteen

Janet looked out the window as the chaise drew near Braemoor.

Unlike the grand manor home where she had grown up and the house in which she had lived after her marriage, Braemoor was a true tower house, a large circular stone edifice that was virtually unbreachable.

Years ago, she had thought Braemoor stark by the standards of her own childhood home. It had also been ill kept. She remembered her first dismay at seeing it, then at meeting the man her father had considered a match for her. He'd been more distasteful. She'd even been frightened of him.

And then she'd seen Neil Forbes in the background, dressed as simply as his cousin had been bedecked with finery. He had worn a simple linen shirt and plaid. His dark eyes had met hers and her heart had fluttered wildly. She had listened to the romantic ballads and had discounted the thought of love at first sight. Her mother had told her that love and respect were things that grew between man and woman.

But in that moment at Braemoor, she knew her parents were wrong and the balladeers were right. The next few days had been magic, so sweet and pure that she still ached at the memories.

"Is that it?" Rachel asked, interrupting her thoughts. "Is that where we are going?"

"Aye, sweetling," Janet said.

"Do you think I can have a pony there?" Annabella asked.

Janet remembered that she had promised them they could have a pony, mayhap even two. But that was before she knew that Braemoor was going to take over her life. "I do not know, love," she said.

She looked at the tower house as the chaise came to a stop. Memories crowded in on her. She had hoped never to see this house again, the house where her dreams—and hopes—had been shattered.

Her thoughts were disrupted as Braemoor opened the door and his gaze, dark and enigmatic, met hers.

He'd stayed away from the occupants of the carriage for much of the previous day. They had awakened at dawn, and despite an obviously painful leg, Braemoor had assisted in harnessing the horses and getting the chaise back on the road. He had remained on the drivers' bench and she had only seen him when they had stopped to rest the horses and allow the lasses to get some exercise. They had stopped at an inn last night, but Braemoor had disappeared after seeing them to their rooms and ordering their supper.

Braemoor had remained quiet and tight-lipped this morning when they left the inn. Only Annabella appeared to affect him as he lifted her this morning into the chaise. Her arms had gone around him and for a moment he hesitated before settling her inside.

There had been raw hunger in his eyes, but it disappeared quickly. Why? What was it about a child that seemed to . . . disconcert him so? It was more, she thought, than simply unfamiliarity. He was good with Annabella. He had obviously enjoyed holding her that night in the carriage. But now he seemed to avoid her, to avoid all of them.

And what would he do now that they were at Braemoor, a place he ruled absolutely?

She reluctantly handed him the lasses, then urged Clara to

descend next so the nursemaid could take Colin. Then Lucy. Braemoor gallantly held his hand out to each of them, easing them down. Then there was no one left but her. He held out his hand. For a moment, she thought about refusing it, then thought that would be childish. She took it, feeling the familiar jolt of awareness, and jerked it away quickly.

He said nothing for a moment, then gave her that half smile that both irritated and intrigued her. "Braemoor is your home," he said softly. "If you need anything, anything at all, just ask."

Her hands tightened in fists at her side. She did not want to feel what she was feeling. She did not want every sense to tingle when he touched her, or even looked at her. She tried to remember the desolation, the pain she felt years ago when he tore her heart to shreds. She had trusted him then. How could she possibly be fool enough to trust him again? "I doubt I will need anything," she said tartly.

"Then I will try to anticipate your desires," he replied.

"Anticipate then that I wish to return to Lochaene. With my children."

"You will," he said.

"When?"

"I canna answer that, my lady."

"Or will not," she amended. She turned away from him and took Colin from Clara. She wanted her son, and the lasses, close. Safe.

"I will let you get reacquainted with Braemoor," he said. "You know about the library. Use it as much as you like."

Annabella sidled up to him. "Do you have a pony?"

He knelt and looked at her. "Nay," he said. "But you will have one," he said.

Janet was stunned by his reply, by the casual way he'd made the promise. Or did he realize it was a promise? To a child, it would be. And he, she knew, was not very good at keeping promises.

"That is . . . not necessary," she said.

"Yes it is. I uprooted them from everything familiar."

That was not exactly true. Lochaene may have been where they lived, but the familiar things were Samson and Delilah, Clara, Lucy, Colin and herself. Even during that hellish journey, she'd felt that the children were safer than they ever had been while their father lived. But she was not ready to say that to Neil.

"We are tired," she said. "And my daughters can use a bath." So could she. They had been too tired last night and the lasses too cranky for a bath.

"I will have it readied." He hesitated, then said, "Trilby will be helping Lucy."

"I do not need anyone else," she said.

"It . . . would be . . . a kindness," he said. "She was Rory's wife's maid. Bethia left . . . at the same time Rory died, and Trilby has been unhappy since. A lady's maid is a long step up from a parlor maid, and there has been no lady . . ."

Janet gazed up at him. "And that matters to you?"

"Aye," he said in a low voice.

"Then we will make use of her," she agreed.

"My thanks," he said simply.

Blast the man for doing it again. She squinted up at him. He looked bland, indifferent, and yet it had not been an indifferent request.

"How is your leg?" she asked, trying to change the subject.

"Raw," he admitted.

"Will you give it some rest?"

"Do you really care, madam?"

She nearly melted under the warmth of his gaze. But then she had been deceived by it before. "Aye, I do not wish to take care of you forever."

"That blow is more wounding than the one struck by the bandit," he replied dryly.

"Is it?" she asked skeptically and turned toward the tower.

He limped beside her. Kevin, she noticed, was unhitching the horses along with a slightly older man who had appeared from the stable. She did not recognize him, but then she had been at Braemoor only a short time years ago and much had happened in the meantime—including a war.

And yet the sight of Braemoor stirred a storm of emotions in her. She had thought she could never return to a place that held such joy, then later such misery. How long could she stay in the shadow of both?

Upon entering the tower house, she noticed it was far cleaner and neater than she had remembered.

"It looks different," she noted.

"My cousin's wife," he said. "Bethia. She transformed Braemoor."

"What happened to her?" she asked. "I heard about your cousin's death, that he must have killed the Black Knave, and that his wife disappeared."

Neil shrugged. "Some say she ran away with the Black Knave. Some say she died with him. I doubt if anyone will ever know."

"You liked her?"

"Aye. She was a difficult person to dislike," he said. "But she had been forced into the marriage with my cousin, and I knew she wasna happy. Still, she changed Braemoor for the better."

Janet tried to remember all she had heard. Her husband had not known she had once loved someone at Braemoor, and he and Marjorie had relished the gossip months ago. The wife of a Forbes running off with a criminal and blackguard, an upstart inheriting an honorable name disgraced by a Jacobite woman.

That Janet had been Jacobite had not quieted their talk at all, in fact they had seemed to relish talking about it in her presence. It showed the treachery of Jacobites, Marjorie had said.

Janet shivered inside. She understood how that woman had felt. She had been bound, as had Janet, to a system that regarded women as little more than broodmares or a means to obtain money and land. They were all pawns. Mayhap

Bethia had found her love. Mayhap Bethia had found a way
out. She hoped so.

Janet's fists clenched. Mayhap she could find one, too.

Will took a drink from the keg of ale Burke had liberated.

"So he lives?"

"Aye," Burke said.

"And the countess cared for him."

"Burke nodded.

"Then she still cares for him." He said it in a low voice.

"Sir?"

"Nothing," he said, berating himself for speaking the
words aloud. It had been a thought. He had not meant to put
voice to it.

"He has taken her to Braemoor," Burke said.

Will looked around the cold, bare cave where his band of
refugees had taken shelter. Food was a constant problem.
Their occasional banditry usually yielded small sums, not
nearly enough to smuggle these people out of the country.
One young lad had a constant cough. The children were thin.

He also knew Cumberland planned an expedition to clean
out these mountains. That would mean moving from one
place to another.

He had never meant to be guardian angel to a group of
refugees, people in danger because of their family name. It
was no matter they were children.

"I think it is time to see whether Braemoor pays his debts
or not," he said.

"And if he does not?"

"Then he is a dead man," Will said.

"We should have killed him when we had a chance,"
Burke muttered.

"Never play all your cards," Will said. "You might need
that jack. Or king."

"'E is naught but Cumberland's man," Burke said. "''E
will betray you."

Will laughed bitterly. "There is nothing to betray. Cumberland already knows there are . . . rebels in these hills."

"'E will never help you," Burke said. "Them kind never do."

"If he does not," Will said, "then mayhap the new widow will. In any event, I want you to take a message to Braemoor. Unfortunately I canna be taking this face anywhere near Braemoor."

Burke scowled.

Will wished he had someone else to send. Burke was as good as any man in a fight. He was excellent at ferreting out information. He was no good at guile. They had found each other in the old woman's hut. Burke, too, had been injured. He had served Robertson of Struan who had disappeared at Culloden. Burke did not know whether his clan chief was dead or had escaped. He only knew he'd been able to crawl away from the battlefield when, like Will, he had been thought dead. His one wish now was to get to France where he hoped to fight England in the new world.

Will knew revenge was Burke's sole goal. His own goal was not much, but his means would be far different. He meant to escape Scotland and somehow make a fortune. Only through enormous amounts of money could you inflict deadly harm. And he had his list of those on whom he wished to inflict harm.

But first he had to get out of the country, and he would not go until he knew those with him could also go. That meant arranging passage on a ship. It meant the kind of money that only someone like Braemoor could get him.

That fact had stayed his hand two weeks ago. That and the card. Murmurings about Braemoor. And the man himself. He had not begged for his life.

Will admired courage. And he had remembered something long ago. Janet Leslie had once been enamored of Braemoor. He knew it had ended badly, which is why he had sent him to her. If the man lived, it would be a sign.

And a debt owed.

He intended on collecting.

"You will go tomorrow," he said, wishing that he could go. But his face was known and his scar far too distinctive. He had to depend on Burke. He could pray the man kept his temper reined.

The room Janet had was far grander than the one she'd had as a girl. It was, according to the lass named Trilby, the same room occupied by the marchioness. "The marquis said you might like a bath, my lady?" Trilby said nervously.

Lucy bristled. "Aye, she would," she said, making it very clear as to who was responsible for Janet's well-being.

Trilby bobbed. "I will see to it and be back to show the others their rooms."

Lucy glared at Trilby as she slipped out the door.

"You do not need someone else serving you, my lady," she said, then clasped her fingers to her mouth as she realized what she had said.

Janet sighed. "In truth, you are all I need, Lucy, but it would be a kindness."

"The manor is very nice," Grace said, as if sensing some discord. She hated discord. "Where will *we* stay?"

"Somewhere close, love," Janet said. She had already decided that.

Samson came over and started to chew on her slippers which were, unfortunately, stiffened with mud from several stops along the way this day. Janet had tried to clean them last evening at the inn but they had been ruined and she had not wanted to destroy yet another pair.

She had changed her gown this morning, but it, too, was travel-stained, with mud clinging to the skirts, and had a distinct odor from where Colin had spit up. She knew her hair looked lank and plain and colorless and her eyes tired.

Janet closed her eyes and sat down on the huge feather bed.

Grace touched her hand. "Should I take Samson and Delilah out?" she asked.

"Can I see the horses?" Rachel added.

"Can I really have a pony?" Annabella chimed in.

Colin broke into a loud wail.

"Aye, aye, we will see about a pony, and yes, Colin, I will feed you," she said, trying to answer all the questions at once.

Grace and Rachel ran out the door, Grace clutching Delilah's basket and Samson nipping at Rachel's heels.

"Clara, you go with them," she said. "Lucy will help me with Colin."

"Aye," Clara said. She hesitated, then uttered traitorous words. "I think the marquis means no 'arm." It was a very long and profound statement for her. She was usually as quiet as her oldest charge, Grace.

"The marquis has his own objectives," she said, "and it is best to remember that."

Clara nodded.

Trilby entered. "Water is being heated," she said. "I can show ye yer daughters' room," she said. "It is down the hall. The marquis thought you would prefer that rather than the nursery upstairs. We have tried to make it verra comfortable."

Janet stared at her. "You knew we were coming?"

"Aye. My lord sent word when 'e called away Jock."

How long had Braemoor planned this?

Time enough, she thought bitterly, to handle the journey better.

But her daughters were excited at being somewhere beyond Lochaene. And their troubles along the way were travails to her but adventures to them. Even Colin had survived quite well.

In truth, she admitted to herself, so had she. Despite the mud and rain and cold, she had found she had a strength she did not know she had.

And now she was ready to do battle with Braemoor. She was not going to bend to his will. Not now. Not ever.

She would start with short rides, then expand them day by

day. Before long, she hoped, no one would notice if she
were gone six hours or more. And in that time, mayhap she
could do what she must.

Neil rested a day. He was impatient, but he knew enough
about his wounds to know it was necessary. There was so
much to do. And with Jock gone, he would have to do most
of it himself.

He had hoped that Janet might inquire about him, might
even pay him a visit, but the day passed without either. He
had asked Torquil whether he had seen the countess, but he
had said nay.

There was no reason for it to be different. He imagined
she was exploring the house with the lasses. They would be
restless after so many hours in the close interior of the
chaise. He dutifully partook of soup and bread and ale.
Torquil had looked at his thigh and had stitched the edges,
which had come loose.

He would have much preferred Janet's gentle hand, but he
had vowed he would not force her to do anything more than
she wished to do. It was just as well, in fact, that she wanted
to stay away from him.

He slept on and off. He was warm. Tired. He hurt nearly
as much as when he was first shot. Or had he merely forgotten the intensity of pain? Finally dawn came, and with it
renewed strength and energy.

He rose, shaved and dressed. He wondered how Janet was
settling in, whether her daughters had been down to the stable. A pony would be his first business and then a visit to the
new properties where he hoped Braemoor's tenants were
building crofts.

He went down to the large dining room.

The three young lasses looked at him from the table.
Clara was there with them. The countess was not.

"I was feared you were dead," Annabella said. "Like my
father."

"Nay, little one. I think it would take more than one journey to kill me."

"Mama said you needed rest," Rachel said. "I wanted to come to see you."

"Me, too," Annabella said.

Grace sat upright in her chair. "Mama said we could read your books."

"Aye."

"Our father never wanted us to have them. He said it would spoil us, like they spoiled . . . Mama."

He wished like hell that Campbell was still alive so he could kill him himself. It was not the first time he'd thought that, but the feeling was growing with fury inside him. Instead, he said mildly, "She is not spoiled at all, and reading is a fine thing."

For the first time since he had met her, Grace favored him with a smile. Its very rarity made it extraordinary. It lit a face that was usually plain. Or mayhap not plain. Just too somber to shine.

She quickly bent over her plate as if embarrassed.

"I read, too," Annabella said, obviously displeased at not being the center of attention.

"She does not," Rachel interjected indignantly. "She is just a bairn."

Grace ate faster. Any discord obviously bothered her. Something shifted inside him. These children touched him as nothing else had. He had not expected it. He had thought of children as, well, something to be avoided. But he had also thought people were something to be avoided, small or large.

Especially women.

He looked around the dining room and thought how much it had improved since his cousin had so reluctantly married. It had not taken long, he discovered later, for both the bride and groom to discover they had something between them other than Cumberland's whims. But Janet would never allow anything to develop between him and her, and neither would he.

Ride out today. Stay away until you can find a way to send her safely back.

But first a pony. He had promised.

He enjoyed a big breakfast as he answered the girls' questions. All kinds of questions. Did he have a mother? Did he have a wife? He had already told them he had no children, but they obviously thought it strange that he had no one.

Not even a friend, come to think of it.

He had never thought that a loss before. Now he did. Now it filled him with a bleak emptiness.

Too soon, Clara came for them. Their mother, he said, was with Colin in her room and had already had breakfast there. Trying to avoid him, no doubt.

The large dining room seemed extraordinarily empty without the sound of childish voices. He looked around the room. The tower house was more than two hundred years old. Some Forbeses had honored it; others had not.

Rory probably had done it more honor than any predecessor, and even that was partly because he hated it so much. Neil remembered how much he had despised Rory, how much he had envied him, how much he had resented him. Those feelings had been so strong that he had not been able to see anything decent in the man. He'd told himself then that he resented Rory because he cared nothing for the tenants.

In truth, neither had Neil. Oh, he cared about order. He'd cared about doing things well. He'd cared about improving the yield from the land because that seemed to make his life worth something, and he had nothing else.

It wasn't until he discovered what Rory had been about that he started looking closer at people, saw what he had never seen before. Selflessness in Rory, integrity in Jock; honesty in Tim, innocence in the children.

Gallantry in Janet.

He was actually beginning to like people. Or at least appreciate them. Some of them.

His uncle had made him distrust everyone. Donald, his cousin, had reinforced that opinion. And Rory, Donald's brother, had always taken great pride in allowing everyone to believe the worst of him.

Bloody hell, but he was becoming maudlin. A ride would shake away those remnants of memories. He needed to check on Braemoor, then tomorrow he would ride up to the new properties. It would take him several days. Several days away from Braemoor, away from eager questions. Away from Janet's tempting presence.

Neil dropped by the village, passing the vacant blacksmith shop. He would have to employ a new farrier. He wondered what had happened to Alister Armstrong, the former farrier. He had disappeared when Rory had, but only one body was found.

Since then he'd had to send for a farrier once a month to keep his horses well shod.

He rode by fields that were nearly ready for harvesting, then continued down a road that led to the property adjoining his. An Englishman had taken the property and was raising horses. He might have some ponies or know where Neil could find one. Otherwise, he would have to go all the way to the town of Fort William, which would take several days.

He nudged his horse into a canter. He thought of Lochaene as he passed fields growing high with wheat. There was not much chance for any kind of crop for Lochaene unless winter held back. The tenants would need a great deal of help this winter.

He was suddenly aware of another rider well behind him on the path. He'd been so lost in his own thoughts that he'd paid no attention, but now he wondered how long the rider had been with him. After the incident with Will, he should be more careful. Well, this time he would plan a little ambush of his own.

Thank God he had his pistol with him. He vowed he
would never be without it again.

He spurred his horse into a canter. There was a turn just
ahead where he could leave the path, ride up ahead and look
down on whomever may be following him. If they were.

He took the turn and guided his horse off the road. He
then wound around a low-lying hill and dismounted, taking
a pistol from the saddlebags. After tying the horse to a tree,
Neil climbed the hill that overlooked the narrow path below.
The rider was not good at either riding or stealth. Neil recognized him.

It would be incredibly foolish to ask him to halt from this
distance. Pistols had no accuracy at this distance, and he had
but one shot.

The man would backtrack when he discovered he'd lost
his prey. Neil decided that he would wait for him to return,
just as Burke and his master had waited for him. The poetic
justice appealed to him.

He went back and mounted his horse, then waited in the
shadow of the hill.

It did not take long. Within minutes, Burke was back-
tracking.

Neil heard the sounds of hoofbeats and loud cursing. The
man would have to learn to be more quiet if he were to remain a live bandit.

What in bloody hell was the man after? Did he want to
finish the job he'd started days ago?

Neil himself felt oddly reckless.

Hell, he had never been reckless even one day of his life.
He had always stood back, uninvolved, weighing the advantages and disadvantages of a situation. The one time he had
been reckless—the early days with Janet—had turned disastrous. Even at Culloden, he'd tried to be detached, protecting a bully of a man as he'd been taught even as his stomach
turned at the killing . . .

So why not be reckless now?

Dammit, he was tired of being cautious!

Pistol in hand, he moved his horse out of the shadows of the hill and onto the road. "Burke!"

The man stopped, looking startled. He started to go after his pistol, then raised his right hand in a gesture of surrender. "Ah, my lord," he said. "Ye got me rightly, you did."

"What do you want?"

"Ah, to see how ye were farin'. I was the one who took ye tae Lochaene," Burke said.

"You just wanted to see after my general welfare?" Neil replied dryly.

"Aye, my lord."

" 'Tis very kind of you, but I doubt that was your sole reason. This is well-patrolled land. Give me one reason I should not turn you over to the English."

"A debt ye owe to Will?"

"For nearly killing me?"

"Fer saving yer bloody life. I would 'ave taken it."

"You have to do better than that. 'Tis no good reason for not turning you over to the magistrate."

Burke shifted in his saddle, his lank brown hair falling around his face. One hand was still up, the other holding the reins. He shrugged. "We knew 'twas possible, but Will thought ye a better mon than tha'."

"How nice. And how very wrong," Neil said. "Now tell me why you were following me or we go to the magistrate."

Burke looked uncomfortable. "Will is callin' in his debt. He wants to see ye. I told him ye were naught but another nob doin' the king's bidding."

"Then why did you come if you believe that?"

Burke shrugged. "I do as he tells me."

"Why?"

The bandit looked uncomfortable but did not answer.

"And what does he want with me?" Neil asked, even as he felt he already knew. Pursuing the matter might well be the worse decision he'd ever made, but that feeling of recklessness persisted. And he was impressed with a man who would risk his life for another. It said a great deal about the enigmatic bandit in the mountains. God knew he did not know a soul who would do the same for him.

"He needs money," Burke said after a slight pause.

"How much?"

"Enough tae get passage to France fer twelve people."

"For Jacobites?"

Burke just stared at him with hard eyes.

"And he trusts me no' to betray him?"

"Nay, but he has no one else," Burke said, adding darkly, "ye will die if ye betray him." It was obvious he did not share Will's opinion of the master of Braemoor.

"You do like threats, even when you are in no position to make them," Neil said, even as he lowered his pistol.

Burke shrugged carelessly. "There are some ready tae kill if anything happens tae me."

Neil doubted it. There was only Burke and his master. Still, he found himself responding in a perfectly irrational way. "I will bring you money tonight. You can take it yourself. 'Tis no need for me to go."

Burke did not look happy. "He wants ye tae come."

Neil studied him for a moment. Taking money into a bandit's lair would indeed be a reckless thing. And yet something about Will intrigued him. "I will meet you at midnight," Neil said. "I have something to do first and it is best we travel at night."

Burke scowled. "Wha' will I do until then?"

"Skulk around. You seem good enough at that." Then he hesitated. "There is a cottage not far from Braemoor. It is deserted at the moment. You can wait there for me. Just take this road past the village, then take the first path to the right."

"Wha' if someone sees me?"

"That, my good fellow, is none of my concern."

Burke glared at him.

"Midnight," Neil said again.

"Aye, but ye better not bring anyone with ye," Burke said in a voice that was nearly a growl.

"Ah, trust between comrades," Neil replied. "'Tis quite touching."

"Will may trust ye. I do not," Burke said. "Remember what I said about betrayal." He turned his horse, heading off the road toward the hills.

Neil watched him disappear.

And wondered what in the bloody hell he was doing.

He dismissed the thought. A pony, at the moment, was more important.

Chapter Seventeen

Janet heard the excited scream as she mounted the stone stairway with a tray full of hot fruit pastries. She barely missed being knocked down as two little whirlwinds passed on the stairs, followed by a barking puppy and a racing kitten. Grace followed at a more sedate pace.

"What . . . ?"

She barely got the word out as Grace stopped. "The marquis . . . is coming. He has two ponies with him."

A promise kept. One, anyway.

Janet turned around and went down the steps with Grace, putting the tray on the table in the hall. Then she followed Grace through the door left open by the children.

The marquis was dismounting as Annabella and Rachel squealed with delight at the sight of two ponies, one white and one a dark bay, on a lead. Both had saddles on them.

Fearless Annabella started to run over to the white one. Rachel more cautiously approached the bay. She knew far better than Annabella never to take an animal by surprise.

Janet started to go to Annabella, but Braemoor reached her first, slowing her. He lifted her up and spoke something into her ear. Annabella grinned at him, then slowly held out her hand and touched the white pony, which shook his head then nuzzled her hand.

"He likes me."

"*She* likes you," Braemoor corrected her, then put her back on the ground. He remained close for a moment, though, then he turned to Grace. "I could only find two ponies, so the three of you will have to share until I find a third." Apology was written all over his face, and Janet felt her heart melting again. The bloody man was always confusing her.

"That is perfectly all right," Grace said in her grown-up voice. "I would rather read."

The little mother. She had always seen to her siblings' needs before her own. Sometimes Janet wished she would have a temper tantrum, be a child for once.

She went over to Grace and put her arms around her.

Rachel had slowly approached the bay pony. She turned back toward Grace. "I will share her," she offered generously.

"Him," Braemoor said. "He's a gelding."

Rachel looked up and beamed at him. "Does he have a name?"

"I did not ask," he said. "So I imagine the three of you will have to name the two of them."

"Can I ride him . . . her . . . now?" Annabella asked in a pleading voice.

Braemoor looked toward Janet for her approval. It was nice, she thought a trifle bitterly, that he was asking for approval for something. He certainly had not heeded her feelings in any other way.

She looked at Annabella and Rachel. They looked at her beseechingly.

Braemoor had won their hearts. He had the trust it had taken her months to earn. She hated the resentment she felt. And the fear.

Would he turn on them as he had turned on her eight years earlier? Once they were no longer a novelty, would he desert them with the swiftness of the stroke of a steel blade? That would be more cruel than their father's contempt. She could not bear that. They trusted so few people. Herself and may-hap Kevin. Why then had they allowed Braemoor to steal their hearts so easily?

She went over and picked up Annabella, hugging her close. She never wanted any of them to feel the desolation, the complete emptiness of being rejected by someone whom they thought loved them. "Of course you can, sweetling," she said and placed her in the saddle. She took the reins, however, which had been tied over the saddle.

She avoided looking at Braemoor but walked the pony around the yard. She was aware of Rachel following on the other pony.

"I want Grace to ride with me," Rachel said from behind, and Janet knew her second daughter was trying to be generous.

Janet looked at Grace and she was backing away. "No," she said. Janet realized then that Grace's smile had been for her sisters' delight. Suspicion was as alive in her eyes as it must be in Janet's own.

Janet turned her eyes back to the path in front of her. She was not going to let her own fears spoil the joy of two little lasses who'd had so little. She would just try to stand between them and disillusionment.

A few more rounds, and she stopped to take Annabella down from the saddle.

"Doan want to get down," Annabella protested.

"Not even if I give you a lesson tomorrow so you can ride her all by yourself?"

Annabella thrust her lip out stubbornly.

"I think the pony is very tired from her walk today," Janet added, hoping that Annabella's soft heart would do the rest.

"You think so?" Annabella asked, the lip receding slightly.

"Aye," she said. "I think she needs some oats. And you can take her a carrot to make her feel at home."

"Awright," she said, holding out her hands to be taken down from the saddle. Janet held her for a moment, then let her down. She went running over to the marquis who had just lowered Rachel. Annabella flung her arms around his neck before he could straighten up. "Thank you. I love you."

Janet wanted to turn her head away but before she did, she saw the incredulous expression cross his face, the softening of his stern eyes, the way his arms went around and held Annabella a moment longer than necessary. Then he let go and straightened, his gaze meeting Janet's.

She expected to see triumph and satisfaction in them. Instead, she saw a pain so deep and so raw that she flinched.

Then he turned away.

She stood there a moment. Stricken. Had she seen what she'd thought she'd seen? Or had it simply been a trick of the sun and shadows?

"I will take them inside," he said.

"I will pay you for the ponies as soon as Lochaene . . ." She realized how meaningless the words were. Lochaene was dependent on him, on his loans. And yet . . .

"They are a gift, Janet," he said. "Please do not take that pleasure from me."

The plea was naked. Not a hint of arrogance or authority.

She turned away from him. She did not want to feel what she was feeling. She was not going to trust him again.

"Janet."

She turned back.

"I am leaving tonight. I will not be back for several days. Tell Torquil if you need anything. The stablelads are very competent."

"I will not need anything," she said.

"Do not try to return to Lochaene," he warned.

What doubt she had about him faded. "You would drag me back again?"

"Aye," he said coolly. "I would."

"And you wish me to promise to be a good prisoner?"

"A contented guest."

"You can bribe my daughters," she said. "But not me."

"'Twas no' a bribe."

"Was it not, my lord?"

"I wish them to be happy here. And safe."

"I felt far safer in my own home than I do as a captive here."

"And your children's safety?"

"I can take care of them myself," she said. "At least they will be protected against promises that are never kept." Janet felt herself flush with color. She had not meant to say that. She had not wanted him to realize how much he had hurt her. How much damage he had done to her years earlier.

His eyes met hers. "That will never happen," he said softly.

"No? And why should I believe you?"

"You probably should not," he said. "But do believe that you are unsafe at Lochaene."

"I do not want to be here." It hurt too blasted much, but she could not tell him that.

A muscle twitched in his cheek. "I will try not to inflict my presence upon you more than necessary."

She felt a twinge of regret. In protecting herself from hurt, was she being unfair? He so confused her that she did not know. She just knew she was terrified of trusting him again. She did not think she could survive another hurt that deep. "Is that why you are leaving?"

"Nay. I have a bit of unfinished business."

Her gaze met his. "You seem to have a lot of unfinished business." She hoped it was not as much a question as it sounded to her. His comings and goings were of no interest to her. It would be best, in truth, if he disappeared completely. Then she would not have all these . . . conflicting emotions.

He looked at her for a long moment, then his gaze dropped, and he took the reins of the ponies and headed for the stable.

Janet took her daughters inside. She had promised carrots for the ponies. But first she would tempt young appetites with the apple pastries she had intended to bring them before the marquis had appeared with the ponies.

Her heat beat unsteadily. Her mind was full of angry words she had not spoken, and thoughts she tried to lock away. Why did he always create such a storm of emotions inside her? And where was he going in the middle of the night?

Could he have some secrets of his own?

Annabella skipped alongside of her and took her hand. "I love the pony," she said.

Janet did not want to ruin what must be one of the truly wonderful moments in Annabella's life. "Have you thought what to name her yet?"

"I think Snow White would be good," Annabella said, looking up at her anxiously for approval.

"I think Snow White is perfect," Janet replied.

"And we can name Rachel's pony prince Charming," Annabella said.

"I think we should consult Rachel and Grace about that first," Janet said.

"But Grace doesna want a pony."

"I think your sister was just being generous."

Annabella considered that possibility. "She can ride Snow White anytime she wants."

"I'm sure that will make her very happy," Janet said.

They went inside and stopped. Samson had obviously sneaked inside while the door was open. The tray holding the pastries was on the floor, along with crumbs and jam. Delilah looked up from where she was licking the tray. Samson, his face smudged with powder and filling, looked out from under a chair, guilt all over his face as he wriggled in ingratiating supplication.

Grace went over to Samson. "Bad dog!" she said.

The puppy lay down and rolled over, his tongue lolling out pitiably.

Torquil appeared then and looked aghast as he saw the remnants of the cook's pastries and the guilty-looking animals. Grace grabbed the puppy she'd just been chastising, clutching him to her. "I spilled the pastries," she said.

His severe face bent a little. "So I noticed, Lady Grace."

Grace straightened at that and tried to look as regal as possible. "I am sorry."

"No harm done," he said with the slightest twitch to his lips. "Cook can make a few more for afternoon tea."

"Tea?"

Janet had not been offered tea in the two days they had been here. But mayhap that was because Braemoor had been indisposed.

"Yes, my lady. My lord asked me to serve it this afternoon. He thought the wee lassies might enjoy it."

And obviously he had not cared whether or not she did.

"Thank you," she said.

"I will serve it in the nursery," he said, referring to the room near Janet's that had been turned to that use. The lasses had been moved there, along with a bed for Colin when he was not with Janet.

So Braemoor would not be joining them. Good riddance. And yet she felt a streak of disappointment.

Janet told herself she felt that way because she just wanted to learn more of his plans. Where he was going. How long he would be gone. Then, and only then, could she make her own plans.

"Thank you," she said. "I understand the marquis is leaving tonight."

A flicker of surprise ran across his face. So he did not yet know. Which meant something might have prompted his sudden journey. But what? What could have happened in the past day?

And was he well enough? She kept telling herself that her only concern was to rid herself of him. And yet he'd been so exhausted upon arriving at Braemoor that she had worried about him. Should he really be taking a long trip again soon? And why in the devil did she even care?

Curse the man, but she did. She did not understand why,

any more than she understood why he had gone to so much trouble to get the ponies.

But she would find out where he was going. And how long he would be gone. And what he intended for her and for Lochaene.

Braemoor came down to supper. He'd planned a good supper tonight since he did not know when he would have another. After their short exchange today, he did not expect Janet to come down for the meal.

She did.

She had apparently asked Torquil for the time he'd planned to eat, and had sworn him to silence. When Neil went down at his usual time of seven, there were two places set at the large table.

He poured himself a glass of wine and waited, remembering how much he hated to eat here alone.

Neil downed the goblet of wine even as Janet entered the room. She looked lovely, even in the black mourning dress. Her eyes were the color of the evening sky and her hair framed her face instead of being pulled back into severe braids or a knot. Her cheeks were the color of rose, not pale as he had noticed at Lochaene. A touch of some color?

He stood. "My lady."

Her gaze met his and held it. "My lord," she replied. "I am pleased you are joining me."

He went over to where she stood and pulled out the chair for her. She sat and waited until he went back to his own seat. "I wanted to thank you," she said. "I was not very . . . gracious earlier. My daughters love the ponies."

"I want you, and the lasses, to enjoy your stay here."

Her eyes regarded him steadily. She played with her wineglass. "When are you leaving?"

"After supper. You wished to say farewell?" he asked dryly.

"No, I just wondered what . . . the restrictions were."

"Restrictions?"

"I am your prisoner, my lord. Mayhap not with bars, but with your threat to take my son away."

"No threat, my lady. I just wanted you to be aware of the danger at Lochaene."

"Then why do I feel as if it were a threat? That I had no choice?" Her eyes bore into his. "Have you ever thought of what it must be like to be a woman, my lord? If not, it might well be informative.

"Everyone," she added quietly, "tells you they know better than you do. Everyone assumes you are too weak or too brainless to manage your own affairs. Everyone assumes that you are content to be a pawn in some game, and that you can never understand the affairs of men.

"My daughters," she continued, "will never learn that from me."

Neil heard the pain in her voice. "I did not intend to imply that," he said. "I find that I am . . . not always good with words. I wanted merely to protect."

"You have never asked what I wanted," she said. "I wrote you because I felt trapped. I do not think I expected an answer. But I had hoped that you remembered something about me. A letter to Cumberland. That was all I wanted, all I hoped for."

"I wanted to do more," he said quietly.

"By putting me in another cage, my lord?"

"I do not want Braemoor to be that for you. I thought—"

"*You* thought. That is the problem, my lord. And now you go away and leave me here. I do not know what is happening with my properties. With my son's inheritance. I do not know your true motives."

"You cannot believe they are honorable?"

"Quite frankly, my lord, no," she said. "You are kind with my children. But then you were kind to me years ago. I do not want them hurt as I was."

He had told himself all these years that he had done the best thing for her. Now he realized he had done the best thing for himself. He had not been able to tell her of the madness in the family. He had not wanted to see fear in her eyes. Nor the rejection he thought he would find.

Was it too late now to tell her that . . . tell her what? That he had not enough respect for her then, either, to tell her the truth?

Had he used his suspicions toward the Campbells as an excuse to be near her, to revive something that had never had a chance, that could never be?

"When I return," he said, "I will take you back to Lochaene."

"No ifs?"

"I hope you will accept having some of my people there."

"People you trust—or people I trust?"

"Someone *you* trust," he said.

"How long will you be gone?"

"I do not know."

He wished he could read her intentions. He did not doubt that her mind was working actively to find some way out of the cage she'd just mentioned. Nor did he fool himself that his words had been heeded. They quite simply meant nothing. He had ensured that years ago.

Torquil appeared, the slightest twinkle in his eyes. He poured wine into her glass and stepped aside as a footman entered with plates of food. Neil knew he had more servants than he needed or wanted, but they needed the positions, and so he had added one by one, most of them, like Torquil, not very competent.

Neil's attention went entirely to his guest. He was fascinated with Janet, with the way she regarded him steadily. He could not quite read her expressions.

She was after something. He steeled himself against a need to say aye to whatever she wanted. He was sure she wanted something he could not give her.

But she merely sipped her wine. "Did Torquil tell you about the pastries?"

He raised an eyebrow. "Evidently not," he replied.

"Samson and Delilah ate all the cook's pastries. I had left them on a table when you arrived with the ponies."

It had been days since they had exchanged pleasantries. She was very definitely up to something. He waited.

"Are you going to Edinburgh? If so, I have some letters. . . ."

He doubted very much whether she had letters. She wanted to know where he was going. "Nay," he said. "I have some properties to the west that I must see to."

Her eyes narrowed. "New properties?"

"Aye."

"Jacobite properties?"

He said nothing.

"Given in service to the butcher?"

"Given to my predecessor for *his* services," he said. "My own were not nearly that deserving."

"Deserving enough to take guardianship of my son," she observed dryly. Then she turned her gaze away. "I meant this to be a pleasant evening," she said.

"You have accomplished your goal, my lady. It is always a pleasant evening when you are at the table."

"A pretty speech," she said.

"An honest one," he replied.

She looked skeptical but said nothing. She tried again. "Will you be going to Lochaene?"

"I do not plan to do so," he said.

"Surely you can tell me if you plan to be away several days or a week or a month."

"I doubt a month, my lady," he said. "But in truth, I do not know. We are starting something new at Calleigh, a property some forty miles from here. The property was deserted when it came to my cousin, and Braemoor has too many tenants. I have offered some of the younger men free land if they will move there and tend sheep. Then we can keep all of Braemoor in farming. I want to see if all is going well. Their trust, like yours, is tenuous at best." That was the truth, but only part of it. He disliked misleading her, but he had no intention of telling her that he, for some inexplicable reason, was going to meet the man responsible for nearly killing him, a man who was wanted by the crown.

She studied him, as if she knew he was holding something back. "If you are going to be gone for any amount of time, I would like to go to Edinburgh."

He raised an eyebrow. "Edinburgh."

"I would like to purchase some cloth to make dresses for my daughters."

"And would you take them with you? And the lad?"

"Aye, I would not leave them," Janet confirmed.

He wondered what she really wanted. He'd never met a woman who cared less about fripperies. Even for the children. In addition, they were all still formally in mourning. Did she plan to make a special plea to Cumberland to have him removed as guardian?

It would do no good, he knew. And the journey could be dangerous, especially if her Campbell in-laws learned of it.

He damned Will. His demand could not come at a worse time but Neil knew he had to leave tonight. Otherwise, Burke would probably lurk around the property, putting everything he'd worked for in jeopardy.

"I think not, Countess," he said at last. "The roads are dangerous. Edinburgh itself is dangerous for those known to be Jacobites."

"And so I am to remain here alone."

"Not alone, madam. You have the children, books, servants. You have horses to ride and ponies to teach your daughters to ride. You need only to go to the village to find some good cloth if you wish to have dresses made." He paused for a moment, then added, "I thought you might welcome my absence."

"To live in someone else's home?"

"Better than one with dangerous enemies."

"I might ride?"

"If you take Kevin. He will stay here with you. 'Tis not because I fear you fleeing, Janet. I do not think you would do that with the children here. But 'tis still dangerous in Scotland. There are desperate men. I would not like to see you harmed when under my protection."

"Your *protection*," she said. "I feel more like a prisoner." She paused, then struck out blindly. "I should have realized there is a reason behind every thing you do. You taught me that lesson well."

It was the second time tonight she had directly mentioned that disastrous time. He wished he could tell her that he had loved her then, loved her as much as a man could ever love a woman, loved her so much that he had let her go. That he still loved her, that it was pure agony to look into her eyes and see that distrust.

Tell her why.

He couldn't. He did not know how to rip out his deepest fears and express them.

And he needed to leave soon if he were to change clothes and meet Burke. For a fleeting second, he wondered if he would be back at all. He knew he was a fool for even considering going. But Will obviously needed something more than money. Something only he could provide. It was the reason he had not been killed.

It has nothing to do with you. How many times had he told himself that in the past few hours?

But he had done damn few bloody good things in his life, and he remembered those children in the mountains, and knew that spending the winter there could kill them.

Rory had left him Braemoor. He had made sure there would be no question that Neil would inherit. He owed his cousin something. He knew what Rory would do. What the Black Knave would do.

He owed it to himself to help the innocents that Rory had fought so hard to protect.

He stood. "I must go, madam. I plan to leave tonight."

Her eyes narrowed. "Tonight? Why not the morning?"

He damned himself. He should have said nothing.

"I wish to be there at dawn."

She just looked at him as if he'd been struck mad. She did not realize how close she was to the truth.

He rose from the table. "I want you to be happy, Janet," he said. "I swear I will get you back to Lochaene as soon as it is safe."

But he saw only doubt written on her face as he bowed, then hurried to his room before he said more than what would be wise.

Chapter Eighteen

The children were all asleep when Janet went upstairs. She leaned down and pulled covers over them, her hands lingering on Annabella for a moment before leaving the side of the bed. She hesitated at the cradle where Colin slept, then leaned down and kissed him lightly. She told Clara that she would leave him with her this night.

When she returned to her room, Lucy was waiting for her. She helped Janet take off her gown and started to brush it out, but it was obvious she was impatient to get away. Kevin, no doubt, was the reason.

That suited Janet's purposes. "I will finish," she said. "You can go and see Kevin. I will not need you again tonight."

Lucy's plain face brightened. "Thank you, my lady."

Janet waited until she knew the girl was gone, then she looked out the door. No one was in the hallways. Not Torquil or Trilby, who had been hovering about, anxious to do anything she could. *Anything you need or want, you need merely to ask. His* words. Well, now she wished to explore.

She was aware of the location of his room down the hall. Other rooms were up on the next floor, including one she knew had once been occupied by his cousin, Rory, the late marquis, before Neil had assumed the title. The nursery had once been there, too, before the current marquis had apparently transformed a room closer to her for the children. An unexpectedly thoughtful act by a man who was a bachelor.

But then everything about him was unexpected . . . puzzling. Mayhap while he was gone she could extract information from the butler or others around Braemoor.

Now, however, she had another goal. She went up the steps and looked at the door to the room once occupied by Rory Forbes. She felt like a thief even as she reminded herself of Neil's words. She was going to use them against him, and something inside rebelled against that.

She tried one door and looked in. Dust layered old pieces of furniture, which included a narrow bed and wardrobe. She went over the wardrobe and opened it. Clothes were neatly folded inside, although they had a musty smell. She went through them. They were a strange combination of the practical and flamboyant: leather trousers together with plaid trews, a simple coat beside a purple waistcoat.

She took out the trousers. They were obviously tailored for a tall man, probably as tall as Neil. She took them and a linen shirt and simple jacket, then replaced everything else back into neat piles. Then she looked out the door. No one was in sight. She crept back down the stairs with her find and hurried into her room.

Then she held up the clothes against her. She would have to do a bit of tailoring herself, but she could manage that. She had cut down clothes for the lasses.

She put a log in the fireplace, watching the dying embers catch. Then she found a needle and thread, and small knife. She dragged a heavy chair over to the window and started cutting as she kept an eye on the stable.

Something was very odd about his leaving tonight. It did not make sense. She wanted to know where he was going. And whether it had anything to do with her. Knowledge was a weapon, and she badly needed one at the moment.

She cut off part of the trouser legs, then tried them on.

They were huge around her waist. She needed a belt. She had not considered that. Another trip would be necessary.

Janet slipped them off, put them in the wardrobe and changed into her shift and dressing gown. She looked again out the room. It was nearly midnight, and all was quiet. Only a few torches in wall sconces gave light. She slipped out the door and closed it quietly behind her and turned, suddenly finding herself face-to-face with Braemoor.

He looked even more startled than she felt. He was dressed in dark clothing and had slung a black cloak around his shoulders.

"My lord," she said.

"My lady," he replied with wry amusement. "I did not expect you to be up this late. Can Torquil fetch you something?"

"I wanted only some milk," she said, "and I can fetch that myself."

His gaze moved up and down her body. His eyes were dark and the shadows did nothing to lighten them, but she saw something like desire flash across his face. "You look much too bonny in that," he said.

The night robe was white, and her hair was down, ready to be braided for the night. She felt naked without the usual armor of petticoats and drawers, without the severe knot and matronly cap. She crossed her arms against her still-full breasts.

Her eyes went back to his face. It was shadowed with new beard, and a lock of thick dark hair fell over his forehead. In all black garments, he looked dangerous, even mysterious. He did not look like the Neil she had come to know in the past several weeks. That Neil was practical and reserved, and sure of himself. A man who had been a stranger and intent on remaining that way. This Neil had a dangerous glint in his eyes. He looked more brigand than lord.

She could not take her gaze from those eyes.

Not even when he bent his head and his lips captured hers and she found herself responding just as she had several weeks ago. Her lips remembered that kiss at Lochaene the night before he had left. The night he was so badly injured. Now he was going out into the night again and fear ran through her.

She did not want to care. But she did. Desperately.

His arms went around her and crushed her to him. His kiss deepened, his tongue entering her mouth.

She cautioned herself. Remember what happened last time. It had obviously meant nothing to him. And yet . . .

Her tongue met his. They tasted each other, then sought those secret, sensitive places that ignited so many feelings. She felt small in his embrace, small and protected, and it was a good feeling. She did not want it to feel good.

She tried to move away, but his grip on her did not relax. He closed his mouth and it left hers, but moved to her cheek. He kissed her with all the gentleness she expected existed in the world, his lips progressing ever so slowly up her face, each touch a tender whisper of a kiss until he reached her forehead. Then his lips rested there, and his arms cradled her.

She felt the hard planes of his body, felt him tense, and her own body melded itself to his. It felt so . . . right, just as it had so long ago. But then there had been a sweetness and exploration, and now the emotions were bolder, stronger, full of such conflicting emotions that they created a blizzard of feelings.

They had been there, inside, untapped. And now they flowed unhampered, sparking and sizzling, hurtling her into a world without limits or barriers. She was so hungry for his touch, for the feel of his body.

One of her hands touched the back of his head, letting the hair tangle between her fingers. Her body ached with internal tension and fierce wanting. She did not know how she could be so wanton now; she only knew she could not let him go, not now, not without scaling that wall he always erected between them.

Janet saw his quiet eyes blaze with fire, felt his hand

stroke her neck. His other arm remained around her, holding her as if he never wanted to let it go.

Neil told himself to stop, but he had never wanted anything as much in his life as to take her inside his room and make love to her, slowly and exquisitely. He wanted her so much it caused gut-wrenching agony. He wanted it even more knowing the bloody fool errand upon which he was about to embark. He felt the passion in her, the passion he had seen in her protection of the girls, in the way she held her son. She had tried to hide it, mayhap even tried to bury it, but it was there. And it was something that had always eluded him. It was, he knew, what had attracted him so many years ago.

Those dark blue eyes had been like a lodestone to someone who had always lived life as an observer.

He put his face next to hers, felt its softness, the smoothness of her skin, and the contact was like a balm to his soul. His arms tightened around her as he tried to capture the feeling and keep it in his mind and heart. For a moment in time, he allowed himself to savor every sensation, to bask in the intimacy of their touch. He belonged here. He had always belonged here.

And he knew he could have it. He could explain why he had done the unforgivable years ago. He could tell her he loved her, had always loved her, would always love her. And in this moment, he knew she would accept it. Accept him.

Dear God, he needed that.

She looked up at him, her gaze steady and searching but also misty with the same sensations flowing through him.

Then what?

A marriage to a man who might turn into a monster.

With a groan, he pulled away. How do you give up every dream you have ever had? Especially when it was so near.

You did, if you had honor.

His hand caught her face and his fingers memorized every feature, every curve, every expression. She was gazing at him with puzzlement now. "I must go," he said, and yet he could not move his hand.

She did not move for a moment. Instead, their gazes locked together. Raw emotions ran through hers—desire, need, hurt, bewilderment. They both seemed unable to move, as if they were locked together by some irresistible force. "Do not go," she finally whispered.

The words made his heart pound. Something large and painful lodged in his throat.

Trust. She was offering trust. She was offering herself. He did not believe he could hurt more. He leaned toward her and his lips brushed hers. It was a farewell kiss, and she knew it. She stepped back, her gaze never moving from his. Her face was set, her teeth worrying her bottom lip.

He wanted to offer her the truth. And his heart.

But nothing had changed. He could never offer her marriage. And he could not bear seeing pity—or horror—in her eyes. Would the truth help, or only make the present—and future—more painful?

His hand touched her face again, then turned toward the stairs. It was more than past time to leave. Burke would be sorely tried.

Mayhap even enough to try to finish what he had started days ago.

Stunned by the impact of her emotions and her own actions, Janet leaned against the other side of the door. How many times would she humiliate herself before learning he did not want her? Why in God's name had she offered herself with those three words? *Do not go.*

Because she would have sworn she saw love in his eyes.

When would she learn not to see what she wanted to see?

The door was too heavy to hear anything, to tell whether he had left or not. She waited for a moment, wondering whether he would knock. Yet deep inside, she knew he would not.

At least he had not seen the clothes on her bed.

She took a deep breath. How could he still affect her this way? What was it she thought she saw in him? Her legs felt weak as she walked to the bed. She was trembling all over. She clung to a post for a moment, then scolded herself. She finally stood upright and took the clothes, then went over to the window and looked down like some imprisoned princess in the fairy tale she had so recently read to the girls.

She had barely reached it when she saw him stride across the courtyard as if he had a meeting with the devil. It was in the square set of his shoulders, the long and yet somehow hesitant steps. He turned and looked up, and she looked down, unwilling to dart out of sight. He stared upward for a moment, then disappeared into the stable.

In minutes, he was riding away on a large dark horse. Together they looked like a shadow. She watched as the horse stretched into a slow trot and he turned right toward the village. She understood that his new properties were west, in the other direction.

Janet slipped off her dressing gown and shift and pulled on the trousers she had just altered. She did not have time to find a belt so she cut a strip from the bed cloth and tied it around her to keep the trousers from slipping away. Then she pulled on the shirt and jacket.

It was too late to follow him. But she could ride off some of her own emotions. *Foolish. It would be a fool thing to do.* He had told her not to ride without an escort. But she had to find a moment of freedom. To feel control for just an hour of time.

She wrapped a cloak around her to cover her costume, though everyone should be abed this night. Then she ran down the stairs, across the hall and through the door toward the stables.

Cautiously, she opened the door. She left the door open slightly while her eyes accustomed themselves to the darkness. Then she went to the tack room. Sleeping quarters for two grooms, including young Jamie, were on the other side of the wall, so she tried to move stealthily. She picked the lightest saddle and found a mare that looked fast. She quickly saddled the animal, then walked the horse outside. Only then did she rise easily into the saddle, remembering how she used to ride astride with her brother a lifetime ago.

She walked the animal down the path that Braemoor had taken. The moon was full, the night a rare clear one.

The horse felt good under her. If she had not been intent on trying to find out where Braemoor was going at this time of night, she would have enjoyed every moment of it.

There had been something about him tonight, though. Something odd and mysterious. She kept trying to tell herself that was the reason she'd lost all remnant of reason. He'd been different.

His horse had been trotting when he'd turned on the road. Mayhap she could make up those few moments of time. Yet she would have to be careful. She did not want him seeing her.

For a few glorious moments she let the mare run. She leaned forward against the wind and her body moved with the smooth easy gait of the mare. The road was straight and she kept her eyes open for anything ahead. Nothing.

She reached the village. An old man was walking unsteadily, apparently having been drinking someplace. She pulled up the horse. "Have you seen anyone riding this way?"

"Nay," he said and trudged on.

Could he be that far in front?

It had been a mad thing to do anyway. She turned the horse and started back. Mayhap she could put her in the stall without anyone knowing. It had been a small adventure, in any event. She had slowed to a walk when she heard horses just ahead. The fields had given way to a stand of trees that ran along a stream. She pulled the mare back into the woods and watched through the trees.

Two riders came from between the trees just ahead and turned back toward Braemoor. She could only see the back of them. One rode well and wore a black cloak; the other rode awkwardly in a way that pricked at her memory. Braemoor was one. She was sure of that. His height gave him away, as did the easy seat.

And the other . . .

And why would he be meeting someone out here in the middle of the night? Why not at Braemoor? She'd had no idea what she might find, or even what she'd hoped to discover. Mayhap she even hoped she would meet him and he would return with her. It had been impulsive and unwise.

She'd just needed to display some independence, some control.

And now she knew no more than she had before.

She waited until the two disappeared from sight, and then she rode to where they had exited the woods. A path. She turned and went down it. It seemed almost to disappear at times, but her mount seemed oblivious to the heavy brush. Finally they emerged in a clearing. A cottage sat alongside a stream.

Although it was a cool night, no smoke rose from the chimney, and shutters covered the windows. After a moment's indecision, she dismounted and went to the door. She knocked several times, but no one answered. After a moment, she opened the door and entered.

The interior smelled musty, and the ashes in the fireplace were cold. The moonlight coming through the door allowed her to see a plate and cup on the table. There was also the smell of an unwashed body lingering in the room. The cottage had obviously been abandoned, yet someone had stayed here, someone who had not used the fireplace. That meant the occupant had not wanted anyone to know he was here.

She sat at the table and looked around. Her eyes became accustomed to the dim light. A large pot sat at the side of the fireplace. How long had it been empty? And who had lived here?

She had not been here before, did not even know it existed. She wondered whether someone had lived here eight years earlier when she visited Braemoor. But then, she had been so consumed with Neil that she had noticed little else.

The questions were intriguing enough to bring her back tomorrow. She might have to escape Kevin, but she could manage that. Maybe the cottage held secrets about Braemoor. Who had he met here? Why had they not come up to the house?

Did it have something to do with her? Or was there some other nefarious reason?

Braemoor and Burke rode fast. Braemoor needed the distraction for a mind constantly recalling every second of his encounter with Janet. How could he have let it happen?

The night robe? Her hair? His upcoming journey, which could well end in disaster?

Whatever, it was well that he had told Burke he would go tonight, rather than in several days. Now he would get this business done, then visit his properties. By then he hoped to have his emotions back in control.

He spurred his mount, leaving a cursing Burke behind again. He knew most of the way, needed help only on the very last part of the journey, and he did not want to be seen with the man. Burke looked exactly like what he was: a cutpurse.

He judged they would reach the mountains by dawn, then could lose themselves in the mist that usually covered the mountains.

The hours droned on. They avoided roads, riding across fields and through the heather-covered fields. Neither of them suggested stopping except to rest and water the horses. Neil had brought along oatmeal, cheese and hard bread, and they shared that at dawn, then started up into the mountains. It was a relentless pace, and hard on the horses, but Scottish animals were bred for sturdiness.

They stopped at one stream to let them drink, and when they were to start again Burke approached him. "I must blindfold you."

"I think not."

"Then you will go no farther."

Neil considered that. "Then you will not have the funds."

Burke had his pistol out now. "I think I will, Braemoor."

No fawning "my lord" here.

"And what would your lord say?"

It was a guess, but when Burke's eyes widened, Neil knew he was right. Will indeed came from the nobility. And his name was obviously not Will. Then who was he?

Neil's curiosity flared even more than it had. He knew from Burke's eyes that he would not go one foot farther until Neil agreed to be blindfolded. It was a stupid thing to do here in the mountains, even if he were not accompanied by a man who had previously tried to kill him. But he had come this far, and his interest in Will had increased with every step. Mayhap it was time to take chances. He shrugged. "All right, but it will be a piece of my clothes, not yours."

Burke shrugged. He was obviously willing to be generous now that he had won this concession.

"How far is it?" Braemoor said.

Burke frowned.

"God's breath, I will know when I arrive whether it has been one hour or three," Braemoor said as he took his dirk from his belt and pulled his shirt out of his trousers, then cut a strip off. "Do you at least trust me to put it on?"

Burke looked startled, then suspicious. He obviously had not expected such cooperation. He snorted, then said, "I will do it."

"Not too tightly," Neil said lightly. "And please remember that to get my money, you must keep me alive."

"You do not have it with you?"

"I am not that big a fool, my friend," he said. "You had a choice between me or the money."

Burke cursed loudly, then roughly took the cloth from Neil's hand and tied it tightly around his eyes.

Neil was holding to the reins and easily found the stirrups to mount. Once in the saddle, he felt the reins jerked away.

After another pause they started moving. For a moment, he wondered whether he really wanted to stake his life on Burke's riding ability, but the man had obviously been in and out of the mountains. He tried to relax. He tried to think of something else, but that meant Janet. He did not know if he was prepared to revisit that kiss.

He tried to turn his mind to the estates, but it kept wandering back to her, to the glazed look in her eyes. How he wanted her to look that way all the time, to look up at him with wonder.

And then his thoughts wandered into dangerous territory: Mayhap his mother's madness would not touch him.

Could he take that chance? More important, could he ask Janet to take that risk?

The questions haunted him as they climbed up the mountain. Mist moistened his face, then rain pelted it like tiny icy needles. After what seemed like hours, they came to a stop. He reached back and pulled the blindfold from his face and found himself in a thicket of trees. He slid from the saddle.

Burke had already dismounted and was leading his horse directly into dense woods. Neil followed as the rain continued to beat down upon him. They wound around a barely visible path, then reached an opening in the mountain. Once inside, he recognized the interior of the cave. A fire heated the interior. The young girl he remembered from before stooped before the heat.

The man who called himself Will appeared from the back of the cave. He was dressed in a kilted plaid that came over his shoulder. His cheeks were covered by new beard which only partially hid the scar that ran down one side of his face. His eyes looked tired, and he seemed thinner than he had before. Neil was startled to see that they were nearly the same height. He had not recalled that, but then he had been on the ground most of the time.

Cold, blue eyes regarded him carefully, then he looked toward Burke. "You did well," he said.

Burke looked uncomfortable. "He came on his own."

"You did not have to force him?"

"Nay," Burke said and cast a pleading look at Neil. He obviously did not want his leader to know that, in fact, Neil had taken *him*.

Will stared at him. Hard. "A trick, my lord?"

Neil shrugged. "I wanted to see the man who would nearly kill me and then say I owed *him*."

"I must say I dinna think you would take it so to heart," the bandit said wryly.

"Then why did you send your man for me?"

"Hope, I suppose," Will said. "Come walk with me."

"In the rain?"

"Why not?"

Neil stared at him for a moment, then nodded his head. "I need to look after my horse. Do you have any oats?"

"Hell, we donna have any food for the wee ones, much less an animal. He will have to satisfy himself with the grass."

"I'll hobble him then. If it is safe."

"From the bloody English? Aye. They do not care for our fine Scottish weather."

He watched as Neil took hobbles from his saddlebag and quickly secured the horse. Burke's mount was tied to a tree. Will apparently saw his disapproval. "I will take care of him after we walk." He led the way to a spot partially sheltered by overhanging rock.

Will leaned against the wall, putting one foot against it. "Why did you come?"

"To tell you the truth, I really do not know."

"I found a jack of spades on you. Also known as the black knave."

"Are you asking me if I am that legend?"

"Aye," Will said softly.

"That is a long jump in reasoning."

"I have also heard that Braemoor was one place where . . . one might find help."

"Is that what stayed your hand?"

"Aye," Will said. "And something else. I heard that the Marquis of Braemoor had been at Lochaene. I had not equated that with an English gentleman until you spoke."

"And that would mean something?"

"If you lived, aye."

"You believed the countess might complete what you started."

"I know you had met before."

"How?"

"Rumor, my lord. I have several spies in the surrounding villages. They help with information for a portion of whatever we take."

"Why would you care about Lochaene?"

"I knew the countess long ago."

Neil did not like the jealousy that rose inside him, nor did he like the intent way the man looked at him.

"You did not answer my question, my lord. Are you the Black Knave? Or do you know who he is?"

"I am a king's man," Neil said.

"So must be the Knave, if he has survived this long."

"I heard he was killed nearly a year ago."

"Then what were you doing with those cards?"

"I happen to like them."

Will was silent for a moment, then said slowly, reluctantly, "I have to get the children out of here before winter or they will never survive. One of them belongs to a clan marked for extinction. Cumberland will kill him if he finds him."

"And you think I can help?"

"I think by being here you show a certain . . . interest."

"It could be a trap."

Will's eyes looked anguished. "I canna go anywhere with this face nor barter for passage with money I do not have."

"Not enough people to kill and rob?"

"The word gets out," Will answered without apology. "The English avoid this area, but soon . . ."

"You would trust me?"

"I donna trust anyone, but I have bloody little choice at the moment. I canna leave these children alone here to travel far, and these woods have been hunted out. I had only hope that you had some association with the Black Knave and that if so you would come willingly." His gaze met Neil's steadily. "You did."

"You have no friends?"

"Most died at Culloden Moor. The others have been hunted down."

"What is your name? I know it is not Will."

"It is unimportant. I do not want to endanger anyone."

"It *is* important . . . if you want my help."

"Why?"

"If I am committing treason, I would rather like to know who I am doing it for."

"*If?*"

"There is a large reward still for the Black Knave, although most consider him dead. What is to prevent you from claiming it once you are safe? A word to someone, and it will be my neck on the line."

Will looked at him for a long time, then asked, "What were you doing at Lochaene?"

"The countess is a widow. I was appointed her son's guardian."

"Why?"

Will's blue eyes were intense, probing. And familiar.

Why had he not noticed it before? Because he had been so bloody ill? Or because he had not wanted to see it? Or had he noticed and buried it somewhere inside? Was that what had brought him here?

"You are a Leslie," he said. It was not a question.

A muscle throbbed in the man's cheek.

"A cousin, mayhap, to Janet Leslie? Or a brother?"

Another silence.

Neil tried again. "Alexander Leslie?"

A muscle throbbed in the man's neck. "Aye," he said after a moment's pause.

"She believes you dead," Neil said with some anger.

Leslie ignored it. "You have not answered my question. Why were you appointed guardian?"

"I asked for it. She wrote me. The Campbells were spending what there was left of her husband's inheritance and keeping her virtually a prisoner."

"Why you?"

"We had . . . met years ago. I was the . . . only one she had to turn to. Everyone else, including you, was dead. Or thought to be."

"I did . . . not know. I knew her husband had died, but I thought . . ."

"Why did you not try to reach her?"

"I was badly wounded. It took nearly six months before I could function again, and then I was marked with the scar. I knew I would be on a wanted list. Both Janet and I would be safer if I were believed dead. Do you think I wanted her to see me hang? Or get her involved now? And she would have tried if she knew I lived. Janet would risk everything for those she loves."

"She has the right to know. She feels all alone."

"She has you, and for that I am grateful."

"I fear she doesna feel the same gratitude."

Alexander straightened. "If you have done her harm . . ."

"I have, but only for her own good."

Alexander's eyes stared at him, weighing him. "Burke was told that a woman had let it be known that a wealthy Englishman would be crossing this way. I did not know if it was Janet. If it had been, she would have had a bloody good reason, and you damn well would have deserved it."

"So that is why you sent me back there? If it had been her, it would have been easy enough to let me die."

"Aye," Alexander said. "Since you are alive, I can only assume you have another enemy."

"So does your sister," Neil said. "One of the Campbells wants her dead. Someone cut her saddle cinch. She is at Braemoor now."

Alexander looked stunned. "I did not know that."

"You should cultivate better spies."

"I have not been able to pay them lately."

"Who are those with you?"

"Orphans I found along the way. As I said, one belongs to an outlawed clan. They have no one else. I was hoping they might find family or friends in France."

"If not?"

Alexander sighed. "Then I will see to them."

Neil tried to equate the man who had ambushed him and would have killed him without a qualm with this protector of children. And as the brother of the woman he loved.

Alexander had not been with his father and sister when they had visited Braemoor years ago. And apparently he'd never been told of Neil's offer of marriage, nor its disastrous aftermath. They had never met elsewhere. The old marquis and his oldest son Donald had rarely left Braemoor. On the rare occasions when they had traveled, Neil had been left at Braemoor.

Janet had spoken of her brother with great pride and affection. According to her, he had been the gentlest, most honorable and bravest of men. Now he had turned to savaging travelers.

"I will make arrangements for passage to France," Neil said abruptly. "But I want to tell Janet you are alive."

"Nay," Alexander said. "Mayhap when I am safe. Not now."

More lies. And, like his own eight years ago, for good purposes. But he was beginning to wonder whether a lie could ever be justified. In the grand cause of protecting someone, exactly how much pain was caused?

"Swear it," Alexander said.

"I will consider it," Neil retorted. "I make no promises."

"You do not know her," Alexander pleaded. "She will come to me. You will not be able to stop her. And it is far too dangerous."

Neil regarded him icily. "Too bad you were not so protective when she married a Campbell."

"I tried," Alexander said. "But she loved those girls. And someone had hurt . . ." His voice broke off as he narrowed his eyes. "You. It was you who—"

"It seems we both failed her," Neil said simply.

"Damn you," Alexander said.

Neil had no defense. Not now. Not for this man. "I have some food I will leave with you. And some money. Enough so that Burke can buy some more food, and even some blankets. I will return as soon as I can arrange passage."

He knew from Alexander's expression that he wanted to refuse the offer, but he would not, For the children's sake, he would not.

Alexander nodded stiffly.

"Burke," Neil said. "Can he be trusted?"

"With my life," Alexander said, not explaining further.

"I will leave as soon as my horse is rested."

Alexander stared at him for several moments, a frown further marring what once must have been a very striking face. Then he turned, left the shelter of the rock overhang and walked into the cave.

Neil waited for several moments. If he'd ever had any doubt of the damage he had done years ago, he knew it now. It was partly because of him that Janet had married a Campbell. And now, because Alexander was right about the danger to her, he would lie to her again.

And this was one lie she would never forgive.

Chapter Nineteen

Janet visited the cottage on the second day after Braemoor left. It had taken her that long to get away from Kevin's anxious eyes. He obviously had divided loyalties.

She knew Braemoor had told him to ride with her because the roads were dangerous. But she was the lady of Lochaene, where he was employed. She saw the conflict in his eyes, and so she had waited until Torquil had sent him on an errand.

The truth was that she wanted to investigate the cottage on her own.

The night Braemoor had left, she had been able to get the horse back to the stables without anyone seeing her. She had spent the next day with her daughters. She'd prowled through the empty rooms, taking clothes that could be cut down for dresses, then reading to the children from a book in the library. She played with Colin. She loved them all more than life itself, and she realized she could bear anything in order to keep them with her—and safe.

At the same time, they made it impossible for her to find safety for them. If she was alone, she would not hesitate for a moment to flee from Braemoor. But how to take four children—the youngest not yet one?

So she tried to tame her restlessness and await her opportunity. On the second afternoon, Kevin was gone, and Jamie was exercising a horse. After helping Clara put the children down for a nap, she saddled a mare.

She quickly rode out of the courtyard before anyone stopped her and down the road to town, hoping that she could find the overgrown path that led to the cottage. She had not yet asked Torquil or anyone about it for fear of showing her interest. She wanted to get there before anyone else did.

Janet found the path after having passed it once. She hoped she would not run into Kevin along the way and was grateful when she finally saw the opening. She guided her horse between two ancient trees, then continued until she found the cottage. It looked lonely, almost as if it were waiting for someone. An overgrown garden sat adjacent to the house. She dismounted, tied her horse to a tree branch and went over to the garden.

She stooped down and readily identified some of the plants. Herbs.

Then she went to the cottage door. It opened easily and she stepped inside, leaving the door open. A layer of dust covered the floor. She raised it with every step she took. How long had it been empty? And who had lived here?

A woman. Little touches told her that. Curtains at the window. Pots of flowers long dead. A rug thrown across the dirt floor.

She wondered why scavengers had not looted it. Was the cottage under Braemoor's protection? If so, why?

She moved around the cottage, looking for more evidence of the man who had ridden out with Braemoor. Who was he? But there were no clues. Then she saw a woman's dress bundled up in a corner. She held it up. The simple garment was made of a good soft wool and obviously meant for a tall and slender woman. Other than that, she saw nothing to mark the owner. She left abruptly, intent on finding out more about the woman from the servants at Braemoor.

She rode back slowly, enjoying the fresh air even while

questions pounded at her. She sought answers as to why Braemoor had left in the middle of the night and met someone secretly in an abandoned cottage. She had once thought him so honest and direct. It had been one of the things she had liked best about him.

Kevin met her halfway back. His eyes were anxious, and she sought to allay that anxiety.

"My lady," he said. "You . . ."

"Do not worry, Kevin," she interrupted. "I am quite safe. I just wanted to go riding and no one was around."

"The marquis . . ."

"I know the marquis worries," she said. "But I needed some fresh air, and this mare needed exercise." She paused, then changed the subject. "Are you planning to wed Lucy?"

The tactic worked. Kevin's face grew even rosier. "Aye," he said. "If she will have me."

"I do not believe there is much doubt about that," she said. "But I am pleased you are not trifling with her."

"Nay, my lady, I would no' do that."

"How are you and young Jamie getting along?"

"He is a good lad," Kevin said. "Quick and willing."

"Has he lived here long?"

"All his life. He was here with his father, who beat him. The marquis indentured him and sent the father away, then freed him." Kevin's words were full of awe and respect.

Janet just wished the marquis would free her. But Kevin's words made her wonder. She kept hearing these small stories. Except they were not small at all. They were very big. She had heard something similar from Torquil. And the cook.

And yet except for a kiss or two, Braemoor showed so little emotion, said so little about other people. She always had the impression of aloneness. Even when he had courted her years ago, he had been quiet about his background, about friends. Now that she thought about it, she had never seen him in friendly conversation with another person.

She had never met anyone as puzzling as Braemoor.

Whenever she thought she understood a little about him, he did something else that completely negated her earlier opinion. She knew, though, that she was going to ask Jamie. And Torquil.

Jamie was not exactly forthcoming. He was shy. Only when she brought Samson and her older girl to see him did he relax.

"You like animals?"

"Aye, the previous mistress had a wee dog."

"Tell me about her."

"She was a fine lady. Like you, my lady. She had the same spirit."

Spirit?

Janet had not thought she had spirit at all recently. She realized suddenly that she had worried so about *feeling* trapped that she had *become* trapped. And by her own hand. Not Braemoor's.

"What happened to her?" She kept hoping *someone* would know more than she'd already been told.

"No one knows, my lady. She disappeared with the Black Knave. They say the marquis went after her and was killed."

They say. The words repeated themselves in his mind. *They say.* It was almost as if the lad did not believe them.

"And the Black Knave?"

"He disappeared at the same time, my lady. Some say the marquis might have killed him before dying himself. Others say he fled the king's justice."

"And no one has heard of the marchioness since?"

"Nay," he replied.

"Who lived in the cottage down the road and in the woods?"

Jamie's eyes widened and he busied himself with Samson, rubbing his ears as the dog's throat rumbled with pleasure.

"Mistress Mary Ferguson. They say she was a witch."

"A witch. Is that why no one goes there?"

"Aye, they say she bewitched the former marquis."

"The one who went after his wife and was killed by the Black Knave?"

"Aye."

"He must have been a busy man." She tried to remember him from her own visit eight years ago, but she did not. He must have been away.

"What was he like?"

Jamie seemed reluctant to say anything.

"Jamie . . . ?"

" 'E gamed," Jamie said.

"And what else?"

Jamie was silent for a moment, then words rushed out of his mouth. "They say 'e was a coward, but I dinna believe it. 'E told my da no' to beat me. 'E was good to me." Tears hovered on the edge of his eyes.

"And the present lord?"

" 'E is different," Jamie said, wiping the tears from his eyes. " 'E got rid of my da, but because Master Rory told him to."

Janet sat on a bundle of hay. It was obvious the lad's loyalty was to the former lord, although it had been Neil who had freed him from a brutal father. Because Neil had replaced the boy's protector?

But if Neil's cousin had been so wonderful, then why had his wife tried to escape him? And why had he betrayed her with Jamie's witch?

So many puzzles. Just as there were about the present marquis. Did Braemoor breed enigmas?

"Did the . . . former marquis and the present one like each other?"

" 'Tis no' fer me to say," Jamie said.

Then the answer was no. She would ask Neil about his predecessor. Mayhap she could learn something from him.

The lad rose. "I 'ave work to do, my lady."

It was obvious that he felt acutely uncomfortable talking about his master. She would find out no more. But she had two other sources: the young maid who had served the marchioness, and Torquil. Of the two, Torquil would be the most difficult. Thus, it was important to have as much information as possible before approaching him.

Trilby first.

Because Neil had suggested it, she had asked Trilby to help Clara with the children. Janet knew that Lucy would never willingly give up being a personal maid to her. She had taken such pride in her elevation.

She went up to the nursery. The lasses were awake with Clara and Trilby. So was Colin, who was raising himself by holding onto the chair. He was ten months old. He would be walking soon, getting into everything. She went over to him and he let go of the chair, raising his arms to her. There was so much trust in that gesture.

She picked him up and held him close to her. She put her head next to his, feeling the softness of his hair. "My big lad," she said, "I will keep you safe no matter what." And no matter the consequences to her. He *was* probably safer here. Her own wounded pride had blinded her to that. So had her fear that the marquis had some ulterior motive in taking Lochaene. But even if he did, would it not be better for her son to be safe than to own an overextended debt-ridden estate?

He squirmed from her embrace, and she looked into his eyes. Deep blue like hers. He looked so serious, as if he understood everything she said. Then he broke into a blinding smile. A charmer. He would be that.

"Can we go for a ride on our ponies?" Rachel pleaded.

They had about five hours before dusk.

"I will ask the cook to bring you tea," she said, "while I feed Colin. Then we will have a riding lesson."

"Really?" Annabella stared up at her, and she realized that she had not been as attentive as she usually was. She had allowed her own fears to reach out and touch them.

"Really," she confirmed. "I will be back for you in an hour."

She balanced Colin in her arms, aware of how quickly he was growing, and made for the door. "Trilby, can you come with me?"

"Oh aye, ma'am," she said, obviously delighted to be asked. Janet only hoped she would be as delighted in a few moments.

She led the way to her room. "Can you get some mush and honey for Colin?"

"Aye, your ladyship."

Janet took her son over to the window as Trilby left. She looked out all too often. Part of her hoped that she would see Neil Forbes, the Marquis of Braemoor, riding in. Another part feared what would happen when he did. Another kiss? Something greater?

Where was he? What was he doing? And why did she care so much?

She sat in a rocking chair and talked to Colin as she often did. "What do you think?"

He looked at her inquisitively as if he understood.

"Do you trust the marquis?"

He gurgled.

"That is not a very good answer."

Colin grinned.

"Is that an aye?"

Colin pulled her ear.

"I want so much for you," she said. "And your sisters. They will never be forced into marriage. But you, my son, will have no problem finding just the right bride."

He mumbled something.

"Ah, love, one of these days you will know the agony and the joy of love."

Just then a knock came at the door.

"Come in."

Trilby entered with a tray in her hands. "Would ye like me to be taking the lad, my lady?"

"Nay, I will do it," she said. "But sit and talk to me."

Looking none too comfortable, Trilby sat.

Janet felt guilty—but not so guilty that she would not ask the questions she wanted answered.

She held Colin and spooned mush into his mouth, getting much of it on her.

Even while feeding her son, she looked toward Trilby. "Tell me about your former mistress."

A smile brightened her face. It was immediately obvious that Trilby had liked the marchioness.

"She was an angel," Trilby said.

"But she ran away from her husband."

"If she did, she had reason. But I think . . ." She stopped.

"What do you think, Trilby?"

"I think she and the marquis . . . loved each other."

"Then why . . . ?"

"I do not know, my lady." She shut her lips tightly.

Mystery upon mystery.

"And the current marquis?"

"What about 'im, my lady?"

Another stone wall. No one seemed to want to discuss the current nor the last marquis.

"I want to thank you for being so kind to my daughters."

She blushed. "They are easy to like."

"How long has Torquil been here?"

"Only since the marquis inherited Braemoor," Trilby said. "He was a footman at first, but then became butler."

Trilby was busying her fingers with each other. She was obviously uncomfortable at the questions. "You may go, Trilby," Janet said. "Thank you."

Trilby stood and bobbed. "It is good to 'ave a lady 'ere again."

Janet sat for a moment and played with Colin, even as her mind ran over the conversation. She discovered she knew even less than she had before. The puzzle was even more difficult to decipher.

Nothing seemed to be as it appeared.

Including the Marquis of Braemoor.

• • •

Neil wondered what in the hell he'd agreed to. He was no hero. No knight. He had not the faintest idea how to find passage for Jacobite refugees.

Subterfuge had never been his strong suit. He always met problems headlong.

And now he was committed to something that could not only get him hanged but also destroy everyone around him. Including Janet and all the people at Braemoor.

It had not even been the fact that Will was really Janet's brother. He knew he had mentally committed himself to trying to get the children out even before he knew of the relationship.

Why had he not considered the fact that he was probably incapable of helping them?

He did not have the connections his cousin obviously had. He did not even know how to go about locating them. Who *had* helped him? And why?

Burke had led him back down the path. He had put the blindfold back on, and Neil had not protested. He was pleased that Will—Alex—was cautious. It also gave Neil time to consider the enormity of the task he'd just undertaken.

Ten children. And two wanted outlaws, one who could not be easily disguised. Even a beard would not cover the scar that ran alongside his face. The lower part, yes. But there was no way of covering the upper part of the jagged scar. It would draw attention to him as if it were a brand.

So any attempt to leave from a Scottish port, or an English one, would be foolish. That left a smuggler, leaving from some isolated beach along the coast. But how could Neil find a smuggler he could trust?

He would return to Braemoor and go through all his cousin's belongings. And the cache at the cottage. Mayhap he could find a hint. A name. An invoice for the brandy that he always had at hand. French brandy. Which meant it had been smuggled. But then there would be no invoice.

Bloody hell.

Mayhap he would go to Edinburgh. Visit taverns. Listen. Was there not an actress that he remembered being mentioned as one of his cousin's many paramours?

First Braemoor. Then Edinburgh.

Satisfied that he had at least the beginning of a plan, he settled in the saddle and tried to relax.

Impossible.

He was on his way back to Braemoor.

And he would lie again to the only person he had ever loved.

Braemoor was dark when Neil returned. It was past midnight. Even the stables were closed. He dismounted and opened the doors. The noise was slight. He found an oil lamp and tinderbox. After several attempts, he lit the lamp and led the horse inside.

The animal was exhausted. Neil took his time in rubbing him down, cooling him even though he hungered for his own bed. He could call Kevin, but he did not want to do that. The lad deserved his sleep.

He finally felt his mount was cool enough to water and feed. After he completed that chore, he quenched the light and left. He would go to the cottage at first light, before the rest of the household was up. If he found nothing there, he would turn to Rory's old apartment.

He strode to the tower house and opened it. Even Torquil was apparently abed, but then he'd had no idea that Neil would return tonight. He went into the great hall where a fire was always kept ablaze. He lit the lamp, then made his way into his office.

It was a comforting room for him. It contained a desk, his ledgers arranged in a neat pile, and books on agriculture lining the bookshelves. He sat down and looked over the ledger for the months when his cousin was lord. Rory always passed the bills to Neil to pay until Rory's wife assumed that role. There was a period of time, then, when he was not sure what payments were made and to whom they were made.

He went through the month when he did not pay those bills. He had looked at them after Bethia and Rory had disappeared, but he'd found nothing amiss. Now he looked again. There was nothing out of the ordinary for a marquis who was known to gamble and spend large amounts of money for clothing.

One draft made him pause. It was not in Bethia's small writing, but in Rory's bold hand. A draft for a hundred pounds made out to an Elizabeth Lewis. Neil had noted before that despite Rory's reputation as a spendthrift and wastrel, he had seldom tapped the Braemoor accounts.

Elizabeth Lewis. Could that be the actress in Edinburgh whose name had been connected to Rory's?

It was a starting place.

He continued his search but found nothing else. His mind was beginning to dull, in any event. The devil take it, but he was weary. How long had it been since he'd slept in a bed? Four days? Five? The days were starting to blur together.

Neil closed the books, took the lamp, and went upstairs. He paused at Janet's door. How he wanted to knock and tell her that the brother she thought dead was alive. He could almost see the joy spread over her face.

Was Alexander right? Would she try to rush to his side? Undoubtedly.

He knew her that well now. So, apparently, did Alexander. She would want to see him and risk everything to do so.

He'd never had any family he cared about. But he *had* loved. He knew what it meant to lose someone.

Tell her.

He'd sworn to her brother he would not. Not until Alexander was safely away.

Damn Alexander!

But he understood. Alexander had already lost everything. He had committed himself to those children, to getting them away safely. He did not want to compromise their safety, nor that of his sister. He was doing the noble thing.

Or was he?

Neil knew damn little about being noble. He was beginning to find out it could be bloody painful.

He had lifted his hand to knock at her door. Now he let it fall and turned toward his own room.

"His lordship is back," Torquil said when Janet went down for breakfast.

Pleasure surged through her even though she realized she had not yet had a chance to question Torquil.

"Has he had breakfast yet?"

"Aye, my lady," Torquil said. "He has already left to go for a ride."

The pleasure died a quick death. He had not even waited to say good morn to her. She wished for a moment she had not tarried upstairs with her daughters and son as they drank hot chocolate and Colin had smeared his face with jam.

Mayhap she could catch up to him.

It was a bright, beautiful day.

She looked down at her dress. It was sturdy enough to ride in.

She took a sweet from the side table. "I do not think I will have breakfast this morning, Torquil," she said. "'Tis too fine a day to stay inside." Before he could register disapproval, she was out the door, hurrying to the stable.

She felt inexplicably happy. Mayhap because she had lost some of her suspicion of the marquis. An enigma, yes. A monster, no. He couldn't fool an entire household.

Kevin and young Jamie were cleaning out stalls.

"I wish to take the mare," she said.

"Do ye wish me to go wi' ye?" Kevin said.

"Nay. The marquis is back," she said as if he had indeed consulted her about his return. "So you need not worry about accompanying me."

Kevin looked none too sure, but he nodded. "I will saddle her."

As he went for a sidesaddle, she walked past the stalls,

finding the gelding that had been missing these past few days. "Where have you been, laddie?"

But he was no more help than anyone at Braemoor had been. She waited impatiently as Kevin finished saddling a mare, then offered his hands to give her a lift up into the saddle.

"Thank you," she said as she hooked her knee around the saddlebow. Before he could offer another objection, she pressed the mare into a fast trot, then a canter. She knew exactly where she was going. She did not know why or how she knew. There was just something about that cottage in the woods that beckoned to her.

Chapter Twenty

Neil rode out early, hoping to avoid Janet. He was not ready yet to look her in the face and not tell her about Alexander. He was not ready, either, to recall—and possibly repeat—the kiss they had shared, the passion that had flared between them. There was, he admitted sadly, a limit to his self-control.

He needed to get some items from the cottage before traveling to Edinburgh. He would then be gone for several weeks. He would go by Lochaene. He would ensure Janet's safety, even if he had to evict the current members of the household. Being in such close proximity to Janet was obviously not a workable solution. Particularly when he was keeping information from her.

For someone who liked stability and normalcy, Neil felt everything was spiraling out of control. He no longer had a firm hold on any part of his life. He was risking everything for an outlaw. He could not control himself around Janet. He was ready to risk Campbell ire by tossing out Janet's Campbell in-laws. He could be sacrificing everything he'd wanted to build here at Braemoor. He was putting all these people, or at least their futures, at risk.

He rode to the loch and watched the sun rise over the rugged hills. Was he waiting for a revelation? He'd never been a religious man. Bloody hell, he'd been the opposite. Man made his own fate, he'd always thought. He was beginning to reconsider that view.

The questions would not go away. Was he doing the right thing in any of this? He could only go by instinct. What if his instincts were wrong?

The biggest question was whether he should tell Janet about Alexander. What if her brother was right? What if she rushed to him, risking her life and that of the children? Or even worse, placed her in an agony of divided loyalties. He knew about that.

But not telling her, not giving her a choice, was taking away her dignity. He knew that, too.

He could try to bring Alexander here. But that would place all his tenants and servants at risk as well as Janet. She would lose everything—children, estates, perhaps freedom—if Cumberland ever discovered she had helped an outlaw.

Damn the man. Neil wished Alexander had never asked for his help. He wished like hell he wasn't Janet's brother.

Neil turned away from the loch. He intended to retrieve some items he might need from the cottage. When he had first discovered them, he had thought to destroy them. Something had stopped him then. A premonition, mayhap. Except he did not believe in premonitions.

He turned back to Braemoor. He rode to the path that led to the cottage. He would take the British uniform, the mustache and theatrical paints he had found. He did not know what he might need, but Rory had apparently found them useful. Mayhap he would, too.

He reached the cottage, grateful that no one ever approached it. Part of the reason, he knew, was that many of the tenants had regarded Mary, the past owner, a witch. He opened the door and went inside. A cup, apparently used by Burke, remained on the table.

A faint aroma of flowers seemed to hover in the air. Mary's herbs, he supposed.

He closed the door and strode over to the hidden place next to the fireplace. He brushed away the dirt, then pulled up the board that covered the cache of clothing and disguises that remained there. He took out the British uniform, then found the box of paints. A wig. A mustache. Eyeglasses. Balls of cotton.

He squatted, putting his weight on the balls of his feet, then piled the items together. He suddenly realized what a poor spy he was. He had nothing to wrap them in. He could hardly strap a British uniform onto a horse. Bloody hell.

He looked around the cottage, and his gaze settled on a dress. He seemed to remember it had been someplace else the last time he had been here. Neil decided it might be wise to lock the door while he was rummaging in contraband. He started for it just as it opened.

Janet stood there. She looked lovely in a dark gray dress. Her eyes seemed even a clearer, darker blue. Her hair was pulled back in a long braid and her face was flushed.

"My lord?"

"What are you doing here?" he asked, trying to move his body in front of his carefully arranged pile.

"That is not much of a greeting," she said.

"How did you know about the cottage?"

"I found it when I was riding." But her eyes blinked, and he knew that was not the entire truth. "I asked the servants about it. They said a woman named Mary lived here."

"Aye," he said simply.

"You were not gone as long as you said you would be."

"I plan to leave again this afternoon."

Her face changed subtly. He would have sworn she was disappointed. The realization both elated and dismayed him.

"I see," she said.

"How are the children?"

"They love the ponies."

He found himself smiling. "Good," he said softly. "I hope they are not unhappy here."

"They like it here. Torquil has been kind."

"Torquil?" he said in disbelief.

"He can be very . . . sweet."

"And Kevin? I see you must have twisted him around your very bonny fingers. You *are* alone?"

"You are back, my lord," she replied. "There is no reason not to allow me to ride alone."

"And when you found the cottage? Were you alone then?"

Indecision slid over her face. He almost had to grin. She was terrible at being sly.

"Aye," she said after a moment.

"Poor Kevin," he said.

"I did not think you intended to keep me prisoner." Her eyes wandered back to the pile next to the fireplace, and the hole that was still uncovered. "What is that?"

"Nothing that concerns you," he replied curtly.

Something flickered in her eyes, and he knew he had made a mistake. Janet was no timid woman. She had a spine of steel, and allowed herself to be controlled only because of her concern for her children.

"There is a British uniform there," she persisted.

He shrugged.

"What would you be doing with a British uniform?"

"It belonged to the former occupants. Mayhap a lover."

Her eyes did not waver from his. "Then what are you doing with it?"

"I thought I might let a tenant use the cottage," he said. "I was looking around when I found the hole there."

Her gaze met his squarely. He knew she knew he was lying. The air heated between them. An expectation clasped them in a silent embrace. He stilled, knowing how close he was to taking her in his arms, to whispering things that must never be said in her ear. He took a step back, trying to break that invisible bond between them.

Her eyes showed that she understood. She looked away, back at the pile, then walked over to it. She stooped and studied the different items. Then she looked back up at him. "A curious assortment."

"I thought so, too," he said carelessly. "They might have belonged to my cousin. He often affected different styles."

"A rather contradictory man," she said.

"You have been asking questions."

"Aye."

"I would think four children would keep you occupied."

"They do," she admitted with a smile.

He stood awkwardly, wanting so much to take her in his arms. Wanting to kiss her. Wanting to pull her next to him. Wanting to reassure her. Wanting to bring joy to her eyes by telling her that Alexander lived.

Her eyes searched his, even as her gaze flitted to the uniform for a moment. "Were you planning to take that somewhere?"

"I doubt if its owner is still around," he said.

"Did the Black Knave disguise himself as a British officer?"

"I have no idea what the Black Knave did," he said.

"And the woman who lived here? Did you like her?"

"Aye," he said. "Though I did not know her well."

"And your cousin? Did you like him?"

"Nay."

"Why not?"

"I did not think he cared for Braemoor. And its people."

"But *you* do," she said. "More than you ever let anyone know."

"I like success, my lady. And profit."

They were dueling now, and despite the danger, he felt exhilarated by the exchange. She always made him feel alive.

"Is it not dangerous to have such items as those on the floor?" she asked. "Can they not endanger success? And profit?"

"They are not mine."

"They are on your property."

"So they are. I plan to do something about that."

"You have no plan to use them?"

"Now, Madam, why would I do that?"

She was eyeing him speculatively. There was a gleam in her eyes that he had not seen recently. He liked it. And he feared it.

"There are many puzzling things about your cousin."

"I did not think so."

"Jamie adored him."

"Jamie is an impressionable lad."

"Trilby said she thinks the marchioness cared for him."

"A silly lass's impressions."

"So lasses are silly?"

"Not all of them. No more than all men are fools."

"It has been my impression that they are."

"I am sure you are exempting present company."

"Oh, I do not think you are a fool, my lord. I am trying to figure out exactly what you are."

"A hard-working farmer, Countess."

"Really?" she said, disbelief obvious in her voice. And meant to be obvious.

If only her eyes did not keep going to the British uniform. If the Black Knave appeared again, she would undoubtedly put two and two together.

"I hope you plan to see my daughters before you go. Their feelings will be wounded if you do not."

Pleasure coursed through him. He could not remember when anyone had actually wanted to see him—other than Alexander, of course, and he had far different reasons than just thinking Neil was an admirable man.

"I will make it a point to do so."

"Are you leaving in the dead of night again?"

That was exactly what he was planning. But Janet was far too suspicious now. "Nay," he said. "At daybreak."

"How long will you be gone this time?"

"I am delighted you care," he replied, avoiding the question.

"You flatter yourself, my lord. I merely was wondering when we might return to our home."

"As soon as it is safe," he said.

She tipped her head and looked at him as though she saw right into his heart. "I thanked you for the ponies. I did not thank you for your protection."

"I did not explain it well," he said uncomfortably.

"I did not want to accept it," Janet replied.

Neil wished they would return to dueling. She was looking altogether too bonny, too approachable. He wanted her to be bristly again.

Tell her. Damn that voice.

He stepped forward. She was so close, he smelled the scent of roses that hovered around her. Light and seductive.

"Ah, lass," he said. " 'Tis hard to be near you without . . ."

"Without . . . ?"

"Doing something we both will regret."

"Why would you regret it?"

"Because there can never be anything between us. You will go home and raise your children and marry again."

"I will never marry again," she said.

"Not ever?" he said, his hand touching her arm.

"My marriage was not of the kind I wish to repeat."

"Not all men are like Alasdair Campbell."

"Are they not?" she asked. "Mayhap not as purposely cruel, but I have seen little to admire in them."

"What of your father and your brother?"

Her face softened. "My father did want what was best for me. He was not sure of Alasdair, but I . . ."

"You?" he prompted when she hesitated.

"I wanted . . . children. I fell in love with his children. And I wanted someone to care about."

A lump caught in his throat. "And you got four of them," he said gently. "They are all very bonny."

"I want them safe. Most of all," she added intensely, "I want them to be safe. And to be among people who love them."

"They will have that. I swear it."

Her eyes searched his for a moment and heat coiled inside

him. He wanted her so badly. He wanted to feel her skin against his hand, her warmth mixed with his. How much longer could he endure this without reaching out his hand? And when he did, they would both be lost.

He forced himself to turn back to the clothes. He went to the woman's dress, took a knife and cut the skirt from it, then wrapped the items in material. She watched every movement.

He felt her eyes even as he stopped and covered the hole again and brushed it over with dirt. She had already seen it. There seemed no sense in ignoring it. That would make it even more obvious.

"Why is it in the floor?" she finally asked.

"Mary was eccentric."

"Truly?" she asked wryly.

"She did not trust anyone," he felt compelled to add.

He saw doubt written on her face. He saw the questions in her eyes.

"Tell me about your brother," he said. He had not wanted to ask the question, but he needed to know more about the man who was going to trust his life to him.

Her face softened. "He was strong and brave and handsome. I thought he was a god. He loved to tease me but he was also my champion. He did not want me to marry Alasdair."

One sign of good judgment.

"I wanted to name my son Alexander, but Alasdair said no son of his would carry a traitor's name." She bit her lip and turned away.

You swore to Alex you would not tell her.

She will never forgive you if you do not.

"We had best go if I am to see the lasses ride their ponies."

"Aye," she said.

She went through the door. She had, evidently, decided not to ask more questions about the clothes. She knew he had them, though. He hoped to God he would not have to use them.

He followed her out, tied his bundle to his horse, then went over to her and put out his hands to help her mount. She stepped lightly into his locked hands and onto the saddle.

"It may not be wise to return here," he said, then instantly realized those words would probably prompt her to do just that. "You do not want to do anything that might affect your children."

"Is that a threat?"

"No, Janet, it is not. I would not threaten you. It is friendly advice. Cumberland's men are still combing the country for refugees and outlaws. I would not like to see you caught in his net."

She looked down at him. Damn, but her eyes were wide and dark and lovely, even when clouded by the uncertainty that made her look vulnerable. And she *was* vulnerable. He had been tossed around like a piece of flotsam himself. He knew exactly how it felt not to have an anchor. A place to belong. A home.

He reached up and put his hand on hers. "I will get you home soon. I swear it."

Her mount took several dancing steps, obviously ready to get back to the stable. The movement took his hand from hers.

He had already said too much this morning. He had felt too much.

He went to his own horse and mounted, then paced the animal into a trot, then a canter, never looking back to see whether she stayed apace.

Janet was silent on the way back. She'd wished immediately she could retract her question about whether his suggestion about her staying away from the cottage was a threat. She had regretted it the instant she'd seen a muscle jerk in his jaw. It *was* unfair. She kept trying to think the worst of him, so she would not remember how much she had once loved him. He seemed to have little interest in renewing that bond despite a kiss here and there. And she'd needed some shield so she would not make a total fool of herself. She'd used anger. She always used it.

After the past few days, after talking to the servants, she knew she had nothing to fear from Neil. He was trying to protect her. And her children. And they were more important than her own life or future.

But he was also keeping something from her. His explanations about the clothes at the cottage made no sense. How did he know they were there? And what would he want with a British uniform? If he had merely meant to destroy them, he could have burned them there.

There was a great deal more to Neil Forbes, the Marquis of Braemoor, than she'd ever thought. It was obvious that he had secrets he planned to keep.

But the air was fresh and clean and she decided not to pursue those thoughts.

She quickened her pace until she rode at his side. He cast a look at her with those serious eyes that had always so appealed to her, but then he turned away until they reached the road to Braemoor. Then he gave her a rare grin and pushed his mount into a gallop. They raced down the road. The wind was blowing against her face, and the sun was shining down on them. The mare stretched under her and Janet felt the strength and power and the wonder of being in control of her.

She felt as if she were seventeen again. And in love. Racing him as she had eight years ago.

Everything had seemed possible then.

He was riding a gelding, she a mare. But her smaller animal easily kept pace with his. She leaned down, and the horse seemed to sense her urgency. She quickened the pace, drawing several feet in front of Braemoor.

She threw her head back and laughed. How she did love

to ride. How she missed it at Lochaene. She also loved the competitiveness of racing Neil. Not Braemoor. *Neil.*

Their horses were neck and neck when they reached the stone fence that led into Braemoor. Neil slowed to a walk. She followed and waited as he dismounted and came over to her. He opened his arms and she slid into them. His hand caught hers. "You ride as well as ever."

She found herself smiling up at him, taking pleasure in being so close, in the way he looked at her.

She could not force herself to move away, not even as she saw Torquil coming down the stairs, a document in his hand.

"Your lordship. A letter from Edinburgh."

He let go of her. She watched as he took it, studied the seal for a moment, then opened it. His mouth tightened as he read it.

"Neil?"

He took her arm in a protective gesture and led her inside the tower house. There was a rigidity to his posture, a tightening of his lips that alarmed her. He so seldom showed any emotion.

Once inside, he led her into his office.

"Reginald has filed a new complaint against you, accusing you of his brother's murder. This time the physician said it is possible. A maid said she heard you threaten to kill him. They are asking for a warrant."

She felt all the recent pleasure drain from her. "He must have bribed them."

"Aye, 'tis possible. He is asking again for custody of his brother's children."

"No!"

"It will not happen," he said. "But Cumberland is back in Edinburgh and he wants this answered. Your brother-in-law has apparently aroused other branches of the Campbells and the king owes much to them."

She felt the blood drain from her face.

"The Forbeses have as much power as the Campbells," he

said. "But Cumberland wants to see both of us in Edinburgh. He knows you are here."

"My dear brother-in-law," she said bitterly. "He is probably accusing me of bewitching you now."

A twinkle came into his eyes. "He would not be far wrong, my lady. But he also underestimates me."

Janet knew at that moment she had never stopped loving him. She had tried. God help her, she had tried.

She had not succeeded.

He did not return that feeling, but even with the sick feeling in her stomach at Cumberland's message, she felt safe for the first time in a very long while.

"When do we go?"

"Tomorrow," he said. "I don't want them to have any more time to stir up trouble."

"What about Braemoor? Your plans . . ."

A shadow crossed his face. "They will have to wait."

"And the children?"

"They will be safe here with your Clara and our Trilby," he said. He hesitated. "Can you do without a maid? If so, we can ride horseback. It would be far quicker."

"Aye," she said. He would be risking much for her. She realized that. She also realized he had done that from the beginning. The Campbells *were* powerful, perhaps the most powerful family in Scotland. If they took on Reginald's cause . . .

He knew the risks, too. She saw it in his face. She had never asked him about his hopes but in the past few weeks, she'd learned they were rooted in Braemoor. How could she ask him to risk it all?

For the children.

"Thank you," she said simply.

"You are welcome, my lady," he said, the side of his lips slipping upward. "Although it might well be premature." Then he moved toward the door. "I would very much like to see the lasses ride their ponies."

Chapter Twenty-one

Neil waited as Janet went up to fetch her daughters. In minutes, they came skipping down the stairs, three little stepping stones.

All three of them curtsied before Neil. He bowed formally to them, and Annabella giggled and looked at him coquettishly through black lashes. That one was going to be a real flirt, he thought with amusement.

"I am most pleased to see you again," he said, truly meaning it.

Annabella beamed up at him. "We are pleathed to see you, too," she said. "I love my pony," she said.

"Can you ride her?"

"As good as mama," she said, then wrinkled her nose. "Almost as good."

"Will you show me?" he asked.

"Aye. Mama said she would let us ride this afternoon."

"And so you will," he said, still not quite sure how to talk to little lasses ranging in age from five to seven. But they did not seem to care. Annabella held out her hand, and he took it, wondering at its tiny size, and the trust that permitted her to put it there. He knew now that their father had terrified them.

Her complete trust was a gift, the finest he had ever known.

He felt infinitely humbled as he walked with her to the paddock. Her fingers seemed so small and fragile in his, like a bird's wing; he feared his own long, rough fingers might hurt her. Yet it was something very, very fine, this small tender moment.

Rachel raced on ahead to see Kevin. Grace walked sedately with Janet, her eyes darting from Annabella to Rachel. Grace apparently was not quite as trusting as her sisters. She still viewed him with cautious eyes. She could accept him as long as he stayed in front of her and made no move to hurt her sisters.

Satan's plague on Campbell. The joy had been drained from Janet, trust from the lasses. God only knew how he would have influenced his son.

He led Annabella, followed by Samson, into the stable. Jamie was there and the two of them saddled the ponies. Neil leaned down and set Annabella on the smallest pony. "Have you named her yet?"

"I liked Snow White, but Rachel said she was sweet as sugar," she said, "so I decided on Sugar. And Rachel's pony is Molasses."

"Then I will have to get a honey-colored horse for Grace," he said seriously.

Annabella thought about that a moment, then grinned. "That is a very good idea," she said in a grown-up tone.

"Thank you," he said, smothering his own grin. She always made him smile. Inside and out.

He led her pony outside, while Jamie led out Molasses. Neil watched as Jamie helped Rachel up, his wiry body stronger than it looked.

"You do not need to lead me," Annabella said grumpily.

They were in a paddock, but still . . . He glanced at Janet and she nodded.

He handed the reins to Annabella and stepped back to stand next to Janet. They watched as the two little lasses walked their ponies around the paddock, showing off their newfound skills.

"You have been teaching them," he said.

"Aye. They are natural riders."

He had to agree as he watched the concentration on their faces. Pleasure coursed through him. Buying the ponies was such a small thing, and yet he could already see how it was giving the lasses both enjoyment and confidence. He also felt a pride he had never known before. Was it a tiny taste of the feelings a parent had for his or her children? He would never know the full joy of fatherhood.

He looked down at Grace. Her gaze followed every move of her sisters as they walked the ponies around. "I will bring you back a pony from Edinburgh," he said.

She regarded him steadily, then said, "You do not have to do it. I really do not mind borrowing one."

His heart went out to her. The lie was in her eyes. She ached for a pony. She could have even demanded one of the two he had bought since she was the oldest. Instead, she had allowed them to be claimed by the two younger girls. He had never heard her ask for anything for herself.

"I promise you the most perfect pony in Edinburgh," he said.

She looked at him through big solemn blue eyes. They were several shades lighter than Janet's, more a cornflower blue than the deep, dark blue of the sea. But they were just as expressive. It was obvious she was not quite sure she believed him. She always looked as if she expected a blow. He knew that feeling too well and it made him ache inside. He wanted to put a hand on her shoulder, but he feared it would startle her more than comfort.

His chest constricted. No child should ever know that kind of fear. Especially a lass.

He leaned down and picked up Samson who was rubbing against his legs. He held the pup a moment, enduring a sloppy swipe of the tongue, then handed him to Grace. "Here, lass, you want to keep him away from the ponies. He could startle them."

Grace clutched the puppy to her chest.

He made himself turn away from her before he leaned down and hugged her. He had missed them all while he was gone, far more than he wanted to admit. He did not even want to think of the emptiness of Braemoor when they and their mother left.

His gaze went to Janet and found hers on him. He managed to smile. "Your lad?"

"Still sleeping. I dinna want to wake him. But now he will keep me awake all night." She looked at him. "I have never been away from him. Can we not take him?"

"We would not be able to move as quickly. With just the two of us, we can go by horseback and be back within four days. If we take a coach and servants, it will take us six or eight, and it is a hard drive."

She seemed to consider his words, then nodded. He saw the reluctance in her eyes, however. And yet they had no choice. He wanted to get to Cumberland before Reginald and his mother did any more damage. And he also had to get back to her brother.

He felt as if he were a jester, balancing any number of balls in the air.

"I will have some men stationed here at the tower house," he said. "They will be safe."

She nodded and looked back at the small figures on the horses. "I know," she said reluctantly.

Janet visited the small chapel on the side of the tower. She had been there several times before but now she felt a compelling need. She dreaded leaving her son. And the lasses. It could be the last time she saw them.

If Cumberland believed Reginald and Marjorie, he might well order her held for trial. Her stomach bunched in knots. What would happen to the children then? Could she depend on Braemoor to look after them? She could not bear the thought of them under the control of Reginald and Louisa.

But she could not take them with her. Braemoor was right: a carriage would take far longer. It would be too difficult a journey for the children. Especially after the last one. And Neil had already spent so much time on her behalf, including the several journeys to Lochaene. Still, she could not quiet the sick feeling she had in the pit of her stomach. Nor the fear that was like a lead weight on her.

Even the thought of being alone with Neil for those days did not help. In truth, they made the prospect even more daunting. She had watched his eyes before he had looked toward her. She had seen them soften. She had even seen the bleak look when he had turned back to her, as though something valuable had been taken from him.

Why did he always try so hard to conceal his feelings, any sign of emotion?

And why could she not control her own? Why did she continue to ache so for him?

She bent her head and prayed. Prayed for her children.

And for herself.

They left at daybreak. She had kept her son with her through the night and had shed a tear on bidding him farewell. She told him that she was doing it for him, that she would be back soon.

She kissed him, rocked him, sang him songs. Her only comfort at leaving him was knowing that Clara loved him nearly as much as she. And then there was Trilby. Lucy. And Grace. All of them would look after Colin.

She had already packed the extra gown that she intended to wear for her audience with Cumberland. It was a particularly plain one. She had no intention of trying to impress the Duke of Cumberland. For the ride, she had chosen a dark blue riding dress and a plain cap. She missed the plaids, but they were gone from Scotland these days. Part of her wanted to flaunt her Leslie heritage, but too much depended on her being cautious and obedient.

God in heaven, but she wished she were a man. She would have options she did not have as a woman. As a mother. Her first duty—her only duty—was to protect the bairns.

She heard a light knock on her door and opened it. Braemoor stood there in leather buckskin breeches, with a white linen shirt and fine tweed coat stretching across his wide shoulders.

She wished her heart would not thump so wildly when she saw him.

"Lucy said you were awake," he said.

"Aye," she said, holding tightly to Colin.

He looked down at her son, and she saw regret in his eyes. He held out her finger and a drowsy Colin took it, holding onto it. "He is a handsome lad."

"And he will be a good man," she said.

"Aye." He hesitated, then said, "We should go. Lucy is outside."

Janet gave Colin one last kiss, then closed her eyes as Lucy took him to the nursery.

Braemoor helped her put her cloak on. "We will be back soon, Janet. I have five men who will stay within the tower house. They have sworn to protect your children with their lives."

A chill ran through her. "You do not think . . . ?"

"Nay. I think Reginald is confident he can work through the Campbells. But I do not want to take any chances."

She nodded. She was becoming accustomed to his quiet efficiency.

He picked up her bundle. It contained her nightdress and robe, her extra dress, brush and comb and change of shift. No more. He put his arm at the crook of her elbow and guided her out the door. "I will have this wrapped in oilcloth," he said.

She forced herself to go down the stairs. An adventure was awaiting her. Hopefully even independence. But dread was a heavy lead ball in her stomach. Cumberland had a reason for wanting to see her.

The day was not one to lift spirits. Fog shielded the hills

and the mist was heavy. She began to wish for the jolting carriage. But Braemoor had instilled her with his own urgency. He took her into the stable. Kevin was holding two saddled horses. As she watched, Braemoor wrapped her belongings in oilcloth, then tied it to the back of her saddle. His own saddlebags were bulging.

"Kevin," she said, "I do not think Rachel and Annabella should ride while I am gone."

"Aye, my lady. But I will make sure they have some carrots to give them."

"Thank you."

"I will look after them," he said.

"Aye," Jamie said, appearing from the back. "I will, too."

She had to smile at his earnest face. "Thank you both," she said.

Braemoor helped her up into the saddle, then vaulted onto his own mount.

He started at a walk, then moved into a canter. She followed, looking back only once. She realized then that Braemoor somehow felt more like home than Lochaene.

Mayhap because it was where her heart now was.

It took them the best part of two days to reach Edinburgh. They'd stayed in an inn overnight; Janet took the only private room they had and Neil stayed in the common room. In truth, Neil often felt more comfortable that way than in a lone bed in a private chamber. He had trained as a soldier and was used to communal lodging.

He was like a fish out of water now, pretending to be a lord. A marquis. He had always wanted that because it represented power. Now he felt the full weight of having people dependent on him.

He was not doing a good job of it. Instead, he was riding around the country like some fool Don Quixote. With the likelihood of not much more success.

He had been moody and quiet along the way, uncertain as to what he was doing. He was almost sure that Cumberland would inquire about his intentions toward Janet. He had not told Janet that Cumberland desired a marriage between them because he did not want her to believe he had encouraged it, or wanted it. But if it was the only way to save her, God help him, what would he do?

And how was he going to get Alex, and his orphans, out of the country?

He'd noticed that she had darted glances at him during the journey. She was obviously trying to understand his mood, but he did not know how to explain all the secrets he carried. He'd never liked deviousness. Now he felt consumed by the lies and nontruths that had become a part of his life. He hated them. He hated keeping even the smallest secret from Janet. She deserved so much more.

At least, he had left enough money with Alex for Burke to buy blankets and food. If only they could avoid the authorities for the next month. It would take at least that long.

Beset by worries, he'd even been curt to Janet. But it had been necessary: A moment's relaxation and he might reveal everything.

They approached Edinburgh at mid-afternoon. The sight of the castle looming above the city was always a bit daunting. Neil turned and looked at Janet. Her eyes were on the great stone edifice. "I have never been to Edinburgh," she said.

That was not unusual for a woman from the Highlands, he knew. He had gathered that her husband had kept her secluded.

"We will not have much time here," he said. "No more than a day, but mayhap you can visit some shops tomorrow afternoon."

"I would like to get some material for dresses for the girls," she said wistfully. "And warm cloaks for winter."

Nothing for herself, he noted, even as he knew her wardrobe was small. He would tend to that another day. He really wanted to give her the moon.

He could not do that, but he might return a brother to her, or at least the knowledge that he lived.

He guided his horse into Edinburgh. He watched as she turned her face from the British soldiers that seemed to crowd the cobbled streets, but her eyes were also alive with interest as her gaze took in the many shops and markets.

"My cousin kept lodgings at an inn called the Fox and Hare. He used to stay there when he was in Edinburgh," Neil said. He'd discovered that from billings received from the inn. Rory had apparently maintained an apartment there; mayhap he could follow some trail from the inn and discover how Rory had helped spirit Jacobites from Scotland. The odds of doing so were dismayingly small, but he had nowhere else to go unless he journeyed to France. That would be his last option.

He had noted the inn when last he was in Edinburgh and he guided them directly to it. Once settled, he would send a messenger to Cumberland at Holyroodhouse to see when they could obtain an audience.

They stopped at the Fox and Hare and they went inside. The proprietor looked at them curiously.

"I am the Marquis of Braemoor," Neil said, still not comfortable with the title or the saying of it. "And this is the Countess of Lochaene. We would like two rooms."

The man frowned, even as his eyes lit in recognition of Neil's name. "I have no room, my lord."

"Ah, but you do, landlord. I noticed in my cousin's accounts that he had paid for a room here. It lasted, I believe, for a year."

The landlord's face paled. "But he is dead, my lord. I thought . . ."

"Aye?" Neil said quietly, but there was steel in his voice.

"I will see what I can do," the landlord said.

Neil did not want to alienate the man completely. He might have information. "We will return after supper," he said. "I expect the rooms to be ready."

"But it was only one."

"Aye, it was, but it seems you have been renting out a room already paid for." Then he decided to relent. "I will pay handsomely to recompense someone for the inconvenience," Neil said. "I will pay triple the cost for a second room for two nights."

The man's face cleared. "I think I can find something."

Neil studied him. "I thought you might. The Braemoor custom could be quite valuable. I am sure you would not abuse it."

"Nay," the man said, bowing. "If I had but known . . ."

"Of course," Neil said equably. "I would like the rooms to be ready when we return. In the meantime I would like a message delivered to His Grace, the Duke of Cumberland, our horses tended and our personal belongings taken to our rooms."

The man bobbed up and down. "I will send someone immediately. Several of his officers stay here. Several were friends to the late . . . to your . . . cousin."

"Friends, or gaming companions?"

The man's expression told Neil it was the latter. Good. Mayhap he would do a bit of gaming himself tonight. But first he had to see that Janet had something to eat.

Janet watched Neil over supper. The landlord had recommended a tavern nearby. His own, he said, was not suitable dining for a lady.

She realized that neither was the inn respectable for a woman staying alone.

The truth was she did not care about her reputation. She cared only about getting back to Lochaene and having the freedom to make it prosper. At least, she told herself that. She did not want to consider how much Braemoor felt like home, or how much she . . . still cared about its lord. He had made it only too clear on the journey from Braemoor that his concern was fulfilling an obligation he felt he owed her.

The tavern was large and noisy. Neil passed a few coins to the tavern keeper, who then led them to a private alcove. Braemoor ordered a large meal, starting with a platter of fruit and cheeses. A bottle of fine wine arrived. She gratefully sipped it, feeling herself relax. Course after course appeared. Roast mutton, crab and oysters appeared on the table. She watched him eat, noticing that he did so carefully, savoring every bite. He was quiet, but then he was always quiet. It was one of the things she liked about him, the companionable silences, but she wondered whether she would ever know what he was thinking.

She was not hungry, and simply nibbled. She could not stop thinking about what Cumberland wanted from her. And why.

"My lady?"

Her gaze returned to his. "You are not eating."

"A little, mayhap," she said.

"Ah, but not enough." He picked up a sugar wafer from a plate and tempted her mouth open with it. Janet licked it, then took it into her mouth, realizing that little crumbs of pastry and sugar sprinkled her lips.

Neil leaned over the narrow table and his lips touched hers. She could taste the wine on his lips and the sugar so recently on her own. His breathing was erratic, and she felt her own body tense with warmth. She heard the crackling of a nearby fire, smelled the aromas of good food mixed with that of wood smoke.

She knew she looked . . . not her best. Her dress was damp and limp. She had tried to tuck her hair neatly into her cap but ringlets had escaped. And yet he made her feel as if she were the most desirable woman on earth.

She thought *he* must be the most desirable man. He exuded strength and confidence. He made her body react in any number of traitorous ways. Most of all, he made her feel as if she were something of worth. And it had been a long time since anyone had made her feel that way.

She reached out and touched his face, her fingers exploring its angles and even the tiny cleft in his chin. They were the only two people in the world, cut off momentarily by the curtain from the rest of the room, deaf to the noise of loud voices, oblivious to the food remaining on the plates.

She took a deep breath. It was only because she was so tired, so uncertain, even frightened, although she hated to admit it. She dropped her hand and straightened.

He gave her a wry smile.

"I am tired, my lord."

He nodded, his eyes shadowed by the darting light of the candle. He rose, and he helped her up. The inn was only a street away, but she was only too aware of him as they walked together, his large protective figure next to hers. She still felt the taste of his lips on hers. She knew she would always feel it.

The rooms were ready. Neil did not know if the innkeeper had asked others to leave, or whether he had the rooms in reserve for some important person. He did not care.

The innkeeper gave him a message with Cumberland's seal. The duke would see them in the morning. Neil saw the apprehension in Janet's face and he started to reach out, then remembered the innkeeper. He turned away. "Give the countess the largest room," he said.

He waited until she was shown to the room and the innkeeper returned and showed him his own. It was across the hall. Neil asked that water be taken to Janet's room for a bath, then he went down to the taproom. It was filled with British soldiers.

He took a moment with the innkeeper, placating him with coins, thanking him profusely and promising to continue his custom.

"I am trying to reach some of the . . . late marquis's friends," he said. "He left gaming debts and I have received claims. I thought they could tell me which are legitimate and which are fraudulent. I do not want the name of Braemoor tainted." It was a damn fool explanation, but the only one he'd been able to construct.

The innkeeper shrugged. "There was Captain Lehgrens."

"Is he here?"

The innkeeper shook his head. "He left for England

months ago. You might find a few men in the taproom who might have known the late lord."

"I also heard he had an . . . alliance with an actress. Elizabeth . . ."

"Elizabeth Lewis," the innkeeper said, his eyes on the purse that Neil held loosely in his fingers. "She used to be at the Edinburgh Theater."

Neil tossed him another crown. "My thanks."

He went into the taproom, where a game of hazard was being played. He introduced himself as Braemoor. A murmur went around the room. Everyone was curious about the new marquis. "You dress more soberly," one officer said.

"Aye," Neil replied with a wry grin.

"Our condolences on Rory's death," one man said. "Heard the Black Knave killed him."

"Aye," Neil said. "That is what they say."

"He must have gotten the Knave before he died. The bastard has disappeared."

"Mayhap the Knave escaped with the Pretender," Neil suggested. Prince Charles had escaped Scotland some eight months earlier, despite the huge reward on his head.

One of the officers shook his head. "We would have heard."

"Poor Elizabeth. She was distraught at your cousin's death," an officer said meanly. "Swore to take vengeance on the Knave. But I would say you did well by his death."

Silence settled around the table as all eyes went to the speakers' face. It was poor manners to make such a statement, even if it were true.

Neil shrugged. "'Twas unfortunate for my cousin, but at least this Knave fellow has not reappeared. Kept everything in an uproar. I keep expecting the bandit to dart out onto the road."

"It has been eight months since anyone heard of him," one of the officers scoffed.

Neil dealt the cards. "Mayhap he was wounded. Or just waiting until His Grace stopped looking for him."

A wail of protest ensued.

He dealt himself a card face up. A black knave. "You see, gentlemen, you never know when he will appear."

Hours later, his purse lighter by twenty crowns, he returned to his room. He had learned that Elizabeth Lewis had left Edinburgh. No one knew where she had gone. She'd been his best hope. But he did have an idea. One that might help both Alexander and his sister. It would depend on what happened in the morning.

Once in his room, he undressed. He took out the deck of cards he had taken from the taproom. No one objected, since he had lost. He said it would be a reminder not to game with the British again. They had all laughed.

He laid the cards on the table and gazed at them for a moment. Mayhap he and Rory had shared more than the same name.

Chapter Twenty-two

They waited for Cumberland for more than two hours. Neil tried to contain his impatience. Janet was totally still, sitting neatly and formally, in a chair in the morning drawing room outside the king's antechamber.

He tried small talk but he was not very good at it, and he knew it. His own mind was occupied with possibilities.

An idea kept nagging at him, and he needed to work it out in his mind. The risk was great, but it had the possibility of solving two very big problems at once.

Could he pull it off?

Finally, a lieutenant entered. "His Grace will see you now," he said.

Janet started to stand, but the lieutenant shook his head. "Just the marquis," he said.

Neil gave her a small smile to encourage her, then followed the lieutenant into the king's antechamber. He exaggerated a limp as he entered.

Cumberland sat at a desk and continued to scribble on a page below him.

"Your Grace," Neil said after a moment.

"Aye, Braemoor. It appears we have more evidence against Countess Lochaene. The dowager countess is demanding her arrest. She also wishes custody of her grandson and granddaughters. Since you seem to have taken a . . . special interest in the lady, I wanted your reaction."

Cumberland was ready to act. Neil knew that from the look in his eyes, like a cat playing with a mouse. Well, this mouse could bite back.

"The physician has changed his original opinion?" Neil asked dryly. "I wonder how a magistrate would view that."

"There is the countess's threat."

"If threats were evidence of crimes, most of Scotland would be convicted," he said. "And England also. Even then, the witnesses to such threats have something to gain."

"Are you accusing the dowager countess of false witness?"

"I accuse no one, Your Grace. I am merely stating a fact."

Cumberland stood. "Do you have a personal interest in this lady?"

"As I told you a month ago, our families were friends."

"And you believe her innocent?"

"Aye, Your Grace."

"You have never married."

"Nay, Your Grace. I have been in no position to do so."

"But you are now."

Neil was silent as Cumberland looked at him speculatively. After a moment, he spoke, "I do not like turmoil between families loyal to England."

"Are you sure that Reginald Campbell is . . ." Neil left the sentence unfinished.

Cumberland's eyes sharpened. "What do you mean?"

"None of his branch of the family marched with you, my lord, and I have heard . . ." He stopped again. Then shrugged. "Unlike some, I do not toss around unfounded accusations."

"I command you to tell me what you mean."

"I was attacked, Your Grace, on my way from Lochaene back to Braemoor. I was left to bleed to death. It was a well-planned ambush. I heard one of the villains say that word had come from the master at Lochaene, that they had been informed that an English gentleman would be traveling that way."

Cumberland frowned. "Why did you not inform me?"

"I was very ill, Your Grace. The countess nursed me back to health and accompanied me to Braemoor because I had urgent business. She feared I might exhaust myself and that the fever might return. I had planned to inform you as soon as my wound healed well enough to travel to Edinburgh." Neil was fabricating as quickly as he could. He wished like hell he had his cousin's wit. "And then you were in England. I thought it news for your ears alone. I came as soon as you sent a message and I knew you had returned."

Cumberland's brows furrowed together. "Why, for God's sake?"

"The man who shot me left a card with me. A jack of spades." Neil pulled out the card he'd been carrying for months. It had dried blood on it.

"The devil you say!" Cumberland exploded. "Are you saying the Black Knave is still alive and here in Scotland? And that Reginald Campbell knows about it?"

"I know only what I heard," Neil said. "I did observe that one of the villains had a stiff arm. He must have been badly wounded at some time. I wished to tell you before anyone else."

"How did you get away?"

"They left me for dead. A traveler found me more that way than not and took me to Lochaene. I would have died had it not been for the countess, Your Grace. All at Lochaene . . . can attest to that."

Cumberland's face had turned crimson. "And you believe Campbell is in league with this . . . bandit?"

"We all know the Black Knave must have had some support, and protection," Neil reminded him gently. "And neither of the Lochaene Campbells fought with you." *As I did.* Neil left the words unsaid, but they hovered in the air. "I also know that Reginald Campbell was in dire need of funds. Was not the Knave a thief as well as a traitor?"

He allowed Cumberland to ponder the words.

"Where did . . . this attack happen?"

"Ten miles from Lochaene."

"What did the fellow look like?"

"I cannot say exactly, Your Grace. I got only a glimpse of him. Stiff arm. Mid height. Dark hair. Short beard. The other man was tall. Red hair. In truth, I do not know that either is the Black Knave. Nor if Reginald has anything to do with them. Or whether . . . ?" He shrugged, leaving Cumberland to finish the thought.

Cumberland looked thoughtful.

"Mayhap there is a reason they do not wish the countess to be around," Neil said after a silence. He had absolutely no regret for what he was doing. Reginald was trying to get Janet hanged. He might have killed Alasdair, his own brother.

It would take a great deal of effort to make anyone believe Reginald could have enough brains to be the Black Knave, but . . . with Alexander's help, Neil thought he could do it.

Neil liked the idea more and more. He thought his cousin might approve.

"Would you be willing to wed the lady?" Cumberland said. "You have apparently taken her under your protection. You must feel that the charges are groundless."

"I do, but she is a new widow, Your Grace. It would not be seemly."

"Anything is seemly if it has my approval," Cumberland replied.

"But a rush to marriage would indeed make it look as if she had not been happy in her marriage," Neil said. "It might give validity to Reginald Campbell's calumnies. It might well be wise to wait until you can determine his true loyalties."

Cumberland's gaze bored into him. "You are sliding away from my question, my dear Braemoor. Would you consider a match with the countess? A woman cannot run that large a property."

"I have placed a manager there who will report to me. I believe that is why Reginald is pressing these charges. He cannot take from the estate as he had been doing. If he can get rid of the countess and myself, then he would be only a step away from the title and freedom to act whichever way he wishes. In the meantime, if he can pay his gambling debts by splitting purses with the Knave, then . . ."

"Are you ready to press those charges yourself?" Cumberland asked.

"Unlike his family, nay. But I would like to know the truth of it. For my poor cousin's sake as much as for the sake of myself and the countess. It would not be politic, or wise, to accuse a Campbell without proof. Mayhap we can set some kind of trap. In the meantime, though, I think the countess should stay at Braemoor for her protection."

Cumberland hesitated. Neil knew he had used every tool he had. His own service, dubious as it was, at Culloden. Rory's supposed death at the hands of the Black Knave. The lack of service by the Lochaene Campbells. And, most of all, the possible capture of the Black Knave. Cumberland had been beside himself with rage when Prince Charles had escaped after six months of hiding.

He also knew the dangerous game he was playing. He could lose everything, including his head. And then the people at Braemoor and Lochaene would lose everything, too.

Cumberland walked over to a map. "Where exactly were you ambushed?"

Neil pointed to a spot ten miles in the opposite direction of the true location.

Cumberland nodded. "I will discover why Campbell did not report the incident."

"It would be better if you did not, Your Grace. If we are to set a trap, he must not believe he's under suspicion."

"What do you suggest?"

"Wait a few weeks," Neil said. "My men can watch him."

"I'll send out patrols to comb those hills," Cumberland said.

"And the blockade?" Neil asked.

"It continues," Cumberland said.

Neil was only too aware of that. Despite the fact that Culloden had taken place more than eighteen months ago, and that most Jacobites had been killed or were waiting in jail somewhere, the English were further strangling Scotland by starving it. He had heard, though, that several ships from Ireland were being allowed to carry oats into Scotland.

He had planted his seed. It was time to leave before he made a mistake. He thought he had countered Reginald's charges against Janet. Cumberland would not move now and risk talk of treason against a branch of one of his most powerful allies.

Cumberland was through, too. "I would like to meet the lady," he said, "and judge for myself."

Neil bowed. "I will fetch her."

Janet was standing when he reentered the drawing room. She was staring fixedly at a portrait of some past Scottish personage. It had been slashed by a sword or bayonet and left in that mangled condition.

Aware that a British lieutenant remained in the room, Neil walked over to her. "His Grace would like to see you," he said.

Momentary panic played in her eyes, then she stiffened. Like so many Jacobite Highlanders, she hated Cumberland. For her children's sake, she had to hide that hatred.

Neil leaned over. "Agree with everything he says."

Her eyes questioned him, but then she nodded. Her silent agreement went straight to his heart. She had not trusted him before. She did now. He knew at that moment he could do no less than trust her.

He put his arm beneath hers and led her in. She curtsied gracefully. "Your Grace," she acknowledged.

A gleam came into his eyes. "I understand now why Braemoor has taken you under his protection."

"I thank you, Your Grace."

Neil thought she looked poised and altogether lovely. But,

then, she always had to him. No resentment showed in her eyes, no fear, though he had felt her tremble earlier.

"Is Braemoor taking good care of you?"

"'Tis she who is taking good care of me," Neil interrupted. He turned to her. "I told His Grace how you saved my life after I was ambushed in the hills. And that you were kind enough to accompany me back to Braemoor since I had a lingering fever."

She turned to Cumberland. "He insisted in getting back to his estate. I feared the fever might return."

"Very kind of you," Cumberland said. "And now, regretfully, I must turn to other matters."

It was a dismissal. Janet curtsied once more.

"Oh, and Braemoor?" Cumberland said as they turned to leave.

"Aye?"

"I miss the brandy your cousin often gifted me with. 'Twas unusually fine."

"I will see whether we have some at Braemoor, my lord."

Cumberland nodded and turned away.

Neither said anything until they left Holyroodhouse. The carriage they had engaged earlier was waiting outside. He told the driver to return them to the inn, then handed her into the coach. He stepped in next to her, meeting her curious gaze. As the coach lurched forward, he took her hand.

"You didn't have a fever when we left Lochaene," she said.

"I may have exaggerated a wee bit," he replied.

"Why?"

"You are very quick, Countess. You did not even blink when I said that."

"You warned me. You have not told me why."

"Scorpions, my lady. Turn them on one other."

A smile started at the edge of her mouth. "Cumberland and my brother-in-law?"

"Aye. It is a mismatch, and we know who will win, but one at a time."

"You have a plan," she said.

"Aye, it is not much of one but it is better than none at all. I have learned to recognize the signs. His Grace had been ready to press charges of murder. A favor to the Campbells."

"Then how . . ."

"The Black Knave," he said.

She started at him. "You?"

"Nay, it would take a far better man than I."

"Those things in the cottage . . ."

He was silent for a moment. It was still hard for him to trust, hard for him to tell anyone his thoughts, or explain himself. It was, in truth, nearly impossible. He had made an art of being alone. He had withdrawn into himself as a lad when his mother stared at him as if he was not there, when he had been taken away and left with a family that wanted only his labor. That wariness increased when he was made companion and bodyguard for a bully. The only time he had lowered the walls around himself was with Janet eight years ago, and then came that devastating pronouncement from the old marquis. He built those walls twice as high, then. He had nearly suffocated himself with walls.

Her hand crept into his, her fingers intertwining with his.

He knew he should unwrap them. Nothing had changed. He was who he was. He was a man who should never create a child. And that meant abstinence. He had been abstinent since that afternoon eight years before. He was feeling every moment of those years now. They had not quieted the need inside. Nor the yearning.

"Neil?"

He realized then that his own hand had tightened around hers. "I did not intend to hurt . . ."

"I know," she said. "You did not hurt me. I just . . . you did not answer."

Trust, he told himself.

Others are at risk.

It was an excuse. It *had* been an excuse. He had lived his life around excuses. And Rory could not be hurt now. He was gone, and with his talents no one would ever find him. "Rory was the Knave," he said.

"But your . . . the late marquis . . . was killed."

"Nay. It was someone else dressed in his clothes. He made his escape with his wife."

Her smile lit the carriage. "Trilby told me she thought they loved each other."

"Then my cousin wasna as devious as he thought he was," Neil said. "I sure as hell did not notice it, but then I was too occupied with resenting him. I believed he was a profligate gambler who would destroy Braemoor." He hesitated, then added, "Instead, he was very careful to protect it despite the fact he hated every inch of the property."

"I would have liked to have met him."

"You probably would have despised him. He wore peacock green waistcoats with trews."

She laughed. "You do not think I would have seen through it?" she asked.

"It is often difficult to see the heart when someone does not want you to," he said, surprising himself. He had not meant to say that, nor wanted to. The longing in him, though, had thrown out the words.

Her hand stilled in his. "Does that not include you, my lord?"

"We are discussing my cousin."

"Are we?"

He pondered the opportunity. He could tell her now why he could not marry her years ago. Could not marry her ever, no matter how much he wanted it. No matter how he ached for it. For her. He could not drag out the words, though, not and endure her pity. It would merely add a complication to an already complicated matter.

It was Janet who changed the subject. "How are you going to turn the scorpions on each other?"

"I have already planted the seed," he said. "Cumberland is going to come to believe that your brother-in-law is either the Black Knave or connected to him."

"Reginald?" she said doubtfully. "He is not intelligent enough. No one would believe that."

"Neither would anyone have believed my cousin was intelligent enough to outwit the entire British army," he said equably. "Everyone believed him a fool and gambler and womanizer."

Her eyes widened. "But how . . . ?"

"The Black Knave must reappear. He will choose targets in and around Lochaene."

She stared at him. "Not . . . you?"

He was not sure whether her question resulted from her lack of faith in his heroic abilities or fear for him. "Nay," he said. "I have no talent for skulking."

"Then . . ."

"The gentlemen who shot me," he said, trying to choose his words carefully. "They are Jacobites and have little use for the English. A theft or two, with a card thrown out, will make Cumberland believe the villain is active again. It will not hurt to turn Cumberland's eyes to that direction. It will make him suspect their charges against you."

"But . . . if they are not involved."

"In what, my lady?" He paused, then added, "I told you the bandits had been informed that an Englishman would be traveling that way. It was a woman from Lochaene who passed the information. Your husband's family wanted me dead."

"A woman? You did not tell me that."

"Nay," he said simply.

Her eyes filled with hurt. "You thought . . ."

"I thought it was Louisa or Marjorie," he said, evading the one moment of doubt he did have. "I told Cumberland that the outlaws said it was Reginald. I also allowed him to believe that one of the men was the Knave or connected to him."

Her eyes widened. "How?"

"I had a jack of spades. It was stained with blood."

"So the Knave lives again," she said. "But will Cumberland not hunt down the outlaws and discover the truth?"

"No' if I can get them out of Scotland. There would be no one left for Cumberland to blame other than . . . your brother-in-law."

She blinked and he knew she was trying to complete the missing parts of the puzzle. "When I left a few days ago," he explained, "I did not go to look at my properties. I met the outlaws in the mountains."

"But they tried to kill you."

"Aye. And considering their circumstances and the fact that they thought they were ambushing a wealthy Englishman, I do not hold it against them. They did deliver me back into your hands."

"Why? You are a wealthy man and if not English, then at least thought to be loyal to the English."

He hesitated, trying to decide what to say. And how much to tell her. "I had the jack of spades with me. It made them think I might have some connection to the Black Knave, and they needed help."

Her eyes regarded him steadily. "And why would you help them?"

"They have children with them," he said simply.

"Children?"

"Aye. Orphans. Some of them are from families outlawed by Cumberland. They could well be imprisoned or transported if captured."

"You would risk everything for them?" Her eyes glowed.

A lump in his throat crowded out his breath. He was no hero. No slayer of dragons. He had been forced into this. And when he finished, she would know he had lied by omission, that he had kept something from her that she'd had every right to know. "It serves my purpose for the moment," he said abruptly and looked outside the carriage at the blackened stone of the city. Blackened from years of coal fires. A stench rose from the city and he longed for the green hills and clean air of Braemoor.

"What can I do?" she asked.

"You can take care of your children," he replied curtly.

"How do you plan to get . . . this gentleman and the children out of Scotland?"

"Damned if I know," he said. "I was hoping to find a way here in Edinburgh, someone whom my cousin knew and used, but I've had little luck."

"You are known as an ally of Cumberland's," she said. "My family were Jacobites. I might be able to find someone who will help. There are some kinsmen near the coast. They did not participate in the rising, but I know their sympathies are with Jacobites."

He turned back to her. "I cannot let you do that. It is dangerous."

She tried to smile. "More dangerous than being called a murderess? More treacherous than Reginald and his family? If one of them tried to kill you . . . and me, then they will try to kill my son. There will be no one to stop them if you are caught. I would rather be endangered by *doing* something than risk my children's life by doing nothing."

A blast of fear filled him. If he were wrong, if he took a misstep, she would pay. She and the children.

"I think Cumberland has given me a way to find a smuggler. I just must find the source of good French brandy, and I do it at his own behest. If a man smuggles brandy, I do not think he would object to smuggling children. If that does not work, then we can discuss alternative plans."

She gazed at him for a moment, then nodded reluctantly. Then she asked the question he was dreading. "Who is it in the mountains?"

He'd known the question was coming. And he knew he could not lie to her. Not now. He had weighed the two sins: breaking his oath to Alexander or lying to Janet. He simply could not do the latter. Not now.

"Your brother."

Her face paled. Her hand tightened in his. Her eyes

looked into his. "It . . . cannot be. He was killed. We were told . . ."

"Alexander is alive," he said.

"How . . . ?"

"He was badly wounded after Culloden," Neil said. "Left for dead. He has been hiding in the mountains these past months with a man named Burke."

Her eyes were huge, searching, and her hands knotted together. "You . . . are sure?"

"Aye," he said.

"You said . . . he was wounded."

Neil nodded.

"How . . . badly?"

"His face was scarred. He limps. But he is well enough to care for children and terrorize poor travelers." He said the last with a wry smile.

"I cannot believe you were terrorized," she said.

"Anyone is terrorized when they are on the wrong end of a pistol, particularly when they already have a bullet in them," he said. "I am only grateful that he and his accomplices are poor shots."

"You said there were children?"

"Aye. Ten of them. He has found them or, as he claims, they found him."

She stilled, her face like a marble statue. Only the expression in her eyes changed. Disbelief. Hope. Joy. Confusion. She was trying to believe him, but it was obvious she could not quite accept it.

He damned himself for being such a clumsy fool. Surely he could have found a better way.

"How . . . long have you known?" Her voice broke but her gaze stayed on his.

It was the question he had most dreaded.

"A week," he said. "I did not know when I was shot and returned to Lochaene. His man showed up here two weeks ago and asked for my . . . help. He wanted money." Neil hesitated, then continued. "I thought I knew why. I also wanted to know why . . . they had not killed me. I went with him. Once I saw his eyes, I knew . . ."

"Why did you not tell me?" The fingers in her fist were intertwined, knotted together so tight that the blood had drained from them.

"I thought you should know. Alexander did not. He feared you would try to see him and endanger yourself. And your children. He did not want to risk that." He reached over and put his hand over hers. She jerked it away.

"I gave him my word, lass."

"You broke it," she observed flatly.

"Aye," he replied. "You had a right to know."

"He did not want to see me?"

"I think he wants it very much," he said, trying to feel his way. "He wants to protect you, lass."

"He could have sent word."

"I think he did," Neil said softly. "He seemed to sense that I had a connection to you. 'Tis another reason I was allowed to live."

"Nay," she said, "there is no connection."

He ached at the dead, hopeless sound in her voice. Only moments earlier it had been filled with excitement and hope. Now the only two people remaining in her life had purposely left her out of theirs. He wanted to touch her, but he knew she would not welcome it now. Her hurt ran too deep for a platitude or caress.

He'd known he would regret giving his word to Alex. In truth, he had regretted it every waking minute since he'd left the blasted man. He knew how she had been used by her husband, then by her brother-in-law. Even worse, he knew that she felt that he had used—and discarded—her years ago.

And now her brother.

The silence was like a scream.

The jolting carriage came to a stop.

"Lass?"

She had looked away. She did not look back when the

coachman opened the door. Instead, she stepped down. After he paid the driver, he started to take her arm, but she drew away. Every inch of her was resistant to him. All the closeness of the earlier moments was gone.

He trailed her up to her room. She looked so brittle that he thought one touch might cause her to shatter into a hundred pieces.

Janet hesitated at the door. She should just feel pure joy at knowing her brother was alive. And she did. Yet . . . she also felt something immeasurably sad at the same time. She had just started to trust Neil. And yet he had not told her the most important thing she could ever know. He'd *known* her brother was alive. He'd *known* and had not told her.

She told herself that he was helping Alexander. And others. She knew she was being terribly ungrateful and she silently berated herself for it. And yet . . . trust was such a fragile thing, and it had been fractured once more. She'd felt like an object to be bargained over, traded, used for too long.

She accepted that he was doing what he probably thought was best for her, just as he had from the beginning. But he had given no thought of making her a part of decisions that concerned her. Her throat clogged with conflicting emotions.

She opened the door and turned to face him. A muscle flexed in his cheek. His dark eyes were questioning.

"I should have told you earlier," he said.

"Aye," she said. "But thank you for helping him."

He raised one eyebrow. "Alexander said I owed him."

"He could always twist words to his favor," she said. *Alive.* She was still trying to sort that out in her mind. *Alive.* The realization was finally sinking in, piercing the odd numbness, the disbelief, that had paralyzed her. Alex was truly alive.

Suddenly, it did not matter that Neil had not told her sooner. He'd told her now. *Alex. Alive.* The words became a refrain in her mind, in her heart.

Janet closed her eyes and leaned against the door.

His arm went out to her. "Janet?"

She took a deep breath, trying to bring all the tumultuous feelings under control. She held out her hand, and he took it, tightening his own fingers around her. She felt its warmth and then he released her hand, and his arms went around her. He pulled her close to him and held her tight.

Her legs barely held her. Her body trembled, then found strength in his.

Alive. Her brother was alive.

She looked up and saw the pain in his face. She had not thought how much the secret must have hurt him. Her hand went up and her fingers touched his face, traced the lips that so seldom smiled.

"I wanted to tell you. It has been haunting me every waking hour."

She nodded, accepting it. "I would never do anything to put Alex or my children in danger," she said. "Alex has not seen me in years. I have grown up."

"Aye, you have," he confirmed.

The sound of footsteps on the stairs startled them and they separated. He leaned leisurely against the door.

A man in a British uniform came lurching toward them. He leered at Janet, then continued on after seeing Neil's glare.

"You had best go inside," he said.

She hesitated.

"I have some business to attend to."

"More secrets?"

"Nay, I am going to try to find some French brandy for His Grace. And through that, a smuggler. The best way to do that is to get some soldiers of the king well in their cups." He touched her arm. "I will call for you in the morning for breakfast."

That brief explanation was a gift.

Her hand caught his. "Thank you." She meant it this time. She meant it with all her heart.

He suddenly grinned. It was totally unexpected and rare

and had a sweetness she had never seen before. The latter did not seem to fit a man bent on cozening the British this night.

Or mayhap it did.

He opened the door. She leaned against it when he closed it. Her hand still burned from his touch.

She listened to his footsteps moving away.

Alive. In hiding. With children. Her brother had never been easy with children. She had to smile thinking of him as a shepherd to a covey of them.

He had been right. She did want to see him. She wanted her brother to meet her son before Alex left Scotland forever.

There had to be a way without hurting the children. There had to be.

Chapter Twenty-three

"Rotten stuff," Neil said, slinging the contents of his tankard to the floor. The four British officers he was treating gave him bleary looks. One nodded with approval.

"My cousin always had far better," he continued with a drunken slur. "Does no one know where to get decent wine?"

"I heard your cousin smuggled it in," one officer smirked.

Neil raised an eyebrow and grinned. "My cousin? He would not do anything unlawful."

"He cheated at cards," one man said darkly.

Another snorted. "He means the man beat him. Braemoor was a generous fellow. So, my friend, are you."

"I try to follow his example," Neil said with a fulsome grin. "In truth, His Grace remarked he would be most grateful if I could find more of that brandy he likes, but I have no idea where Rory obtained it."

"His Grace?" one of the earlier speakers asked, obviously impressed.

"Aye, I had an audience with him this very day and he asked about the brandy. I would be extremely grateful if anyone knows its source."

"How grateful, my lord?"

"Most grateful," Neil said. "About fifty pounds grateful."

Several officers straightened in their chairs. Fifty pounds was a fortune. But they all knew what he was asking: the name of a smuggler.

"And it *is* for His Grace." Neil licked his lips. "Though I must admit I do miss good brandy. As do my friends." When silence followed, he yelled for another pitcher of ale and listened to a ribald joke about a Scotsman.

He hid his temper behind a fatuous grin. He had taken insults all his life, and he had never been one to mix in politics or take on hopeless causes. But he had changed these past months since Culloden. Mayhap it had been his cousin. Mayhap Janet. Even Alexander. It might even have been the one-sided battle itself. He did not know. He only felt a fierce pride for those Scots who had given up everything for their country, and contempt for these people who feasted on his Scotland.

But now was not the time to show it.

He finally finished his tankard and rose. "I thank you for a fine evening," he said, "but I have not my cousin's constitution, God rest his soul. I need fresh air before . . ."

He lurched out and down the street, despite the fact that his rooms were right above. He stopped several buildings down and leaned against a wall. He'd cast his net. He could see whether it caught anything.

Neil's head was bobbing when he heard a voice. "Did you mean what you said about the fifty pounds?"

He looked up. The person addressing him had been sitting at another table. Neil saw that he was dressed in plain clothes, not a uniform, but he could see little else in the fog that blanketed the city.

" 'Bout what?" Neil asked drunkenly. "Ah, the brandy. Aye. I meant it. Who are you?"

"The name is not important," the man said. "The information is."

"Then tell me where I can find some of this brandy. If it is as you say, then I will pay you."

"Now," the man said. "You will pay me now."

"Do I look like a fool?"

"Aye," his companion said.

"An honest answer. However, I am not *that* much a fool. I would need proof."

"A small keg?"

"A small keg is not enough for my needs."

"Nay, but you will know I have access."

"I had planned to leave tomorrow."

The stranger's jaw twitched. Then, "How do I know you are not an informer?"

"My friend, I do not need to be an informer. I am rather wealthy." He paused, then decided to play another card. "I know that my cousin often saw an actress. I thought she might know a good source of brandy. But apparently she has left Edinburgh."

Something flickered in the stranger's eyes.

Neil waited to see whether greed or caution would win.

It was greed. "I will have the keg in an hour. Where should I take it?"

"I have a room at the inn. It is the third left on the second floor."

The man backed away and disappeared into the foggy night. Neil remained where he was for a moment, still lolling against the building in the event that someone else had taken his bait.

After several moments, he returned to the inn, passed by the taproom and went up the steps. He stopped midway, realizing he'd lost his drunken swagger. He was obviously not cut out for subterfuge. Neil wondered how his cousin had managed his charade for so long.

He hesitated outside Janet's room. He'd known it was awkward that she had not brought a maid with her. But he had not known if they would have to move rapidly. If she was to be arrested, he would have united her with her brother, gathered the children and tried to get them out of the country. But now they had time. Perhaps she could still salvage a life at Lochaene.

And that was what he wanted.

Aye, it was what had to be.

Still, he knocked lightly on the door. If she were asleep, he hoped he would not wake her, but if she could not sleep—as he expected—he could answer some of her questions. He could not stay long since he expected a visitor, but he knew she must be anxious about Alexander. She would want to know more. She had been too stunned to react earlier.

The door opened. She was still fully dressed.

He slipped inside and closed the door behind him.

She looked beautiful. Her hair was loose and fell down her back, the tawny shade catching streaks of gold from a roaring fire in the hearth. Her blue eyes appeared even darker than before and were roiling with emotion.

He opened his arms and she slipped into them. Her body moved instinctively to nestle with his. He leaned down and kissed her forehead. It was a mistake. A second later, his lips were moving over her face with a tenderness he'd confined within himself for years.

Their lips met. He heard her small moan, and subdued the one rising in his own throat. It was as if they both had been waiting for this all their lives. He was seized by a need so strong and powerful that he could think of nothing else. There had always been electricity between them, a smoldering fire, but now it was an inferno.

He needed to leave. He needed to leave this moment. But just then she stood on tiptoe, her body fitting his like a glove, her lips so very inviting. He deepened his kiss, and it became something desperate and wild and abandoned. His mouth played with her lips and, feeling her mouth open to him, his tongue reached out and explored greedily. Her tongue met his, shyly at first, then eagerly, and they teased each other until all their senses reeled.

Neil felt a craving he had never known before as his body tensed and responded to hers. They moved even closer, bodies pressing against each other with a need as elemental as a violent Highland storm and the warmth of a summer sun.

His lips caressed her with a possessiveness that jolted him, and he drew away, his eyes searching her face. Dear God, how he wanted her. In so many ways. He knew he had been waiting for this all his life, this explosive mixture of sweetness and ferocity, of the need to give and take at the same time.

He saw the smoldering desire in her eyes and his heart warred between craving and caution. The former won. He shook his head in defeat and saw the realization reflected in her eyes.

Neil felt her hand on his face, exploring it, and his hand captured it, bringing it to his mouth. He kissed it simply, first the palm, then the back, and he was plunged into waves of longing he could no longer suppress.

Janet knew the second it happened. It was as if a curtain had been lifted from his eyes. She felt his hands hesitate, then run up and down the side of her body with such gentleness that her heart ached. Her husband had never been gentle. He'd always taken her roughly.

Neil's touch, so tender and even reverent, wiped away any doubts she had.

She willed him to continue when she sensed his momentary hesitation. Her hands went up to tangle themselves in his hair, to touch and caress the back of his neck. She knew now she had never stopped loving him. God knew she had tried. But they were like gunpowder and fire. Suppressed hunger radiated between them.

All her tumultuous emotions of the past few days erupted, tearing down every emotional barrier she'd tried so hard to build. The anger was gone. The distrust had faded. After her initial anger, she realized how much he had done. Quietly, without ever asking for anything, he was risking death to save her brother. He had been willing to forfeit his own future for her safety. He had patiently tried to make her children happy and comfortable.

She looked up at his roughly hewn face and thought how beloved it was. And irresistible to her. She loved the dark brows, the serious eyes, the hard planes of his cheeks. Her lips moved from his lips and nuzzled his ear. She felt his body respond, knew she was igniting a firestorm of desire. Her fingers unbuttoned his waistcoat, and he shrugged it off onto the floor. His neckcloth went next, leaving a plain linen shirt and breeches. His fingers were equally as occupied. They were busy untying the ribbons of her gown. He was clumsy at it, and that pleased her. But still it did not take him long to finish and the dress dropped to her feet, and she stood there in only her chemise and petticoat.

She trembled as he moved closer to her, and she felt the throbbing of his need as their bodies met, melded. The burning inside intensified. She had never known something this powerful existed. She had been attracted to him years earlier, and they had traded kisses and embraces. There had even been a yearning curiosity, but nothing like this raging need that roared through her.

"Ah, lass," he whispered in her ear. It seemed almost a sigh of surrender. But she had no time to analyze it because his lips were brushing kisses along her neck, lingering at the hollow at her throat. Unfettered by the loose, low-cut shift, they moved down to her breasts, licking first the left, then the right, leaving trails of liquid fire as he went. Each new touch aroused more sensations until she thought she would explode with the exquisite need undulating within her.

He took off her petticoat, and she stood clothed only in the short linen shift. He looked at it for a very long moment. His dark eyes were glittering with passion and yes, recklessness. It was as if he were someone else tonight. She smelled spirits, but she did not care. She cared only about having his arms around her.

Most of all, she wanted his body connected to hers in the most intimate way. She wanted him bound to the deepest essence of her.

She had always wanted it. She had wanted it when he had

first come to Lochaene, but she had not allowed herself to dream again, and so she had pushed him away and tried to despise him.

She touched the thongs on his breeches.

He stilled. "I canna stay now, lass. I am expecting a visitor." His voice was hoarse to her ears, thick with the passion that bound them. "It may be our solution to getting your brother out of Scotland."

She leaned against him. She wanted him now, here. She thought for a moment she wanted it more than anything in the world. But that was not true. Most of all, she wanted him, and Alex and Colin and her daughters, safe.

"I will come back if you agree," he said as his hand touched her cheek.

"Will you?"

"It would not be wise."

"And you are always wise."

"Nay, or I would not have stopped here this night." His fingers played with her hair, touching her shoulders.

"I will wait for you."

He leaned down. "It may be late," he warned.

Every part of her body was crying out for him. She feared letting him go. Mayhap it *would* be as it had been eight years ago.

"Nay, lass," he said as if reading her mind. "I will not do that to you again. But I must tell you something first, and I have not the time now."

Ominous. It was ominous. But he was relacing his trousers, and the moment was broken. But he would be back. She struggled for the trust she needed.

So she merely nodded and accompanied him as he shrugged on his waistcoat, then carelessly tied the neck cloth. Then he leaned over and kissed her. "If you are asleep," he said, "I will not wake you."

Before she could respond he was out the door.

•　　•　　•

Janet sat before the fire and waited. She did not need the warmth, though. She felt on fire.

Would he indeed be back? Or would he greet her in the morning with a cool, regretful glance? Could she stand that?

She watched the flickering flames in the fireplace. What else did he have to tell her? It could not be any worse than hiding the fact that her brother was alive.

Because they had traveled by horseback, she had not brought a separate shift for sleeping. She felt more than a little naked, but she had no wish to put her dress back on. She went to the bed and took a blanket from it and wrapped it around her, then sat down again.

She thought about those weeks so many years ago, when she was young and sure and ever so happy. She'd been so convinced she had found her true love, the one man who could make her happy. She remembered the way he had smiled shyly at her, at the reserved quiet way he'd courted her. He'd had a lonely dignity that had appealed to everything in her. He still had it. That, she knew, was why she trusted him now, and made her wonder why he had rejected her years ago. He had not seemed feckless then. He certainly was not today. Then why had he disappeared so abruptly?

Was that what he wanted to explain?

She listened for footsteps passing, then grew drowsy.

She missed Colin. It was the first time she had ever been away from him. Her arms felt empty and she found herself listening for his garbled sounds. She curled up in the chair. Neil had locked the room and taken the key. He had also promised not to wake her if she were asleep. She had to make sure she was not asleep.

She did nod off. But she woke when she heard the door open. She turned around and watched Neil enter. He had shed his waistcoat and carried a keg and a tankard with him. "Would you share a glass with me?"

He had that odd reckless look again. It added another dimension to him, an intriguing one.

"Aye," she said. "What happened?"

"I have a name of a smuggler on the coast. I will make a trip down there and see if I can get passage for your brother."

He filled the tankard and offered it to her. She took a sip, felt the rich warmth flow through her. She'd often had wine, but she had never had brandy, and she found the smooth rich taste to her liking.

"It is a very good brandy," he said with half smile.

She handed it back to him. She hadn't needed the warmth provided by the spirits and the fire. His smile did that. As did his touch as his fingers brushed hers.

"I wish I could go with you," she said longingly.

"I know," he said. "But it takes far more bravery to stay when you want to go. Your children need you."

"Aye," she said. "And I miss them. This is the first time I have been away." She was silent for a moment. "I would like to see Alex."

He sighed. "I will try to arrange something."

She studied him. She was no longer sleepy and his eyes were alert though guarded.

Janet stood, the blanket falling from her, and reached for his hand, then led him to the bed. She sat while he still stood but he kept her fingers clasped in hers.

His hand was warm. That heat coursed through her. She waited for him to speak.

After a moment, he sat next to her and touched her face in a gesture so longing and so tender, that terror struck her. She knew suddenly that she was not going to like what he had to say. Her fingers tightened around his.

She knew she should feel some kind of shame at being clad only in her thin shift. But even when she'd been so angry, she'd never felt awkward with him. She realized then that they unconsciously shared an intimacy, a bond, an attachment that had never dissipated.

She leaned against him. "What is it?"

His fingers tightened around her hand. "Lass, you are so very bonny." The words hovered in the air as he hesitated, then continued. "I meant everything I told you eight years ago." Each word, she thought, sounded painful.

"Then why . . . ?"

"When I told my uncle I wished to marry you, he explained something I did not know," he said.

She did not ask the question. He would continue in his own way, and she feared the coming words. She felt the tenseness in his body, the hardening clasp of his fingers against hers.

"I was taken from my mother when I was but a lad," he said. "She was . . . quiet, always rocking in a chair. I canna remember her ever saying a word."

She was watching him. She saw a muscle flex in his cheek, the granite look of his face, the agony in his eyes.

"I did not miss her because she had never . . . really been there," he said. "My grandfather was a bitter man, and ill. One day, a stranger simply came and took me. I was trained and educated with the son of the Marquis of Braemoor and told I was to be his companion and bodyguard. It was not until much later that I learned that my father had been brother to the marquis."

A knot of apprehension twisted her stomach.

After a timeless second, he continued. "The day . . . I asked for your hand, my uncle told me my mother had been mad and had killed herself after I left. Her mother, too, had been mad. The . . . illness tainted the entire line for centuries." He paused. "I did not know. I swear it," he said with a vulnerable catch in his voice. "I could have that taint, Janet. I could well end up mad. And I can have no children. I could not do that to you."

Her fingers tightened around his. His words slashed at her heart because she knew what they had cost him. And yet . . . something else lightened in her as she suddenly understood what had happened eight years earlier.

She could not speak for a moment. She had not known what to expect. She had expected an explanation of why he had left so abruptly years ago. A youthful indiscretion. The loss of her dowry when her father refused her hand. So many things. But never this.

And now she knew why her father had been so against the match and had whisked her away.

"Why did you not tell me?"

"Your father convinced me not to. He said you were too loyal. He said you would not accept it, that you might never marry if I could not. We . . . both wanted you to wed and have bairns of your own."

"My papa?" She felt the tears well in her eyes. He had known how unhappy she had been. If only he had explained . . .

"He thought he was doing the best thing for you. . . ."

"No one knows the best thing for someone else," she said painfully.

He was silent.

She swallowed through the lump in her throat. He had loved her. He had loved her enough to make her hate him. "Why did you not tell me when you came to Lochaene?"

"I did not think this would happen," he said. "I thought . . . I could try to help, then leave. I did not think . . ."

"That love lingers?" she finished.

"Aye. At least not on your part, after . . ."

She touched his face. There was so much pain in his voice. In his eyes. She knew now how much love he had to give. She had tried not to see it, but it had been there all along. With the girls. With the way he looked down at her son. With the restrained but ever so tender caresses he had given to her.

He had so much love in him, and he'd tried so hard to smother it that he'd isolated himself from everyone. Raw pain twisted inside her and she fought a wave of quiet despair. He was telling her this now for a reason. He was telling her that they could not be together. Ever.

But she didn't want him to see her pain. He'd had too much himself.

"I have children now," she said quietly. "I do not need more."

His gaze sharpened. " 'Tis not just children, lass. It is the fact that I might well go mad some day. I could not . . . inflict that on you. I remember my mother, the bewilderment when I touched her. . . ." .

There was a finality in his voice.

"We have *now*," she said.

"Aye," he said wistfully. "We have now."

She lifted her head until her lips touched his cheek. His large hand tenderly pushed a curl from her face and his lips touched her forehead, then her eyes, now awash with tears. His hands had never been so gentle as when he cupped her face in them and lifted it toward him as if trying to memorize everything on it.

"I have always loved you, lass," he said. "I want you to know that."

Her heart almost broke then.

Her hands pulled him to her and neither for his sake or her own could she deny the deep aching need to be with him, to feel his heart next to hers, to have him join with her, regardless of the consequences.

His arms went around hers and he held her tight, resting his head against hers. "This is so unwise," he said in a broken voice.

"I do not care," she whispered. "We will worry about tomorrow later, and I want tonight."

"What is left of it," he said wryly, but there was a rough emotion to his voice. His lips caught hers again, and her mouth opened. Swirling eddies of desire enveloped them both, tumbling them along in a flood that eclipsed everyone and everything except each other.

A whisper in the back of her mind warned her. But it was as a willow in the wind, unsubstantial compared to the power of her feelings, to the need that battered her very soul. It was not physical need as much as the need to bring a smile to his face, to light those eyes that were so filled with anguish.

She felt the tension in his body, the barely restrained passion in his hands, which moved seductively now at the small of her back. Their touch sent sensations shooting through her.

Janet leaned back in his arms, seeking a respite from the emotions battering her, emotions that overruled every sensible part of her. More . . . intimacy was only going to make it more difficult to lose him, and she knew she *would* lose him. He had made that clear.

He pushed a curl back from her face. "I will not leave my seed in you, Janet."

She did not care. Whatever will she had, he destroyed with a touch. Her heart thudded so hard she thought he must hear it. She felt his need and any doubts dissolved into immense longing.

His mouth melded to her and her hands tightened on the linen shirt that molded to his body as he leaned toward her. Then her thoughts faded as his kiss deepened, his tongue roaming and stroking and seducing as shudder after shudder flooded her body.

His hands lifted her shift over her body then caressed her breasts, which she felt swell and tingle and ache. It was a courting of her body, and it responded in magical ways she never knew possible. Her husband had taken his rights. He had never prepared her, nor caressed her, nor touched her with any love.

She had never known that a man could make her body sing. Every touch was like a bow across the strings of a fiddle. It hummed and responded to his slightest touch, each stroke of his fingers leading toward a crescendo.

Her fingers unlaced his breeches. He gave her a small smile and he leaned down, pulling off his boots, then shrugged off his breeches. She saw the still raw ugly scar from the bullet wound, and her fingers ran over it. His body shivered slightly as she did so and she drew them back.

"Nay, lass. It is not pain that made me react." He caught her fingers and brought them to his mouth, nibbling lightly on them. Then he released them and his fingers went to her face, then her hair. "I . . . dreamed of this," he said, his voice barely audible.

She leaned against him, feeling the strength beneath the shirt, the hard muscles of his chest. She could even hear the beating of his heart. She had never felt as close to another human being, had never known that this kind of intimacy existed, had never realized the splendor of it.

His hands guided her down on the bed, then stroked her until she felt as if she would explode with need. She looked up at him, and the same tumultuous excitement glittered in his eyes. His mouth moved to her breasts, first one, then the other, his tongue teasing and leaving hot wakes in its path. Then his fingers moved to the most intimate part of her, caressing, arousing until her body was alive with sizzling fires.

He moved next to her. He angled himself above her and she felt his manhood reach out to her, pulsing with need. Her body trembled with expectation, with wanting, and the core of her was a pool of warmth.

When at last he entered her, he did so with a slow magic. He moved deliberately, teasing every sense, going deeper until the sensations became so thunderous, so fiery, so full of splendor that nothing mattered except this one moment in time. And then the universe exploded; pieces of stars floated down to earth. . . .

He left her then, quickly, pulling away and spilling his seed on a blanket. He then stood and went to the window, keeping his eyes averted, but she saw his clenched fists. Dear God, she wanted to go to him. He looked so alone, standing there. And she felt alone now that he had left her.

His self-control told her he would not change his mind.

He turned around. His face was granite again. He came over to her and sat down, taking her hand. The muscle in his cheek rippled.

"I do not care about your mother," she said.

"I do," he said. "I knew what it was like as a child. I would not subject your son to that."

"You do not know anything for sure," she argued.

"I know enough, lass."

Her heart screamed at the hopelessness in his eyes, the gathering sense of loss in herself.

He brushed away a curl from her face, just as he had done earlier, but now there was a resignation about him.

"I had best go and let you get some sleep."

"Stay with me tonight," she pleaded. She did not care about pride now, about regrets. She only wanted the warmth of him next to her for a few hours. He would leave tomorrow to do something very dangerous on her behalf and that of her brother. She could not let him leave like this.

His lips turned into a half smile. "I am not sure I can keep away from you."

"I hope not."

"You are a wanton lass," he said as his fingers tightened around hers.

"Aye."

His gaze met hers. Then he nodded.

He went to the candle and blew it out, then lowered himself into the bed beside her. She moved into his arms and he held her there.

Neither moved the rest of the night.

Chapter Twenty-four

Neil rode hard the next day. He did so because he had much to do. He also hurried because he needed to throw the devil off his back. Neil imagined he sat there, leering at him.

Janet was on her way back to Braemoor, accompanied by two men he'd hired and a fat palomino pony he'd found the morning before they had left Edinburgh.

He had taken great care in selecting the bodyguards. Both were Scotsmen who had come highly recommended by the innkeeper. He had then checked on them through other sources, and made sure they would receive no money until they arrived safely at Braemoor.

He had not wanted to do it, but he'd had no choice. If he had taken Janet back, he would have lost at least four days. From what his informant told him, there would be a delivery of French goods on the coast this week. He had to be there.

And he could not take Janet with him. She had bairns that needed her far more than he, or Alex, did. It had nearly shattered what composure he had left to let her go alone. He had seen the look in her eyes, the knowledge that last night would be the only one they would have. She had stretched up and kissed him, slowly and wistfully and lovingly.

It was a memory he would always have. He carried it with him now.

He dug his heels into his mount.

He knew he had a day of hard riding to reach Alex's mountain lair and explain what was needed from him. Then two days to the coast. Finally, three more days to ride back to Braemoor. He could only hope that Cumberland would delay any action on Janet until then. He was almost convinced that the small seeds he'd planted might make him hesitate.

If only Alex could accomplish his part.

He stopped only long enough to rest and water his mount, then traveled on, only too aware of his weariness. He'd had little sleep in the past few days and nearly none at all last night. And he had dropped enough information to Cumberland that the duke might well have sent out patrols. Neil knew he had to skirt roads and be cautious.

As he climbed up into the Highlands, he felt more alive than at any other time in his life. The grass was greener, the sun brighter, the air fresher. If he could not have Janet, at least she had given him something he had never had before. He had known love.

He had wanted to improve his properties, and the lot of people on those properties, but there had been a distance between them and him. He had eyed it as an intellectual problem. It was part of the wall he had built around himself.

But since he'd been with Janet, watched her gentle ways with her children and with servants, and watched them bloom under that care, he knew he would never see people as an intellectual problem again.

He slept briefly when clouds cloaked the moon and he could no longer ride safely. But it was a restless sleep, plagued by images, by the many things he must do, and do right unless lives were to be lost. It was a burden he had not wanted, and yet . . .

He was riding again at daybreak, and reached Alex's lair by noon. He whistled as he drew near, then waited. He whistled again, and in minutes he heard an answer. He dismounted and led his weary mount.

Alex and one of the young lads met him.

"Braemoor?" Alex acknowledged.

"I have some news," Neil said.

Alex turned to the boy, a gangly youth of approximately thirteen years. "Go inside and tell the others it is a friend."

Friend. The word sounded very good to Neil. Now that he thought about it, he had never had one. That was a sad admission for anyone.

When the lad disappeared through the trees, Alex turned to him, questions in his eyes.

Neil did not know how to be indirect or to soften the blow. "The Campbell family has gone to Cumberland with accusations that Janet murdered her husband. His Grace did not say whether he believed them or not but I suspect he is under pressure by the Campbell family." He paused, then added, "Reginald is from one of the lesser branches of the family, but he can still call on them."

Alex's lips tightened in a grim line. "I will kill Campbell."

"That would not help Janet. It would only convince Cumberland that Reginald was right."

Fury clouded Alex's eyes.

"There *is* something you can do."

Alex raised an eyebrow in question.

"You can become the Black Knave."

"*You* said he was dead."

"I want to resurrect him."

"Why?"

"I told Cumberland I was wounded by the Black Knave, that I was sure that there was a connection to Reginald. He will have patrols east of here. I told him that was where I was attacked."

"Go on," Alex said, an edge in his voice.

"The Black Knave must strike near Lochaene. He must steal. He must leave cards. He must somehow drop Reginald's name."

"I do not look anything like Reginald."

"It doesna matter. The Black Knave takes many different forms. There have been so many differing descriptions, I am sure Cumberland believes he has associates. The goal is to throw so much suspicion on Reginald that any charges he might make would never be considered."

"He's a Campbell. No one would suspect him of being the Knave."

Neil hesitated. This was not his secret to tell. Rory had staged his own death to protect Braemoor. But Neil expected Alex to trust him, so he would have to trust Alex in return. He'd never done that before. Just as he'd never had a friend. The knowledge felt like a damnation.

"Neither did anyone suspect Forbes of being the Knave," Neil said.

Alex's brows arched upward. "You said . . ."

"I did not lie. I said I was not the Knave. My cousin was."

Alex's brows knitted together. "I heard of him, even met him once. He was a fool."

"Was he?" Neil asked. "I thought so, too. I had nothing but contempt for him. I thought he had run from Culloden because he was a coward. He turned out to be the bravest man I've ever known."

Alex's gaze locked on his. "Where is he now?"

"Safe somewhere. I do not know where. I only know he went to great effort to make everyone believe he was killed by the Knave. He wanted to protect the people at Braemoor." He hesitated, then added, "You are the only man in Scotland other than myself who now knows."

Alex nodded his understanding.

"I also know a French ship is smuggling brandy to the coast. It should be there this week. I plan to meet the captain and try to make arrangements for your passage. You will have only three or four weeks to bring the Knave back to life."

Alex shook his head. "You do not waste time."

"I never saw a reason to do so," Neil said. "Every moment you stay in Scotland you are a threat to Janet."

"Why do you care so much?" Alex asked.

Neil drew in a deep breath. "I . . . admire her."

"Is that all?"

"That is all there ever can be," he said with as much finality as he could put into his voice.

Alex studied him for a long moment.

"There is something else," Neil said. "Janet knows you are alive."

Dark blue eyes so like Janet's glared at him. "You gave me your promise."

Neil nodded. "Aye, I did. And I meant to keep it. But I told her I knew someone who needed to flee Scotland and might be able to imitate the Knave. She asked your name. I could not lie about something that important to her." He hesitated, then continued. "She has children. She would do nothing to endanger them, not even to see you. But she told me to tell you she loves you. You canna know the joy the news gave her."

Alex's hard face softened. "I have missed her. It was hell realizing she did not know. But I truly thought it better for her not to know until I escaped Scotland."

Neil did not reply. Alex had not seen his sister in several years, had not seen his sister since she'd become a mother. She had a mother lion's protectiveness of her children.

"I am going to do my best to see that you meet before you leave," he said.

Alex's lips bent into a half smile. Because of the scar it would always be a half smile. "I knew there was a reason I did not let Burke kill you. I had this strange feeling that I should not. If I was Irish, I would say it was the faeries."

"Then you will be the Knave?"

"With pleasure, my lord."

"Where is Burke?"

"Getting supplies, thanks to you."

"I asked you before whether or no' you could trust him."

"Aye, and my answer is the same. But I will not tell him about your cousin."

"Send him to Braemoor. There are some items there that you might be able to use. Janet can show him where they are. And you might well use a mask."

"I would like to go myself."

" 'Tis too dangerous for both of you," Neil replied. "If you were caught anywhere around Braemoor she would be the one to pay. And the children. Reginald would most certainly have her tried."

A visible shudder ran through Alex's body. "That bastard."

"He will pay," Neil said. "In a way he will not expect."

Alex stared at him for a moment. "You fought at Culloden?"

"Aye. With Cumberland," Neil said evenly.

"And you saw the error of your ways?"

"I ran into the Leslies," Neil said simply.

Alex held out his hand. "I thank you for everything you are doing."

Neil extended his hand while discomfort roiled around inside him. He did not want thanks. He did not even want to be here. He was a fraud. One that was stumbling around with little idea of whether anything was going to succeed. He might well be readying the hangman's noose for them all.

But Alex's grip was strong and he found himself returning it, their eyes meeting.

Neil released it. "Do you have some food for both myself and the horse? And I need a few hours' sleep. Then I am bound for the coast."

"Aye," Alex said and led Neil inside the cave. It was dark and damp, but a small smoky fire burned toward the back. Although Neil had been in the cave briefly on his last visit, the children had melted into its back recesses, and he had really seen very little of them. Now they seemed assured that he was, indeed, a friend.

Still, too-large eyes in too-small faces regarded him warily. Only God knew what had happened to them in the year since Culloden. He remembered the young lass who had washed his face on his first visit here. And the oldest lad. He must be the one wanted by Cumberland. The others ranged in age from eight to about thirteen.

He was given a bowl of oatmeal, several hard biscuits and a cup of bad ale.

"We have no meat," Alex said.

"I do not need it," Neil said.

The wee lass who had tried so solemnly to nurse him weeks ago came over to him. "Alex said you were going to help us." Her lips quivered.

"I hope so," he said. "What is your name, lass?"

"Sophie McSparren," she said.

He wanted to ask what had happened to her family, but that was not a question one asked these days. Not of a child.

The child sat next to him but she said nothing else. She just watched him as if judging. He wanted to reach out and hug her. He had no right. He might well have killed her father. Damn it all to hell.

He finished as quickly as he could. Alex showed him a corner in the back where he could sleep, and he led the girl away. Neil watched the outlaw get down on one knee and talk to her. There was a gentleness in the gesture. Gentleness in a man who had cold-bloodedly intended to kill him.

Neil closed his eyes. Damn, but he was tired, and he had a long ride ahead of him tonight.

With mixed emotions, Janet approached Braemoor. The escorts Neil had hired in Edinburgh had been respectful and polite. She had stopped at the same inn where she and Neil had stayed a few day earlier. She kept remembering the companionship of that ride, even at the pace Neil had set.

She missed him with every step her mount took. She missed stealing glances at him. She missed his hands, which reached out to catch her as she dismounted. And his face, as he had told her about his mother, haunted her.

She also missed, almost beyond belief, holding her son

and singing a lullaby to the lasses. She missed their hands in
hers, and seeing the happiness on their faces as they rode the
ponies.

And then she longed to see Alex before he left Scotland,
and her life, forever.

Her heart felt torn in three different directions. The simple truth was that her greatest duty was to those who could
not protect themselves.

They reached Braemoor in the late afternoon. She did not
wait for her escorts to help her dismount. She slid off the
horse herself and nearly ran to the door, opening it herself.

Torquil appeared seemingly out of nowhere. His grave
face broke into a hint of a smile when he saw her.

"The children?" she asked.

"Fine as the day," he said, then hesitated. "Some horse-
men came by, saying they represented your brother-in-law.
They tried to take the young lord." He straightened, pride radiating from him. "I took my musket to them, as did young
Kevin and the men the marquis had asked to stay here."

Her heart pounded wildly. She should have suspected. At
least Neil had. "Thank you," she said, reaching out her hand
to take his. Then she turned to the two soldiers standing behind her. "These men escorted me. The marquis promised
them twenty pounds, good wine and a fine meal."

Torquil nodded. "Your lasses will be pleased to see you. I
will take care of these gentlemen."

Janet turned to the two men. "Thank you for taking such
good care of me."

The face of one of the men flushed with pleasure. "It was
our honor, my lady."

She stayed no longer, but mounted the steps with unlady-
like haste. She headed first for the nursery. All four children
were there. Colin was on the floor playing with Samson.
Grace had obviously been reading and the other two were
painting pictures, with more paint on them than on the can-
vases. All three jumped up when she walked in.

Colin reached the table, and using one of its legs, stood

up, wobbling slightly. He let go to hold out his two arms to her and took an unsteady step toward her. She reached him before he fell and picked him up, holding him close to her. "Ah, my wee love," she said, her heart skipping a beat. His first faltering step. *The first she had seen.* Had he taken a step without her? She did not want to miss even one of those milestones in his life.

Still holding him tight, she stooped and received the hugs of her daughters. Annabella's kiss was especially moist and enthusiastic. When Janet had become their stepmother, she had been the first to embrace her unhesitatingly. It had taken Grace the longest time, but now even her eyes filled with pleasure at seeing her stepmother.

Janet's heart swelled with emotion. She was back with them. Thanks to Neil. She rested a hand on Grace's shoulder. "I think there is something special for you outside."

Grace's eyes had widened. "A pony."

"Aye. From the marquis."

Grace stood silently for a moment, as if she could not believe it. Janet could not ever remember Grace receiving a gift from her father. Her own Christmas gifts to Grace had been made-over dresses and homemade dolls. Alasdair had always said there was no money for fripperies.

"Can we ride our ponies?" Annabella asked.

"I think Grace's new pony will be tired, but you may all go look at her."

Clara, who was behind them, shook her head. It was so rare that the nursemaid ever refused the lasses anything, Janet hesitated, then spoke to Grace. "Will you find Lucy first and tell her I am back? Then I will go with you."

Obviously disappointed, Grace looked at her for a moment.

"I will be there in a moment," Janet assured her.

Grace nodded reluctantly, then took Annabella's hand, Rachel following behind.

When the three were gone, Clara closed the door behind them. "Someone came tae take Colin," she said. "Said his uncle had sent for 'im. Torquil would no let him do it, but Jamie has seen them skulking about when he rode tae the village. We 'ave not been letting them go out alone."

Janet clutched Colin closer to her. The lasses were of no value to Reginald except for purposes of bargaining, a way to get her back to Lochaene. He knew she loved the lasses as much as she did Colin. Or mayhap they still had hoped to take Colin.

She balanced Colin in one arm and held the other out to clasp Clara's. "Thank you."

"They are like my own," Clara said awkwardly.

Janet nodded. "We will be very careful."

"The lasses have been told not to go outside the manor without someone with them."

"Good," she said, relieved beyond belief that she had not tried to go with Neil. She wished she could reach him, but it seemed he had left sufficient help behind. Still, she could not let go of Colin. She knew she would not let him out of her sight until Neil returned.

And when they returned to Lochaene . . . ?

Janet had lost all her enthusiasm for the return. She would lose Neil then. Yet Lochaene was still her son's heritage. She had to protect it for him, no matter what the cost to her.

Still holding a squirming Colin, she went down the stairs to the kitchen where the lasses were talking to her maid, Lucy. All three held carrots.

Lucy curtsied. "'Tis glad I am to see you back," she said.

"Even if there is more work?" Janet teased.

"I barely knew what to do wi' myself," Lucy replied.

"With Kevin around?"

Lucy's face reddened. "Aye, my lady."

"Thank you for helping Trilby and Clara take such good care of the children."

Lucy bobbed again.

"I have some candy for them, and some for you and Clara and Trilby, too," she said.

"Oh, miss," Lucy said with a huge grin.

Holding Colin, Janet took her daughters outside. Either Kevin or Jamie had evidently already taken the pony into the barn, and they walked over to it. Kevin had unsaddled her mare, and the saddle was on the stall door. Jamie was admiring the palomino pony. The two horses her escorts had been riding had been unsaddled and put into stalls.

The two—Kevin and Jamie—worked well together, she noted, almost like brothers. It was obvious that Jamie looked up to Kevin.

Grace gingerly stepped up to the pony and ran her fingers down its velvety neck as Rachel and Annabella also admired her. The pony seemed to preen, as if knowing she was the center of adulation.

Her eyes glowing, Grace held out her other hand with the piece of carrot and the pony crunched it in its mouth, then nuzzled her fingers. She giggled, and the sound made Janet's heart leap. It came so rarely.

Kevin greeted her with a big grin, and then inquired, "My lord did not come back?"

"Nay," she said, watching the lad's face fall. Well, Neil had made one friend.

"He will be back in several days," she said as she ran a hand along the mare's neck. She had been ridden hard. "Give her extra feed when she has cooled. The others, too."

"Will the escorts be staying?"

"Nay, they will leave on the morrow. They will stay in the hall tonight."

The lasses had gone over to the ponies. She lowered her voice. "Clara told me what happened. Do you think we need more protection?"

He visibly puffed at being asked the question. "Nay, my lady. We can take care of Braemoor. But I would not be riding alone."

She nodded. She remembered the cut cinch only too well. And now she had no intention of leaving the children, not even for a short ride. Neil had been right. How could she have discounted his warnings so flippantly?

Annabella came running over to her, Samson at her heels. "Can I ride my pony? Kevin said I couldna until you came back."

She looked at Kevin. He nodded.

"I think that is a fine idea," she said. "But we will stay in the paddock. Grace's pony is probably tired from her long journey."

Grace looked up. "I can wait," she said, but her eyes glittered with disappointment.

"Oh, I do not think a turn or two around the paddock will be too much," she said.

Janet helped Annabella on her pony as Kevin assisted Grace. Then Kevin helped Rachel. The three rode the ponies out into the paddock, Kevin leading Annabella's. Grace beamed with pride, and Janet silently blessed Neil for remembering and for having taken the time to purchase the pony. She had known how anxious he was to be on his way, and yet . . . he kept his promise to a lass who'd had few dreams.

He was the kind of man who would always keep his promises.

The reminder was hurtful. She could forget neither the determination nor the hopelessness in his eyes when he had said he loved her but could never marry her.

Unless he was wrong, and madness did not haunt his family. She already knew from the servants that the old marquis had been cruel and selfish. He probably would not have hesitated for a moment to destroy his nephew in order to win a fine dowry for his son. He had not known that she would refuse Donald, and that her father would give her a choice.

As she watched her daughters and clung to her son, a part of her started to question the truth of Neil's background. There must be someone who would know the truth of it. She would start this evening with Torquil.

Suddenly buoyed by the prospect, she allowed herself to relax and enjoy the grins on her lasses' faces.

• • •

Neil sat in the Pelican Tavern, nursing his sixth glass of ale. Or was it the seventh? God knew he had spent enough time here to nearly consume all its limited offerings. He had asked for brandy but had been told there was none available. It was hinted that it might be available later.

That had been enough for Neil. The man in Edinburgh had the right of it. But, then, he had known a considerable sum awaited him if the information proved correct.

Neil realized he was spending money at an ungodly rate. He had never done that before. Even when he'd come into the inheritance, he'd weighed the merits of each pence spent. Only something that improved the estates met with his approval and even then he sought ways to reduce costs. Money had been too dear to him. He had not ever thought he could spend it with abandon. But now he had paid huge sums for information, had purchased three ponies, had hired bodyguards, had given considerable money to Alex for his orphans, and now he was prepared to pay a fortune for their passage.

Had he gone completely mad? Or was life making sense to him for the first time ever?

He had watched the comings and goings in the tavern for two days. He'd been told only that the proprietors of the tavern had been suppliers of brandy. The man in Edinburgh had known no more. Neil only hoped it was enough.

How do you approach people and ask them if they are smugglers?

And not get killed in the doing?

Neil did not have a bloody idea. He just waited and watched.

He'd waited and watched last night, too. And the night before. He stayed until closing hours, feigning drunkenness, then staggered outside and pretended to pass out.

The tavern was full each night, and everyone seemed to know each other. He was ignored. Shunned. His tailored, albeit soiled, clothing set him apart. He explained that he was to meet someone here this weekend and had taken rooms at a nearby inn.

He did not miss the covert looks nor the suspicion in people's eyes. Outside of asking for the brandy, he'd said nothing about smuggling. It was obvious, though, that they all knew what he wanted.

The owner called for the closing. It was an hour earlier than the tavern had closed the night before. The tavern cleared out quicker, too. A knot of expectancy twisted his stomach. "Jus' one more," he mumbled, holding up his tankard.

He was the last patron. The owner gave him a sour look. "Nay. Ye must leave."

Neil was uncertain what to do. He had no disguise. He could be identified if he ripped out his question, and had been wrong. "Doan wanta go."

"I donna give a farthing what ye want," the innkeeper said. "Not get out before some of my boys help ye out."

Neil stumbled out of his chair, gave the man a bleary look and made for the door. Once out, he leaned against the outside of the building. A knot of men outside watched him. He staggered down the street and fell at an angle where he could see. The men were still watching. No one offered assistance. He worked at getting up, but not too hard, then turned toward the inn where he had a room.

Instead of going in, however, he went down to the next road and turned, then doubled back through the alley. Keeping to the shadows, he quickly found himself near the back of the Pelican. A stout man stood there, obviously on guard. Neil was certain then. Tonight was the night, and it would do no good to try to follow anyone from the tavern. They were obviously very careful.

Bloody hell. Neil realized his only chance was to ride down to the beach and hope to see some kind of signal.

He hurried back to the inn and went to his room, where he'd left his saddlebags. But the moment he went inside he knew he was not alone. His saddlebags were not where he'd left them, and when he shut the door he found someone be-hind it—a very large someone, who was pointing his own pistol at him.

"Mus' be wrong room," Neil said.

"Right room, gent."

Neil looked longingly toward the saddlebags, now emptied of their contents.

The stranger studied him. "Now who in the devil are ye?"

So much for his sleuthing skills. "Someone who wishes to make a contract," Neil replied.

"What kind of contract?"

"I have goods I need shipped. A friend in Edinburgh said I might find a ship here."

"Then why did ye no' ask?"

"One does not go around asking whether someone is a smuggler and keep his head."

The man permitted himself a small smile. "Who told ye about us?"

"I canna say."

"Tall? Stout?"

"Nay."

"Tim, no doubt," his visitor said. "Ye know too much."

Neil had no answer to that. "I can make it worthwhile to someone if I can make that contract."

"Are ye alone?"

"Aye," Neil replied. He knew it was dangerous to make such an admission. It would be far easier to kill him. Yet it would be equally dangerous to lie. He suspected he had been watched ever since he arrived here. Was that why the tavern closed earlier? Not because a shipment was due?

"How worthwhile?"

"Five hundred quid."

"For passage or for information?"

"Both." How easily he'd said that.

"Only an Englishman or a Scots traitor 'as that much scratch."

Neil had damned little reply to that. But he did have hope.

Scots traitor. Those words meant that these men were probably Jacobite sympathizers as well as smugglers. He resorted to the truth. "'Tis a Jacobite and Jacobite bairns that need passage. Two men and ten orphans. I must find them a ship."

The man stared at him for a moment, then shrugged. "I will take ye to the meeting place. But if the Frenchie says kill ye, ye will be fish bait."

Neil nodded his understanding.

The man gestured him out and Neil obeyed, wondering whether he would survive this night.

Chapter Twenty-five

The three lasses ate in the main dining room at Braemoor along with Colin, who chattered away in some indecipherable language. It was time, she knew, that they begin to learn table manners. Her husband had banned them from the dining room with its crystal, and after his death she had not wanted to subject them to joyless Reginald, Louisa and Marjorie.

So now seemed a good time. And she also had an ulterior motive. She wanted to linger and talk to Torquil about the Marquis of Braemoor. He must know something about his family. Trilby had told her that the marquis had brought him from his old home.

She could have just sought him out, but she had not wanted to do that. She only wanted to begin the conversation naturally. She certainly did not want him to report to his master that she had been intruding into his privacy.

Even though that was exactly what she was doing.

She knew he had soft spot for the lasses and for Colin, though he tried to look dignified and severe.

The evening meal did not go exactly as planned. Annabella spilled her milk and decided she did not like anything on her plate. Rachel did not stop asking questions about the whereabouts of the marquis and Grace just pushed her food around.

"Where's Neil?" Annabella whined. "I want him."

Neil. She raised an eyebrow. "He is 'my lord,' sweetling," she said gently. "You should use his title."

"He told me to call him Neil," Annabella contended, her eyes filling with tears.

"He did," Grace spoke up. "I heard him."

Janet was not quite sure how to handle that. But just then Rachel dropped her silver spoon, and Grace scolded her for being careless. Poor Torquil scurried around, retrieving spoons and cleaning spills, even while she tried to tempt the lasses into eating what was on their plates. But she knew they missed Braemoor, that they wanted to ride their ponies outside the paddock and that they did not understand the new restrictions on their activities.

She and Clara took turns feeding and holding Colin. He had his own bowl of oatmeal, which he enjoyed throwing over the room, and Torquil hurried to clean it.

When they were finally finished, she gave Colin to Clara to take upstairs to remove oatmeal from his face and clothing. Trilby, who had turned out to have a winning way with the lasses, took them away. Torquil was still cleaning up various spots.

Janet thought he was much too old to be bending down and scrubbing floors, and she found a cloth and joined him. "My lady," he said with horror.

"'Tis my son's mess," she said. "And I am quite bored with doing nothing. Trilby says the marchioness who did live here used to scrub the floors. 'Twas a sight to see, Trilby said."

"I was not at Braemoor then," Torquil said, scrubbing even harder. His voice was full of disapproval.

"When did you come?"

"Eight months ago, after the marquis inherited the title."

He certainly had made himself at home in eight months. He terrified the other servants, or at least they claimed so, even as a twinkle sparkled in their eyes. Everyone seemed to like the gruff, good-hearted Torquil, who had taken his new responsibilities very seriously.

She scrubbed a little harder.

"Where did he find you?"

"At 'is old home on the sea."

"Tell me about it."

"No' much tae tell. It was a great, dark place. 'Tis falling apart."

"My lord told me his family had all died."

His brows knit together. "Aye. His mother died when he was but a wee lad. But he had already been taken away. Her father, the old lord, died shortly after."

"And no one inherited."

" 'Twas nothing tae inherit. The castle was falling down, the lands played out. The old master was in debt. 'Twas taken over by the crown for taxes, but no one wanted it. 'Twas cursed, everyone said."

"Why?" She tried to keep her voice level.

His face worked and his eyes clouded. "The lady threw herself from the tower."

His lips clamped shut then, as if he had said too much.

"My lord told me about his mother," she said gently.

Torquil's eyes narrowed, and he regarded her warily.

"He said she had been sick." It was both a comment and a question.

Torquil bent back to the spot he was scrubbing. She wondered about that. He could have called in one of the maids, but he seemed to take a proprietary interest in every aspect of Braemoor. He had, in fact, been given the power to make payments while Neil was absent. The trust obviously went two ways.

Janet thought he was not going to answer. But after a moment's silence, he did. "She was a bonny lass. Kind . . . and trusting. Everyone loved her."

So had he, she knew suddenly.

His mouth clamped shut suddenly.

"What happened?" she asked, prodding him as gently as she could.

"Gaston Forbes visited," he said bitterly. "He told her he loved her, and she thought she loved him. He . . . seduced her, then left. The bastard had offered for the hand of another woman wi' a larger dowry and it was accepted. She wrote him when she discovered she was with child but he never answered."

"Her fa was furious. Although she had only a small dowry and the land was poor, he had depended on a good marriage. His only hope was tae keep the matter quiet. He dinna want anyone to know of her disgrace and told everyone she was visiting relatives. But he had no heirs and when the young master was born, her father claimed the child had been orphaned, and told the world he'd legally adopted him. His mother . . ."

He stopped. "I should not be talking of these things." He stood, but he was trembling, and she would have sworn he was fighting back tears.

She put a hand on his sleeve. She hesitated. One did not confide in servants. But she must know. "It is important, Torquil. The marquis was told by his uncle that his mother was mad, and so was her mother. He believes his blood is tainted."

"Nay," he said as he slowly got to his feet. "Tha' canna be right. I remember her mother dying of a cancer. She died the year before the Lady Johana met the man who betrayed her." His anger was obvious.

"She was not mad?"

"Nay."

"Would the family try to hide the real cause?"

"I was a groom, my lady, and servants talk. I heard nothing about madness."

"But Johana?"

His eyes flickered and he turned away. She saw a glint of tears in them. She realized he had cared far more for his mistress than he would probably ever admit.

"When she refused tae deny her son, her father kept her imprisoned, hoping to bend her tae his will. It was foolish. Too many people knew, but the earl was desperate. I . . . agreed to help her escape. She wanted tae take Neil with her. Her father caught her on the steps after a maid let her out of her room. One of the servants told me he took the boy, who was no more than two, and hit her. She fell down the steps and hit her head on the stones. She was never the same again."

"She never spoke again. She just . . . sat. She did not even know me. She stayed that way for years. Then one day the lad was taken away, and I dinna know then what happened tae him. Several days after he left, Lady Johana fell from the tower. Three months later, the earl died."

"And the castle?"

"All the furniture was sold. The servants were discharged."

"And you?"

"I couldna leave," he said, lifting his chin defiantly. "Someone had to see tae her grave."

"And now?"

"My lord employed someone to see tae it. He said he needed me." The last was said proudly. "He has even taught me tae do sums, so I could be of more help."

More likely, Braemoor knew Torquil needed *him*. She was learning that Braemoor's acts of kindnesses were always hidden under some pretext.

"Would anyone know anything about Johana's mother?" she asked.

"Her family was English. I think . . . it may ha' been Wadsworth."

"And the marquis never asked you about her?"

"Nay," he said.

Because he thought he knew.

A lump as large as a piece of coal lodged in her throat. What if he had been wrong? What if his uncle had lied to him? Then she could have married him years ago. It would not have mattered if they had little.

But then she wouldn't have Colin and the lasses.

God took away, and He gave.

But perhaps it had not been God at all. It had been the late marquis. A pox on his soul.

"My lady?"

"We must find out more," she said. "Mayhap hire a solicitor to make inquiries."

Torquil shook his head. "No' without my lord's approval." He started to back out. "I should no' have said so much."

She watched him disappear. He left, his head high.

She remained there a moment. She wanted to go after him, but she knew he would say no more. Not tonight. His loyalty to Neil was complete. As it had been to Neil's mother.

Janet went up the stairs, the story echoing in her mind. Her heart hurt for the woman who had been hidden away, the mother whose son was stolen. But now she had hope. Neil's mother had apparently been badly injured. Johana had not been mad, at least not before hitting her head, and that had a physical cause, not a hereditary one.

But would it be enough for Neil, especially after he had lived these past eight years under the cloud?

She did not think so.

If only they could find out.

She had the control of Lochaene funds. She needed only to find a solicitor. She did not trust the one that served Lochaene and she had not yet found a new one. The village nearby had none. Again she knew the hopelessness that had too often filled her. Other than Neil, she knew no one she could trust.

But Braemoor must have a solicitor.

And Torquil would know who it was.

But would Torquil help her?

• • •

Alexander Leslie tied the mask around the lower part of his face, leaving only his eyes revealed. A shock of russet hair covered the only visible part of his scar.

He had a jack of spades with him, the one Braemoor had given him. Burke, on the other side of the road, was also masked. He had been in the village when he had seen a fancy coach stop at the inn. He'd soon discovered it was an Englishman recently gifted with Scots land. For services to King George, no doubt.

The village was three miles from Lochaene.

Mayhap they would fetch enough to repay Braemoor at least part of the sums the man was spending. Despite his words to Braemoor, it galled Alex to take so much from any man, much less one who had fought with Cumberland. Only the children had made him do so.

They were his one reason for living now. He had lost everything else. His family's land. His clan members. His legacy. Even the face he'd grown up with. But the old woman who had saved his life had harbored five of the bairns. She had begged him to help them find a way to France, where she hoped other Scottish refugees would care for them. The others . . . well, they had come one by one.

He'd been hesitant to roam far from the cave, because he was all they had. But now he had a reason. He could do this to help his sister. That was very important to him.

They had already felled a log across the road. Now they waited and hoped there would be no British patrols.

It was several hours later when Fergus, one of the youngsters, came riding toward them. He had been watching the road from a vantage point. Thank God they still had Braemoor's mount from their unfortunate—or was it fortunate—original meeting. The man had said nothing about it on his subsequent visits. Alex was not sure whether Braemoor had forgotten about it or thought Alex needed the horse more than he did. He now suspected the latter.

The man confounded him. Confused him. But by God, Alex hoped he was no more than a very odd angel.

He and Burke mounted their horses. They were just around a curve, and the tree would keep the carriage from going forward. It would be nearly impossible to turn it on such a narrow road.

They heard the hooves, the jangling of harnesses, the turning creak of wheels, and then it was in sight, a great lumbering, ostentatious coach drawn by four matched black horses.

The driver's eyes had been on the road and started to slow the coach when he saw the log in the road. Then he saw Alex and Burke and frantically tried to hold back the horses.

A head popped out of the window, then back in. Time enough to aim a pistol, Alex knew. He pointed his pistol at the man. "Stand and deliver," he said.

The driver lifted his hands and the horses stood nervously. Burke, on the other side, slipped off his horse and went over to the door on the opposite side of the coach. He jerked it open.

"Get down," Alex ordered the driver.

The man stepped down, and Alex swung one leg over the saddle and slipped down. He flipped the man's coat with his pistols. "No weapons?"

The driver shook his head, his eyes pure fright.

"Go toward the back of the coach and stand where I can see you."

The driver did as he was told. Alex then approached his side of the coach, hoping that any pistol inside the carriage had been taken. It had been. A stout man dressed in velvet finery sat inside, Burke's gun aimed for his sizeable stomach. A pistol lay uselessly beside him. Alex leaned over and took it. "My lord, I thank you for another weapon. And now your purse and jewelry, if you please."

"Blackguard, you will pay for this. The Duke of Cumberland—"

"The butcher, you mean," Alex said. "He will be able to do nothing. Has he not already tried to take the Black Knave? 'Tis impossible, my lord. I am like the Scottish mist.

I will plague you until you leave Scotland. And you can tell your grand duke that. And now you are wasting my time. If you wish to keep that waistcoat without a hole through the center, then I will take the purse and those rings. The belt buckle, too, I think. Gold, my lord? Paid for by the blood of good Scots?"

The man was shaking now. He handed Alex a fat purse attached to his belt, then reluctantly undid the gold belt. Burke reached out and took it.

"Now your rings, my lord—and hurry. I am getting impatient and might well cut off your fingers to get them."

The Englishman yanked at his rings. Three came off. The other did not. Alex played with his knife.

"I beg you," the Englishman said.

"I do like to see an Englishman beg a Scot," Alex said. "In truth, I enjoy it so much, I will leave you the ring as a memento. Along with this." He flipped over a card. "And tell your lord Cumberland that the Black Knave has enjoyed his holiday but now intends to make the English pay."

"You will never get away."

"Oh I have friends, my lord. Important friends. And now I leave you to contemplate your transgressions against my countrymen." He nodded to Burke, whose one foot was inside the carriage. "Cut the traces."

The Englishman came halfway up on his feet before Alex shoved him back down. "I would not do that. My friend cares for the English even less than I do."

"But you cannot leave us here."

"Of course I can. You can walk, my lord. You look as if you need activity."

Burke cut the traces, then headed for his horse. Alex closed the coach door and glared at the driver. "Do not do anything foolish." Then he sprinted several steps to his horse, mounted, and dug his heels into the horse's sides.

Neil stood on the beach, his hands tied behind him and six burly and surly smugglers surrounding him. He hoped like hell that the Frenchman was a reasonable sort. He watched as a longboat neared the shore. Eight men handled the oars and Neil saw casks piled in the middle. A second boat was also appearing out of a mist.

For a while, neither he nor his captors believed contact would be made. The mist obscured the flashes of light. The smugglers had been swinging lanterns from three parts of the beach, and an hour passed before Neil had seen the bare glimmer of light from sea and alerted the others.

And now he was wondering whether he should have been so accommodating.

A man in a dark blue coat jumped out of the longboat and approached Neil and the smugglers. The lantern had been dimmed, but Neil saw a handsome man with a dark beard. "*Mon ami,*" he said with great good humor. "And who do you have here?"

"I found him spying on us. He said he was looking for a Frenchman."

The captain looked him over, completing the survey by taking the lantern and holding it up, looking straight into Neil's eyes. "Monsieur?"

Neil studied him just as obviously. The man was lean but Neil had the impression of power. The man's eyes looked as cold as the sea he'd just left. "I have two adults and ten children who need passage to France. I will pay any amount you ask."

"You are that wealthy?"

"More like desperate," Neil admitted.

"And how can I trust you?"

Neil looked at the men around him. "May I speak to you alone?"

Still holding the lantern, the Frenchman nodded and took his arm, guiding him a distance down the beach as the smugglers started to unload casks. "My cousin was Rory Forbes," he said.

"Should that mean anything to me?"

"I had hoped so. I believe he had some transactions with a French captain."

"There is more than one smuggler, monsieur."

"Ones who like gold, I hoped."

"Your name, monsieur?"

Neil did not want to give it. And yet he had already admitted his relationship to Rory. It would not take the authorities long to make the connection. In for a pence, in for a pound, he thought, thinking that cliches were cliches for a reason. They were too often true. "Braemoor," he said. "The Marquis of Braemoor."

"Ahhhhh," the Frenchman said, his face clearing. "But you do not resemble him."

"Nay," Neil said, confident now he had met the same man who had served Rory's needs.

"He did not mention you."

"We were not friends," Neil admitted honestly.

The Frenchman raised an eyebrow. "Then why are you here?"

"As I said, I have friends who wish to leave the country."

"Enemies of the crown?"

"If one could call a child of six or ten that."

"And your interest in them?"

"Only to find them safety."

The Frenchman's eyes seemed to pierce him, then he took out a knife with his free hand. "Turn around," he said.

Neil did so and felt the knife slicing the ropes binding him. Gratefully, his hands massaged his wrists for a moment. Then he turned his attention back to the Frenchman. "You will do it?"

"The price is a thousand quid."

"Five hundred," Braemoor said.

"You offered any price," the Frenchman reminded him.

"Aye," Neil said. "But I thought the French liked to bargain."

"For Rory's cousin, I agree," the Frenchman said with a grin.

Neil hesitated, then said, "He is well?"

"Well and free with his lovely wife," the Frenchman said and held out his hand. "I am Renard."

Neil took it. "No more questions?"

"*Mon ami,* if anything were to happen to me, your life would not be worth a pence. I have friends."

It was a clear warning, one he believed.

They returned to the smugglers, who had already unloaded the first boat and had nearly finished with the second. The casks were piling up on the beach.

"When can my friends expect you?"

"The next new moon," the Frenchman said. "Twenty days from now. I like the dark."

"They will be here."

"And the money?"

"It will be here, too." He reached down into the purse contained in his cloak. "Here is fifty quid," he said, tossing the purse to the Frenchman. He had already given half of its contents to the smugglers.

"*Bon,*" the Frenchman said. "Send your *amis* to Jack. The owner of the Pelican. He knows the signals. And he hates the English. He will not betray them."

"*Merci,*" Neil replied.

The captain grinned. "I enjoy outfoxing the damned English." Then he turned away and talked to Jack for a moment. Money was exchanged. Then the tall Frenchman jumped into the boat and it pulled away.

Janet looked through the ledger on Braemoor's desk in his office. Torquil, she knew, was in the kitchen. She did not have much time.

She knew that he would never countenance what she was about to do. It was the marquis's business, he would say.

But now it was hers, too. After the night in Edinburgh, it most definitely was her business.

She found what she wanted. The name of his solicitor in

Edinburgh. She quickly wrote it down, then closed the journal and made her escape.

Edwin Prentis, Esq.

She sat down at the table in her room; one eye on Colin who was now careening from one fixed object to another. He had discovered that legs were faster than knees.

"Dear sir," she started. *"I am writing on behalf of the Marquis of Braemoor. He is trying to find members of his mother's family and would like you to instigate a search. His grandmother's maiden name was Wadsworth. Please do not contact them, but direct your reply to me."*

She addressed it. She would have to get back into his office and use his seal.

She fingered it for several moments, wondering if she were doing the right thing. She recalled the granite look of Neil's face when he had talked about his past. He had accepted it, that much was clear. She was not sure whether he would choose to reopen what was obviously a raw wound. But at least she would have a name for him.

And then it would be up to him as to whether he cared enough about her to fight not only her enemies but his own secret ones.

Chapter Twenty-six

Home. Odd how the word had so much meaning now.

It was not the stone edifice. It was the woman and children inside.

His heart speeded as he approached. He had thought of little more than Janet on his journey back from his coast. He had detoured to see Alex on the return, and had discovered a man well pleased with himself.

It had taken two days from the coast to see Alex and another two days to get back to Braemoor, and that was only by riding day and night. He had been away from Janet for more than a week, and it seemed a century. He did not know what he would do when she, and the children, left for good. A rare joy would leave his life.

But that would be a while. In the meantime, he would enjoy her. And her lasses and the bairn. He yearned to protect her, care for her, bring smiles and laughter to her face, and to her heart.

And his own. God knew it had been bereft for a long time. Bereft and lonely and hardened. No matter what the future held, it was good to feel again.

The sun was setting behind Braemoor. No mist today, or fog, or rain. Instead, rays hit the gray of the stone and appeared to bring it to life.

Then he saw Janet, and the red of the sun reflected the gold in her hair. She was bending over, balancing Colin as he tottered away from her toward his oldest sister. Then Rachel said something, and she looked in his direction. Neil saw her blinding smile, and it made his heart ricochet in his chest. He thought about seeing it every day, then quickly crushed that thought.

Janet loved children. She had every right to have more of her own. And she had every right to be loved as a woman should be loved, not only in part. Not with shadows lurking ominously about.

He rode to her and slid down wearily from the saddle. Annabella launched herself at him, and he reached out and took her up in his arms and whirled her around once, relishing her laughter and treasuring her hug. Then he let her down, and somehow his hand caught hers, and her warmth flowed through him, filling every empty part.

Then Grace was in front of him, her usually solemn eyes shining. "Thank you for the pony."

He stooped down as he had seen Alex do and looked directly into her blue eyes. "You are welcome, lass."

"I love him."

"Well, God created ponies to be loved." The words surprised him, but they apparently delighted her.

Her smile widened. "I will take very good care of him."

"You take good care of everyone," he observed. And she did, with her earnest face and too-serious eyes. Now, though, they glowed.

"*I* take good care of mine, too," Annabella protested at losing his attention.

"You do not," Rachel disagreed. "Jamie has to help *you*."

"She's not the grown lass you are," Neil interjected.

Rachel straightened up, a satisfied look on her face.

Colin, evidently sensing he was being left out, tottered over to him, and Neil released Annabella's hand to catch him just as he started to fall. Colin grinned at him, and Neil found himself grinning back. "Adventuresome little lad," he said.

Colin gurgled his assent and his hand touched Neil's face.

The touch was quizzical, the small hand soft. But there was a trust in the gesture that made him melt inside. He swallowed hard. Here was everything he'd never even dared to dream about. He was chagrined to feel moisture building behind his eyes.

He handed Colin to his mother and saw the warm understanding in her eyes.

"I need a bath," he said awkwardly, only too aware that he had been riding nearly nonstop for six days and he smelled more like a horse than the horse did.

"And some food, I would suppose," she said.

"Aye, that would be welcome."

"And you have news?"

"Aye. It is good, lass, but must wait." He did not want the small children involved. They could not tell secrets they had not heard.

Then he noticed Kevin standing not far away. A musket was nearby, leaning against the stable. He raised an eyebrow in question.

"Later," Janet said, her gaze going back to the children.

He nodded. His hand touched Colin's mop of brown hair, then he turned and went into the house.

The children would eat with Clara this evening. Their manners had improved in the last three nights, but she needed—wanted—time alone with Neil.

He appeared in the dining room, his hair still wet and slightly curling. He was dressed in his usual preference of clothes: dark breeches, top boots, and a white linen shirt laced at the neck. He looked virile and handsome in the casual attire. She knew he disdained the usual fripperies such as padded breeches and knee buckles. But austerity suited him.

He bowed slightly. "My lady."

She curtsied. "My lord."

The words were said in low and intense voices and Janet knew they sounded more like a love song than a courtesy. The room, in truth, sizzled with emotions. She wanted to reach out and touch him, but instead simply stood there, her legs as wobbly as Colin's had been.

He offered her his arm and seated her, then sat opposite.

"Why did Kevin have a weapon?"

"Two men came here while we were in Edinburgh. Torquil told me they intended to take Colin back to Lochaene. They said it was by Reginald's order. He refused, and the men you left here, along with Kevin and Jamie, told them to leave. Kevin, however, has seen them nearby. I have not gone anywhere or let the children out alone since."

"They must have been waiting for us to leave," Neil said. "I will have men comb the area tomorrow. If they are still here, I will know exactly what Reginald intended."

"If anything happens to Colin, Reginald inherits," she said, worrying her lip.

"He must have believed it was a surety that Cumberland would arrest you." Neil took a sip of wine. "It suits our plan that he lost this round. He should be very susceptible to an offer by the Black Knave. We must now prepare for our great masquerade ball."

"Ball?" Janet asked. She knew only the barest outline of what he had been plotting; only that he would somehow throw suspicion on Reginald.

He grinned. "Aye, I think it is time for the new Marquis of Braemoor to emerge in society. That, of course, will be the occasion. Everyone will come. Curiosity will compel them. Mayhap even His Grace may honor us. Or some of his staff."

"And my role?"

"Ghostly," he said. "Your brother and I worked out the details," he said. "He apparently makes a very believable Black Knave."

She sat and listened, her amazement growing at the audacity of his plan. The one problem that had worried her conscience—that Reginald might not be guilty of the accidents—was solved. If he did not act to harm her or the children, then Neil's plan would not work.

"When?"

"The ball will be in three weeks. Alexander will be on a ship in three and a half weeks."

"And I will never see him again," Janet said sadly. " 'Tis hard to find him, only to lose him again."

"There are ways, Janet," he said.

"And the children with him?"

"He makes a fine surrogate father," Neil said. "He will make sure they are safe."

" 'Tis difficult to imagine him that way. He was always a rake."

Something crossed Neil's face.

"Neil?"

"I told you he had been scarred. I want you to be prepared."

Joy coursed through her. "I will see him?"

"I am trying to arrange a brief meeting," he said.

She hugged the thought, the hope. "Thank you," she whispered.

He nodded. "Now we will work on the invitations tomorrow," he said. "We will have to employ more people to help us."

"I do not think we will have any problem doing that," she said.

"Nay. I have not done yet all I wanted to do. It will give some enough to survive more comfortably through the winter."

"I have interfered with your plans," she said sadly.

"Nay, lass," he said. "You have taught me to care about life again, and it will make me a far better landlord."

There was a sadness in his eyes. She wondered whether she should tell him what she had learned from Torquil or wait until she heard more from the solicitor. She did not want to raise his hopes only to have them dashed.

She would wait. Then, regardless of the answer, she would tell him.

They ate, he more hungrily than she had ever seen him. She wondered how much he'd had in the past week. She could not even imagine how much he'd given up for her. And now he was risking even more. He was committing treason.

She was no longer hungry. She remembered how he looked when Colin reached out his hand to his face. The wistful longing in his eyes. He was a man filled with love. He'd tried to suppress it because he thought he had no right to it, and that hurt her more than anything else. She would gladly become his wife under any conditions. But she knew he would never agree.

So, instead, she watched him eat. He did it as carefully, even methodically, as he did most things. But now she knew that other side of him: daring and loving. But controlled. Even his recklessness was controlled.

Torquil hovered over them both, taking away dishes and replacing them with new ones. His eyes were more anxious than ever. She wondered how much he had heard. Or whether he would tell Neil about her questions.

Neil rose and went to her side of the table, pulling the chair out for her. She stood and looked up at him. She was inches away, but his expression told her it might as well be a mile. Still, his hand touched her cheek. "Good night, Janet."

She nodded, wishing he would take her with him. But he had that determined glint in his eyes that were red from exhaustion. She had meant to ask him whether he wanted to say good night to the children, but mayhap tomorrow.

Instead, she turned and walked from the room and up the stairs, aware that he was not behind her, that he had gone into his office.

She missed him already.

•   •   •

The lasses woke her up. They jumped on the bed and gig-gled like the little girls they were. At one time she had thought she would never hear the sound; they had been so terrified of their father.

Colin was gurgling in his bed. "Grace, will you get your brother?"

Grace immediately went over to Colin and picked him up, cradling him as if she were the mother. He grinned at her. "He needs changing," she said.

"Aye, I would think so," she said, stretching and clearing the lasses off the bed. She gave each one a kiss and sent them off to the nursery to get dressed. Then she changed Colin. Clara could do it, but she took pleasure in every mo-ment with him, unlike Louisa, who wanted as little to do with the chores of motherhood as possible. She liked to see him smile when she touched him, liked to listen to him chat-ter. It would not be long before he disdained such closeness.

She finished and set him on the floor where he promptly started exploring with those unsteady but now plump little legs. She brushed her hair to a fine sheen, then put on a clean chemise. She thought about wearing a corset, then decided against it. She was already slender and she had enjoyed the freedom she had since her husband's death. Instead, she chose a simple dress that laced in front. She had just about finished when Lucy appeared with a tray with hot chocolate, some buns and a bowl of fruit. "The master sent this up for you, my lady," she said. Her face fell when she saw that her mistress was already dressed. "I dinna mean to be late."

"I would have called you had I needed you," she said. "The marquis?"

"He went riding," she said.

She wished he had asked her to go, too. But she knew now why he was trying to distance himself. She only hoped she could discover the truth about his family, and that that truth would be the one that she wanted.

•   •   •

Alex watched as Reginald Campbell rode away from Lochaene. He was a poor rider, and apparently made up for his discomfort by taking it out on the animal.

Sympathy flooded Alex for the horse. And for his sister, who had lived in this household for three years. He would enjoy this role.

Alex had been waiting now for two days for his chance. He had to meet Reginald alone. He had to prompt Reginald into making an offer that the Black Knave could not refuse. And now that the Black Knave had made his presence known with three robberies, he should have no problem in convincing the man that Cumberland's nemesis had returned.

He fell in behind Campbell. The man was dressed for visiting, not for a ride, and thus would take the road. Alex knew exactly where he wanted to intercept him. Thank God that Braemoor had taken the Lochaene carriage, leaving Campbell with few options of transportation.

Alex also knew that Braemoor had cut off Campbell's income. He must be desperate by now.

He rode at a leisurely pace. The road was a lonely one, though it wended to the main road to Edinburgh. He wondered whether that was Reginald's destination. Well, he would not make it. Not today. At least not as quickly as he had expected.

Alex knew he had to strike before they reached the more heavily trafficked Edinburgh road.

He veered off the road and skirted it, prodding his horse into a gallop. He'd been familiar with this land even before the past year. Lochaene and his own family's land had not been that far apart. And in the last few months, he had crisscrossed it, had hidden among its hills and moors.

He continued to ride hard until he emerged at a point that Reginald would have to pass. He waited until he heard hoofbeats, then rode out to meet him, pistol in hand.

Reginald's mount came to a stop. The man's florid face paled when he saw the mask and pistol.

Alex bowed and flipped a jack of spades toward him. It landed on the ground, but Reginald knew its significance.

"What do you want?" he blustered.

"That you leave the road, at the moment," Alex said. He used his free hand to gesture toward the forest on their left.

"And if I refuse?"

"You will not live beyond the next moment."

Reginald guided his horse in the direction Alex had indicated. Once out of sight of the road, Alex told him to dismount. Reginald did not move.

Alex audibly sighed. "I am a man of little patience."

Reginald dismounted.

"Do you have a weapon?"

Silence.

Alex sighed again, his thumb moving back on the flintlock.

"Aye," Reginald said.

"Ah, a truthful man, albeit reluctantly."

Alex swung down from his horse and went to Reginald's saddlebags. They were bulging. He found the pistol, put it in his own saddlebags, and bowed mockingly. "Thank you, my lord. And now for your ransom, I will take your purse and jewelry."

"I . . . I have no money. Only a few coins. I am . . . a poor man."

"That is unfortunate for you."

"I thought . . . you assisted people in leaving Scotland."

"For a price," Alex said. "But I do have my needs, and the English, and those who serve them, appear to have all the wealth. I feel that separating the two is my sworn duty. And now, my lord, I must decide what to do with you since you have none."

Speculation suddenly came into Reginald's eyes, just as Braemoor had predicted. "I have none now, but I can promise you much if . . ."

Alex's apparent but silent interest prompted him to continue.

"If a certain lady has an accident," Reginald said, watching his eyes closely. It was obvious he felt safe enough making the offer to a much-wanted fugitive.

"A lady?"

"A murderess. She killed my brother so she could control his estate. It would be justice," he added pompously.

"Ah, justice. A noble aim, indeed. And how much could I expect for administering this . . . justice?"

"Sanctuary at my estate," Reginald said. "And a hundred quid."

"Why should I believe you? It could be a trap. The reward on my head is more than that."

Alex saw that Reginald's eyes were gleaming now. He obviously thought he had finally found a way to dispose of the one obstacle in his path. His proposal had not been rejected outright. And he was still alive. Alex could almost read his mind. Greed. It did strange things to reason. Reginald believed he could get rid of both of them. The interesting thing about not very intelligent men was that they always thought they were smarter than they actually were. And they often thought other men were as venal as they themselves might be.

"I give you my oath," Reginald said.

Alex threw back his head and laughed. "You ask me to murder someone, then offer your word. Surely I must have something stronger than that."

Reginald was growing more confident. "What would you suggest?"

"The Lochaene seal," Alex said. "And a note saying you owe me one hundred quid."

The man stared at him. "How did you know about Lochaene?"

Alex looked at the fingernails of his left hand in a gesture of careless contempt. "I know everything. I followed you from there."

"Why me?"

"You are the last gentry around with money. I have already relieved the others of valuables."

Alex knew Reginald must have heard of the Black Knave thefts. He should be wondering now how many others he'd not heard about. "I willna put anything in writing."

"You can say it is a gambling debt," Alex said. "And it is to be made out to . . . John Burke. I will return the seal when I receive the money."

"Why the seal?"

Alex shrugged. "If it is a trap and I am taken, there will be many questions about the seal. I would not want you tempted, my lord-to-be."

He watched Reginald struggle with himself. The men he had sent to Braemoor to retrieve his nephew had not returned. Braemoor's factor had cut him out from all funds. And now there was not the action he had expected on his accusations toward his sister-in-law. In truth, he must be desperate.

"I do not have the seal," Reginald finally said.

"I am sure there must be one at Lochaene."

"Aye," Reginald replied after a moment.

"I will meet you back here tomorrow."

"I am on my way to Edinburgh," Reginald said.

"Not if you want . . . justice," Alex said.

Reginald weighed that for a moment. He undoubtedly had been making a trip to Edinburgh to try to see Cumberland and find out why he had heard nothing about Janet. Now he had a chance to put an end to his problems immediately.

He nodded.

"In the meantime, I will take that ring you are wearing," Alex said, "and your purse. You must have a few quid."

"I want it back," Reginald said.

"Aye, why not, if I have my hundred quid."

Reginald struggled to take it off his finger and reluctantly handed it to Alex. "My pistol."

"I find I am in need of it," Alex said, tossing the ring in the air and catching it. "You are fortunate I do not take your horse. Poor beast. You ride like a sack of oats." Then he went to his horse and mounted, his pistol still in his hand. "You may mount now," Alex said. "Tomorrow, you just ride down this road. Alone. I will meet you along the way. Leave Lochaene at noon. Bring the seal. And the paper. Oh, and do not betray me. I know your estate, and I have friends."

Then he disappeared into the trees before Reginald could have any second thoughts.

Days passed in a flurry of activity. Janet kept hoping she would hear something from the solicitor. He would not have had time to make inquiries in London, of course, but mayhap there was some information in Edinburgh.

But she did not have time to think about it. There were dresses to be made, invitations to be written and sent, menus to plan.

Neil was rarely about. That was by design, Janet thought. If she rose early enough, which she often did because Colin did, she might see him riding out. He had told her that his men combed the area but found no strangers. They were probably gone now. He had sent others to deliver invitations and they already had a slew of acceptances. As he had guessed, curiosity, if not friendship, prompted them.

He usually came back so late she had already put the children to bed. She still kept close watch on them, refusing to let them far from her sight. But she missed Neil. She particularly missed seeing his eyes light up with pleasure when he watched the lasses or held Colin. He would be a wonderful father.

And husband. Thoughtful. Tender. Protective.

It had been no different this morning. She had risen early, but still not early enough. She looked out to see the sun rise. She saw Neil riding away. She knew Neil was visiting the tenants, solving disputes, giving advice on crops, even taking food to those short of it. As if he feared he might not be here to do it.

She yearned to go with him, to ride alongside him, to visit

with the women and hear problems. But he had shut her out since that first day he had returned. The few times she did see him, his mouth was grim, his face set, his eyes bleak. Only when he glimpsed the children did he relax. She left the window. Colin was still asleep and she did not want to wake him. He always looked so peaceful when he was asleep, completely different from the little whirlwind he became later in the day.

She went over to the dress hanging in the wardrobe. Unrelenting black. She would look like a corpse.

Neil had employed a dressmaker to design the dress, had sent for her from a small village twenty-five miles away. It was a severe black gown with a high neck and full sleeves. The dressmaker added an overdress of dark gray gauze that gave her an ethereal appearance. A little powder and her face would be nearly white.

Sighing, she sat in a chair and watched Colin. She thought of her brother, and chewed on her lip. He was out there somewhere, his life forfeited if he made the slightest mistake. And Neil's, too. Yet here she was, watching her child sleep.

She reached out and touched him and wished him a lifetime of peace.

Chapter Twenty-seven

Neil rapped lightly on the door of Janet's room. The lasses, he knew, were asleep in their beds.

He had waited outside the nursery door and heard Janet tell a story, then sing a lullaby. Then he had left, not wanting her to know he was skulking around. And he was not. He had returned from a long ride and mounted the steps to his own room. He had merely been walking by when he heard her soft voice and had been compelled to stay.

But now he could avoid her no longer. Her brother was within riding distance, and he owed her this last chance to see him. Alex had simply appeared on the road, surprising him.

She opened the door, dressed in her nightshift, her tawny hair falling down her back.

She smiled uncertainly. "Neil?"

"I wonder if you would like to go for a ride?"

"Tonight?"

"Tonight," he said.

"I will have to take Colin to the nursery. I do not like leaving him alone."

"I will take him while you change . . . into something more practical," he said, pleased that she asked no questions. She simply trusted him. It was a far cry from several weeks ago.

He picked up Colin, who stretched and gave him a be-
atific smile. Neil found himself grinning back. It was probably a foolish grin, but he did not care. The child felt so right
in his arms.

Neil looked at Janet and saw her sweet, gentle smile, and
his heart swelled. And swelled even more when he thought
how happy she would be in an hour. He had a gift for her. A
dangerous one to be sure, but now he realized safety and
practicality were not everything. Their gazes met and there
was understanding between them. He felt warm and even
dizzy. The air grew thick with strong emotions. He found it
hard to swallow.

Had he been wrong to refuse love? Had he allowed his
uncle to poison his life and leave him doubting every moment of it? Janet was obviously willing to risk what he had
not. He had thought honor demanded it, but had he really
been protecting a heart afraid to love?

He balanced Colin in one arm and reached out to touch
her hair with the other. Her hand caught it, wrapped her fingers in his and brought it to his cheek, the soft back of her
hand running along his cheek. The gesture was so loving
that his heart slammed into his ribs.

How he had longed for it all his life.

But Alex was waiting. And he wanted to see her eyes
when she saw her brother.

He brought her hand down and leaned over and kissed her
with the same tenderness she had offered him. What a fool
he had been these ten days to try to avoid her! He had
thought he had the will to do so. And now he saw it for what
it was: arrogant, foolish pride.

"I will be back in a few moments," he said.

"I will be ready," she said softly.

Janet had no idea what Neil intended. A midnight ride was
so unlike him. Or was it? She smiled to herself at that
thought.

She knew almost immediately they were going to the

loch. They had not been there together in more than eight years, but she knew every turn and climb on the short journey. She had taken it enough times in her dreams.

He leaned over at one point and touched her gloved hands, and it was as if he had poured warm molasses through that spot and it slowly filled her entire being. She had never felt so protected and wanted and . . . loved. He had not said the words, but he conveyed them to her in every action and every gesture.

They reached the loch where they had once exchanged kisses. Hills rose up around it, and in the moonlight she saw the flashes of white—the sheep—that dotted them. The moon was wedge-shaped tonight, but the night was clear and stars crowded the midnight sky.

He dismounted and helped her off her horse, holding her a moment longer than necessary. Then he whistled, a series of sounds that sounded like the call of a night bird. She looked at him anxiously, then saw a dark figure appear from behind a hill.

As he neared, she knew familiarity. The lanky build, the arrogant steps, the height.

She ran to him and into his arms, her body shuddering with the pure delight she felt, with the relief and the release of the silent grief she'd buried inside her.

Alex's arms closed around her. "My bonny little sister," he whispered.

She buried her head against his familiar chest, remembering how he had comforted her when she fell from her first pony or an older boy teased her or when she had returned to her home years ago in desperate misery. He had not asked questions, but had merely been there. He had been silent when she'd agreed to marry Alasdair, asking only if she was sure.

They shared parents and family and memories. They shared blood. And they were the only two left. No, there was Colin now.

She looked up at his face, shielded by the collar of his

cloak and a pulled-down cap. She tugged it up, so she could see his face in the light of the part moon and the stars.

Neil had warned her, so she was able to keep her shock to herself. Her handsome brother, the bonny braw lad who had drawn women as flowers drew bees. A jagged scar ran down his cheek, from the side of his eye down to below his mouth.

He smiled ruefully but only one side of his mouth turned upward. "I'm sorry, moppet. I did not want you to see this, but by God I could not leave without saying good-bye."

It was oddly poignant to hear his old nickname for her. "Do you think a small thing like a wee scar would bother me?" she said softly. "When Neil told me you were alive . . . but I could not see you . . ." Her fingers touched his cheek lovingly. "I thought my heart would break."

"And is it mended now?" he queried softly.

"Aye. I will miss you. I can bear it now, though. I do not think I could if . . ."

"I think you can bear anything. You have become stronger than any of us," he said. "Braemoor has told me about . . . your husband and his family. I only wish . . ."

She shook her head and took his hand in hers. "I want only to talk about you. Neil said you are caring for a covey of children."

The rueful smile again. "More truthfully, they care for me."

"What are you going to do with them?" she asked.

"Find homes for them in Paris among the refugees."

"And then?"

"Make a fortune, moppet. What else?"

That sounded like the brother she remembered. Dauntless, self-confident, brash.

"Who is taking care of the children now?"

"A man named Burke and one of the older lads."

She glanced toward Neil. His back was toward them and he was staring out at the loch.

Alex's fingers tightened in hers. "You like him."

"Aye," Alex said. "Even if he did fight with Cumberland."

That was a great admission from her brother, whose passions had always been fiery and unforgiving.

"And you?" he asked her with amusement.

"Aye," she said, mocking him. "But he has reservations."

"He loves you."

"As much as he will let himself."

"Ah, moppet, I will place my wager on you."

"I do not want to let you go."

"I will keep in touch. Some way. I promise."

She leaned against him, knowing that she might never see him again. But she knew he would always be with her, no matter the distance between them. And she would have pleasant, wonderful memories of him. Not terrible thoughts about what might have happened to him. Even the scar meant nothing next to his life.

It was a glorious moment. Neil and her brother. Together. Allies, at least for now. She did not want to break the moment, but knew she must. Every moment here was dangerous for him.

"And Reginald? Did he do as Neil thought he would?" She could not bear to say the words, to ask forthrightly whether someone wanted her dead.

"Aye," Alex said softly. "Braemoor is a good judge of men. And cowards." He hesitated, then said, "I will need your ring, moppet."

Janet nodded, trying not to let him know how she felt. She had lived with Reginald and his wife, and while they had not agreed on many things, she'd not thought him capable of paying someone to murder her. She took off the ring her husband had given her and handed it to her brother. Its absence on her finger gave her an odd sense of freedom.

"I have to go," he said. "I should no' have come, but Braemoor . . ." He hesitated. "Take care of him," Alex grinned. "He has a reckless streak I don't think he quite understands."

"I will not see you again?"

"Nay, I think not. Braemoor has arranged passage to France."

She stood up on her tiptoes. He was taller than Neil, but not by much.

"Be safe," she said.

He nodded, then strode over to Neil. He said something to him that she could not hear and then he disappeared as quickly as he had appeared.

She walked over to Neil. "Thank you," she said, struggling against the lump in her throat. "That was the finest gift anyone could give me."

"You are welcome, lass."

She was reminded that he had no family, apparently never had one except a mother believed mad and a grandfather who had handed him away. Well, he had a family now.

But she only took his hand in hers, her fingers interlocking with his. And together they walked back to their horses, a new intimacy silent between them.

They both saw to their own horses rather than wake either Kevin or Jamie. Neil had told him earlier that they were not to stay up. One of them had left an oil lantern hanging from a rafter.

They left the stalls at the same time, nearly running into each other. Neil felt as if he were one of two lodestones, unable to move in any direction other than hers. He simply could not fight any longer. He did not want to.

Their lips met in a fiery collision. His arms went around her, and her body fused against his. He felt the softness of her form and the urgency already ruling it. Ruling his as well. He deepened his kiss and savored the bonding, warm and tender and right. Very right. He knew now no man could foretell the future, and if she were willing to take risks, then how could he not take them?

After a moment, he released her lips and his gaze met hers. Asking.

A sweet softness came into her eyes. He put an arm around her and guided her toward the tower house. He did not care who saw, or what tales might be told. He cared about nothing but keeping her at his side.

Once in her room, he closed the door, and his mouth melded against hers, searching, exploring, reaching. Her body was taut with need, and his own was burning. Then with a moan of long denial, he unbuttoned the front of her riding habit. Her hands in turn worked on the ties of his breeches.

She paused, looking at him with questions in her eyes. "You will not regret . . ."

"One thing your brother taught me," he said, "is that life is fragile and no one can predict what will happen. You . . . and Alex . . . tonight . . . it was dangerous, and a month ago I would have thought too dangerous." His hand touched her chin. "It was worth it."

She caught his hand. "Aye, my lord. Now when I think of him, I can think of him as he was tonight, not lying mutilated and untended on some battlefield. You told me he lived, but I do not think my heart truly believed it until tonight." She held his hand tight. "No one can predict the future. You can only seize and cherish the chances given you."

His heart pounded against his ribs. He had lived with caution for so long. He had lived with the ghost of his mother for so long. Now he was thirty, and there was no sign of madness.

"A child . . ."

"A child will be loved," she said fiercely. Something shadowed her eyes, but then quickly moved away and they were full of longing and the anguish of denial.

She finished her job of unclothing him and he her. Her body was so soft, softer than he remembered. But that night in Edinburgh, they had been lost in the throes of guilt and need. He ran his hands along the curves of her body, then threaded his fingers through her hair. "You are the very breath to me," he whispered.

Janet looked up at him, startled delight in her eyes at his words. He realized he had said far too few endearments to her. "Aye," he said. "And the sun and moon and stars."

She stood on tiptoes and matched her lips to his. He crushed her to him, feeling her body instinctively meld into his. His lips courted her at first, questioning, seducing. He deepened the kiss, emotion turning it fierce, and he made demanding, hungry forays into her mouth. Her arms tightened around his shoulders and her fingers played with the back of his neck, igniting blazes that spread like wildfire into his loins.

He picked her up and carried her to the bed and gently laid her down, his own hard body resting next to her, his hand skimming over her body in movements so light and tender they brought a low sigh from her. Then he leaned over and his tongue licked the hardening nipple of her breast. He felt her shudder with sensation. His own body was raging with its own need.

Desire surged through him as his lips found hers again and played against them, nibbling tenderly, teasing. She exchanged kiss for kiss, her lips and mouth eagerly seeking and receiving, her hands exploring him just as he had her.

He had never known a touch could be so gentle and yet so much like a fiery brand. The dichotomy of the sensations was in itself an aphrodisiac—not that he needed one. His blood already felt like fire in his veins. Her body tensed, moved erratically, signaling her need. He moved, balanced himself above her, teasing her until she moaned with need and he entered, slowly, wanting her to feel every delicious sensation that he was feeling. Then he invaded further, filling her and moving with a rhythm that became more and more primitive as her body moved with his in an elemental dance that left them both without will or choice. The rhythm quickened. Thrust and another thrust. He stopped breathing as pleasure became ecstasy, and they became one in a brilliant moment of splendor.

• • •

Alex met Reginald on the same road where they had met before.

As instructed by the Marquis of Braemoor, Alex sent Burke with a sealed letter for Reginald. Burke, who was a master of furtiveness, was to leave it at the front door of Lochaene. Alex wanted Reginald to believe the Black Knave could appear and disappear at will.

The note said that the Black Knave had accomplished his mission. Reginald was to meet him as he had before to receive proof and to conclude their business arrangement.

Alex did not think Reginald had the fortitude to refuse the meeting. Nor could the man set a trap without implicating himself.

So this would be the final piece to be put into place. Alex knew he had to convince Reginald to attend Braemoor's ball. He should have received his invitation.

As an additional precaution, Alex met Reginald a mile closer to Lochaene than their previous meeting. And, as before, he appeared out of nowhere, mask back on his face and pistol leveled at Reginald.

"My dear Campbell," he said. "You will ride towards those trees until we cannot be seen from the road."

Reginald Campbell silently turned his mount into the woods, then stopped a distance from the rarely traveled road.

"Dismount," Alex ordered. He noticed that this time Campbell rode an old horse and wore no jewelry. He grinned at that. The man would not have a weapon either, he thought, but he slid down from his own horse and checked Campbell's saddle and his person. Nothing.

"You are learning, sir," he said equably.

"You have news for me?" Reginald said.

Alex shrugged. "She is dead." He tossed him Janet's ring. There was dried blood on it.

Reginald studied it for a moment. "How did she die? I have heard nothing."

"You would not. Braemoor is holding a ball in two days'

time. Cumberland is attending. I do not think Braemoor wants Cumberland to know of the lady's death until he gets his hands on your estates."

"How do you know that?"

"How do I know so much about you? I have spies everywhere, my dear Campbell." Then he seemed to relent. "I have someone in Braemoor's employ. I know that he had forbidden the lady to ride alone, but she paid scant attention. She had a very regrettable accident on the road and was thrown from her horse."

Reginald nodded. "She often rode off without telling anyone. And I know she did not want to leave Lochaene. He forced her and left his man here to guard his interests. Probably to rob us blind."

Alex continued as if Reginald had not spoken at all. "I waited to see whether anyone would find the body. From a distance, that is. He came after her and found the body. I saw him take it not far away through the woods and leave it there, apparently for the animals. He must be as greedy as you are. As was his cousin. I rather enjoyed skewering *him*," Alex said.

His cold words apparently were convincing. Or mayhap Reginald saw himself in everyone else. Satisfaction swept his face. "There is a ball in three days' time. I did not plan to go, but now I will. I will demand to see her."

"I would not appear too early were I you," Alex warned. "You do not want anyone to suspect you had anything to do with her disappearance." He hesitated, then added in an ominous voice, "I expect my payment by this time next week. That will give you time to fetch the children and take over their guardianship," he said, lifting his pistol again and rubbing the barrel against Reginald's neck.

"It . . . it will take longer."

"Sell some jewelry. Borrow money. I do not care how you do it, but do not disappoint me."

Reginald believed it. Alex could feel his fear. And he felt no guilt at all for putting it there. Or for what he was about to do to Reginald. The man had been willing to pay an outlaw money to kill Janet, and he might well have killed his own brother.

Alex mounted. He eyed Reginald's horse, wishing he could take it for the children. It would be a long journey to the sea from his cave. The older lads would have to walk.

Hell, why not? "Do not bother to mount, Campbell. Your horse will be part of the payment you owe me."

"But . . ." Reginald blustered.

"You can say you were thrown," Alex said, smiling under the mask. "No one would doubt that."

He leaned down and took the reins from Reginald's hands and galloped off without looking back. He thought he had baited the hook rather well.

Chapter Twenty-eight

The days before the ball were feverish. Janet planned the menu, saw to the purchase of food, hired additional staff and supervised the cleaning of the tower house.

Neil was often gone. After they had made love following the meeting with her brother, he had ridden to his most recently acquired property, a trip of three days. Before he left, he made sure she was well protected.

"I must see that they have food and feed for the winter," he said, and she knew he worried that something might go wrong, and he might not be able to see to it later. It was that practical, caring part of him that she loved. She also knew that when he returned tonight, she would have to leave and stay in Mary's cottage for several days. In the event that Reginald arrived early, she had to be missing. The servants would be told she had urgent business at Lochaene, and the trip would be too difficult for the children. She did not even want to think about being away from her son that long, but it was a small enough price to pay for safety for them all.

And Neil would visit. She knew now he would visit. He had not said anything about marriage, but she saw the love shine in his eyes. She still saw pain in his face, an anguish that pierced her heart every time she saw it. She prayed every day she would hear from the solicitor and she could soothe the worry from his brow.

Yet once he had broken through that reserve the other night, he had touched her whenever they were alone. He had done it with a gentleness and protectiveness that brought a flooding warmth to her heart. She only hoped that he would be here tonight before she left in the morning for Mary's cottage.

Once Lucy left, Janet went over to Colin's bed. He had been active all day, exploring every nook and cranny. She and Clara really had to watch him now that he walked, or jolted from one object to another, gazing up at her with bright blue eyes that asked her to share his pride in his growing confidence.

He slept now, a thumb in his mouth. He looked more content than she had ever seen him. Mayhap, she thought, because there was no tension in this house. Everyone regarded him with love, even the servants. No one glared at him or looked on him with hatred or jealousy. She wanted him to have that security now. She wanted him and her daughters to feel nothing but love and safety.

After the ball . . .

She sat next to his bed as she had done so many times, thinking about the wonder that he was, that the lasses were. Then she went over to the window and looked outside. Fog made it all but impossible to see the road. It completely obscured the moon, which would be waning in a few days. Her brother would sail then.

But now she had her memories, good memories of his rueful smile and his love, and she had Neil. And the children. It was so much more than she had ever expected.

She waited, but no one came. Restless, she took the candle lamp and padded down to the library. She would need some books at Mary's cottage. She looked among the volumes, then stretched upward to pick one from the shelves. Then she felt rather than heard him. The air was suddenly warmer, electric. Every one of her senses was aware, tingling. She turned and he was there, his lips curved into a smile although his eyes were weary. His dark cloak was wet and his hair damp and curling. He looked magnificent to her.

"I saw a light in here," he said.

"I was getting a book to read at the cottage."

His arms went around her, and she leaned against him. His lips touched her forehead. "I am sorry we have to go through this charade."

"I know," she said, "but as long as you are nearby . . ."

"Aye, and Kevin," he said. "I want him to stay out there with you when I cannot be."

"You have told him?"

"Aye, and he has sworn not to tell another living soul, not even your Lucy," he said.

"I will miss Colin."

"Aye, I know. I will try to find a way to bring him to you."

She looked up and their gazes met. "The tenants?"

"They are fine. There is one young lad who shows signs of leadership. I left some funds with him."

"You are a good man, my lord."

His face colored. "Nay. I did no' do what a good man would. I did not see despair when it was before my eyes. I did not want to see it. I was too concerned with myself and what I felt were injustices against me to see those committed against others."

"Most people never see them," she said gently, her fingers going to his face. Her gaze rested on his eyes. Despite the lines of exhaustion, his eyes glittered with intensity and she felt his coiled, controlled strength. He was tense, just as she was tense, both of them unsure as to their next step. Did he regret the night they'd made love?

A muscle leaped along his tightened jaws, then his arms went around her. "I missed you," he said in a hoarse whisper before his lips clamped on hers in a fiery clash. "God, I missed you." His lips touched hers with a hungering need that slashed at her heart, then he deepened the kiss, his mouth fusing with hers passionately, even savagely. She responded with a frantic need of her own.

Her hands played with the back of his neck, with hair dampened by Highland fog, and she knew a want so deep and fierce she could scarcely bear it. Their lips melded, dueled, loved. Tenderness turned savage, hungry, then gentle again, like mist after a heavy storm. His lips lingered on hers for a moment, then he released them, his fingers threading through her hair. "I have never been so eager, nor fearful, of returning home," he said with a wry smile.

"Do not ever be fearful," she said. "Not of me."

"Ah, but you are a fearful wench," he said. "You possess a magic that has enveloped me."

"Then I hope the spell will last forever."

Anguish swept across his face, and she knew he still had not forgotten his vow, nor accepted that he had broken it.

"You are tired, my lord," she said, taking his hand and starting toward the door.

"The books?"

"I will fetch them in the morning."

His fingers tightened around hers. She took the candle in her other hand and led the way past her room and to his own. She could not stay here this night. Colin might wake and she did not want the household to know what had happened between them.

She had not been in his room before. It was spartan in comparison to other rooms, furnished with a wardrobe, a table, a chair and a narrow bed. It was a soldier's room, she thought, and she reminded herself that he had been that.

She set the candle down and turned to him. He stood perfectly still, and she untied his cloak, then unbuttoned the jerkin he wore over his customary shirt with flowing sleeves. Then she went to the table that contained a tray with a bottle of spirits and glasses. She poured a sizeable portion into a glass and handed it to him.

He took one sip, then another.

His gaze met hers. "I will go," she said. "You need rest."

"You rest me," he said. "You make me content."

"Not always."

"Nay, for truth. You are like fire in my blood as well as a cool resting place, lass. 'Tis a heady combination."

"When this is over . . ."

"When this over," he finished, "we will talk. Cumberland would like nothing more than a marriage between us. But the risks are great, lass, and you must be sure." He put a finger to her lips as she started to speak. "No, lass. Not now. And now you had best return to your son. I will visit you at the cottage."

She stood on tiptoes and kissed him slowly, a promise in every deliberately seductive touch.

Then she broke away and walked out the door and to her room.

The sound of strings tuning up filled the great hall as carriage after carriage arrived and gaily dressed and masked passengers descended and entered.

Neil tried to hide his anxiety. Where in the hell was Reginald Campbell? All the planning, all the preparations would be for naught if he did not appear.

At least one of his prayers had been answered. Cumberland had arrived earlier in the day with several of his officers. He had asked about Janet and Neil had told him what he had told everyone, that she had to go to Lochaene but was expected back at any time.

They'd shared a drink together and Neil had presented him with a keg of the brandy he had bought from the smugglers. Cumberland took a sip, then nodded his head. "I should arrest you just as I should have arrested your cousin," he said as he licked his lips. "But no one else has been able to find me its like in this godforsaken country."

"And I would not risk arrest for anyone but you, Your Grace," Neil retorted. "I was but following your suggestion."

Cumberland chuckled. "You have your cousin's wit."

Cumberland had retired then until the ball. Neil noticed he took the brandy with him.

The guests who were staying overnight arrived during the afternoon. Each time a carriage—or a horseman—approached, Neil went out to meet them, trying to feign a welcome jocularity he did not feel. He only wanted this night over.

In between greeting guests, he agonized over whether Reginald had taken the bait. He had not heard from Alex; they had agreed Alex should start for the coast. It was essential that he and the children be there for the meeting, and they would be dodging English patrols. But Neil felt sure that either Alex or Burke would have communicated with him if they thought Reginald would not be coming.

The carriages became a steady stream at nine o'clock, and slowed by ten. Neil went inside the hall. Guests in colorful costumes, including jesters and harlequins, filled the great hall and the corridors. Laughter spilled out as guests tried to guess the identity of one another. Some, like him, merely wore formal clothing along with elegant masks. He had donned a dark blue velvet waistcoat trimmed with silver, an overcoat of the same material, a ruffled shirt, stock with a diamond solitaire, white silk stocking and shoes with silver buckles. He wore a plain powdered wig tied back in a queue. He felt a fraud in the finery, some of which once belonged to his cousin, some of which he had ordered in Edinburgh.

But it was important that he look prosperous and settled for his neighbors. He knew many regarded him as a bastard upstart, just as they had his cousin. He did not give a rat's ass for their opinion, except he wanted no interference with what many would believe were his almost revolutionary plans for his estates.

The costume ball had been an especially attractive draw to those he wanted to attend. It was more an English entertainment than a dour Presbyterian Scottish one.

He bent his ear and listened to conversation, trying to look interested even as he kept an eye on the door. He also fended off advances from any number of young lasses. Bastard or not, he was now a wealthy and unattached marquis, and a valuable catch.

He had almost given up when a doorman opened the great door. "The honorable Reginald Campbell," he announced.

Lucy gave Janet's hair one last look. She had drawn it back into a French knot in back of her head, from which a few long curls fell over her right shoulder.

The maid was beside herself with excitement. "I am so pleased ye arrived in time for the ball," she said. "Ye must have ridden day and night."

"Aye," said Janet who had slipped in the servants' entrance and up the servants' stairs just an hour earlier and made her way to her room shielded by a long cloak and hood. She then went by the nursery. Clara and Trilby were looking after the children, but both had on their best dresses, and she knew they hoped to sneak down and watch from the stairs.

Grace and Rachel jumped up with large grins on their faces. Annabella was playing on the floor with Colin, and she waited until Janet leaned down and hugged them. "I missed you all."

"Are you going to the ball, mama?" Grace asked.

"Aye, but it is to be a surprise, and you are not to tell anyone. 'Tis a secret between you and me." She gave each of her daughters a hug. "I missed you," she said again, then she went to Colin and picked him up. She had been away from him for three days, except for a short visit when Neil had brought him to the cottage.

She turned to Clara. "I want someone with the children all evening," she said.

"Aye, my lady," Clara said. "Can we take turns and peek out?"

"Aye," she said, "but I do not want you to tell anyone but the marquis that I have returned." Then she gave them an impish grin. "I am in mourning and I do not want anyone to know my identity. If anyone asks, I have not returned."

Both Clara and Trilby nodded their heads.

She had seen Neil for several moments. Everything was ready, he said. Kevin would be watching for Reginald and replace whatever was in his saddlebags with a few of the Black Knave's belongings.

She wished she could feel a moment's sympathy for Reginald, but she could not. He had endangered the lives of her children as well as her own.

She only hoped she could play her part well enough. She had to unmask in front of Cumberland and Reginald. And wait for his reaction. Had Neil judged him well? So much depended on it. She would never feel safe as long as Reginald plotted. Nor, she feared even more, would her son ever be safe.

She donned the black dress, and Lucy helped her with the gauze overdress that gave the illusion that she floated in the air.

"Lucy?" she said.

"Aye, my lady?"

"You are to stay on the top step and watch for the marquis. When he approaches the stairs and winks at you, you come for me."

"The marquis? Winking?"

"Aye," Janet said, trying to keep amusement from her voice. The marquis was winking quite often this days.

Lucy bobbed, then disappeared out the door, and Janet sat down to wait for her entrance.

Neil felt a moment of amusement. Reginald was red-faced, his silk waistcoat rumpled and his boots mud-splattered. The honorable Reginald Campbell must have really hurried to get to Braemoor.

But he had a look of absolute triumph on his face.

"Reginald," Neil said. "So good of you to come. His Grace the Duke of Cumberland has also honored me with his presence." He allowed that to penetrate for a moment. He had Cumberland's ear. "Where is your lovely wife?"

"She could not come," Reginald said bitterly with an accusing look at him. "We did not have a carriage and she cannot ride that far."

"Mayhap I should have sent it back to Lochaene," Neil said musingly.

Reginald visibly tried to control his anger. "And my sister-in-law?" he asked spitefully. "She is well?"

Neil waited a fraction of an instant longer than necessary. "Aye," he said and started to turn around.

"I want to see her. And my nephew."

"My dear Campbell, first you must refresh yourself."

"Where is my sister-in-law?"

"She is in mourning," Neil said airily.

"Is she in the Tower house?"

"I am not sure what you mean."

"It seems plain enough. Is my sister-in-law here? I want to see her."

His voice was rising steadily. Neil saw faces turn toward him.

"I am sorry. You cannot."

"You have no right."

"I have every right. You are in my home."

"And the countess is my sister-in-law," Reginald countered. "Her well-being is my concern." His gaze went around the room. "I am going to ask Cumberland to demand that you produce her."

"No!" Neil said with alarm.

A quietly triumphant look came into Reginald's eyes. "It is my right as the man in the family."

"She is in mourning," Neil protested with, he hoped, desperation in his voice.

Reginald ignored him and started to push through the crowded revelers. He found Cumberland in a corner with several men.

"Your Grace," Reginald said as he bowed.

"Campbell," the duke acknowledged with evident displeasure.

"I must talk to you," Reginald plodded on stubbornly.

Neil sighed audibly, then said, "Let us go into the library."

Cumberland's displeasure obviously deepened, but he nodded curtly.

Neil paused at the steps and looked up. Lucy was there. Good. He winked.

He led Cumberland and Reginald into his study. He went to a decanter and poured a glass of brandy for Cumberland, then one for himself. He pointedly ignored Reginald. Then he went and opened the curtains which looked out over the gardens.

He suggested a chair to Cumberland, one to the side of the window. Then Neil moved in front of the window, positioning himself so that Reginald's gaze would be directed toward the window.

"What is it, Campbell?" Cumberland asked impatiently.

"I want to see my sister-in-law, and Braemoor refuses to produce her." Reginald's voice sounded like a whine. He seemed to sense that. He drew himself up stiffly. "I am responsible for her."

Cumberland turned to Neil.

"She is in mourning," Neil said.

"I think she is dead." Reginald blurted it out.

Cumberland gave Campbell a puzzled look. "Why would you think that?"

"Because . . . because . . ." Reginald stuttered.

Puzzlement turned to impatience. Cumberland frowned. "Do you have proof for that kind of accusation?"

"Just ask him where my sister-in-law is. She is dead, I tell you. The proof is . . . she is not here," Reginald said. "And it is my duty to protect my nephew."

Neil raised an eyebrow and looked out. Reginald's eyes followed him. A slender figure walked across the garden, the gauze overdress flowing in the wind, then she turned and looked directly into the library.

Reginald turned white. "It cannot be. 'Tis a specter."

Neil looked out. "I see nothing."

"It is Janet. But she is dead." His hands were shaking.

"Why do you think she is dead?" Neil asked, his brows knitting together in puzzlement.

Reginald took a step back. "She is dead, I tell you. He said . . ."

"Who said what?" Neil said.

Reginald looked up and suddenly realized what he'd said. His gaze turned toward Cumberland whose face had turned to ice.

"Speak, man," Cumberland said. "Who said the countess was dead?"

"I . . . I . . . was . . ." Reginald's face fell.

"You believed the countess was dead. Why?"

Neil looked outside. She was gone.

"It was a specter, I tell you." Reginald protested. "Ask to see her," he pleaded.

Neil stiffened. "The countess said someone shot at her a week or more ago, but she told only me. No one else knew."

Cumberland stared at Reginald. "No one else could have known unless it was you who shot at her, or someone on your behest."

Reginald was desperate now. "The Black Knave. It was the Black Knave. He threatened me . . . he . . ."

Cumberland looked at Neil. "Get my officers. I want this man under arrest."

Neil hesitated. "Do you really believe . . ."

Reginald was trembling now. "I . . . did nothing."

"Aye," Cumberland said in answer to Neil's question.

Neil left the room to fetch the officers. He couldn't help but feel a little sorry for Reginald and his confusion, the same pity he would feel for a rabid wolf.

The arrest of a Campbell only heightened the success of the ball. Guests stayed until dawn. Neil had breakfast served on the morning after the last ball he hoped he would ever hold.

Cumberland left at midday, his prisoner bound on his own horse. His Grace had checked the saddlebags and found some interesting items, including a pistol, a suit of black clothes, a jack of spades and the queen of hearts.

As soon as Reginald had seen the items, he knew exactly what had happened, and he started to claim that he had been duped.

His words to Cumberland in Braemoor's library, though, had convicted him.

Janet had come down to watch them ride away. Reginald had turned and seen her, and despair had filled his face.

The last guest left by noon.

"What will happen to him?" Janet said as they went up to his room.

"Do you care?"

"Aye," she said. "I find I do."

"I will see whether I can convince Cumberland to transport him," he said. "Cumberland can prove attempted murder, but not that he is the Black Knave." He grinned. "In any event, I want the Knave to live on."

"And Reginald's family. Louisa? The baby?"

"I will make sure they have enough money to live well but quietly in Edinburgh," he said. "Along with Marjorie. I do not want any of them at Lochaene." He hesitated, then added, "But that is your decision. Not mine."

"How can I ever thank you?" she said.

"Your safety is sufficient thanks."

They were at the top of the stairs, their rooms in opposite directions. Servants were busy cleaning up the last remnants of the ball which, she knew, would be discussed for years to come.

She took his hand and led him into the nursery. Clara was changing Colin's diapers. She curtseyed, with a smile on her face. "Lucy and Kevin are with the lasses, fetching roses," she said. "I thought ye might like some sleep."

"Aye," Janet said. "But first I had to see my big lad and mayhap we can take them all out to the loch on a picnic later this afternoon. I have not spent much time with them." She looked up at Neil. He nodded with a smile.

Janet leaned over and kissed Colin and took over from Clara, finishing the job and lifting him up. He put his small arms around her neck, giving her a big hug. "You are safe now, my lad," she whispered into his ear.

He pulled away and looked at Neil, then held out his hands for him, too.

Janet watched as he took Colin gingerly, then with more assurance. He grinned at the lad, and Colin grinned back. A bit of male acknowledgment, she thought wistfully. She did not know what would happen now. Whether Neil could overcome his fears enough to make her part of his life, or whether she would return to Lochaene.

That had been what she wanted. Had it not? To be her own mistress, to have the freedom of a man. She could have that now. Neil had just made it possible.

So why was she not elated?

The loch looked beautiful in the midday sun. The rays bounced off its surface, spreading what looked like golden trails across the dark blue surface.

Annabella rode with her. Colin rode with Neil, and the two oldest lasses rode their own ponies. They had been riding daily, and were good little riders, but Neil had fixed leads to their ponies.

It was their first expedition on the ponies and their excitement was catching. Janet realized how much they had been neglected in the past week, and she had ordered a particularly tasteful supper. There were roasted chickens and tarts and pastries. There had been much to choose from after the ball.

She and Neil had had three hours' sleep—enough, she thought, to sustain her until tonight. More important than anything, though, was giving the children a sense of freedom and joy. And being with them. She had missed her time with them.

They stopped at a spot above the loch, the spot where he had taken her before. It was far enough from the water to be safe for Colin. Neil lifted Colin down, then dismounted and took their lunch and blanket from the saddle, then helped each of the lasses dismount while Janet lowered Annabella. He came over to her and caught her in his arms. They were not quite steady, and she knew he felt the same heated reaction as she.

She had to force herself to step back. She stood next to him and looked down at the loch below. The dreary weather of yesterday was gone. The sun was bright in a cloudless sky and a gentle breeze brushed the fields of wild heather.

The children spread out, Annabella and Rachel playing with a ball as Grace played with Colin. Janet and Neil spread out a blanket and sat, watching them. Listening to their laughter. Seeing the smiles in their eyes.

They were happy. Some of the ghosts would persist, Janet knew. But Neil had taken away their fear of men. They would never again flinch when one walked into a room.

He had given them all so much. She reached out her hand and their fingers intertwined. "I love you," she said simply.

His eyes clouded but his fingers tightened around hers.

"I did not tell you something," she said. She had planned to wait until she had heard something from the solicitor, but now she knew she must tell him. He had already opened his heart to her, but now she had to give him the same hope that she had.

He raised an eyebrow in question.

"I talked to Torquil about your mother," she said. "He does not remember events the way your uncle described them."

He stiffened. For a moment she felt guilt at prying into his past without his knowledge. But she continued on. "He never said anything because he did not know what your uncle had told you," she stumbled on.

Still no words, no change in his eyes. His fingers, though, continued to hold onto her as if she were a lifeline. "He . . .

said your mother hit her head. That she was fine until then. And he knew nothing about her mother . . . being mad. In truth, he believes she died of a cancer."

A muscle worked along the side of his tightened jaw.

"I . . . I wrote your solicitor and asked him to make queries," she said. "I should have asked you first, but I . . . did not want to . . . raise your hopes."

"Have you heard back?" he asked.

She shook her head.

He released her hand and stood, his eyes going to the loch. Her heart shriveled as she saw the naked pain sweep across his face. He did not believe her. Or he resented her going behind his back. But she'd had to tell him. There had been too many secrets, too many misunderstandings, too many lies.

She stood and went to stand next to him. Silently. Waiting.

Seconds passed. Then minutes. She heard the children's loud voices in play, but she was frozen in this one second of time.

"A lie?" he said at last.

"Aye, I believe so."

His eyes closed, then fluttered open. "So much time . . . wasted."

"We can make up for it," she said, her hand sneaking over to his and bringing it up to her mouth. She kissed the back of it, thinking how strong it was. And how tender. How infinitely dear.

No accusations. No questions as to why she had not immediately told him. Neil Forbes, the Marquis of Braemoor, was a unique man, she knew. She had never known such quiet strength.

He disentangled her hand and for a second she felt he might pull away. Instead, he put his arms around her and pulled her close. "If . . . it is true," he said, "will you wed me?"

Something shifted inside her and she looked up at him, at

the face that had never left her dreams, at the eyes that were now glittering with moisture. "Only," she said, "if you do not put conditions on it. I will wed you, whether true or not."

He started to say something, but she put her fingers on his lips, cutting off the words. "For better or for worse, in sickness and in health," she repeated from memory. "If you are not willing to make those vows, then . . ."

She did not finish the sentence. His lips captured hers, tender at first and filled with warmth and yearning. Her free hand went up to his face, a gentle shining avowal of love. She felt his momentary hesitation and she stepped back to look at his face. This had to be his decision.

Neil did not understand why his eyes were blurred as Janet stood in front of him, her eyes full of love. Her touch had shattered what little resistence he had remaining.

She was right. He would have taken her if the risk were reversed. How could he do less, even if . . . even if . . .

His soul soared with hope, the hope that she had given him with the love that was unconditional, with the tenderness he'd never known that he'd so wanted.

"Forever," he said, knowing it was true, that love was so much stronger than fear. He had been a slow student. "I love you," he said, his voice breaking. "I have always loved you." He paused. "You are already my heart queen. Will you be my wife?"

"Aye," she said as his lips came hard down on hers, and the kiss was fire and storm, then gentled to a promise.

They heard a giggle behind them. Then another. Reluctantly, they parted to see four sets of eyes looking up at them, all of them shining with approval.

"You will have a large family," she whispered.

"Aye," he said, emotion clogging his throat, knowing he had reached the heaven he had never thought could be his.

Epilogue

The letter came on the day Janet was to wed Neil.

The timing, she thought, was like a blessing.

A messenger brought it at daybreak. It came from Paris via the French smuggler. A scribbled message three months earlier had assured her that Alex and his children had reached the coast of Scotland safely.

Now she knew that the French ship had also successfully run the English blockade. Alex was safe in Paris.

She read it again as Lucy wound her freshly washed and scented hair in back of her head. One curl fell down across her shoulder.

My dearest friend,

We are safe in Paris. I hope soon to find families for the children. My own plans are indefinite. A new friend has heard of some opportunities in the diamond trade, and we are considering a partnership—his money and my wit. He believes anyone who eluded the English for more than a year can elude anyone.

I did not thank our friend properly. I hope you will do that for me, and I expect that some day we will meet again and I can make some repayment.

I wish you Godspeed in all that you do.

There was no signature, but she recognized Alex's bold writing, if not his newfound caution.

Diamonds. She should have known he would not settle for some ordinary trade. She suddenly smiled at a momentary whimsy. The Black Knave. Neil called her his heart queen. Mayhap Alexander would be the diamond king.

She looked back in the mirror. Lucy had laced the hair with a string of pearls Neil had given Janet as a wedding gift.

It was five months since her husband's death but neither she nor Neil had been willing to wait, particularly after they had learned the truth about Neil's family. The solicitor had confirmed that Neil's maternal grandmother had died quite sanely of a cancer. There was no trace of madness in his family.

She had been willing, in any event, to marry Neil. Nay, not willing, but eager. Together they could conquer anything. She loved him to the very height her soul could reach and never more than when she'd discovered the lengths he had gone to protect her. But because of her husband's recent death, they had decided to wait. And despite her pledge, he'd also wanted to wait until the solicitor she had contacted had discovered the truth of his heritage. He'd lived with it far too long to be able to discard his fears easily.

And then there had been much to do. Reginald was, at Neil's request, transported to America as a bond servant for fourteen years. Janet had not wanted his blood on her hands and both she and Neil knew that transportation—virtual slavery—could be an even worse punishment than a quick death.

Neil had established a small annuity for Marjorie and Louisa, mostly because of Louisa's child. The one condition was that they never return to Lochaene.

Jock had agreed to stay at Lochaene as a steward. Janet and the children had moved back for a while, only to find it a very lonely place. The lasses wanted to be with Neil. She

wanted Neil also. Independence was not all she believed it
would be, not when her heart lay over the mountains.

And Jock, she had discovered, had established a rapport
with the tenants and was a fine manager. Lochaene, at last,
was becoming a happy estate. It did not need her.

Then one day at Lochaene—when she was working in the
gardens, trying to rebuild them—she looked up and saw
Neil riding toward her.

She had started running toward him.

It had been all the answer he needed.

He had taken her in his arms and kissed her for what
seemed an eternity. Then he looked down at her. "I cannot
live without my heart queen one day longer," he said. "I ha'
tried and cannot."

And now today they would wed. It was to be a small
wedding. Only the tenants and a few neighbors had been invited. Neil had, in truth, picked a date when he knew Cumberland would be in England. He had not wanted the duke
to be present.

A knock came at the door. Three lasses, all dressed in finery, stood there with huge smiles on their faces. Clara was
behind them with Colin. He held out his arms. "Mama?"

She took him. "Aye, my bonny lad, and I am going to
marry your new papa."

Colin grinned broadly as if he understood exactly what
she was saying.

They must be an odd group, she thought as she went
down the stairs, through the door to the small chapel. She
handed Colin to Grace, and her daughters started down the
aisle. Her gaze went straight to Neil, who stood at the altar.
Clad in a deep blue tailcoat, with a white waistcoat, dark
trousers and a dark blue neck cloth, he looked magnificent.

Just as she took a step toward him, a dog suddenly
scooted under her dress, an orange-colored cat behind him.

"They wanted to come, too," Annabella explained as she
crawled under the blue silk of Janet's dress and gathered up
the cat.

Samson peered out from under the silk. Rachel grabbed him. "I will put them away," she said.

Janet recalled the day Samson had wet on Neil. She remembered his wry smile and the way her heart had responded. "Nay," she said. "They are members of the family, too."

She looked up toward Neil, who was trying to keep from laughing. He winked.

Her heart filled with love for him, for that wink. Weeks ago, she would never have believed it possible. So much had seemed impossible.

Now everything was possible.

Following three little lasses, their arms full of Colin and animals, she reached Neil. He held out his hand to her and his fingers laced around hers, just as their hearts had bonded together.

And together they heard the words, "Dearly beloved . . ."